"GO SLOW, OLD MAN; GO SLOW"
—*A Millionaire of Rough-and-Ready*

"ARGONAUT EDITION" OF
THE WORKS OF BRET HARTE

A WAIF OF THE PLAINS

IN THE CARQUINEZ WOODS
SNOW BOUND AT EAGLE'S
A MILLIONAIRE OF ROUGH-AND-READY

BY

BRET HARTE

ILLUSTRATED

VIGILANS ET AUDAX

P. F. COLLIER & SON
NEW YORK

CONTENTS

	PAGE
A MILLIONAIRE OF ROUGH-AND-READY . . .	3
DEVIL'S FORD	83
A WAIF OF THE PLAINS	159
IN THE CARQUINEZ WOODS	265
SNOW-BOUND AT EAGLE'S	375

A MILLIONAIRE OF ROUGH-AND-READY

PROLOGUE

THERE was no mistake this time: he had struck gold at last!

It had lain there before him a moment ago—a misshapen piece of brown-stained quartz, interspersed with dull yellow metal; yielding enough to have allowed the points of his pick to penetrate its honeycombed recesses, yet heavy enough to drop from the point of his pick as he endeavored to lift it from the red earth.

He was seeing all this plainly, although he found himself, he knew not why, at some distance from the scene of his discovery, his heart foolishly beating, his breath impotently hurried. Yet he was walking slowly and vaguely; conscious of stopping and staring at the landscape, which no longer looked familiar to him. He was hoping for some instinct or force of habit to recall him to himself; yet when he saw a neighbor at work in an adjacent claim, he hesitated, and then turned his back upon him. Yet only a moment before he had thought of running to him, saying, "By Jingo! I've struck it," or "D—n it, old man, I've got it"; but that moment had passed, and now it seemed to him that he could scarce raise his voice, or, if he did, the ejaculation would appear forced and artificial. Neither could he go over to him coolly and tell his good fortune; and, partly from this strange shyness, and partly with a hope that another survey of the treasure might restore him to natural expression, he walked back to his tunnel.

Yes; it was there! No mere "pocket" or "deposit," but

a part of the actual vein he had been so long seeking. It was there, sure enough, lying beside the pick and the débris of the "face" of the vein that he had exposed sufficiently, after the first shock of discovery, to assure himself of the fact and the permanence of his fortune. It was there, and with it the refutation of his enemies' sneers, the corroboration of his friends' belief, the practical demonstration of his own theories, the reward of his patient labors. It was there, sure enough. But, somehow, he not only failed to recall the first joy of discovery, but was conscious of a vague sense of responsibility and unrest. It was, no doubt, an enormous fortune to a man in his circumstances: perhaps it meant a couple of hundred thousand dollars, or more, judging from the value of the old Martin lead, which was not as rich as this, but it required to be worked constantly and judiciously. It was with a decided sense of uneasiness that he again sought the open sunlight of the hillside. His neighbor was still visible on the adjacent claim; but he had apparently stopped working, and was contemplatively smoking a pipe under a large pine-tree. For an instant he envied him his apparent contentment. He had a sudden fierce and inexplicable desire to go over to him and exasperate his easy poverty by a revelation of his own new-found treasure. But even that sensation quickly passed, and left him staring blankly at the landscape again.

As soon as he had made his discovery known, and settled its value, he would send for his wife and her children in the States. He would build a fine house on the opposite hillside, if she would consent to it, unless she preferred, for the children's sake, to live in San Francisco. A sense of a loss of independence—of a change of circumstances that left him no longer his own master—began to perplex him, in the midst of his brightest projects. Certain other relations with other members of his family, which had lapsed by absence and his insignificance, must now be taken up anew. He must do something for his sister Jane, for his brother William, for his wife's poor connections. It would be unfair to him to say that he contemplated those things with any other instinct than that of generosity; yet he was conscious of being already perplexed and puzzled.

Meantime, however, the neighbor had apparently finished his pipe, and, knocking the ashes out of it, rose suddenly, and ended any further uncertainty of their meeting by walking over directly towards him. The treasure-finder advanced a few steps on his side, and then stopped irresolutely.

"Hollo, Slinn!" said the neighbor, confidently.

"Hollo, Masters," responded Slinn, faintly. From the sound of the two voices a stranger might have mistaken their relative condition. "What in thunder are you mooning about for? What's up?" Then, catching sight of Slinn's pale and anxious face, he added abruptly, "Are you sick?"

Slinn was on the point of telling him his good fortune, but stopped. The unlucky question confirmed his consciousness of his physical and mental disturbance, and he dreaded the ready ridicule of his companion. He would tell him later; Masters need not know *when* he had made the strike. Besides, in his present vagueness, he shrank from the brusque, practical questioning that would be sure to follow the revelation to a man of Masters' temperament.

"I'm a little giddy here," he answered, putting his hand to his head, "and I thought I'd knock off until I was better."

Masters examined him with two very critical gray eyes. "Tell ye what, old man!—if you don't quit this dog-goned foolin' of yours in that God-forsaken tunnel you'll get loony! Times you get so tangled up in follerin' that blind lead o' yours you ain't sensible!"

Here was the opportunity to tell him all, and vindicate the justice of his theories! But he shrank from it again; and now, adding to the confusion, was a singular sense of dread at the mental labor of explanation. He only smiled painfully, and began to move away. "Look you!" said Masters, peremptorily, "ye want about three fingers of straight whiskey to set you right, and you've got to take it with me. D—n it, man, it may be the last drink we take together! Don't look so skeered! I mean—I made up my mind about ten minutes ago to cut the whole d——d thing, and light out for fresh diggings. I'm sick of getting only grub wages out o' this hill. So that's what I mean by saying it's the last drink you and me'll take together. You know my ways: sayin' and doin' with me's the same thing."

It was true. Slinn had often envied Masters' promptness of decision and resolution. But he only looked at the grim face of his interlocutor with a feeble sense of relief. He was *going*. And he, Slinn, would not have to explain anything!

He murmured something about having to go over to the settlement on business. He dreaded lest Masters should insist upon going into the tunnel.

"I suppose you want to mail that letter," said Masters, drily. "The mail don't go till to-morrow, so you've got time to finish it, and put it in an envelope."

Following the direction of Masters' eyes, Slinn looked down and saw, to his utter surprise, that he was holding an unfinished pencilled note in his hand. How it came there, when he had written it, he could not tell; he dimly remembered that one of his first impulses was to write to his wife, but that he had already done so he had forgotten. He hastily concealed the note in his breast-pocket, with a vacant smile. Masters eyed him half contemptuously, half compassionately.

"Don't forget yourself and drop it in some hollow tree for a letter-box," he said. "Well—so long!—since you won't drink. Take care of yourself," and, turning on his heel, Masters walked away.

Slinn watched him as he crossed over to his abandoned claim, saw him gather his few mining utensils, strap his blanket over his back, lift his hat on his long-handled shovel as a token of farewell, and then stride light-heartedly over the ridge.

He was alone now with his secret and his treasure. The only man in the world who knew of the exact position of his tunnel had gone away forever. It was not likely that this chance companion of a few weeks would ever remember him or the locality again; he would now leave his treasure alone—for even a day perhaps—until he had thought out some plan and sought out some friend in whom to confide. His secluded life, the singular habits of concentration which had at last proved so successful had, at the same time, left him few acquaintances and no associates. And in all his well-laid plans and patiently-digested theories for finding the treasure, the means and methods of working it and disposing of it had never entered.

And now, at the hour when he most needed his faculties, what was the meaning of this strange benumbing of them!

Patience! He only wanted a little rest—a little time to recover himself. There was a large boulder under a tree in the highway of the settlement—a sheltered spot where he had often waited for the coming of the stage-coach. He would go there, and when he was sufficiently rested and composed he would go on.

Nevertheless, on his way he diverged and turned into the woods, for no other apparent purpose than to find a hollow tree. "A hollow tree." Yes! that was what Masters had said; he remembered it distinctly; and something was to be done there, but what it was, or why it should be done, he could not tell. However, it was done, and very luckily, for his limbs could scarcely support him further, and reaching that boulder he dropped upon it like another stone.

And now, strange to say, the uneasiness and perplexity which had possessed him ever since he had stood before his revealed wealth dropped from him like a burden laid upon the wayside. A measureless peace stole over him, in which visions of his new-found fortune, no longer a trouble and perplexity, but crowned with happiness and blessing to all around him, assumed proportions far beyond his own weak, selfish plans. In its even-handed benefaction, his wife and children, his friends and relations, even his late poor companion of the hillside, met and moved harmoniously together; in its far-reaching consequences there was only the influence of good. It was not strange that this poor finite mind should never have conceived the meaning of the wealth extended to him; or that conceiving it he should faint and falter under the revelation. Enough that for a few minutes he must have tasted a joy of perfect anticipation that years of actual possession might never bring.

The sun seemed to go down in a rosy dream of his own happiness, as he still sat there. Later, the shadows of the trees thickened and surrounded him, and still later fell the calm of a quiet evening sky with far-spaced passionless stars, that seemed as little troubled by what they looked upon as he was by the stealthy creeping life in the grasses and underbrush at his feet. The dull patter of soft little feet in the soft dust of the road, the gentle gleam of moist and wondering little eyes on the branches and in the mossy edges of the boulder, did not disturb him. He sat patiently through it all, as if he had not yet made up his mind.

But when the stage came with the flashing sun the next morning, and the irresistible clamor of life and action, the driver suddenly laid his four spirited horses on their haunches before the quiet spot. The express messenger clambered down from the box, and approached what seemed to be a heap of cast-off clothes upon the boulder.

"He don't seem to be drunk," he said, in reply to a querulous interrogation from the passengers. "I can't make him out. His eyes are open, but he cannot speak or move. Take a look at him, Doc."

A rough unprofessional-looking man here descended from the inside of the coach, and, carelessly thrusting aside the other curious passengers, suddenly leant over the heap of clothes in a professional attitude.

"He is dead," said one of the passengers.

The rough man let the passive head sink softly down again. "No such luck for him," he said curtly, but not unkindly. "It's a stroke of paralysis—and about as big as they make 'em. It's a toss-up if he ever speaks or moves again as long as he lives."

CHAPTER I

WHEN Alvin Mulrady announced his intention of growing potatoes and garden "truck" on the green slopes of Los Gatos, the mining community of that region, and the adjacent hamlet of "Rough-and-Ready," regarded it with the contemptuous indifference usually shown by those adventurers towards all bucolic pursuits. There was certainly no active objection to the occupation of two hillsides, which gave so little promise to the prospector for gold that it was currently reported that a single prospector, called "Slinn," had once gone mad or imbecile through repeated failures. The only opposition came, incongruously enough, from the original pastoral owner of the soil, one Don Ramon Alvarado, whose claim for seven leagues of hill and valley, including the now prosperous towns of Rough-and-Ready and Red Dog, was met with simple derision from the squatters and miners. "Looks ez ef we woz goin' to travel three thousand miles to open up his d——d old wilderness, and then pay for the increased valoo we give it—don't it? Oh, yes, certainly!" was their ironical commentary. Mulrady might have been pardoned for adopting this popular opinion; but by an equally incongruous sentiment, peculiar, however, to the man, he called upon Don Ramon, and actually offered to purchase the land, or "go shares" with him in the agricultural profits. It was alleged that the Don was so struck with this concession that he not only granted the land, but struck up a quaint reserved friendship for the simple-minded agriculturist and his family. It is scarcely necessary to add that this intimacy was viewed by the miners with the contempt that it deserved. They would have been more contemptuous, however, had they known the opinion that Don Ramon entertained of their particular vocation, and which he early confided to Mulrady.

"They are savages who expect to reap where they have not sown; to take out of the earth without returning anything to it but their precious carcasses; heathens, who worship the mere stones they dig up." "And was there no Spaniard who ever dug gold?" asked Mulrady, simply. "Ah, there are Spaniards and Moors," responded Don Ramon, sententiously. "Gold has been dug, and by caballeros; but no good ever came of it. There were Alvarados in Sonora, look you, who had mines of *silver,* and worked them with peons and mules, and lost their money—a gold mine to work a silver one—like gentlemen! But this grubbing in the dirt with one's fingers, that a litle gold may stick to them, is not for caballeros. And then, one says nothing of the curse."

"The curse!" echoed Mary Mulrady, with youthful feminine superstition. "What is that?"

"You knew not, friend Mulrady, that when these lands were given to my ancestors by Charles V., the Bishop of Monterey laid a curse upon any who should desecrate them. Good! Let us see! Of the three Americanos who founded yonder town, one was shot, another died of a fever—poisoned, you understand, by the soil—and the last got himself crazy of aguardiente. Even the scientifico,[1] who came here years ago and spied into the trees and the herbs: he was afterwards punished for his profanation, and died of an accident in other lands. But," added Don Ramon, with grave courtesy, "this touches not yourself. Through me, *you* are of the soil."

Indeed, it would seem as if a secure if not a rapid prosperity was the result of Don Ramon's manorial patronage. The potato patch and market garden flourished exceedingly; the rich soil responded with magnificent vagaries of growth; the even sunshine set the seasons at defiance with extraordinary and premature crops. The salt pork and biscuit consuming settlers did not allow their contempt of Mulrady's occupation to prevent their profiting by this opportunity for changing their diet. The gold they had taken from the soil presently began to flow into his pockets in exchange for his more modest treasures. The little cabin, which barely sheltered his family

---

[1] Don Ramon probably alluded to the eminent naturalist Douglas, who visited California before the gold excitement, and died of an accident in the Sandwich Islands.

—a wife, son, and daughter—was enlarged, extended, and refitted, but in turn abandoned for a more pretentious house on the opposite hill. A whitewashed fence replaced the rudely-split rails, which had kept out the wilderness. By degrees, the first evidences of cultivation —the gashes of red soil, the piles of brush and undergrowth, the bared boulders, and heaps of stone—melted away, and were lost under a carpet of lighter green, which made an oasis in the tawny desert of wild oats on the hillside. Water was the only free boon denied this Garden of Eden; what was necessary for irrigation had to be brought from a mining ditch at great expense, and was of insufficient quantity. In this emergency Mulrady thought of sinking an artesian well on the sunny slope beside his house; not, however, without serious consultation and much objection from his Spanish patron. With great austerity Don Ramon pointed out that this trifling with the entrails of the earth was not only an indignity to Nature almost equal to shaft-sinking and tunneling, but was a disturbance of vested interests. "I and my fathers, San Diego rest them!" said Don Ramon, crossing himself, "were content with wells and cisterns, filled by Heaven at its appointed seasons; the cattle, dumb brutes though they were, knew where to find water when they wanted it. But thou sayest truly," he added, with a sigh, "that was before streams and rain were choked with hellish engines, and poisoned with their spume. Go on, friend Mulrady, dig and bore if thou wilt, but in a seemly fashion, and not with impious earthquakes of devilish gunpowder."

With this concession Alvin Mulrady began to sink his first artesian shaft. Being debarred the auxiliaries of steam and gunpowder, the work went on slowly. The market garden did not suffer meantime, as Mulrady had employed two Chinamen to take charge of the ruder tillage, while he superintended the engineering work of the well. This trifling incident marked an epoch in the social condition of the family. Mrs. Mulrady at once assumed a conscious importance among her neighbors. She spoke of her husband's "men"; she alluded to the

well as "the works"; she checked the easy frontier familiarity of her customers with pretty Mary Mulrady,
her seventeen-year-old daughter. Simple Alvin Mulrady
looked with astonishment at this sudden development of
the germ planted in all feminine nature to expand in
the slightest sunshine of prosperity. "Look yer, Malviny;
ain't ye rather puttin' on airs with the boys that want to
be civil to Mamie? Like as not one of 'em may be makin'
up to her already." "You don't mean to say, Alvin
Mulrady," responded Mrs. Mulrady, with sudden severity,
"that you ever thought of givin' your daughter to a
common miner, or that I'm goin' to allow her to marry
out of our own set?" "Our own set!" echoed Mulrady
feebly, blinking at her in astonishment, and then glancing
hurriedly across at his freckle-faced son and the two
Chinamen at work in the cabbages. "Oh, you know what
I mean," said Mrs. Mulrady sharply; "the set that we
move in. The Alvarados and their friends! Doesn't the
old Don come here every day, and ain't his son the right
age for Mamie? And ain't they the real first families here—all the same as if they were noblemen? No,
leave Mamie to me, and keep to your shaft; there never
was a man yet had the least *sabe* about these things, or
knew what was due to his family." Like most of his
larger minded, but feebler equipped sex, Mulrady was too
glad to accept the truth of the latter proposition, which
left the meannesses of life to feminine manipulation, and
went off to his shaft on the hillside. But during that
afternoon he was perplexed and troubled. He was too
loyal a husband not to be pleased with this proof of an
unexpected and superior foresight in his wife, although
he was, like all husbands, a little startled by it. He tried
to dismiss it from his mind. But looking down from the
hillside upon his little venture, where gradual increase
and prosperity had not been beyond his faculties to control and understand, he found himself haunted by the
more ambitious projects of his helpmate. From his own
knowledge of men, he doubted if Don Ramon, any more
than himself, had ever thought of the possibility of a
matrimonial connection between the families. He doubted

if he would consent to it. And unfortunately it was this very doubt that, touching his own pride as a self-made man, made him first seriously consider his wife's proposition. He was as good as Don Ramon, any day! With this subtle feminine poison instilled in his veins, carried completely away by the logic of his wife's illogical premises, he almost hated his old benefactor. He looked down upon the little Garden of Eden, where his Eve had just tempted him with the fatal fruit, and felt a curious consciousness that he was losing its simple and innocent enjoyment forever.

Happily, about this time Don Ramon died. It is not probable that he ever knew the amiable intentions of Mrs. Mulrady in regard to his son, who now succeeded to the paternal estate, sadly partitioned by relatives and lawsuits. The feminine Mulradys attended the funeral, in expensive mourning from Sacramento; even the gentle Alvin was forced into ready-made broadcloth, which accented his good-natured but unmistakably common presence. Mrs. Mulrady spoke openly of her "loss"; declared that the old families were dying out; and impressed the wives of a few new arrivals at Red Dog with the belief that her own family was contemporary with the Alvarados, and that her husband's health was far from perfect. She extended a motherly sympathy to the orphaned Don Cæsar. Reserved, like his father, in natural disposition, he was still more gravely ceremonious from his loss; and, perhaps from the shyness of an evident partiality for Mamie Mulrady, he rarely availed himself of her mother's sympathizing hospitality. But he carried out the intentions of his father by consenting to sell to Mulrady, for a small sum, the property he had leased. The idea of purchasing had originated with Mrs. Mulrady.

"It'll be all in the family," had observed that astute lady, "and it's better for the looks of the things that we shouldn't be his tenants."

It was only a few weeks later that she was startled by hearing her husband's voice calling her from the hillside as he rapidly approached the house. Mamie was in her room putting on a new pink cotton gown, in honor of an expected visit from young Don Cæsar, and Mrs. Mulrady was tidying the house in view of the same event. Something in the tone of her good man's voice, and the unusual circumstance of his return to the house before work was done, caused her, however, to drop her dusting cloth, and run to the kitchen door to meet him. She saw him running through the rows of cabbages, his face shining with perspiration and excitement, a light in his eyes which she had not seen for years. She recalled, without sentiment, that he looked like that when she had called him—a poor farm hand of her father's—out of the brush heap at the back of their former home, in Illinois, to learn the consent of her parents. The recollection was the more embarrassing as he threw his arms around her, and pressed a resounding kiss upon her sallow cheek.

"Sakes alive! Mulrady!" she said, exorcising the ghost of a blush that had also been recalled from the past with her housewife's apron, "what are you doin', and company expected every minit?"

"Malviny, I've struck it; and struck it rich!"

She disengaged herself from his arms, without excitement, and looked at him with bright but shrewdly observant eyes.

"I've struck it in the well—the regular vein that the boys have been looking fer. There's a fortin' fer you and Mamie: thousands and tens of thousands!"

"Wait a minit."

She left him quickly, and went to the foot of the stairs. He could hear her wonderingly and distinctly. "Ye can take off that new frock, Mamie," she called out.

There was a sound of undisguised expostulation from Mamie.

"I'm speaking," said Mrs. Mulrady, emphatically.

The murmuring ceased. Mrs. Mulrady returned to her husband. The interruption seemed to have taken off the keen edge of his enjoyment. He at once abdicated his momentary elevation as a discoverer, and waited for her to speak.

"Ye haven't told any one yet?" she asked.

"No. I was alone, down in the shaft. Ye see, Malviny, I wasn't expectin' of anything." He began, with an attempt at fresh enjoyment, "I was just clearin' out, and hadn't reckoned on anythin'."

"You see, I was right when I advised you taking the land," she said, without heeding him.

Mulrady's face fell. "I hope Don Cæsar won't think" —he began, hesitatingly. "I reckon, perhaps, I oughter make some sorter compensation—you know."

"Stuff!" said Mrs. Mulrady, decidedly. "Don't be a fool. Any gold discovery, anyhow, would have been yours—that's the law. And you bought the land without any restrictions. Besides, you never had any idea of this!"—she stopped, and looked him suddenly in the face —"had you?"

Mulrady opened his honest, pale-gray eyes widely.

"Why, Malviny! You know I hadn't. I could swear!"

"Don't swear, and don't let on to anybody but what you *did* know it was there. Now, Alvin Mulrady, listen to me." Her voice here took the strident form of action. "Knock off work at the shaft, and send your man away at once. Put on your things, catch the next stage to Sacramento at four o'clock, and take Mamie with you."

"Mamie!" echoed Mulrady, feebly.

"You want to see Lawyer Cole and my brother Jim at once," she went on, without heeding him, "and Mamie wants a change and some proper clothes. Leave the rest to me and Abner. I'll break it to Mamie, and get her ready."

Mulrady passed his hands through his tangled hair, wet with perspiration. He was proud of his wife's energy and action; he did not dream of opposing her, but somehow he was disappointed. The charming glamour and joy of his discovery had vanished before he could fairly dazzle her with it; or, rather, she was not dazzled with it at all. It had become like business, and the expression "breaking it" to Mamie jarred upon him. He would have preferred to tell her himself; to watch the color come into her delicate oval face, to have seen her soft eyes light with an innocent joy he had not seen in his wife's; and he felt a sinking conviction that his wife was the last one to awaken it.

"You ain't got any time to lose," she said, impatiently, as he hesitated.

Perhaps it was her impatience that struck harshly upon him; perhaps, if she had not accepted her good fortune so confidently, he would not have spoken what was in his mind at the time; but he said gravely, "Wait a minit, Malviny; I've suthin' to tell you 'bout this find of mine that's sing'lar."

"Go on," she said, quickly.

"Lyin' among the rotten quartz of the vein was a pick," he said, constrainedly; "and the face of the vein sorter looked ez if it had been worked at. Follerin' the line outside to the base of the hill there was signs of there having been an old tunnel; but it had fallen in, and was blocked up."

"Well?" said Mrs. Mulrady, contemptuously.

"Well," returned her husband, somewhat disconnectedly, "it kinder looked as if some feller might have discovered it before."

"And went away, and left it for others! That's likely —ain't it?" interrupted his wife, with ill-disguised intolerance. "Everybody knows the hill wasn't worth that for prospectin'; and it was abandoned when we came here. It's your property and you've paid for it. Are you goin' to wait to advertise for the owner, Alvin Mulrady, or are you going to Sacramento at four o'clock to-day?"

Mulrady started. He had never seriously believed in the possibility of a previous discovery; but his conscientious nature had prompted him to give it a fair consideration. She was probably right. What he might have thought had she treated it with equal conscientiousness he did not consider. "All right," he said simply. "I reckon we'll go at once."

"And when you talk to Lawyer Cole and Jim, keep that silly stuff about the pick to yourself. There's no use of putting queer ideas into other people's heads because you happen to have 'em yourself."

When the hurried arrangements were at last completed, and Mr. Mulrady and Mamie, accompanied by a taciturn and discreet Chinaman, carrying their scant luggage, were on their way to the high road to meet the up stage, the father gazed somewhat anxiously and wistfully into his daughter's face. He had looked forward to those few moments to enjoy the freshness and *naïveté* of Mamie's youthful delight and enthusiasm as a relief to his wife's practical, far-sighted realism. There was a pretty pink suffusion in her delicate cheek, the breathless happiness of a child in her half-opened little mouth, and a beautiful absorption in her large gray eyes that augured well for him.

"Well, Mamie, how do we like bein' an heiress? How do we like layin' over all the gals between this and 'Frisco?"

"Eh?"

She had not heard him. The tender beautiful eyes were engaged in an anticipatory examination of the remembered shelves in the "Fancy Emporium" at Sacramento; in reading the admiration of the clerks; in glancing down a little criticisingly at the broad cowhide brogues that strode at her side; in looking up the road for the stage-coach; in regarding the fit of her new gloves—everywhere but in the loving eyes of the man beside her.

He, however, repeated the question, touched with her charming preoccupation, and passing his arm around her little waist.

"I like it well enough, pa, you know!" she said, slightly disengaging his arm, but adding a perfunctory little squeeze to his elbow to soften the separation. "I always had an idea *something* would happen. I suppose I'm looking like a fright," she added; "but ma made me hurry to get away before Don Cæsar came."

"And you didn't want to go without seeing him?" he added, archly.

"I didn't want him to see me in this frock," said Mamie, simply. "I reckon that's why ma made me change," she added, with a slight laugh.

"Well I reckon you're allus good enough for him in any dress," said Mulrady, watching her attentively; "and more than a match for him *now*," he added, triumphantly.

"I don't know about that," said Mamie. "He's been rich all the time, and his father and grandfather before him; while we've been poor and his tenants."

His face changed; the look of bewilderment, with which he had followed her words, gave way to one of pain, and then of anger. "Did he get off such stuff as that?" he asked, quickly.

"No. I'd like to catch him at it," responded Mamie, promptly. "There's better nor him to be had for the asking now."

They had walked on a few moments in aggrieved silence, and the Chinaman might have imagined some misfortune had just befallen them. But Mamie's teeth shone again between her parted lips. "La, pa! it ain't that! He cares everything for me, and I do for him; and if ma hadn't got new ideas—" She stopped suddenly.

"What new ideas?" queried her father, anxiously.

"Oh, nothing! I wish, pa, you'd put on your other boots! Everybody can see these are made for the farrows. And you ain't a market gardener any more."

"What am I, then?" asked Mulrady, with a half-pleased, half-uneasy laugh.

"You're a capitalist, *I* say; but ma says a landed proprietor." Nevertheless, the landed proprietor, when he reached the boulder on the Red Dog highway, sat down in somewhat moody contemplation, with his head bowed over the broad cowhide brogues, that seemed to have already gathered enough of the soil to indicate his right to that title. Mamie, who had recovered her spirits, but had not lost her preoccupation, wandered off by herself in the meadow, or ascended the hillside, as her occasional impatience at the delay of the coach, or the following of some ambitious fancy, alternately prompted her. She was so far away at one time that the stage-coach, which finally drew up before Mulrady, was obliged to wait for her.

When she was deposited safely inside, and Mulrady had climbed to the box beside the driver, the latter remarked, curtly,—

"Ye gave me a right smart skeer, a minit ago, stranger."

"Ez how?"

"Well, about three years ago, I was comin' down this yer grade, at just this time, and sittin' right on that stone, in just your attitude, was a man about your build and years. I pulled up to let him in, when, darn my skin! if he ever moved, but sorter looked at me without speakin'. I called to him, and he never answered, 'cept with that idiotic stare. I then let him have my opinion of him, in mighty strong English, and drove off, leavin' him there. The next morning, when I came by on the up-trip, darn my skin! if he wasn't thar, but lyin' all of a heap on the boulder. Jim drops down and picks him up. Doctor Duchesne, ez was along, allowst it was a played-out prospector, with a big case of paralysis, and we expressed him through to the County Hospital, like so much dead freight. I've allus been kinder superstitious about passin' that rock, and when I saw you jist now, sittin' thar, dazed like, with your head down like the other chap, it rather threw me off my centre."

In the inexplicable and half-superstitious uneasiness that this coincidence awakened in Mulrady's unimaginative mind, he was almost on the point of disclosing his good fortune to the driver, in order to prove how preposterous was the parallel, but checked himself in time.

"Did you find out who he was?" broke in a rash passenger. "Did you ever get over it?" added another unfortunate.

With a pause of insulting scorn at the interruption, the driver resumed, pointedly, to Mulrady: "The pint of the whole thing was my cussin' a helpless man, ez could neither cuss back nor shoot; and then afterwards takin' you for his ghost layin' for me to get even." He paused again, and then added, carelessly, "They say he never kem to enuff to let on who he was or whar he kem from; and he was eventooally taken to a 'Sylum for Doddering

Idjits and Gin'ral and Permiskus Imbeciles at Sacramento. I've heerd it's considered a first-class insti-
tooshun, not only for them ez is paralyzed and can't talk,
as for them ez is the reverse and is too chipper. Now,"
he added, languidly turning for the first time to his miserable questioners, "how did *you* find it?"

CHAPTER II

WHEN the news of the discovery of gold in Mulrady
shaft was finally made public, it .created an excitement
hitherto unknown in the history of the country. Half of
Red Dog and all Rough-and-Ready were emptied upon
the yellow hills surrounding Mulrady's, until their circling
camp fires looked like a besieging army that had invested
his peaceful pastoral home, preparatory to carrying it by
assault. Unfortunately for them, they found the various
points of vantage already garrisoned with notices of
"preëmption" for mining purposes in the name of the
various members of the Alvarado family. This stroke of
business was due to Mrs. Mulrady, as a means of molli-
fying the conscientious scruples of her husband and of
placating the Alvarados, in veiw of some remote contingency. It is but fair to say that this degradation of his
father's Castilian principles was opposed by Don Cæsar.
"You needn't work them yourself, but sell out to them
that will; it's the only way to keep the prospectors from
taking it without paying for it at all," argued Mrs. Mulrady. Don Cæsar finally assented; perhaps less to the
business arguments of Mulrady's wife than to the simple
suggestion of Mamie's mother. Enough that he realized
a sum in money for a few acres that exceeded the last
ten years' income of Don Ramon's seven leagues.

Equally unprecedented and extravagant was the realization of the discovery in Mulrady's shaft. It was alleged
that a company, hastily formed in Sacramento, paid him
a million of dollars down, leaving him still a controlling
two-thirds interest in the mine. With an obstinacy, however, that amounted almost to a moral conviction, he re-

fused to include the house and potato-patch in the property. When the company had yielded the point, he declined, with equal tenacity, to part with it to outside speculators on even the most extravagant offers. In vain Mrs. Mulrady protested; in vain she pointed out to him that the retention of the evidence of his former humble occupation was a green blot upon their social escutcheon.

"If you will keep the land, build on it, and root up the garden." But Mulrady was adamant.

"It's the only thing I ever made myself, and got out of the soil with my own hands; it's the beginning of my fortune, and it may be the end of it. Mebbee I'll be glad enough to have it to come back to some day, and be thankful for the square meal I can dig out of it."

By repeated pressure, however, Mulrady yielded the compromise that a portion of it should be made into a vineyard and flower-garden, and by a suitable coloring of ornament and luxury obliterate its vulgar part. Less successful, however, was that energetic woman in another effort to mitigate the austerities of their earlier state. It occurred to her to utilize the softer accents of Don Cæsar in the pronunciation of their family name, and privately had "Mulrade" take the place of Mulrady on her visiting card. "It might be Spanish," she argued with her husband. "Lawyer Cole says most American names are corrupted, and how do you know that yours ain't?" Mulrady, who would not swear that his ancestors came from Ireland to the Carolinas in '98, was helpless to refute the assertion. But the terrible Nemesis of an un-Spanish, American provincial speech avenged the orthographical outrage at once. When Mrs. Mulrady began to be addressed orally, as well as by letter, as "Mrs. Mulraid," and when simple amatory effusions to her daughter rhymed with "lovely maid," she promptly refused the original vowel. But she fondly clung to the Spanish courtesy which transformed her husband's baptismal name, and usually spoke of him—in his absence—as "Don Alvino." But in the presence of his short, square figure, his orange tawny hair, his twinkling gray eyes, and *retroussé* nose, even that dominant woman withheld his title. It was currently reported at Red Dog that a distinguished foreigner had one day approached Mulrady with the formula, "I believe I have the honor of addressing Don Alvino Mulrady?" "You kin bet your boots, stranger, that's me," had returned that simple hidalgo.

Although Mrs. Mulrady would have preferred that Mamie should remain at Sacramento until she could join her, preparatory to a trip to "the States" and Europe, she yielded to her daughter's desire to astonish Rough-and-Ready, before she left, with her new wardrobe, and unfold in the parent nest the delicate and painted wings with which she was to fly from them forever. "I don't want them to remember me afterwards in those spotted prints, ma, and like as not say I never had a decent frock until I went away." There was something so like the daughter of her mother in this delicate foresight that the touched and gratified parent kissed her, and assented. The result was gratifying beyond her expectation. In that few weeks' sojourn at Sacramento, the young girl seemed to have adapted and assimilated herself to the latest modes of fashion with even more than the usual American girl's pliancy and taste. Equal to all emergencies of style and material, she seemed to supply, from some hitherto unknown quality she possessed, the grace and manner peculiar to each. Untrammeled by tradition, education, or precedent, she had the Western girl's confidence in all things being possible, which made them so often probable. Mr. Mulrady looked at his daughter with mingled sentiments of pride and awe. Was it possible that this delicate creature, so superior to him that he seemed like a degenerate scion of her remoter race, was his own flesh and blood? Was she the daughter of her mother, who even in her remembered youth was never equipped like this? If the thought brought no pleasure to his simple, loving nature, it at least spared him the pain of what might have seemed ingratitude in one more akin to himself. "The fact is, we ain't quite up to her style," was his explanation and apology. A vague belief that in another and a better world than this he might approximate and understand this perfection somewhat soothed and sustained him.

It was quite consistent, therefore, that the embroidered cambric dress which Mamie Mulrady wore one summer afternoon on the hillside at Los Gatos, while to the critical feminine eye at once artistic and expensive, should not seem incongruous to her surroundings or to herself in the eyes of a general audience. It certainly did not seem so to one pair of frank, humorous ones that glanced at her from time to time, as their owner, a young fellow of five-and-twenty, walked at her side. He was the new editor of the "Rough-and-Ready Record," and, having been her fellow-passenger from Sacramento, had already once or twice availed himself of her father's invitation to call upon them. Mrs. Mulrady had not discouraged this mild flirtation. Whether she wished to disconcert Don Cæsar for some occult purpose, or whether, like the rest of her sex, she had an overweening confidence in the unheroic, unseductive, and purely platonic character of masculine humor, did not appear.

"When I say I'm sorry you are going to leave us, Miss Mulrady," said the young fellow, lightly, "you will comprehend my unselfishness, since I frankly admit your departure would be a positive relief to me as an editor and a man. The pressure in the Poet's Corner of the 'Record' since it was mistakingly discovered that a person of your name might be induced to seek the 'glade' and 'shade' without being 'afraid,' 'dismayed,' or 'betrayed,' has been something enormous, and, unfortunately, I am debarred from rejecting anything, on the just ground that I am myself an interested admirer."

"It's dreadful to be placarded around the country by one's own full name, isn't it?" said Mamie, without, however, expressing much horror in her face.

"They think it much more respectful than to call you 'Mamie,'" he responded, lightly; "and many of your admirers are middle-aged men, with a mediæval style of compliment. I've discovered that amatory versifying wasn't entirely a youthful passion. Colonel Cash is about as fatal with a couplet as with a double-barreled gun, and scatters as terribly. Judge Butts and Dr. Wilson have both discerned the resemblance of your gifts to those of Venus, and their own to Apollo. But don't undervalue those tributes, Miss Mulrady," he added, more seriously. "You'll have thousands of admirers where you are going; but you'll be willing to admit in the end, I think, that none were more honest and respectful than your subjects at Rough-and-Ready and Red Dog." He stopped, and added in a graver tone, "Does Don Cæsar write poetry?"

"He has something better to do," said the young lady, pertly.

"I can easily imagine that," he returned, mischievously; "it must be a pallid substitute for other opportunities."

"What did you come here for?" she asked, suddenly.

"To see you."

"Nonsense! You know what I mean. Why did you ever leave Sacramento to come here? I should think it would suit you so much better than this place."

"I suppose I was fired by your father's example, and wished to find a gold mine."

"Men like you never do," she said, simply.

"Is that a compliment, Miss Mulrady?"

"I don't know. But I think that you think that it is."

He gave her the pleased look of one who had unexpectedly found a sympathetic intelligence. "Do I? This is interesting. Let's sit down." In their desultory rambling they had reached, quite unconsciously, the large boulder at the roadside. Mamie hesitated a moment, looked up and down the road, and then, with an already opulent indifference to the damaging of her spotless skirt, sat herself upon it, with her furled parasol held by her two little hands thrown over her half-drawn-up knee. The young editor, half sitting, half leaning, against the stone, began to draw figures in the sand with his cane.

"On the contrary, Miss Mulrady, I hope to make some money here. You are leaving Rough-and-Ready because you are rich. We are coming to it because we are poor."

"We?" echoed Mamie, lazily, looking up the road.

"Yes. My father and two sisters."

"I am sorry. I might have known them if I hadn't

been going away." At the same moment, it flashed across her mind that, if they were like the man before her, they might prove disagreeably independent and critical. "Is your father in business?" she asked.

He shook his head. After a pause, he said, punctuating his sentences with the point of his stick in the soft dust, "He is paralyzed, and out of his mind, Miss Mulrady. I came to California to seek him, as all news of him ceased three years since; and I found him only two weeks ago, alone, friendless—an unrecognized pauper in the county hospital."

"Two weeks ago? That was when I went to Sacramento."

"Very probably."

"It must have been very shocking to you?"

"It was."

"I should think you'd feel real bad?"

"I do, at times." He smiled, and laid his stick on the stone. "You now see, Miss Mulrady, how necessary to me is this good fortune that you don't think me worthy of. Meantime I must try to make a home for them at Rough-and-Ready."

Miss Mulrady put down her knee and her parasol. "We mustn't stay here much longer, you know."

"Why?"

"Why, the stage-coach comes by at about this time."

"And you think the passengers will observe us sitting here?"

"Of course they will."

"Miss Mulrady, I implore you to stay."

He was leaning over her with such apparent earnestness of voice and gesture that the color came into her cheek. For a moment she scarcely dared to lift her conscious eyes to his. When she did so, she suddenly glanced her own aside with a flash of anger. He was laughing.

"If you have any pity for me, do not leave me now," he repeated. "Stay a moment longer, and my fortune is made. The passengers will report us all over Red Dog as engaged. I shall be supposed to be in your father's secrets, and shall be sought after as a director of all the new companies. The 'Record' will double its circulation; poetry will drop out of its columns, advertising rush to fill its place, and I shall receive five dollars a week more salary, if not seven and a half. Never mind the consequences to yourself at such a moment. I assure you there will be none. You can deny it the next day—*I* will deny it—nay, more, the 'Record' itself will deny it in an extra edition of one thousand copies, at ten cents each. Linger a moment longer, Miss Mulrady. Fly, oh fly not yet. They're coming—hark! oh! By Jove, it's only Don Cæsar!"

It was, indeed, only the young scion of the house of Alvarado, blue-eyed, sallow-skinned, and high-shouldered, coming towards them on a fiery, half-broken mustang, whose very spontaneous lawlessness seemed to accentuate and bring out the grave and decorous ease of his rider. Even in his burlesque preoccupation the editor of the "Record" did not withhold his admiration of this perfect-horsemanship. Mamie, who, in her wounded *amour propre,* would like to have made much of it to annoy her companion, was thus estopped any ostentatious compliment.

Don Cæsar lifted his hat with sweet seriousness to the lady, with grave courtesy to the gentleman. While the lower half of this Centaur was apparently quivering with fury, and stamping the ground in his evident desire to charge upon the pair, the upper half, with natural dignity, looked from the one to the other, as if to leave the privilege of an explanation with them. But Mamie was too wise, and her companion too indifferent, to offer one. A slight shade passed over Don Cæsar's face. To complicate the situation at that moment, the expected stage-coach came rattling by. With quick feminine intuition, Mamie caught in the faces of the driver and the expressman, and reflected in the mischievous eyes of her companion, a peculiar interpretation of their meeting, that was not removed by the whispered assurance of the editor that the passengers were anxiously looking back "to see the shooting."

The young Spaniard, equally oblivious of humor or curiosity, remained impassive.

"You know Mr. Slinn, of the 'Record," said Mamie, "don't you?"

Don Cæsar had never before met the Señor Esslinn. He was under the impression that it was a Señor Robinson that was of the "Record."

"Oh, *he* was shot," said Slinn. "I'm taking his place."

"Bueno! To be shot too? I trust not."

Slinn looked quickly and sharply into Don Cæsar's grave face. He seemed to be incapable of any double meaning. However, as he had no serious reason for awakening Don Cæsar's jealousy, and very little desire to become an embarrassing third in this conversation, and possibly a burden to the young lady, he proceeded to take his leave of her. From a sudden feminine revulsion of sympathy, or from some unintelligible instinct of diplomacy, Mamie said, as she extended her hand, "I hope you'll find a home for your family near here. Mamma wants pa to let our old house. Perhaps it might suit you, if not too far from your work. You might speak to ma about it."

"Thank you; I will," responded the young man, pressing her hand with unaffected cordiality.

Don Cæsar watched him until he had disappeared behind the wayside buckeyes.

"He is a man of family—this one—your countryman?"

It seemed strange to her to have a mere acquaintance spoken of as "her countryman"—not the first time nor the last time in her career. As there appeared no trace or sign of jealousy in her questioner's manner, she answered briefly but vaguely:

"Yes; it's a shocking story. His father disappeared some years ago, and he has just found him—a helpless paralytic—in the Sacramento Hospital. He'll have to support him—and they're very poor."

"So, then, they are not independent of each other always—these fathers and children of Americans!"

"No," said Mamie, shortly. Without knowing why, she felt inclined to resent Don Cæsar's manner. His

serious gravity—gentle and high-bred as it was, undoubtedly—was somewhat trying to her at times, and
seemed even more so after Slinn's irreverent humor.
She picked up her parasol, a little impatiently, as if
to go.

But Don Cæsar had already dismounted, and tied his
horse to a tree with a strong lariat that hung at his
saddle-bow.

"Let us walk through the woods towards your home.
I can return alone for the horse when you shall dismiss me."

They turned in among the pines that, overcrowding
the hollow, crept partly up the side of the hill of Mulrady's shaft. A disused trail, almost hidden by the waxen-
hued yerba buena, led from the highway, and finally lost
itself in the undergrowth. It was a lovers' walk; they
were lovers, evidently, and yet the man was too self-
poised in his gravity, the young woman too conscious
and critical, to suggest an absorbing or oblivious passion.

"I should not have made myself so obtrusive to-day
before your friend," said Don Cæsar, with proud hu-
mility, "but I could not understand from your mother
whether you were alone or whether my company was
desirable. It is of this I have now to speak, Mamie.
Lately your mother has seemed strange to me; avoiding
any reference to our affection; treating it lightly, and
even as to-day, I fancy, putting obstacles in the way
of our meeting alone. She was disappointed at your
return from Sacramento where, I have been told, she
intended you to remain until you left the country; and
since your return I have seen you but twice. I may be
wrong. Perhaps I do not comprehend the American
mother; I have—who knows?—perhaps offended in
some point of etiquette, omitted some ceremony that was
her due. But when you told me, Mamie, that it was
not necessary to speak to *her* first, that it was not the
American fashion—"

Mamie started, and blushed slightly.

"Yes," she said hurriedly, "certainly; but ma has been
quite queer of late, and she may think—you know—that

since—since there has been so much property to dispose of, she ought to have been consulted."

"Then let us consult her at once, dear child! And as to the property, in Heaven's name, let her dispose of it as she will. Saints forbid that an Alvarado should ever interfere. And what is it to us, my little one? Enough that Doña Mameta Alvarado will never have less state than the richest bride that ever came to Los Gatos."

Mamie had not forgotten that, scarcely a month ago, even had she loved the man before her no more than she did at present, she would still have been thrilled with delight at these words! Even now she was moved—conscious as she had become that the "state" of a bride of the Alvarados was not all she had imagined, and that the bare adobe court of Los Gatos was open to the sky and the free criticism of Sacramento capitalists!

"Yes, dear," she murmured with a half childlike pleasure, that lit up her face and eyes so innocently that it stopped any minute investigation into its origin and real meaning. "Yes, dear; but we need not have a fuss made about it at present, and perhaps put ma against us. She wouldn't hear of ou. marrying now; and she might forbid our engagement."

"But you are going away."

"I should have to go to New York or Europe *first,* you know," she answered, naively, "even if it were all settled. I should have to get things! One couldn't be decent here."

With the recollection of the pink cotton gown, in which she had first pledged her troth to him, before his eyes, he said, "But you are charming now. You cannot be more so to me. If I am satisfied, little one, with you as you are, let us go together, and then you can get dresses to please others."

She had not expected this importunity. Really, if it came to this, she might have engaged herself to some one like Slinn; he at least would have understood her. He was much cleverer, and certainly more of a man of the world. When Slinn had treated her like a child, it was with the humorous tolerance of an admiring superior, and not the didactic impulse of a guardian. She did not say this, nor did her pretty eyes indicate it, as in the instance of her brief anger with Slinn. She only said gently,—

"I should have thought you, of all men, would have been particular about your wife doing the proper thing. But never mind! Don't let us talk any more about it. Perhaps as it seems such a great thing to you, and so much trouble, there may be no necessity for it at all."

I do not think that the young lady deliberately planned this charmingly illogical deduction from Don Cæsar's speech, or that she calculated its effect upon him; but it was part of her nature to say it, and profit by it. Under the unjust lash of it, his pride gave way.

"Ah, do you not see why I wish to go with you?" he said, with sudden and unexpected passion. "You are beautiful; you are good; it has pleased Heaven to make you rich also; but you are a child in experience, and know not your own heart. With your beauty, your goodness, and your wealth, you will attract all to you—as you do here—because you cannot help it. But you will be equally helpless, little one, if *they* should attract *you*, and you had no tie to fall back upon."

It was an unfortunate speech. The words were Don Cæsar's; but the thought she had heard before from her mother, although the deduction had been of a very different kind. Mamie followed the speaker with bright but visionary eyes. There must be some truth in all this. Her mother had said it; Mr. Slinn had laughingly admitted it. She *had* a brilliant future before her! Was she right in making it impossible by a rash and foolish tie? He himself had said she was inexperienced. She knew it; and yet, what was he doing now but taking advantage of that inexperience? If he really loved her, he would be willing to submit to the test. She did not ask a similar one from him; and was willing, if she came out of it free, to marry him just the same. There was something so noble in this thought that she felt for a moment carried away by an impulse of compassionate unselfishness, and smiled tenderly as she looked up in his face.

"Then you consent, Mamie?" he said, eagerly, passing his arm around her waist.

"Not now, Cæsar," she said, gently disengaging herself. "I must think it over; we are both too young to act upon it rashly; it would be unfair to you, who are so quiet and have seen so few girls—I mean Americans —to tie yourself to the first one you have known. When I am gone you will go more into the world. There are Mr. Slinn's two sisters coming here—I shouldn't wonder if they were far cleverer and talked far better than I do—and think how I should feel if I knew that only a wretched pledge to me kept you from loving them!" She stopped, and cast down her eyes.

It was her first attempt at coquetry, for, in her usual charming selfishness, she was perfectly frank and open; and it might not have been her last, but she had gone too far at first, and was not prepared for a recoil of her own argument.

"If you admit that it is possible—that it is possible to you!" he said, quickly.

She saw her mistake. "We may not have many opportunities to meet alone," she answered, quietly; "and I am sure we would be happier when we meet not to accuse each other of impossibilities. Let us rather see how we can communicate together, if anything should prevent our meeting. Remember, it was only by chance that you were able to see me now. If ma has believed that she ought to have been consulted, our meeting together in this secret way will only make matters worse. She is even now wondering where I am, and may be suspicious. I must go back at once. At any moment some one may come here looking for me."

"But I have so much to say," he pleaded. "Our time has been so short."

"You can write."

"But what will your mother think of that?" he said, in grave astonishment.

She colored again as she returned, quickly, "Of course,

you must not write to the house. You can leave a letter somewhere for me—say, somewhere about here. Stop!" she added, with a sudden girlish gayety, "see, here's the very place. Look there!"

She pointed to the decayed trunk of a blasted syca-more, a few feet from the trail. A cavity, breast high, half filled with skeleton leaves and pine-nuts, showed that it had formerly been a squirrel's hoard, but for some reason had been deserted.

"Look! it's a regular letter-box," she continued, gayly, rising on tip-toe to peep into its recesses. Don Cæsar looked at her admiringly; it seemed like a return to their first idyllic love-making in the old days, when she used to steal out of the cabbage rows in her brown linen apron and sun-bonnet to walk with him in the woods. He recalled the fact to her with the fatality of a lover already seeking to restore in past recollections some-thing that was wanting in the present. She received it with the impatience of youth, to whom the present is all sufficient.

"I wonder how you could ever have cared for me in that holland apron," she said, looking down upon her new dress.

"Shall I tell you why?" he said, fondly, passing his arm around her waist, and drawing her pretty head nearer his shoulder.

"No—not now!" she said, laughingly, but struggling to free herself. "There's not time. Write it, and put it in the box. There," she added, hastily, "listen!—what's that?"

"It's only a squirrel," he whispered reassuringly in her ear.

"No; it's somebody coming! I must go! Please! Cæsar, dear! There, then—"

She met his kiss half-way, released herself with a lithe movement of her wrist and shoulder, and the next moment seemed to slip into the woods, and was gone.

Don Cæsar listened with a sigh as the last rustling ceased, cast a look at the decayed tree as if to fix it in

I Bret Harte   v. 2

his memory, and then slowly retraced his steps towards his tethered mustang.

He was right, however, in his surmise of the cause of that interruption. A pair of bright eyes had been watching them from the bough of an adjacent tree. It was a squirrel, who, having had serious and prior intentions of making use of the cavity they had discovered, had only withheld examination by an apparent courteous discretion towards the intruding pair. Now that they were gone he slipped down the tree and ran towards the decayed stump.

CHAPTER III

APPARENTLY dissatisfied with the result of an investigation, which proved that the cavity was unfit as a treasure hoard for a discreet squirrel, whatever its value as a receptacle for the love-tokens of incautious humanity, the little animal at once set about to put things in order. He began by whisking out an immense quantity of dead leaves, disturbed a family of tree-spiders, dissipated a drove of patient aphides browsing in the bark, as well as their attendant dairymen, the ants, and otherwise ruled it with the high hand of dispossession and a contemptuous opinion of the previous incumbents. It must not be supposed, however, that his proceedings were altogether free from contemporaneous criticism; a venerable crow sitting on a branch above him displayed great interest in his occupation, and, hopping down a few moments afterwards, disposed of some worm-eaten nuts, a few larvæ, and an insect or two, with languid dignity and without prejudice. Certain incumbrances, however, still resisted the squirrel's general eviction; among them a folded square of paper with sharply defined edges, that declined investigation, and, owing to a nauseous smell of tobacco, escaped nibbling as it had apparently escaped insect ravages. This, owing to its sharp angles, which persisted in catching in the soft decaying wood in his whirlwind of house-cleaning, he allowed to remain. Having thus, in a general way, prepared for the coming winter, the self-satisfied little rodent dismissed the subject from his active mind.

His rage and indignation a few days later may be readily conceived, when he found, on returning to his new-made home, another square of paper, folded like the first, but much fresher and whiter, lying within the cavity, on top of some moss which had evidently been placed there for the purpose. This he felt was really more than he could bear, but it was smaller, and with a few energetic kicks and whisks of his tail he managed to finally dislodge it through the opening, where it fell ignominiously to the earth. The eager eyes of the ever-attendant crow, however, instantly detected it; he flew to the ground, and, turning it over, examined it gravely. It was certainly not edible, but it was exceedingly rare, and, as an old collector of curios, he felt he could not pass it by. He lifted it in his beak, and, with a desperate struggle against the superincumbent weight, regained the branch with his prize. Here, by one of those delicious vagaries of animal nature, he apparently at once discharged his mind of the whole affair, became utterly oblivious of it, allowed it to drop without the least concern, and eventually flew away with an abstracted air, as if he had been another bird entirely. The paper got into a manzanita bush, where it remained suspended until the evening, when, being dislodged by a passing wild-cat on its way to Mulrady's hen-roost, it gave that delicately sensitive marauder such a turn that she fled into the adjacent county.

But the troubles of the squirrel were not yet over. On the following day the young man who had accompanied the young woman returned to the trunk, and the squirrel had barely time to make his escape before the impatient visitor approached the opening of the cavity, peered into it, and even passed his hand through its recesses. The delight visible upon his anxious and serious face at the disappearance of the letter, and the apparent proof that it had been called for, showed him to have been its original depositor, and probably awakened a remorseful recollection in the dark bosom of the omnipresent crow, who uttered a conscious-stricken croak from the bough above him. But the young man quickly disappeared again, and the squirrel was once more left in undisputed possession.

A week passed. A weary, anxious interval to Don Cæsar, who had neither seen nor heard from Mamie since their last meeting. Too conscious of his own self-respect to call at the house after the equivocal conduct of Mrs. Mulrady, and too proud to haunt the lanes and approaches in the hope of meeting her daughter, like an ordinary lover, he hid his gloomy thoughts in the monastic shadows of the courtyard at Los Gatos, or found relief in furious riding at night and early morning on the highway. Once or twice the up-stage had been overtaken and passed by a rushing figure as shadowy as a phantom horseman, with only the star-like point of a cigarette to indicate its humanity. It was in one of these fierce recreations that he was obliged to stop in early morning at the blacksmith's shop at Rough-and-Ready, to have a loosened horseshoe replaced, and while waiting picked up a newspaper. Don Cæsar seldom read the papers, but noticing that this was the "Record," he glanced at its columns. A familiar name suddenly flashed out of the dark type like a spark from the anvil. With a brain and heart that seemed to be beating in unison with the blacksmith's sledge, he read as follows:—

"Our distinguished fellow-townsman, Alvin Mulrady, Esq., left town day before yesterday to attend an important meeting of directors of the Red Dog Ditch Company, in San Francisco. Society will regret to hear that Mrs. Mulrady and her beautiful and accomplished daughter, who are expecting to depart for Europe at the end of the month, anticipated the event nearly a fortnight, by taking this opportunity of accompanying Mr. Mulrady as far as San Francisco, on their way to the East. Mrs. and Miss Mulrady intend to visit London, Paris, and Berlin, and will be absent three years. It is possible that Mr. Mulrady may join them later at one or other of those capitals. Considerable disappointment is felt that a more extended leave-taking was not possible, and that, under the circumstances, no opportunity was offered for a 'send off' suitable to the condition of the parties and the esteem in which they are held in Rough-and-Ready."

The paper dropped from his hands. Gone! and without a word! No, that was impossible! There must be some mistake; she had written; the letter had miscarried; she must have sent word to Los Gatos, and the stupid messenger had blundered; she had probably appointed another meeting, or expected him to follow to San Francisco. "The day before yesterday!" It was the morning's paper—she had been gone scarcely two days—it was not too late yet to receive a delayed message by post, by some forgetful hand—by—ah—the tree!

Of course it was in the tree, and he had not been there for a week! Why had he not thought of it before? The fault was his, not hers. Perhaps she had gone away, believing him faithless, or a country boor.

"In the name of the Devil, will you keep me here till eternity!"

The blacksmith stared at him. Don Cæsar suddenly remembered that he was speaking, as he was thinking—in Spanish.

"Ten dollars, my friend, if you have done in five minutes!"

The man laughed. "That's good enough American," he said, beginning to quicken his efforts. Don Cæsar again took up the paper. There was another paragraph that recalled his last interview with Mamie:—

"Mr. Harry Slinn, Jr., the editor of this paper, has just moved into the pioneer house formerly occupied by Alvin Mulrady, Esq., which has already become historic in the annals of the county. Mr. Slinn brings with him his father—H. J. Slinn, Esq.,—and his two sisters. Mr. Slinn, Sen., who has been suffering for many years from complete paralysis, we understand is slowly improving; and it is by the advice of his physicians that he has chosen the invigorating air of the foothills as a change to the debilitating heat of Sacramento."

The affair had been quickly settled, certainly, reflected Don Cæsar, with a slight chill of jealousy, as he thought of Mamie's interest in the young editor. But the next moment he dismissed it from his mind; all except a dull consciousness that, if she really loved him—Don Cæsar —as he loved her, she could not have assisted in throwing into his society the young sisters of the editor, who she expected might be so attractive.

Within the five minutes the horse was ready, and Don Cæsar in the saddle again. In less than half an hour he was at the wayside boulder. Here he picketed his horse, and took the narrow foot-trail through the hollow. It did not take him long to reach their old trysting-place. With a beating heart he approached the decaying trunk and looked into the cavity. There was no letter there!

A few blackened nuts and some of the dry moss he had put there were lying on the ground at its roots. He could not remember whether they were there when he had last visited the spot. He began to grope in the cavity with both hands. His fingers struck against the sharp angles of a flat paper packet: a thrill of joy ran through them and stopped his beating heart; he drew out the hidden object, and was chilled with disappointment.

It was an ordinary-sized envelope of yellowish-brown paper, bearing, besides the usual government stamp, the official legend of an express company, and showing its age as much by this record of a now obsolete carrying service as by the discoloration of time and atmosphere. Its weight, which was heavier than that of any ordinary letter of the same size and thickness, was evidently due to some loose enclosures, that slightly rustled and could be felt by the fingers, like minute pieces of metal or grains of gravel. It was within Don Cæsar's experience that gold specimens were often sent in that manner. It was in a state of singular preservation, except the address, which, being written in pencil, was scarcely discernible, and even when deciphered appeared to be incoherent and unfinished. The unknown correspondent had written "dear Mary," and then "Mrs. Mary Slinn," with an unintelligible scrawl following for the direction. If Don Cæsar's mind had not been lately preoccupied with the name of the editor, he would hardly have guessed the superscription.

In his cruel disappointment and fully aroused indigna-tion, he at once began to suspect a connection of circumstances which at any other moment he would have thought purely accidental, or perhaps not have considered at all. The cavity in the tree had evidently been used as a secret receptacle for letters before; did Mamie know it at the time, and how did she know it? The apparent age of the letter made it preposterous to suppose that it pointed to any secret correspondence of hers with young Mr. Slinn; and the address was not in her handwriting. Was there any secret previous intimacy between the families? There was but one way in which he could connect this letter with Mamie's faithlessness. It was an infamous, a grotesquely horrible idea, a thought which sprang as much from his inexperience of the world and his habitual suspiciousness of all humor as anything else! It was that the letter was a brutal joke of Slinn's—a joke perhaps concocted by Mamie and himself—a parting insult that should at the last moment proclaim their treachery and his own credulity. Doubtless it contained a declaration of their shame, and the reason why she had fled from him without a word of explanation. And the enclosure, of course, was some significant and degrading illustration. Those Americans are full of those low conceits; it was their national vulgarity.

He had the letter in his angry hand. He could break it open if he wished and satisfy himself; but it was not addressed to *him,* and the instinct of honor, strong even in his rage, was the instinct of an adversary as well. No; Slinn should open the letter before him. Slinn should explain everything, and answer for it. If it was nothing—a mere accident—it would lead to some general explanation, and perhaps even news of Mamie. But he would arraign Slinn, and at once. He put the letter in his pocket, quickly retraced his steps to his horse, and, putting spurs to the animal, followed the high road to the gate of Mulrady's pioneer cabin.

He remembered it well enough. To a cultivated taste, it was superior to the more pretentious "new house." During the first year of Mulrady's tenancy, the plain square log-cabin had received those additions and attractions which only a tenant can conceive and actual experience suggest; and in this way the hideous right angles were broken with sheds, "lean-to" extensions, until a certain picturesqueness was given to the irregularity of outline, and a home-like security and companionship to the congregated buildings. It typified the former life of the great capitalist, as the tall new house illustrated the loneliness and isolation that wealth had given him. But the real points of vantage were the years of cultivation and habitation that had warmed and enriched the soil, and evoked the climbing vines and roses that already hid its unpainted boards, rounded its hard outlines, and gave projection and shadow from the pitiless glare of a summer's long sun, or broke the steady beating of the winter rains. It was true that pea and bean poles surrounded it on one side, and the only access to the house was through the cabbage rows that once were the pride and sustenance of the Mulradys. It was this fact, more than any other, that had impelled Mrs. Mulrady to abandon its site; she did not like to read the history of their humble origin reflected in the faces of their visitors as they entered.

Don Cæsar tied his horse to the fence, and hurriedly approached the house. The door, however, hospitably opened when he was a few paces from it, and when he reached the threshold he found himself unexpectedly in the presence of two pretty girls. They were evidently Slinn's sisters, whom he had neither thought of nor included in the meeting he had prepared. In spite of his preoccupation, he felt himself suddenly embarrassed, not only by the actual distinction of their beauty, but by a kind of likeness that they seemed to bear to Mamie.

"We saw you coming," said the elder, unaffectedly.

"You are Don Cæsar Alvarado. My brother has spoken of you."

The words recalled Don Cæsar to himself and a sense of courtesy. He was not here to quarrel with these fair strangers at their first meeting; he must seek Slinn else-where, and at another time. The frankness of his re-ception and the allusion to their brother made it appear impossible that they should be either a party to his dis-appointment, or even aware of it. His excitement melted away before a certain lazy ease, which the conscious-ness of their beauty seemed to give them. He was able to put a few courteous inquiries, and, thanks to the paragraph in the "Record," to congratulate them upon their father's improvement.

"Oh, pa is a great deal better in his health, and has picked up even in the last few days, so that he is able to walk round with crutches," said the elder sister. "The air here seems to invigorate him wonderfully."

"And you know, Esther," said the younger, "I think he begins to take more notice of things, especially when he is out-of-doors. He looks around on the scenery, and his eye brightens, as if he knew all about it; and some-times he knits his brows, and looks down so, as if he was trying to remember."

"You know, I suppose," exclaimed Esther, "that since his seizure his memory has been a blank—that is, three or four years of his life seem to have been dropped out of his recollection."

"It might be a mercy sometimes, Señora," said Don Cæsar, with a grave sigh, as he looked at the delicate features before him, which recalled the face of the ab-sent Mamie.

"That's not very complimentary," said the younger girl, laughingly; "for pa didn't recognize us, and only remembered us as little girls."

"Vashti!" interrupted Esther, rebukingly; then, turn-ing to Don Cæsar, she added, "My sister, Vashti, means that father remembers more what happened before he came to California, when we were quite young, than he does of the interval that elapsed. Dr. Duchesne says it's a singular case. He thinks that, with his present progress, he will recover the perfect use of his limbs; though his memory may never come back again."

"Unless— You forget what the doctor told us this morning," interrupted Vashti again, briskly.

"I was going to say it," said Esther, a little curtly. "*Unless* he has another stroke. Then he will either die or recover his mind entirely."

Don Cæsar glanced at the bright faces, a trifle heightened in color by their eager recital and the slight rivalry of narration, and looked grave. He was a little shocked at a certain lack of sympathy and tenderness towards their unhappy parent. They seemed to him not only to have caught that dry, curious toleration of helplessness which characterizes even relationship in its attendance upon chronic suffering and weakness, but to have acquired an unconscious habit of turning it to account. In his present sensitive condition, he even fancied that they flirted mildly over their parent's infirmity.

"My brother Harry has gone to Red Dog," continued Esther; "he'll be right sorry to have missed you. Mrs. Mulrady spoke to him about you; you seem to have been great friends. I s'pose you knew her daughter, Mamie; I hear she is very pretty."

Although Don Cæsar was now satisfied that the Slinns knew nothing of Mamie's singular behavior to him, he felt embarrassed by this conversation. "Miss Mulrady is very pretty," he said, with grave courtesy; "it is a custom of her race. She left suddenly," he added with affected calmness.

"I reckon she did calculate to stay here longer—so her mother said; but the whole thing was settled a week ago. I know my brother was quite surprised to hear from Mr. Mulrady that if we were going to decide about this house we must do it at once; he had an idea himself about moving out of the big one into this when they left."

"Mamie Mulrady hadn't much to keep her here, considerin' the money and the good looks she has, I reckon," said Vashti. "She isn't the sort of girl to throw herself away in the wilderness, when she can pick and choose elsewhere. I only wonder she ever come back from Sacramento. They talk about papa Mulrady having *business* at San Francisco, and *that* hurrying them off! Depend upon it, that 'business' was Mamie herself. Her wish is gospel to them. If she'd wanted to stay and have a farewell party, old Mulrady's business would have been nowhere."

"Ain't you a little rough on Mamie," said Esther, who had been quietly watching the young man's face with her large languid eyes, "considering that we don't know her, and haven't even the right of friends to criticise?"

"I don't call it rough," returned Vashti, frankly, "for I'd do the same if I were in her shoes—and they're four-and-a-halves, for Harry told me so. Give me her money and her looks, and you wouldn't catch me hanging round these diggings—goin' to choir meetings Saturdays, church Sundays, and buggy-riding once a month —for society! No—Mamie's head was level—you bet!"

Don Cæsar rose hurriedly. They would present his compliments to their father, and he would endeavor to find their brother at Red Dog. He, alas! had neither father, mother, nor sister, but if they would receive his aunt, the Doña Inez Sepulvida, the next Sunday, when she came from mass, she should be honored and he would be delighted. It required all his self-possession to deliver himself of this formal courtesy before he could take his leave, and on the back of his mustang give way to the rage, disgust and hatred of everything connected with Mamie that filled his heart. Conscious of his disturbance, but not entirely appreciating their own share in it, the two girls somewhat wickedly prolonged the interview by following him into the garden.

"Well, if you *must* leave now," said Esther, at last, languidly, "it ain't much out of your way to go down through the garden and take a look at pa as you go. He's somewhere down there, near the woods, and we don't like to leave him alone too long. You might pass the time of day with him; see if he's right side up. Vashti and I have got a heap of things to fix here yet; but if anything's wrong with him, you can call us. So-long."

Don Cæsar was about to excuse himself hurriedly; but that sudden and acute perception of all kindred sorrow which belongs to refined suffering, checked his speech. The loneliness of the helpless old man in this atmosphere of active and youthful selfishness touched him. He bowed assent, and turned aside into one of the long perspectives of bean-poles. The girls watched him until out of sight.

"Well," said Vashti, "don't tell *me*. But if there wasn't something between him and that Mamie Mulrady, I don't know a jilted man when I see him."

"Well, you needn't have let him *see* that you knew it, so that any civility of ours would look as if we were ready to take up with her leavings," responded Esther, astutely, as the girls reëntered the house.

Meantime, the unconscious object of their criticism walked sadly down the old market-garden, whose rude outlines and homely details he once clothed with the poetry of a sensitive man's first love. Well, it was a common cabbage field and potato patch after all. In his disgust he felt conscious of even the loss of that sense of patronage and superiority which had invested his affection for a girl of meaner condition. His self-respect was humiliated with his love. The soil and dirt of those wretched cabbages had clung to him, but not to her. It was she who had gone higher; it was he who was left in the vulgar ruins of his misplaced passion.

He reached the bottom of the garden without observing any sign of the lonely invalid. He looked up and down the cabbage rows, and through the long perspective of pea-vines, without result. There was a newer trail leading from a gap in the pines to the wooded hollow, which undoubtedly intersected the little path that he and Mamie had once followed from the high road. If the old man had taken this trail he had possibly over-tasked his strength, and there was the more reason why he should continue his search, and render any assistance if required. There was another idea that occurred to him, which eventually decided him to go on. It was that both these trails led to the decayed sycamore stump, and that the older Slinn might have something to do with the mysterious letter. Quickening his steps through the field, he entered the hollow, and reached the intersecting trail as he expected. To the right it lost itself in the dense woods in the direction of the ominous stump; to the left it descended in nearly a straight line to the highway, now plainly visible, as was equally the boulder on which he had last discovered Mamie sitting with young Slinn. If he were not mistaken, there was a figure sitting there now; it was surely a man. And by that half-bowed, helpless attitude, the object of his search!

It did not take him long to descend the track to the highway and approach the stranger. He was seated with his hands upon his knees, gazing in a vague, absorbed fashion upon the hillside, now crowned with the engine-house and chimney that marked the site of Mulrady's shaft. He started slightly, and looked up, as Don Cæsar paused before him. The young man was surprised to see that the unfortunate man was not as old as he had expected, and that his expression was one of quiet and beatified contentment.

"Your daughters told me you were here," said Don Cæsar, with gentle respect. "I am Cæsar Alvarado, your not very far neighbor; very happy to pay his respects to you as he has to them."

"My daughters?" said the old man, vaguely. "Oh, yes! nice little girls. And my boy Harry. Did you see Harry? Fine little fellow, Harry."

"I am glad to hear that you are better," said Don Cæsar, hastily, "and that the air of our country does you no harm. God benefit you, señor," he added, with a profoundly reverential gesture, dropping unconsciously into the religious habit of his youth. "May he protect you, and bring you back to health and happiness!"

"Happiness?" said Slinn, amazedly. "I am happy— very happy! I have everything I want: good air, good food, good clothes, pretty little children, kind friends—"

He smiled benignantly at Don Cæsar. "God is very good to me!"

Indeed, he seemed very happy; and his face, albeit crowned with white hair, unmarked by care and any disturbing impression, had so much of satisfied youth in it that the grave features of his questioner made him appear the elder. Nevertheless, Don Cæsar noticed that his eyes, when withdrawn from him, sought the hillside with the same visionary abstraction.

"It is a fine view, Señor Esslinn," said Don Cæsar.

"It is a beautiful view, sir," said Slinn, turning his happy eyes upon him for a moment, only to rest them again on the green slope opposite.

"Beyond that hill which you are looking at—not far, Señor Esslinn—I live. You shall come and see me there—you and your family."

"You—you—live there?" stammered the invalid, with a troubled expression—the first and only change to the complete happiness that had hitherto suffused his face. "You—and your name is—is Ma—"

"Alvarado," said Don Cæsar, gently. Cæsar Alvarado."

"You said Masters," said the old man, with sudden querulousness.

"No, good friend. I said Alvarado," returned Don Cæsar, gravely.

"If you didn't say Masters, how could *I* say it? I don't know any Masters."

Don Cæsar was silent. In another moment the happy tranquillity returned to Slinn's face; and Don Cæsar continued:—

"It is not a long walk over the hill, though it is far by the road. When you are better you shall try it. Yonder little trail leads to the top of the hill, and then—"

He stopped, for the invalid's face had again assumed its troubled expression. Partly to change his thoughts, and partly for some inexplicable idea that had suddenly seized him, Don Cæsar continued:—

"There is a strange old stump near the trail, and in it

a hole. In the hole I found this letter." He stopped again—this time in alarm. Slinn had staggered to his feet with ashen and distorted features, and was glancing at the letter which Don Cæsar had drawn from his pocket. The muscles of his throat swelled as if he was swallowing; his lips moved, but no sound issued from them. At last, with a convulsive effort, he regained a disjointed speech, in a voice scarcely audible.

"My letter! my letter! It's mine! Give it me! It's my fortune—all mine! In the tunnel—hill! Masters stole it—stole my fortune! Stole it all! See, see!"

He seized the letter from Don Cæsar with trembling hands, and tore it open forcibly: a few dull yellow grains fell from it heavily, like shot, to the ground.

"See, it's true! My letter! My gold! My strike! My—my—my God!"

A tremor passed over his face. The hand that held the letter suddenly dropped sheer and heavy as the gold had fallen. The whole side of his face and body nearest Don Cæsar seemed to drop and sink into itself as suddenly. At the same moment, and without a word, he slipped through Don Cæsar's outstretched hands to the ground. Don Cæsar bent quickly over him, but no longer than to satisfy himself that he lived and breathed, although helpless. He then caught up the fallen letter, and, glancing over it with flashing eyes, thrust it and the few specimens in his pocket. He then sprang to his feet, so transformed with energy and intelligence that he seemed to have added the lost vitality of the man before him to his own. He glanced quickly up and down the highway. Every moment to him was precious now; but he could not leave the stricken man in the dust of the road; nor could he carry him to the house; nor, having alarmed his daughters, could he abandon his helplessness to their feeble arms. He remembered that his horse was still tied to the garden fence. He would fetch it, and carry the unfortunate man across the saddle to the gate. He lifted him with difficulty to the boulder, and ran rapidly up the road in the direction of his tethered steed. He had not proceeded far when he heard

the noise of wheels behind him. It was the up stage
coming furiously along. He would have called to the
driver for assistance, but even through that fast-sweeping
cloud of dust and motion he could see that the man was
utterly oblivious of anything but the speed of his rushing
chariot, and had even risen in his box to lash the infu-
riated and frightened animals forward.

An hour later, when the coach drew up at the Red
Dog Hotel, the driver descended from the box, white,
but taciturn. When he had swallowed a glass of whiskey
at a single gulp, he turned to the astonished express
agent, who had followed him in.

"One of two things, Jim, hez got to happen," he said,
huskily. "Either that there rock hez got to get off the
road, or *I* have. I've seed *him* on it agin!"

CHAPTER IV

No further particulars of the invalid's second attack
were known than those furnished by Don Cæsar's brief
statement, that he had found him lying insensible on the
boulder. This seemed perfectly consistent with the theory
of Dr. Duchesne; and as the young Spaniard left Los
Gatos the next day, he escaped not only the active reporter of the "Record," but the perusal of a grateful paragraph in the next day's paper recording his prompt
kindness and courtesy. Dr. Duchesne's prognosis, however, seemed at fault; the elder Slinn did not succumb to
this second stroke, nor did he recover his reason. He
apparently only relapsed into his former physical weakness, losing the little ground he had gained during the
last month, and exhibiting no change in his mental condition, unless the fact that he remembered nothing of his
seizure and the presence of Don Cæsar could be considered as favorable. Dr. Duchesne's gravity seemed to give
that significance to this symptom, and his cross-questioning of the patient was characterized by more than his
usual curtness.

"You are sure you don't remember walking in the

garden before you were ill?" he said. "Come, think again. You must remember that." The old man's eyes wandered restlessly around the room, but he answered by a negative shake of his head. "And you don't remember sitting down on a stone by the road?"

The old man kept his eyes resolutely fixed on the bed-clothes before him. "No!" he said, with a certain sharp decision that was new to him.

The doctor's eye brightened. "All right, old man; then don't."

On his way out he took the eldest Miss Slinn aside. "He'll do," he said, grimly: "he's beginning to lie."

"Why, he only said he didn't remember," responded Esther.

"That was because he didn't want to remember," said the doctor, authoritatively. "The brain is acting on some impression that is either painful and unpleasant, or so vague that he can't formulate it; he is conscious of it, and won't attempt it yet. It's a heap better than his old self-satisfied incoherency."

A few days later, when the fact of Slinn's identification with the paralytic of three years ago by the stage-driver became generally known, the doctor came in quite jubilant.

"It's all plain now," he said, decidedly. "That second stroke was caused by the nervous shock of his coming suddenly upon the very spot where he had the first one. It proved that his brain still retained old impressions, but as this first act of his memory was a painful one, the strain was too great. It was mighty unlucky; but it was a good sign."

"And you think, then—" hesitated Harry Slinn.

"I think," said Dr. Duchesne, "that this activity still exists, and the proof of it, as I said before, is that he is trying now to forget it, and avoid thinking of it. You will find that he will fight shy of any allusion to it, and will be cunning enough to dodge it every time."

He certainly did. Whether the doctor's hypothesis was fairly based or not, it was a fact that, when he was first taken out to drive with his watchful physician, he apparently took no notice of the boulder—which still remained on the roadside, thanks to the later practical explanation of the stage-driver's vision—and curtly refused to talk about it. But, more significant to Duchesne, and perhaps more perplexing, was a certain morose abstraction, which took the place of his former vacuity of contentment, and an intolerance of his attendants, which supplanted his old habitual trustfulness to their care, that had been varied only by the occasional querulousness of an invalid. His daughters sometimes found him regarding them with an attention little short of suspicion, and even his son detected a half-suppressed aversion in his interviews with him.

Referring this among themselves to his unfortunate malady, his children, perhaps, justified this estrangement by paying very little attention to it. They were more pleasantly occupied. The two girls succeeded to the position held by Mamie Mulrady in the society of the neighborhood, and divided the attentions of Rough-and-Ready. The young editor of the "Record" had really achieved, through his supposed intimacy with the Mulradys, the good fortune he had jestingly prophesied. The disappearance of Don Cæsar was regarded as a virtual abandonment of the field to his rival: and the general opinion was that he was engaged to the millionaire's daughter on a certain probation of work and influence in his prospective father-in-law's interests. He became successful in one or two speculations, the magic of the lucky Mulrady's name befriending him. In the superstition of the mining community, much of this luck was due to his having secured the old cabin.

"To think," remarked one of the augurs of Red Dog, French Pete, a polyglot jester, "that while every d——d fool went to taking up claims where the gold had already been found no one thought of stepping into the old man's old *choux* in the cabbage-garden!" Any doubt, however, of the alliance of the families was dissipated by the intimacy that sprang up between the elder Slinn and the millionaire, after the latter's return from San Francisco.

It began in a strange kind of pity for the physical weakness of the man, which enlisted the sympathies of Mulrady, whose great strength had never been deteriorated by the luxuries of wealth, and who was still able to set his workmen an example of hard labor; it was sustained by a singular and superstitious reverence for his mental condition, which, to the paternal Mulrady, seemed to possess that spiritual quality with which popular ignorance invests demented people.

"Then you mean to say that during these three years the vein o' your mind, so to speak, was a lost lead, and sorter dropped out o' sight or follerin'?" queried Mulrady, with infinite seriousness.

"Yes," returned Slinn, with less impatience than he usually showed to questions.

"And durin' that time, when you was dried up and waitin' for rain, I reckon you kinder had visions?"

A cloud passed over Slinn's face.

"Of course, of course!" said Mulrady, a little frightened at his tenacity in questioning the oracle. "Nat'rally, this was private, and not to be talked about. I meant, you had plenty of room for 'em without crowdin'; you kin tell me some day when you're better, and kin sorter select what's points and what ain't."

"Perhaps I may some day," said the invalid, gloomily, glancing in the direction of his preoccupied daughters; "when we're alone."

When his physical strength had improved, and his left arm and side had regained a feeble but slowly gathering vitality, Alvin Mulrady one day surprised the family by bringing the convalescent a pile of letters and accounts, and spreading them on a board before Slinn's invalid chair, with the suggestion that he should look over, arrange, and docket them. The idea seemed preposterous, until it was found that the old man was actually able to perform this service, and exhibited a degree of intellectual activity and capacity for this kind of work that was unsuspected. Dr. Duchesne was delighted, and divided with admiration between his patient's progress and the millionaire's sagacity. "And there are envious people," said the enthusiastic doctor, "who believe that a man like him, who could conceive of such a plan for occupying a weak intellect without taxing its memory or judgment, is merely a lucky fool! Look here. May be it didn't require much brains to stumble on a gold mine, and it is a gift of Providence. But, in my experience, Providence don't go round buyin' up d——d fools, or investin' in dead beats."

When Mr. Slinn, finally, with the aid of crutches, was able to hobble every day to the imposing counting-house and the office of Mr. Mulrady, which now occupied the lower part of the new house, and contained some of its gorgeous furniture, he was installed at a rosewood desk behind Mr. Mulrady's chair, as his confidential clerk and private secretary. The astonishment of Red Dog and Rough-and-Ready at this singular innovation knew no bounds; but the boldness and novelty of the idea carried everything before it. Judge Butts, the oracle of Rough-and-Ready, delivered its decision: "He's got a man who's physically incapable of running off with his money, and has no memory to run off with his ideas. How could he do better?" Even his own son, Harry, coming upon his father thus installed, was for a moment struck with a certain filial respect, and for a day or two patronized him.

In this capacity Slinn became the confidant not only of Mulrady's business secrets, but of his domestic affairs. He knew that young Mulrady, from a freckle-faced slow country boy, had developed into a freckle-faced fast city man, with coarse habits of drink and gambling. It was through the old man's hands that extravagant bills and shameful claims passed on their way to be cashed by Mulrady; it was he that at last laid before the father one day his signature perfectly forged by the son.

"Your eyes are not ez good ez mine, you know, Slinn," said Mulrady, gravely. "It's all right. I sometimes make my *y*'s like that. I'd clean forgot to cash that check. You must not think you've got the monopoly of disremembering," he added, with a faint laugh.

Equally through Slinn's hands passed the record of the lavish expenditure of Mrs. Mulrady and the fair Mamie, as well as the chronicle of their movements and fashionable triumphs. As Mulrady had already noticed that Slinn had no confidence with his own family, he did not try to withhold from them these domestic details, possibly as an offset to the dreary catalogue of his son's misdeeds, but more often in the hope of gaining from the taciturn old man some comment that might satisfy his innocent vanity as father and husband, and perhaps dissipate some doubts that were haunting him.

"Twelve hundred dollars looks to be a good figger for a dress, ain't it? But Malviny knows, I reckon, what ought to be worn at the Tooilleries, and she don't want our Mamie to take a back seat before them furrin' princesses and gran' dukes. It's a slap-up affair, I kalkilate. Let's see. I disremember whether it's an emperor or a king that's rulin' over thar now. It must be suthin' first class and A I, for Malviny ain't the woman to throw away twelve hundred dollars on any of them small-potato despots! She says Mamie speaks French already like them French Petes. I don't quite make out what she means here. She met Don Cæsar in Paris, and she says, 'I think Mamie is nearly off with Don Cæsar, who has followed her here. I don't care about her dropping him *too* suddenly; the reason I'll tell you hereafter. I think the man might be a dangerous enemy.' Now, what do you make of this? I allus thought Mamie rather cottoned to him, and it was the old woman who fought shy, thinkin' Mamie would do better. Now, I am agreeable that my gal should marry any one she likes, whether it's a dook or a poor man, as long as he's on the square. I was ready to take Don Cæsar; but now things seem to have shifted round. As to Don Cæsar's being a dangerous enemy if Mamie won't have him, that's a little too high and mighty for me, and I wonder the old woman don't make him climb down. What do you think?"

"Who is Don Cæsar?" asked Slinn.

"The man what picked you up that day. I mean,"

continued Mulrady, seeing the marks of evident ignorance on the old man's face,—"I mean a sort of grave,
genteel chap, suthin' between a parson and a circus-
rider. You might have seen him round the house talkin'
to your gals."

But Slinn's entire forgetfulness of Don Cæsar was
evidently unfeigned. Whatever sudden accession of
memory he had at the time of his attack, the incident
that caused it had no part in his recollection. With the
exception of these rare intervals of domestic confidences
with his crippled private secretary, Mulrady gave himself up to money-getting. Without any especial faculty
for it—an easy prey often to unscrupulous financiers—
his unfailing luck, however, carried him safely through,
until his very mistakes seemed to be simply insignificant
means to a large significant end and a part of his original
plan. He sank another shaft, at a great expense, with a
view to following the lead he had formerly found,
against the opinions of the best mining engineers, and
struck the artesian spring he did *not* find at that time,
with a volume of water that enabled him not only to
work his own mine, but to furnish supplies to his less
fortunate neighbors at a vast profit. A league of tangled forest and cañon behind Rough-and-Ready, for
which he had paid Don Ramon's heirs an extravagant
price in the presumption that it was auriferous, furnished
the most accessible timber to build the town, at prices
which amply remunerated him. The practical schemes
of experienced men, the wildest visions of daring dreams
delayed or abortive for want of capital, eventually fell
into his hands. Men sneered at his methods, but bought
his shares. Some who affected to regard him simply
as a man of money were content to get only his name
to any enterprise. Courted by his superiors, quoted by
his equals, and admired by his inferiors, he bore his
elevation equally without ostentation or dignity. Bidden
to banquets, and forced by his position as director or
president into the usual gastronomic feats of that civilization and period, he partook of simple food, and continued his old habit of taking a cup of coffee with milk

and sugar at dinner. Without professing temperance, he drank sparingly in a community where alcoholic stimulation was a custom. With neither refinement nor an extended vocabulary, he was seldom profane, and never indelicate. With nothing of the Puritan in his manner or conversation, he seemed to be as strange to the vices of civilization as he was to its virtues. That such a man should offer little to and receive little from the companionship of women of any kind was a foregone conclusion. Without the dignity of solitude, he was pathetically alone.

Meantime, the days passed; the first six months of his opulence were drawing to a close, and in that interval he had more than doubled the amount of his discovered fortune. The rainy season set in early. Although it dissipated the clouds of dust under which Nature and Art seemed to be slowly disappearing, it brought little beauty to the landscape at first, and only appeared to lay bare the crudenesses of civilization. The unpainted wooden buildings of Rough-and-Ready, soaked and dripping with rain, took upon themselves a sleek and shining ugliness, as of second-hand garments; the absence of cornices or projections to break the monotony of the long straight lines of downpour made the town appear as if it had been recently submerged, every vestige of ornamentation swept away, and only the bare outlines left. Mud was everywhere; the outer soil seemed to have risen and invaded the houses even to their most secret recesses, as if outraged Nature was trying to revenge herself. Mud was brought into the saloons and bar-rooms and express offices, on boots, on clothes, on baggage, and sometimes appeared mysteriously in splashes of red color on the walls, without visible conveyance. The dust of six months, closely packed in cornice and carving, yielded under the steady rain a thin yellow paint, that dropped on wayfarers or unexpectedly oozed out of ceilings and walls on the wretched inhabitants within. The outskirts of Rough-and-Ready and the dried hills round Los Gatos did not appear to fare much better; the new vegetation had not yet made much head-

way against the dead grasses of the summer; the pines
in the hollow wept lugubriously into a small rivulet that
had sprung suddenly into life near the old trail; everywhere was the sound of dropping, splashing, gurgling,
or rushing waters.

More hideous than ever, the new Mulrady house lifted
itself against the leaden sky, and stared with all its
large-framed, shutterless windows blankly on the prospect, until they seemed to the wayfarer to become mere
mirrors set in the walls, reflecting only the watery landscape, and unable to give the least indication of light
or heat within. Nevertheless, there was a fire in Mulrady's private office that December afternoon, of a
smoky, intermittent variety, that sufficed more to record
the defects of hasty architecture than to comfort the
millionaire and his private secretary, who had lingered
after the early withdrawal of the clerks. For the next
day was Christmas, and, out of deference to the near
approach of this festivity, a half-holiday had been given
to the employés. "They'll want, some of them, to spend
their money before to-morrow; and others would like to
be able to rise up comfortably drunk Christmas morning," the superintendent had suggested. Mr. Mulrady had
just signed a number of checks indicating his largess to
those devoted adherents with the same unostentatious,
undemonstrative, matter-of-fact manner that distinguished his ordinary business. The men had received
it with something of the same manner. A half-humorous "Thank you, sir"—as if to show that, with their patron, they tolerated this deference to a popular custom, but were a little ashamed of giving way to it—expressed their gratitude and their independence.

"I reckon that the old lady and Mamie are having a
high old time in some of them gilded pallises in St.
Petersburg or Berlin about this time. Them diamonds
that I ordered at Tiffany ought to have reached 'em
about now, so that Mamie could cut a swell at Christmas with her war-paint. I suppose it's the style to give
presents in furrin' countries ez it is here, and I allowed
to the old lady that whatever she orders in that way she

is to do in Californy style—no dollar-jewelry and gal-
vanized-watches business. If she wants to make a
present to any of them nobles ez has been purlite to her,
it's got to be something that Rough-and-Ready ain't
ashamed of. I showed you that pin Mamie bought me
in Paris, didn't I? It's just come for my Christmas
present. No! I reckon I put it in the safe, for them
kind o' things don't suit my style: but s'pose I orter
sport it to-morrow. It was mighty thoughtful in Mamie,
and it must cost a lump; it's got no slouch of a pearl
in it. I wonder what Mamie gave for it?"

"You can easily tell; the bill is here. You paid it yesterday," said Slinn. There was no satire in the man's
voice, nor was there the least perception of irony in Mulrady's manner, as he returned quietly,—

"That's so; it was suthin' like a thousand francs; but
French money, when you pan it out as dollars and cents,
don't make so much, after all." There was a few moments' silence, when he continued, in the same tone of
voice, "Talkin' o' them things, Slinn, I've got suthin'
for you." He stopped suddenly. Ever watchful of any
undue excitement in the invalid, he had noticed a slight
flush of disturbance pass over his face, and continued
carelessly, "But we'll talk it over to-morrow; a day or
two don't make much difference to you and me in such
things, you know. P'raps I'll drop in and see you. We'll
be shut up here."

"Then you're going out somewhere?" asked Slinn, mechanically.

"No," said Mulrady, hesitatingly. It had suddenly
occurred to him that he had nowhere to go if he wanted
to, and he continued, half in explanation, "I ain't reckoned much on Christmas, myself. Abner's at the
Springs; it wouldn't pay him to come here for a day—
even if there was anybody here he cared to see. I
reckon I'll hang round the shanty, and look after things
generally. I haven't been over the house upstairs to put
things to rights since the folks left. But *you* needn't
come here, you know."

He helped the old man to rise, assisted him in putting on his overcoat, and than handed him the cane which had lately replaced his crutches.

"Good-by, old man! You musn't trouble yourself to say 'Merry Christmas' now, but wait until you see me again. Take care of yourself."

He slapped him lightly on the shoulder, and went back into his private office. He worked for some time at his desk, and then laid his pen aside, put away his papers methodically, placing a large envelope on his private secretary's vacant table. He then opened the office door and ascended the staircase. He stopped on the first landing to listen to the sound of rain on the glass skylight, that seemed to echo through the empty hall like the gloomy roll of a drum. It was evident that the searching water had found out the secret sins of the house's construction, for there were great fissures of discoloration in the white and gold paper in the corners of the wall. There was a strange odor of the dank forest in the mirrored drawing-room, as if the rain had brought out the sap again from the unseasoned timbers; the blue and white satin furniture looked cold, and the marble mantels and centre tables had taken upon themselves the clamminess of tombstones. Mr. Mulrady, who had always retained his old farmer-like habit of taking off his coat with his hat on entering his own house, and appearing in his shirt-sleeves, to indicate domestic ease and security, was obliged to replace it, on account of the chill. He had never felt at home in this room. Its strangeness had lately been heightened by Mrs. Mulrady's purchase of a family portrait of some one she didn't know, but who, she had alleged, resembled her "Uncle Bob," which hung on the wall beside some paintings in massive frames. Mr. Mulrady cast a hurried glance at the portrait that, on the strength of a high coat-collar and high top curl—both rolled with equal precision and singular sameness of color—had always glared at Mulrady as if *he* was the intruder; and, passing through his wife's gorgeous bedroom, entered the little dressing-room, where he still slept on the smallest of cots, with hastily improvised surroundings, as if he was a bailiff in "possession." He didn't linger here long, but, taking a key from a drawer, continued up the staircase, to the ominous funeral marches of the beating rain on the skylight, and paused on the landing to glance into his son's and daughter's bedrooms, duplicates of the *bizarre* extravagance below. If he were seeking some characteristic traces of his absent family, they certainly were not here in the painted and still damp blazoning of their later successes. He ascended another staircase, and, passing to the wing of the house, paused before a small door, which was locked. Already the ostentatious decorations of wall and passages were left behind, and the plain lath-and-plaster partition of the attic lay before him. He unlocked the door, and threw it open.

CHAPTER V

THE apartment he entered was really only a lumber-room or loft over the wing of the house, which had been left bare and unfinished, and which revealed in its meagre skeleton of beams and joints the hollow sham of the whole structure. But in more violent contrast to the fresher glories of the other part of the house were its contents, which were the heterogeneous collection of old furniture, old luggage, and cast-off clothing, left over from the past life in the old cabin. It was a much plainer record of the simple beginnings of the family than Mrs. Mulrady cared to have remain in evidence, and for that reason it had been relegated to the hidden recesses of the new house, in the hope that it might absorb or digest it. There were old cribs, in which the infant limbs of Mamie and Abner had been tucked up; old looking-glasses, that had reflected their shining, soapy faces, and Mamie's best chip Sunday hat; an old sewing-machine, that had been worn out in active service; old patchwork quilts; an old accordion, to whose long drawn inspirations Mamie had sung hymns; old pictures, books, and old toys. There were one or two old chromos, and, stuck in an old frame, a colored print from the "Illustrated London News" of a Christmas gath-

ering in an old English country house. He stopped and
picked up this print, which he had often seen before, gazing at it with a new and singular interest. He wondered
if Mamie had seen anything of this kind in England, and
why couldn't he have had something like it here, in their
own fine house, with themselves and a few friends? He
remembered a past Christmas, when he had bought Mamie
that now headless doll with the few coins that were left
him after buying their frugal Christmas dinner. There
was an old spotted hobby-horse that another Christmas
had brought to Abner—Abner, who would be driving a
fast trotter to-morrow at the Springs! How everything
had changed! How they all had got up in the world, and
how far beyond this kind of thing—and yet—yet it would
have been rather comfortable to have all been together
again here. Would *they* have been more comfortable?
No! Yet then he might have had something to do, and
been less lonely to-morrow. What of that? He *had*
something to do: to look after this immense fortune.
What more could a man want, or should he want? It
was rather mean in him, able to give his wife and children everything they wanted, to be wanting anything
more. He laid down the print gently, after dusting its
glass and frame with his silk handkerchief, and slowly
left the room.

The drum-beat of the rain followed him down the staircase, but he shut it out with his other thoughts, when he
again closed the door of his office. He set diligently to
work by the declining winter light, until he was interrupted by the entrance of his Chinese waiter to tell him
that supper—which was the meal that Mulrady religiously
adhered to in place of the late dinner of civilization—
was ready in the dining-room. Mulrady mechanically
obeyed the summons; but on entering the room the oasis
of a few plates in a desert of white table-cloth which
awaited him made him hesitate. In its best aspect, the
high dark Gothic mahogany ecclesiastical sideboard and
chairs of this room, which looked like the appointments
of a mortuary chapel, were not exhilarating; and to-day,
in the light of the rain-filmed windows and the feeble rays

of a lamp half-obscured by the dark shining walls, it was most depressing.

"You kin take up supper into my office," said Mulrady, with a sudden inspiration. "I'll eat it there."

He ate it there, with his usual healthy appetite, which did not require even the stimulation of company. He had just finished, when his Irish cook—the one female servant of the house—came to ask permission to be absent that evening and the next day.

"I suppose the likes of your honor won't be at home on the Christmas Day? And it's me cousins from the old counthry at Rough-and-Ready that are invitin' me."

"Why don't you ask them over here?" said Mulrady, with another vague inspiration. "I'll stand treat."

"Lord preserve you for a jinerous gintleman! But it's the likes of them and myself that wouldn't be at home here on such a day."

There was so much truth in this that Mulrady checked a sigh as he gave the required permission, without saying that he had intended to remain. He could cook his own breakfast: he had done it before; and it would be something to occupy him. As to his dinner, perhaps he could go to the hotel at Rough-and-Ready. He worked on until the night had well advanced. Then, overcome with a certain restlessness that disturbed him, he was forced to put his books and papers away. It had begun to blow in fitful gusts, and occasionally the rain was driven softly across the panes like the passing of childish fingers. This disturbed him more than the monotony of silence, for he was not a nervous man. He seldom read a book, and the county paper furnished him only the financial and mercantile news which was part of his business. He knew he could not sleep if he went to bed. At last he rose, opened the window, and looked out from pure idleness of occupation. A splash of wheels in the distant muddy road and fragments of a drunken song showed signs of an early wandering reveller. There were no lights to be seen at the closed works; a profound darkness encompassed the house, as if the distant pines in the hollow had moved up and round it. The silence was broken now only by the occasional sighing of wind and rain. It was not an inviting night for a perfunctory walk; but an idea struck him—he would call upon the Slinns, and anticipate his next day's visit! They would probably have company, and be glad to see him: he could tell the girls of Mamie and her success. That he had not thought of this before was a proof of his usual self-contained isolation, that he thought of it now was an equal proof that he was becoming at last accessible to loneliness. He was angry with himself for what seemed to him a selfish weakness.

He returned to his office, and, putting the envelope that had been lying on Slinn's desk in his pocket, threw a *serape* over his shoulders, and locked the front door of the house behind him. It was well that the way was a familiar one to him, and that his feet instinctively found the trail, for the night was very dark. At times he was warned only by the gurgling of water of little rivulets that descended the hill and crossed his path. Without the slightest fear, and with neither imagination nor sensitiveness, he recalled how, the winter before, one of Don Cæsar's vaqueros, crossing this hill at night, had fallen down the chasm of a landslip caused by the rain, and was found the next morning with his neck broken in the gully. Don Cæsar had to take care of the man's family. Suppose such an accident should happen to him? Well, he had made his will. His wife and children would be provided for, and the work of the mine would go on all the same; he had arranged for that. Would anybody miss him? Would his wife, or his son, or his daughter? No. He felt such a sudden and overwhelming conviction of the truth of this that he stopped as suddenly as if the chasm had opened before him. No! It was the truth. If he were to disappear forever in the darkness of the Christmas night there was none to feel his loss. His wife would take care of Mamie; his son would take care of himself, as he had before—relieved of even the scant paternal authority he rebelled against. A more imaginative man than Mulrady would have combated or have followed out this idea, and then dismissed it; to the millionaire's matter-of-fact mind it was a deduction that, having once presented itself to his perception, was already a recognized fact. For the first time in his life he felt a sudden instinct of something like aversion towards his family, a feeling that even his son's dissipation and criminality had never provoked. He hurried on angrily through the darkness.

It was very strange; the old house should be almost before him now, across the hollow, yet there were no indications of light! It was not until he actually reached the garden fence, and the black bulk of shadow rose out against the sky, that he saw a faint ray of light from one of the lean-to windows. He went to the front door and knocked. After waiting in vain for a reply, he knocked again. The second knock proving equally futile, he tried the door; it was unlocked, and, pushing it open, he walked in. The narrow passage was quite dark, but from his knowledge of the house he knew the "lean-to" was next to the kitchen, and, passing through the dining-room into it, he opened the door of the little room from which the light proceeded. It came from a single candle on a small table, and beside it, with his eyes moodily fixed on the dying embers of the fire, sat old Slinn. There was no other light nor another human being in the whole house.

For the instant Mulrady, forgetting his own feelings in the mute picture of the utter desolation of the helpless man, remained speechless on the threshold. Then, recalling himself, he stepped forward and laid his hand gayly on the bowed shoulders.

"Rouse up out o' this, old man! Come! this won't do. Look! I've run over here in the rain, jist to have a sociable time with you all."

"I knew it," said the old man, without looking up; "I knew you'd come."

"You knew I'd come?" echoed Mulrady, with an uneasy return of the strange feeling of awe with which he regarded Slinn's abstraction.

"Yes; you were alone—like myself—all alone!"

"Then, why in thunder didn't you open the door or

sing out just now?" he said, with an affected *brusquerie*
to cover his uneasiness. "Where's your daughters?"

"Gone to Rough-and-Ready to a party."

"And your son?"

"He never comes here when he can amuse himself
elsewhere."

"Your children might have stayed home on Christmas
Eve."

"So might yours."

He didn't say this impatiently, but with a certain abstracted conviction far beyond any suggestion of its being
a retort. Mulrady did not appear to notice it.

"Well, I don't see why us old folks can't enjoy ourselves without them," said Mulrady, with affected cheer-
fulness. "Let's have a good time, you and me. Let's see
—you haven't any one you can send to my house, hev
you?"

"They took the servant with them," said Slinn, briefly.
"There is no one here."

"All right," said the millionaire, briskly. "I'll go
myself. Do you think you can manage to light up
a little more, and build a fire in the kitchen while
I'm gone? It used to be mighty comfortable in the old
times."

He helped the old man to rise from his chair, and
seemed to have infused into him some of his own energy.
He then added, "Now, don't you get yourself down again
into that chair until I come back," and darted out into
the night once more.

In a quarter of an hour he returned with a bag on his
broad shoulders, which one of his porters would have
shrunk from lifting, and laid it before the blazing hearth
of the now lighted kitchen. "It's something the old
woman got for her party, that didn't come off," he said,
apologetically. "I reckon we can pick out enough for a
spread. That darned Chinaman wouldn't come with me,"
he added, with a laugh, "because, he said, he'd knocked
off work 'allee same, Mellican man!' Look here, Slinn,"
he said, with a sudden decisiveness, "my pay-roll of the
men around here don't run short of a hundred and fifty

dollars a day, and yet I couldn't get a hand to help me bring this truck over for my Christmas dinner."

"Of course," said Slinn, gloomily.

"Of course; so it oughter be," returned Mulrady, shortly. "Why, it's only their one day out of 364; and I can have 363 days off, as I am their boss. I don't mind a man's being independent," he continued, taking off his coat and beginning to unpack his sack—a common "gunny bag"—used for potatoes. "We're independent ourselves, ain't we, Slinn?"

His good spirits, which had been at first labored and affected, had become natural. Slinn, looking at his brightened eye and fresher color, could not help thinking he was more like his own real self at this moment than in his counting-house and offices—with all his simplicity as a capitalist. A less abstracted and more observant critic than Slinn would have seen in this patient aptitude for real work, and the recognition of the force of petty detail, the dominance of the old market-gardener in his former humble, as well as his later more ambitious, successes.

"Heaven keep us from being dependent upon our children!" said Slinn, darkly.

"Let the young ones alone to-night; we can get along without them, as they can without us," said Mulrady, with a slight twinge as he thought of his reflections on the hillside. "But look here, there's some champagne and them sweet cordials that women like; there's jellies and such like stuff, about as good as they make 'em, I reckon; and preserves, and tongues, and spiced beef—take your pick! Stop, let's spread them out." He dragged the table to the middle of the floor, and piled the provisions upon it. They certainly were not deficient in quality or quantity. "Now, Slinn, wade in."

"I don't feel hungry," said the invalid, who had lapsed again into a chair before the fire.

"No more do I," said Mulrady; "but I reckon it's the right thing to do about this time. Some folks think they can't be happy without they're getting outside o' suthin', and my directors down at 'Frisco can't do any business without a dinner. Take some champagne, to begin with."

He opened a bottle, and filled two tumblers. "It's past twelve o'clock, old man, so here's a merry Christmas to you, and both of us ez is here. And here's another to our families—ez isn't."

They both drank their wine stolidly. The rain beat against the windows sharply, but without the hollow echoes of the house on the hill. "I must write to the old woman and Mamie, and say that you and me had a high old time on Christmas Eve."

"By ourselves," added the invalid.

Mr. Mulrady coughed. "Nat'rally—by ourselves. And her provisions," he added, with a laugh. "We're really beholden to *her* for 'em. If she hadn't thought of having them—"

"For somebody else, you wouldn't have had them— would you?" said Slinn, slowly, gazing at the fire.

"No," said Mulrady, dubiously. After a pause he began more vivaciously, and as if to shake off some disagreeable thought that was impressing him, "But I mustn't forget to give you *your* Christmas, old man, and I've got it right here with me." He took the folded envelope from his pocket, and, holding it in his hand with his elbow on the table, continued, "I don't mind telling you what idea I had in giving you what I'm goin' to give you now. I've been thinking about it for a day or two. A man like you don't want money—you wouldn't spend it. A man like you don't want stocks or fancy investments, for you couldn't look after them. A man like you don't want diamonds and jewellery, nor a gold-headed cane, when it's got to be used as a crutch. No, sir. What you want is suthin' that won't run away from you; that is always there before you and won't wear out, and will last after you're gone. That's land! And if it wasn't that I have sworn never to sell or give away this house and that garden, if it wasn't that I've held out agin the old woman and Mamie on that point, you should have *this* house and *that* garden. But, mebbee, for the same reason that I've told you, I want that land to keep for myself. But I've selected four acres of the hill this side of my shaft, and here's the deed of it. As soon as you're ready, I'll put you up a house

3   v. 2

as big as this—that shall be yours, with the land, as long as you live, old man; and after that your children's."

"No; not theirs!" broke in the old man, passionately. "Never!"

Mulrady recoiled for an instant in alarm at the sudden and unexpected vehemence of his manner. "Go slow, old man; go slow," he said, soothingly. "Of course, you'll do with your own as you like." Then, as if changing the subject, he went on cheerfully: "Perhaps you'll wonder why I picked out that spot on the hillside. Well, first, because I reserved it after my strike in case the lead should run that way, but it didn't. Next, because when you first came here you seemed to like the prospect. You used to sit there looking at it, as if it reminded you of something. You never said it did. They say you was sitting on that boulder there when you had that last attack, you know; but," he added, gently, "you've forgotten all about it."

"I have forgotten nothing," said Slinn, rising, with a choking voice. "I wish to God I had; I wish to God I could!"

He was on his feet now, supporting himself by the table. The subtle generous liquor he had drunk had evidently shaken his self-control, and burst those voluntary bonds he had put upon himself for the last six months; the insidious stimulant had also put a strange vigor into his blood and nerves. His face was flushed, but not distorted; his eyes were brilliant, but not fixed; he looked as he might have looked to Masters in his strength three years before on that very hillside.

"Listen to me, Alvin Mulrady," he said, leaning over him with burning eyes. "Listen, while I have brain to think and strength to utter, why I have learnt to distrust, fear, and hate them! You think you know my story. Well, hear the truth from *me* to-night, Alvin Mulrady, and do not wonder if I have cause."

He stopped, and, with pathetic inefficiency, passed the fingers and inward-turned thumb of his paralyzed hand across his mouth, as if to calm himself. "Three years ago I was a miner, but not a miner like you! I had experience, I had scientific knowledge, I had a theory, and the patience and energy to carry it out. I selected a spot that had all the indications, made a tunnel, and, without aid, counsel or assistance of any kind, worked it for six months, without rest or cessation, and with scarcely food enough to sustain my body. Well, I made a strike; not like you, Mulrady, not a blunder of good luck, a fool's fortune—there, I don't blame you for it—but in perfect demonstration of my theory, the reward of my labor. It was no pocket, but a vein, a lead, that I had regularly hunted down and found—a fortune!

"I never knew how hard I had worked until that morning; I never knew what privations I had undergone until that moment of my success, when I found I could scarcely think or move! I staggered out into the open air. The only human soul near me was a disappointed prospector, a man named Masters, who had a tunnel not far away. I managed to conceal from him my good fortune and my feeble state, for I was suspicious of him—of any one; and as he was going away that day I thought I could keep my secret until he was gone. I was dizzy and confused, but I remember that I managed to write a letter to my wife, telling her of my good fortune, and begging her to come to me; and I remember that I saw Masters go. I don't remember anything else. They picked me up on the road, near that boulder, as you know."

"I know," said Mulrady, with a swift recollection of the stage-driver's account of his discovery.

"They say," continued Slinn, tremblingly, "that I never recovered my senses or consciousness for nearly three years; they say I lost my memory completely during my illness, and that by God's mercy, while I lay in that hospital, I knew no more than a babe; they say, because I could not speak or move, and only had my food as nature required it, that I was an imbecile, and that I never really came to my senses until after my son found me in the hospital. They *say* that—but I tell you to-night, Alvin Mulrady," he said, raising his voice to a hoarse outcry, "I tell you that it is a lie! I came to my senses a week after I lay on that hospital cot; I kept my senses and memory ever after during the three years that I was there, until Harry brought his cold, hypocritical face to my bedside and recognized me. Do you understand? I, the possessor of millions, lay there a pauper. Deserted by wife and children—a spectacle for the curious, a sport for the doctors—*and I knew it!* I heard them speculate on the cause of my helplessness. I heard them talk of excesses and indulgences—I, that never knew wine or woman! I heard a preacher speak of the finger of God, and point to me. May God curse him!"

"Go slow, old man; go slow," said Mulrady, gently.

"I heard them speak of me as a friendless man, an outcast, a criminal—a being whom no one would claim. They were right; no one claimed me. The friends of others visited them; relations came and took away their kindred; a few lucky ones got well; a few, equally lucky, died! I alone lived on, uncared for, deserted.

"The first year," he went on more rapidly, "I prayed for their coming. I looked for them every day. I never lost hope. I said to myself, 'She has not got my letter; but when the time passes she will be alarmed by my silence, and then she will come or send some one to seek me.' A young student got interested in my case, and, by studying my eyes, thought that I was not entirely imbecile and unconscious. With the aid of an alphabet, he got me to spell my name and town in Illinois, and promised by signs to write to my family. But in an evil moment I told him of my cursed fortune, and in that moment I saw that he thought me a fool and an idiot. He went away, and I saw him no more. Yet I still hoped. I dreamed of their joy at finding me, and the reward that my wealth would give them. Perhaps I was a little weak still, perhaps a little flighty, too, at times; but I was quite happy that year, even in my disappointment, for I had still hope!"

He paused, and again composed his face with his paralyzed hand; but his manner had become less excited, and his voice was stronger.

"A change must have come over me the second year, for I only dreaded their coming now and finding me so altered. A horrible idea that they might, like the student, believe me crazy if I spoke of my fortune made me pray to God that they might not reach me until after I had regained my health and strength—and found my fortune. When the third year found me still there—I no longer prayed for them—I cursed them! I swore to myself that they should never enjoy my wealth; but I wanted to live, and let them know I had it. I found myself getting stronger; but as I had no money, no friends, and no-where to go, I concealed my real condition from the doctors, except to give them my name, and to try to get some little work to do to enable me to leave the hospital and seek my lost treasure. One day I found out by acci-, dent that it had been discovered! You understand—my treasure!—that had cost me years of labor and my rea-son; had left me a helpless, forgotten pauper. That gold I had never enjoyed had been found and taken possession of by another!"

He checked an exclamation from Mulrady with his hand. "They say they picked me up senseless from the floor, where I must have fallen when I heard the news—I don't remember—I recall nothing until I was confronted, nearly three weeks after, by my son, who had called at the hospital, as a reporter for a paper, and had acciden-tally discovered me through my name and appearance. He thought me crazy, or a fool. I didn't undeceive him. I did not tell him the story of the mine to excite his doubts and derision, or, worse (if I could bring proof to claim it), have it perhaps pass into his ungrateful hands. No; I said nothing. I let him bring me here. He could do no less, and common decency obliged him to do that."

"And what proof could you show of your claim?" asked Mulrady, gravely.

"If I had that letter—if I could find Masters," began Slinn, vaguely.

"Have you any idea where the letter is, or what has become of Masters?" continued Mulrady, with a matter-of-fact gravity, that seemed to increase Slinn's vagueness and excite his irritability.

"I don't know—I sometimes think—" He stopped, sat

down again, and passed his hands across his forehead.
"I have seen the letter somewhere since. Yes," he went
on, with sudden vehemence, "I know it, I have seen it!
I—" His brows knitted, his features began to work convulsively; he suddenly brought his paralyzed hand down,
partly opened, upon the table. "I *will* remember where."

"Go slow, old man; go slow."

"You asked me once about my visions. Well, that is
one of them. I remember a man somewhere showing me
that letter. I have taken it from his hands and opened it,
and knew it was mine by the specimens of gold that were
in it. But where—or when—or what became of it, I
cannot tell. It will come to me—it *must* come to me
soon."

He turned his eyes upon Mulrady, who was regarding
him with an expression of grave curiosity, and said bitterly, "You think me crazy. I know it. It needed only
this."

"Where is this mine," asked Mulrady, without heeding him.

The old man's eyes swiftly sought the ground.

"It is a secret, then?"

"No."

"You have spoken of it to any one?"

"No."

"Not to the man who possesses it?"

"No."

"Why?"

"Because I wouldn't take it from him."

"Why wouldn't you?"

"Because that man is yourself!"

In the instant of complete silence that followed they
could hear that the monotonous patter of rain on the
roof had ceased.

"Then all this was in *my* shaft, and the vein I
thought I struck there was *your* lead, found three years
ago in *your* tunnel. Is that your idea?"

"Yes."

"Then I don't *sabe* why you don't want to claim it."

"I have told you why I don't want it for my children.

I go further, now, and I tell you, Alvin Mulrady, that I was willing that your children should squander it, as they were doing. It has only been a curse to me; it could only be a curse to them; but I thought you were happy in seeing it feed selfishness and vanity. You think me bitter and hard. Well, I should have left you in your fool's paradise, but that I saw to-night, when you came here, that your eyes had been opened like mine. You, the possessor of my wealth, my treasure, could not buy your children's loving care and company with your millions, any more than I could keep mine in my poverty. You were to-night lonely and forsaken, as I was. We were equal, for the first time in our lives. If that cursed gold had dropped down the shaft between us into the hell from which it sprang, we might have clasped hands like brothers across the chasm."

Mulrady, who in a friendly show of being at his ease had not yet resumed his coat, rose in his shirt-sleeves, and, standing before the hearth, straightened his square figure by drawing down his waistcoat on each side with two powerful thumbs. After a moment's contemplative survey of the floor between him and the speaker, he raised his eyes to Slinn. They were small and colorless; the forehead above them was low, and crowned with a shock of tawny reddish hair; even the rude strength of his lower features was enfeebled by a long, straggling, goat-like beard; but for the first time in his life the whole face was impressed and transformed with a strong and simple dignity.

"Ez far ez I kin see, Slinn," he said, gravely, "the pint between you and me ain't to be settled by our children, or wot we allow is doo and right from them to us. Afore we preach at them for playing in the slumgullion, and gettin' themselves splashed, perhaps we mout ez well remember that that thar slumgullion comes from our own sluice-boxes, where we wash our gold. So we'll just put *them* behind us, so," he continued, with a backward sweep of his powerful hand towards the chimney, "and goes on. The next thing that crops up ahead of us is your three years in the hospital, and wot you went through at that

time. I ain't sayin' it wasn't rough on you, and that you
didn't have it about as big as it's made; but ez you'll
allow that you'd hev had that for three years, whether
I'd found your mine or whether I hadn't, I think we can
put *that* behind us, too. There's nothin' now left to prospect but your story of your strike. Well, take your own
proofs. Masters is not here; and if he was, accordin' to
your own story, he knows nothin' of your strike that day,
and could only prove you were a disappointed prospector
in a tunnel; your letter—that the person you wrote to
never got—*you* can't produce; and if you did, would be
only your own story without proof! There is not a
business man ez would look at your claim; there isn't
a friend of yours that wouldn't believe you were crazy,
and dreamed it all; there isn't a rival of yours ez wouldn't
say ez you'd invented it. Slinn, I'm a business man—I
am your friend—I am your rival—but I don't think you're
lyin'—I don't think you're crazy—and I'm not sure your
claim ain't a good one!

"Ef you reckon from that that I'm goin' to hand you
over the mine to-morrow," he went on, after a pause,
raising his hand with a deprecating gesture, "you're mistaken. For your own sake, and the sake of my wife and
children, you've got to prove it more clearly than you
hev; but I promise you that from this night forward I
will spare neither time nor money to help you to do it.
I have more than doubled the amount that you would have
had, had you taken the mine the day you came from the
hospital. When you prove to me that your story is true—
and we will find some way to prove it, if it *is* true—that
amount will be yours at once, without the need of a word
from law or lawyers. If you want my name to that in
black and white, come to the office to-morrow, and you
shall have it."

"And you think I'll take it now?" said the old man
passionately. "Do you think that your charity will bring
back my dead wife, the three years of my lost life, the
love and respect of my children? Or do you think that
your own wife and children, who deserted you in your
wealth, will come back to you in your poverty? No!

Let the mine stay, with its curse, where it is—I'll have none of it!"

"Go slow, old man; go slow," said Mulrady, quietly, putting on his coat. "You will take the mine if it is yours; if it isn't, I'll keep it. If it is yours, you will give your children a chance to sho what they can do for you in your sudden prosperity, as I shall give mine a chance to show how they can stand reverse and disappointment. If my head is level—and I reckon it is—they'll both pan out all right."

He turned and opened the door. With a quick revulsion of feeling, Slinn suddenly seized Mulrady's hand between both of his own, and raised it to his lips. Mulrady smiled, disengaged his hand gently, and saying soothingly, "Go slow, old man; go slow," closed the door behind him, and passed out into the clear Christmas dawn.

For the stars, with the exception of one that seemed to sparkle brightly over the shaft of his former fortunes, were slowly paling. A burden seemed to have fallen from his square shoulders as he stepped out sturdily into the morning air. He had already forgotten the lonely man behind him, for he was thinking only of his wife and daughter. And at the same moment they were thinking of him; and in their elaborate villa overlooking the blue Mediterranean at Cannes were discussing, in the event of Mamie's marriage with Prince Rosso e Negro, the possibility of Mr. Mulrady's paying two hundred and fifty thousand dollars, the gambling debts of that unfortunate but deeply conscientious nobleman.

CHAPTER VI

WHEN Alvin Mulrady reëntered his own house, he no longer noticed its loneliness. Whether the events of the last few hours had driven it from his mind, or whether his late reflections had repeopled it with his family under pleasanter auspices, it would be difficult to determine. Destitute as he was of imagination, and matter-of-fact in his judgments, he realized his new situation as calmly as he would have considered any business proposition. While he was decided to act upon his moral convictions purely, he was prepared to submit the facts of Slinn's claim to the usual patient and laborious investigation of his practical mind. It was the least he could do to justify the ready and almost superstitious assent he had given to Slinn's story.

When he had made a few memoranda at his desk by the growing light, he again took the key of the attic, and ascended to the loft that held the tangible memories of his past life. If he was still under the influence of his reflections, it was with very different sensations that he now regarded them. Was it possible that these ashes might be warmed again, and these scattered embers rekindled? His practical sense said No! whatever his wish might have been. A sudden chill came over him; he began to realize the terrible change that was probable, more by the impossibility of his accepting the old order of things than by his voluntarily abandoning the new. His wife and children would never submit. They would go away from this place, far away, where no reminiscence of either former wealth or former poverty could obtrude itself upon them. Mamie—his Mamie—should never go back to the cabin, since desecrated by Slinn's daughters, and take their places. No! Why should she?—because of the half-sick, half-crazy dreams of an old vindictive man?

He stopped suddenly. In moodily turning over a heap of mining clothing, blankets, and india-rubber boots, he had come upon an old pickaxe—the one he had found in the shaft; the one he had carefully preserved for a year, and then forgotten! Why had he not remembered it before? He was frightened, not only at this sudden resurrection of the proof he was seeking, but at his own fateful forgetfulness. Why had he never thought of this when Slinn was speaking? A sense of shame, as if he had voluntarily withheld it from the wronged man, swept over him. He was turning away, when he was again startled.

This time it was by a voice from below—a voice calling him—Slinn's voice. How had the crippled man got here so soon, and what did he want? He hurriedly laid aside the pick, which, in his first impulse, he had taken to the door of the loft with him, and descended the stairs. The old man was standing at the door of his office awaiting him.

As Mulrady approached, he trembled violently, and clung to the doorpost for support.

"I had to come over, Mulrady," he said, in a choked voice; "I could stand it there no longer. I've come to beg you to forget all that I have said; to drive all thought of what passed between us last night out of your head and mine forever! I've come to ask you to swear with me that neither of us will ever speak of this again forever. It is not worth the happiness I have had in your friendship for the last half-year; it is not worth the agony I have suffered in its loss in the last half-hour."

Mulrady grasped his outstretched hand. "P'raps," he said, gravely, "there mayn't be any use for another word, if you can answer one now. Come with me. No matter," he added, as Slinn moved with difficulty; "I will help you."

He half supported, half lifted the paralyzed man up the three flights of stairs, and opened the door of the loft. The pick was leaning against the wall, where he had left it. "Look around, and see if you recognize anything."

The old man's eyes fell upon the implement in a half-frightened way, and then lifted themselves interrogatively to Mulrady's face.

"Do you know that pick?"

Slinn raised it in his trembling hands. "I think I do; and yet—"

"Slinn! is it yours?"

"No," he said hurriedly.

"Then what makes you think you know it?"

"It has a short handle like one I've seen."

"And is isn't yours?"

"No. The handle of mine was broken and spliced. "'was too poor to buy a new one."

"Then you say that this pick which I found in my shaft is not yours?"

"Yes."

"Slinn!"

The old man passed his hand across his forehead, looked at Mulrady, and dropped his eyes. "It is not mine," he said simply.

"That will do," said Mulrady, gravely.

"And you will not speak of this again?" said the old man, timidly.

"I promise you—not until I have some more evidence."

He kept his word, but not before he had extorted from Slinn as full a description of Masters as his imperfect memory and still more imperfect knowledge of his former neighbor could furnish. He placed this, with a large sum of money and the promise of a still larger reward, in the hands of a trustworthy agent. When this was done he resumed his old relations with Slinn, with the exception that the domestic letters of Mrs. Mulrady and Mamie were no longer a subject of comment, and their bills no longer passed through his private secretary's hands.

Three months passed; the rainy season had ceased, the hillsides around Mulrady's shaft were bridal-like with flowers; indeed, there were rumors of an approaching fashionable marriage in the air, and vague hints in the "Record" that the presence of a distinguished capitalist might soon be required abroad. The face of that distinguished man did not, however, reflect the gayety of nature nor the anticipation of happiness; on the contrary, for the past few weeks, he had appeared disturbed and anxious, and that rude tranquillity which had characterized him was wanting. People shook their heads; a few suggested speculations; all agreed on extravagance.

One morning, after office hours, Slinn, who had been watching the careworn face of his employer, suddenly rose and limped to his side.

"We promised each other," he said, in a voice trembling with emotion, "never to allude to our talk of Christmas Eve again unless we had other proofs of what I told you then. We have none; I don't believe we'll ever have any more. I don't care if we ever do, and I break that promise now because I cannot bear to see you unhappy and know that this is the cause."

Mulrady made a motion of deprecation, but the old man continued—

"You are unhappy, Alvin Mulrady. You are unhappy because you want to give your daughter a dowry of two hundred and fifty thousand dollars, and you will not use the fortune that you think may be mine."

"Who's been talking about a dowry?" asked Mulrady, with an angry flush.

"Don Cæsar Alvarado told my daughter."

"Then that is why he has thrown off on me since he returned," said Mulrady, with sudden small malevolence, "just that he might unload his gossip because Mamie wouldn't have him. The old woman was right in warnin' me agin him."

The outburst was so unlike him, and so dwarfed his large though common nature with its littleness, that it was easy to detect its feminine origin, although it filled Slinn with vague alarm.

"Never mind him," said the old man, hastily; "what I wanted to say now is that I abandon everything to you and yours. There are no proofs; there never will be any more than what we know, than what we have tested and found wanting. I swear to you that, except to show you that I have not lied and am not crazy, I would destroy them on their way to your hands. Keep the money, and spend it as you will. Make your daughter happy, and, through her, yourself. You have made me happy through your liberality; don't make me suffer through your privation."

"I tell you what, old man," said Mulrady, rising to his feet, with an awkward mingling of frankness and shame in his manner and accent, "I should like to pay that money for Mamie, and let her be a princess, if it would make her happy. I should like to shut the lantern jaws of that Don Cæsar, who'd be too glad if anything happened to break off Mamie's match. But I shouldn't touch that capital—unless you'd lend it to me. If you'll take a note from me, payable if the property ever becomes yours, I'd thank you. A mortgage on the old house and garden, and the lands I bought of Don Cæsar, outside the mine, will screen you."

"If that pleases you," said the old man, with a smile, "have your way; and if I tear up the note, it does not concern you."

It did please the distinguished capitalist of Rough-and-Ready; for the next few days his face wore a brightened expression, and he seemed to have recovered his old tranquillity. There was, in fact, a slight touch of consequence in his manner, the first ostentation he had ever indulged in, when he was informed one morning at his private office that Don Cæsar Alvarado was in the counting-house, desiring a few moments' conference. "Tell him to come in," said Mulrady, shortly. The door opened upon Don Cæsar—erect, sallow, and grave. Mulrady had not seen him since his return from Europe, and even his inexperienced eyes were struck with the undeniable ease and grace with which the young Spanish-American had assimilated the style and fashion of an older civilization. It seemed rather as if he had returned to a familiar condition than adopted a new one.

"Take a cheer," said Mulrady.

The young man looked at Slinn with quietly persistent significance.

"You can talk all the same," said Mulrady, accepting the significance. "He's my private secretary."

"It seems that for that reason we might choose another moment for our conversation," returned Don Cæsar, haughtily. "Do I understand you cannot see me now?"

Mulrady hesitated. He had always revered and recognized a certain social superiority in Don Ramon Alvarado; somehow his son—a young man of half his age, and once a possible son-in-law—appeared to claim that recognition also. He rose, without a word, and preceded Don Cæsar up-stairs into the drawing-room.

The alien portrait on the wall seemed to evidently take sides with Don Cæsar, as against the common intruder, Mulrady.

"I hoped the Señora Mulrady might have saved me this interview," said the young man, stiffly; "or at least have given you some intimation of the reason why I seek it. As you just now proposed my talking to you in the presence of the unfortunate Señor Esslinn himself, it appears she has not."

"I don't know what you're driving at, or what Mrs. Mulrady's got to do with Slinn or you," said Mulrady, in angry uneasiness.

"Do I understand," said Don Cæsar, sternly, "that Señora Mulrady has not told you that I entrusted to her an important letter, belonging to Señor Esslinn, which I had the honor to discover in the wood six months ago, and which she said she would refer to you?"

"Letter?" echoed Mulrady, slowly; "my wife had a letter of Slinn's?"

Don Cæsar regarded the millionaire attentively. "It is as I feared," he said, gravely. "You do not know, or you would not have remained silent." He then briefly recounted the story of his finding Slinn's letter, his exhibition of it to the invalid, its disastrous effect upon him, and his innocent discovery of the contents. "I believed myself at that time on the eve of being allied with your family, Señor Mulrady," he said, haughtily; "and when I found myself in the possession of a secret which affected its integrity and good name, I did not choose to leave it in the helpless hands of its imbecile owner, or his sillier children, but proposed to trust it to the care of the Señora, that she and you might deal with it as became your honor and mine. I followed her to Paris, and gave her the letter there. She affected to laugh at any pretension of the writer, or any claim he might have on your bounty; but she kept the letter, and, I fear, destroyed it. You will understand, Señor Mulrady, that when I found that my attentions were no longer agreeable to your daughter, I had no longer the right to speak to you on the subject, nor could I, with-

out misapprehension, force her to return it. I should
have still kept the secret to myself, if I had not since
my return here made the nearer acquaintance of Señor
Esslinn's daughters. I cannot present myself at his
house, as a suitor for the hand of the Señorita Vashti,
until I have asked his absolution for my complicity in
the wrong that has been done to him. I cannot, as a
caballero, do that without your permission. It is for
that purpose I am here."

It needed only this last blow to complete the humilia-
tion that whitened Mulrady's face. But his eye was
none the less clear and his voice none the less steady
as he turned to Don Cæsar.

"You know perfectly the contents of that letter?"

"I have kept a copy of it."

"Come with me."

He preceded his visitor down the staircase and back
into his private office. Slinn looked up at his employer's
face in unrestrained anxiety. Mulrady sat down at his
desk, wrote a few hurried lines, and rang a bell. A
manager appeared from the counting-room.

"Send that to the bank."

He wiped his pen as methodically as if he had not
at that moment countermanded the order to pay his
daughter's dowry, and turned quietly to Slinn.

"Don Cæsar Alvarado has found the letter you wrote
you wife on the day you made your strike in the tunnel
that is now my shaft. He gave the letter to Mrs. Mulrady; but he has kept a copy."

Unheeding the frightened gesture of entreaty from
Slinn, equally with the unfeigned astonishment of Don
Cæsar, who was entirely unprepared for this revelation
of Mulrady's and Slinn's confidences, he continued, "He
has brought the copy with him. I reckon it would be
only square for you to compare it with what you remember of the original."

In obedience to a gesture from Mulrady, Don Cæsar
mechanically took from his pocket a folded paper, and
handed it to the paralytic. But Slinn's trembling fingers
could scarcely unfold the paper; and as his eyes fell

upon its contents, his convulsive lips could not articulate a word.

"P'raps I'd better read it for you," said Mulrady, gently. "You kin follow me and stop me when I go wrong."

He took the paper, and, in dead silence, read as follows:—

"DEAR WIFE,—I've just struck gold in my tunnel, and you must get ready to come here with the children, at once. It was after six months' hard work; and I'm so weak I . . . It's a fortune for us all. We should be rich even if it were only a branch vein dipping west towards the next tunnel, instead of dipping east, according to my theory—"

"Stop!" said Slinn, in a voice that shook the room.

Mulrady looked up.

"It's wrong, ain't it?" he asked, anxiously; "it should be *east* towards the next tunnel."

"No! *It's right! I* am wrong! We're all wrong!"

Slinn had risen to his feet, erect and inspired. "Don't you see," he almost screamed, with passionate vehemence, "it's *Masters' abandoned tunnel* your shaft has struck? Not mine! It was Masters' pick you found! I know it now!"

"And your own tunnel?" said Mulrady, springing to his feet in excitement. "And *your* strike?"

"Is still there!"

The next instant, and before another question could be asked, Slinn had darted from the room. In the exaltation of that supreme discovery he regained the full control of his mind and body. Mulrady and Don Cæsar, no less excited, followed him precipitately, and with difficulty kept up with his feverish speed. Their way lay along the base of the hill below Mulrady's shaft, and on a line with Masters' abandoned tunnel. Only once he stopped to snatch a pick from the hand of an astonished Chinaman at work in a ditch, as he still kept on his way, a quarter of a mile beyond the shaft. Here he stopped before a jagged hole in the hillside. Bared to the sky and air, the very openness of its abandonment, its unpropitious position, and distance from the strike in Mulrady's shaft had no doubt preserved its integrity from wayfarer or prospector.

"You can't go in there alone, and without a light," said Mulrady, laying his hand on the arm of the excited man. "Let me get more help and proper tools."

"I know every step in the dark as in the daylight," returned Slinn, struggling. "Let me go, while I have yet strength and reason! Stand aside!"

He broke from them, and the next moment was swallowed up in the yawning blackness. They waited with bated breath until, after a seeming eternity of night and silence, they heard his returning footsteps, and ran forward to meet him. As he was carrying something clasped to his breast, they supported him to the opening. But at the same moment the object of his search and his burden, a misshapen wedge of gold and quartz, dropped with him, and both fell together with equal immobility to the ground. He had still strength to turn his fading eyes to the other millionaire of Rough-and-Ready, who leaned over him.

"You—see," he gasped, brokenly, "I was not—crazy!"

No. He was dead!

DEVIL'S FORD

CHAPTER I

It was a season of unequalled prosperity in Devil's Ford. The half a dozen cabins scattered along the banks of the North Fork, as if by some overflow of that capricious river, had become augmented during a week of fierce excitment by twenty or thirty others, that were huddled together on the narrow gorge of Devil's Spur, or cast up on its steep sides. So sudden and violent had been the change of fortune, that the dwellers in the older cabins had not had time to change with it, but still kept their old habits, customs, and even their old clothes. The flour pan in which their daily bread was mixed stood on the rude table side by side with the "prospecting pans," half full of gold washed up from their morning's work; the front windows of the newer tenements looked upon the one single thoroughfare, but the back door opened upon the uncleared wilderness, still haunted by the misshapen bulk of bear or the nightly gliding of catamount.

Neither had success as yet affected their boyish simplicity and the frankness of old frontier habits; they played with their new-found riches with the naive delight of children, and rehearsed their glowing future with the importance and triviality of school-boys.

"I've bin kalklatin'," said Dick Mattingly, leaning on his long-handled shovel with lazy gravity, "that when I go to Rome this winter, I'll get one o' them marble sharps to chisel me a statoo o' some kind to set up on the spot where we made our big strike. Suthin' to remember it by, you know."

"What kind o' statoo—Washington or Webster?"

asked one of the Kearney brothers, without looking up from his work.

"No—I reckon one o' them fancy groups—one o' them Latin goddesses that Fairfax is always gassin' about, sorter leadin', directin' and bossin' us where to dig."

"You'd make a healthy-lookin' figger in a group," responded Kearney, critically regarding an enormous patch in Mattingly's trousers. "Why don't you have a fountain instead?"

"Where'll you get the water?" demanded the first speaker, in return. "You know there ain't enough in the North Fork to do a week's washing for the camp—to say nothin' of its color."

"Leave that to me," said Kearney, with self-possession. "When I've built that there reservoir on Devil's Spur, and bring the water over the ridge from Union Ditch, there'll be enough to spare for that."

"Better mix it up, I reckon—have suthin' half statoo, half fountain," interposed the elder Mattingly, better known as "Maryland Joe," "and set it up afore the Town Hall and Free Library I'm kalklatin' to give. Do *that*, and you can count on me."

After some further discussion, it was gravely settled that Kearney should furnish water brought from the Union Ditch, twenty miles away, at a cost of two hundred thousand dollars, to feed a memorial fountain erected by Mattingly, worth a hundred thousand dollars, as a crowning finish to public buildings contributed by Maryland Joe, to the extent of half a million more. The disposition of these vast sums by gentlemen wearing patched breeches awakened no sense of the ludicrous, nor did any doubt, reservation, or contingency enter into the plans of the charming enthusiasts themselves. The foundation of their airy castles lay already before them in the strip of rich alluvium on the river bank, where the North Fork, sharply curving round the base of Devil's Spur, had for centuries swept the detritus of gulch and canon. They had barely crossed the threshold of this treasure-house, to find themselves rich men; what possibilities of affluence might be theirs when they had fully exploited their possessions? So confident were they of that ultimate prospect, that the wealth already thus obtained was religiously expended in engines and machinery for the boring of wells and the conveyance of that precious water which the exhausted river had long since ceased to yield. It seemed as if the gold they had taken out was by some ironical compensation gradually making its way back to the soil again through ditch and flume and reservoir.

Such was the position of affairs at Devil's Ford on the 13th of August, 1860. It was noon of a hot day. Whatever movement there was in the stifling air was seen rather than felt in a tremulous, quivering, upward-moving dust along the flank of the mountain, through which the spires of the pines were faintly visible. There was no water in the bared and burning bars of the river to reflect the vertical sun, but under its direct rays one or two tinned roofs and corrugated zinc cabins struck fire, a few canvas tents became dazzling to the eye, and the white wooded corral of the stage office and hotel insupportable. For two hours no one ventured in the glare of the open, or even to cross the narrow, unshadowed street, whose dull red dust seemed to glow between the lines of straggling houses. The heated shells of these green unseasoned tenements gave out a pungent odor of scorching wood and resin. The usual hurried, feverish toil in the claim was suspended; the pick and shovel were left sticking in the richest "pay gravel;" the toiling millionaires themselves, ragged, dirty, and perspiring, lay panting under the nearest shade, where the pipes went out listlessly, and conversation sank to monosyllables.

"There's Fairfax," said Dick Mattingly, at last, with a lazy effort. His face was turned to the hillside, where a man had just emerged from the woods, and was halting irresolutely before the glaring expanse of upheaved gravel and glistening boulders that stretched between him and the shaded group. "He's going to make a break for it," he added, as the stranger, throwing his linen coat over his head, suddenly started into an Indian trot through the pelting sunbeams toward them. This strange act was perfectly understood by the group, who knew that in that intensely dry heat the danger of exposure was lessened by active exercise and the profuse perspiration that followed it. In another moment the stranger had reached their side, dripping as if rained upon, mopping his damp curls and handsome bearded face with his linen coat, as he threw himself pantingly on the ground.

"I struck out over here first, boys, to give you a little warning," he said, as soon as he had gained breath. "That engineer will be down here to take charge as soon as the six o'clock stage comes in. He's an oldish chap, has got a family of two daughters, and—I—am—d——d if he is not bringing them down here with him."

"Oh, go long!" exclaimed the five men in one voice, raising themselves on their hands and elbows, and glaring at the speaker.

"Fact, boys! Soon as I found it out I just waltzed into that Jew shop at the Crossing and bought up all the clothes that would be likely to suit you fellows, before anybody else got a show. I reckon I cleared out the shop. The duds are a little mixed in style, but I reckon they're clean and whole, and a man might face a lady in 'em. I left them round at the old Buckeye Spring, where they're handy without attracting attention. You boys can go there for a general wash-up, rig yourselves up without saying anything, and then meander back careless and easy in your store clothes, just as the stage is coming in, *sabe?*"

"Why didn't you let us know earlier?" asked Mattingly aggrievedly; "you've been back here at least an hour."

"I've been getting some place ready for *them,*" returned the new-comer. "We might have managed to put the man somewhere, if he'd been alone, but these women want family accommodation. There was nothing left for me to do but to buy up Thompson's saloon."

"No?" interrupted his audience, half in incredulity, half in protestation.

"Fact! You boys will have to take your drinks under canvas again, I reckon! But I made Thompson let those gold-framed mirrors that used to stand behind the bar go into the bargain, and they sort of furnish the room. You know the saloon is one of them patent houses you can take to pieces, and I've been reckoning you boys will have to pitch in and help me to take the whole shanty over to the laurel bushes, and put it up agin Kearney's cabin."

"What's all that?" said the younger Kearney, with an odd mingling of astonishment and bashful gratification.

"Yes, I reckon yours is the cleanest house, because it's the newest, so you'll just step out and let us knock in one o' the gables, and clap it on to the saloon, and make *one* house of it, don't you see? There'll be two rooms, one for the girls and the other for the old man."

The astonishment and bewilderment of the party had gradually given way to a boyish and impatient interest.

"Hadn't we better do the job at once?" suggested Dick Mattingly.

"Or throw ourselves into those new clothes, so as to be ready," added the younger Kearney, looking down at his ragged trousers. "I say, Fairfax, what are the girls like, eh?"

All the others had been dying to ask the question, yet one and all laughed at the conscious manner and blushing cheek of the questioner.

"You'll find out quick enough," returned Fairfax, whose curt carelessness did not, however, prevent a slight increase of color on his own cheek. "We'd better get that job off our hands before doing anything else. So, if you're ready, boys, we'll just waltz down to Thompson's and pack up the shanty. He's out of it by this time, I reckon. You might as well be perspiring to some purpose over there as gaspin' under this tree. We won't go back to work this afternoon, but knock off now, and call it half a day. Come! Hump your-selves, gentlemen. Are you ready? One, two, three, and away!"

In another instant the tree was deserted; the figures of the five millionaires of Devil's Ford, crossing the fierce glare of the open space, with boyish alacrity, glistened in the sunlight, and then disappeared in the nearest fringe of thickets.

CHAPTER II

SIX hours later, when the shadow of Devil's Spur had crossed the river, and spread a slight coolness over the flat beyond, the Pioneer coach, leaving the summit, began also to bathe its heated bulk in the long shadows of the descent. Conspicuous among the dusty passengers, the two pretty and youthful faces of the daughters of Philip Carr, mining superintendent and engineer, looked from the windows with no little anxiety towards their future home in the straggling settlement below, that occasionally came in view at the turns of the long zigzagging road. A slight look of comical disappointment passed between them as they gazed upon the sterile flat, dotted with unsightly excrescences that stood equally for cabins or mounds of stone and gravel. It was so feeble and inconsistent a culmination to the beautiful scenery they had passed through, so hopeless and imbecile a conclusion to the preparation of that long picturesque journey, with its glimpses of sylvan and pastoral glades and cañons, that, as the coach swept down the last incline, and the remorseless monotony of the dead level spread out before them, furrowed by ditches and indented by pits, under cover of shielding their cheeks from the impalpable dust that rose beneath the plunging wheels, they buried their faces in their handkerchiefs, to hide a few half-hysterical tears. Happily, their father, completely absorbed in a practical, scientific, and approving contemplation of the topography and material resources of the scene of his future labors, had no time to notice their defection. It was not until the stage drew up before a rambling tenement bearing the inscription, "Hotel and Stage Office," that he became fully aware of it.

"We can't stop *here,* papa," said Christie Carr decidedly, with a shake of her pretty head. "You can't expect that."

Mr. Carr looked up at the building; it was half grocery, half saloon. Whatever other accommodations it contained must have been hidden in the rear, as the flat roof above was almost level with the raftered ceiling of the shop.

"Certainly," he replied hurriedly; "we'll see to that in a moment. I dare say it's all right. I told Fairfax we were coming. Somebody ought to be here."

"But they're not," said Jessie Carr indignantly; "and the few that were here scampered off like rabbits to their burrows as soon as they saw us get down."

It was true. The little group of loungers before the building had suddenly disappeared. There was the flash of a red shirt vanishing in an adjacent doorway; the fading apparition of a pair of high boots and blue overalls in another; the abrupt withdrawal of a curly blond head from a sashless window over the way. Even the saloon was deserted, although a back door in the dim recess seemed to creak mysteriously. The stage-coach, with the other passengers, had already rattled away.

"I certainly think Fairfax understood that I—" began Mr. Carr.

He was interrupted by the pressure of Christie's fingers on his arm and a subdued exclamation from Jessie, who was staring down the street.

"What are they?" she whispered in her sister's ear. "Nigger minstrels, a circus, or what?"

The five millionaires of Devil's Ford had just turned the corner of the straggling street, and were approaching in single file. One glance was sufficient to show that they had already availed themselves of the new clothing bought by Fairfax, had washed, and one or two had shaved. But the result was startling.

Through some fortunate coincidence in size, Dick Mattingly was the only one who had achieved an entire new suit. But it was of funereal black cloth, and although relieved at one extremity by a pair of high riding boots, in which his too short trousers were tucked, and at the other by a tall white hat, and cravat of aggressive yellow, the effect was depressing. In agreeable contrast, his brother, Maryland Joe, was attired in a thin fawn-colored summer overcoat, lightly worn open, so as to show the unstarched bosom of a white embroidered shirt, and a pair of nankeen trousers and pumps.

The Kearney brothers had divided a suit between them, the elder wearing a tightly-fitting, single-breasted blue frock-coat and a pair of pink striped cotton trousers, while the younger candidly displayed the trousers of his brother's suit, as a harmonious change to a shining black alpaca coat and crimson neckerchief. Fairfax, who brought up the rear, had, with characteristic unselfishness, contented himself with a French workman's blue blouse and a pair of white duck trousers. Had they shown the least consciousness of their finery, or of its absurdity, they would have seemed despicable. But only one expression beamed on the five sunburnt and shining faces—a look of unaffected boyish gratification and unrestricted welcome.

They halted before Mr. Carr and his daughters, simultaneously removed their various and remarkable head coverings, and waited until Fairfax advanced and severally presented them. Jessie Carr's half-frightened smile took refuge in the trembling shadows of her dark lashes; Christie Carr stiffened slightly, and looked straight before her.

"We reckoned—that is—we intended to meet you and the young ladies at the grade," said Fairfax, reddening a little as he endeavored to conceal his too ready slang, "and save you from trapesing—from dragging yourselves up grade again to your house."

"Then there *is* a house?" said Jessie, with an alarming frank laugh of relief, that was, however, as frankly reflected in the boyishly appreciative eyes of the young men.

"Such as it is," responded Fairfax, with a shade of anxiety, as he glanced at the fresh and pretty costumes of the young women, and dubiously regarded the two Saratoga trunks resting hopelessly on the veranda. "I'm afraid it isn't much, for what you're accustomed to. But," he added more cheerfully, "it will do for a day or two, and perhaps you'll give us the pleasure of showing you the way there now."

The procession was quickly formed. Mr. Carr, alive only to the actual business that had brought him there, at once took possession of Fairfax, and began to disclose his plans for the working of the mine, occasionally halting to look at the work already done in the ditches, and to examine the field of his future operations. Fairfax, not displeased at being thus relieved of a lighter attendance on Mr. Carr's daughters, nevertheless from time to time cast a paternal glance backwards upon their escorts, who had each seized a handle of the two trunks, and were carrying them in couples at the young ladies' side. The occupation did not offer much freedom for easy gallantry, but no sign of discomfiture or uneasiness was visible in the grateful faces of the young men. The necessity of changing hands at times with their burdens brought a corresponding change of cavalier at the lady's side, although it was observed that the younger Kearney, for the sake of continuing a conversation with Miss Jessie, kept his grasp of the handle nearest the young lady until his hand was nearly cut through, and his arm worn out by exhaustion.

"The only thing on wheels in the camp is a mule wagon, and the mules are packin' gravel from the river this afternoon," explained Dick Mattingly apologetically to Christie, "or we'd have toted—I mean carried—you and your baggage up to the shant—the—your house. Give us two weeks more, Miss Carr—only two weeks to wash up our work and realize—and we'll give you a pair of 2.40 steppers and a skeleton buggy to meet you at the top of the hill and drive you over to the cabin. Perhaps you'd prefer a regular carriage; some ladies do. And a nigger driver. But what's the use of planning anything? Afore that time comes we'll have run you up a house on the hill, and you shall pick out the

spot. It wouldn't take long—unless you preferred brick.
I suppose we could get brick over from La Grange, if
you cared for it, but it would take longer. If you could
put up for a time with something of stained glass and a
mahogany veranda—"

In spite of her cold indignation, and the fact that she
could understand only a part of Mattingly's speech,
Christie comprehended enough to make her lift her clear
eyes to the speaker, as she replied freezingly that she
feared she would not trouble them long with her company.

"Oh, you'll get over that," responded Mattingly, with
an exasperating confidence that drove her nearly frantic,
from the manifest kindliness of intent that made it impossible for her to resent it. "I felt that way myself at
first. Things will look strange and unsociable for a
while, until you get the hang of them. You'll naturally
stamp round and cuss a little—" He stopped in conscious
consternation.

With ready tact, and before Christie could reply, Maryland Joe had put down the trunk and changed hands
with his brother.

"You mustn't mind Dick, or he'll go off and kill himself with shame," he whispered laughingly in her ear.
"He means all right, but he's picked up so much slang
here that he's about forgotten how to talk English,
and it's nigh on to four years since he's met a young
lady."

Christie did not reply. Yet the laughter of her sister
in advance with the Kearney brothers seemed to make
the reserve with which she tried to crush further familiarity only ridiculous.

"Do you know many operas, Miss Carr?"

She looked at the boyish, interested, sunburnt face so
near to her own, and hesitated. After all, why should
she add to her other real disappointments by taking this
absurd creature seriously?

"In what way?" she returned, with a half smile.

"To play. On the piano, of course. There isn't one
nearer here than Sacramento; but I reckon we could get

a small one by Thursday. You couldn't do anything on a banjo?" he added doubtfully; "Kearney's got one."

"I imagine it would be very difficult to carry a piano over those mountains," said Christie laughingly, to avoid the collateral of the banjo.

"We got a billiard-table over from Stockton," half bashfully interrupted Dick Mattingly, struggling from his end of the trunk to recover his composure, "and it had to be brought over in sections on the back of a mule, so I don't see why—" He stopped short again in confusion, at a sign from his brother, and then added, "I mean, of course, that a piano is a heap more delicate, and valuable, and all that sort of thing, but it's worth trying for."

"Fairfax was always saying he'd get one for himself, so I reckon it's possible," said Joe.

"Does he play?" asked Christie.

"You bet," said Joe, quite forgetting himself in his enthusiasm. "He can snatch Mozart and Beethoven bald-headed."

In the embarrassing silence that followed this speech the fringe of pine wood nearest the flat was reached. Here there was a rude "clearing," and beneath an enormous pine stood the two recently joined tenements. There was no attempt to conceal the point of junction between Kearney's cabin and the newly-transported saloon from the flat—no architectural illusion of the palpable collusion of the two buildings, which seemed to be telescoped into each other. The front room or living room occupied the whole of Kearney's cabin. It contained, in addition to the necessary articles for housekeeping, a "bunk" or berth for Mr. Carr, so as to leave the second building entirely to the occupation of his daughters as bedroom and boudoir.

There was a half-humorous, half-apologetic exhibition of the rude utensils of the living room, and then the young men turned away as the two girls entered the open door of the second room. Neither Christie nor Jessie could for a moment understand the delicacy which kept these young men from accompanying them into the room they had but a few moments before decorated and arranged with their own hands, and it was not until they turned to thank their strange entertainers that they found that they were gone.

The arrangement of the second room was rude and *bizarre,* but not without a singular originality and even tastefulness of conception. What had been the counter or "bar" of the saloon, gorgeous in white and gold, now sawn in two and divided, was set up on opposite sides of the room as separate dressing-tables, decorated with huge bunches of azaleas, that hid the rough earthenware bowls, and gave each table the appearance of a vestal altar.

The huge gilt plate-glass mirror which had hung behind the bar still occupied one side of the room, but its length was artfully divided by an enormous rosette of red, white, and blue muslin—one of the surviving Fourth of July decorations of Thompson's saloon. On either side of the door two pathetic-looking, convent-like cots, covered with spotless sheeting, and heaped up in the middle, like a snow-covered grave, had attracted their attention. They were still staring at them when Mr. Carr anticipated their curiosity.

"I ought to tell you that the young men confided to me the fact that there was neither bed nor mattress to be had on the Ford. They have filled some flour sacks with clean dry moss from the woods, and put half a dozen blankets on the top, and they hope you can get along until the messenger who starts to-night for La Grange can bring some bedding over."

Jessie flew with mischievous delight to satisfy herself of the truth of this marvel. "It's so, Christie," she said laughingly—"three flour-sacks apiece; but I'm jealous: yours are all marked '*superfine,*' and mine '*middlings.*'"

Mr. Carr had remained uneasily watching Christie's shadowed face.

"What matters?" she said drily. "The accommodation is all in keeping."

"It will be better in a day or two," he continued, casting a longing look towards the door—the first refuge of masculine weakness in an impending domestic emergency. "I'll go and see what can be done," he said feebly, with a sidelong impulse towards the opening and freedom. "I've got to see Fairfax again to-night any way."

"One moment, father," said Christie, wearily. "Did you know anything of this place and these—these people —before you came?"

"Certainly—of course I did," he returned, with the sudden testiness of disturbed abstraction. "What are you thinking of? I knew the geological strata and the— the report of Fairfax and his partners before I consented to take charge of the works. And I can tell you that there is a fortune here. I intend to make my own terms, and share in it."

"And not take a salary or some sum of money down?" said Christie, slowly removing her bonnet in the same resigned way.

"I am not a hired man, or a workman, Christie," said her father sharply. "You ought not to oblige me to remind you of that."

"But the hired men—the superintendent and his workmen—were the only ones who ever got anything out of your last experience with Colonel Waters at La Grange, and—and we at least lived among civilized people there."

"These young men are not common people, Christie; even if they have forgotten the restraints of speech and manners, they're gentlemen."

"Who are willing to live like—like negroes."

"You can make them what you please."

Christie raised her eyes. There was a certain cynical ring in her father's voice that was unlike his usual hesitating abstraction. It both puzzled and pained her.

"I mean," he said hastily, "that you have the same opportunity to direct the lives of these young men into more regular, disciplined channels that I have to regulate and correct their foolish waste of industry and material here. It would at least beguile the time for you."

Fortunately for Mr. Carr's escape and Christie's uneasiness, Jessie, who had been examining the details of the living-room, broke in upon this conversation.

"I'm sure it will be as good as a perpetual picnic. George Kearney says we can have a cooking-stove under the tree outside at the back, and as there will be no rain for three months we can do the cooking there, and that will give us more room for—for the piano when it comes; and there's an old squaw to do the cleaning and washing-up any day—and—and—it will be real fun."

She stopped breathlessly, with glowing cheeks and sparkling eyes—a charming picture of youth and trustfulness. Mr. Carr had seized the opportunity to escape.

"Really, now, Christie," said Jessie confidentially, when they were alone, and Christie had begun to unpack her trunk, and to mechanically put her things away, "they're not so bad."

"Who?" asked Christie.

"Why, the Kearneys, and Mattinglys, and Fairfax, and the lot, provided you don't look at their clothes. And think of it! they told me—for they tell one *everything* in the most alarming way—that those clothes were bought to please *us*. A scramble of things bought at La Grange, without reference to size or style. And to hear these creatures talk, why, you'd think they were Astors or Rothschilds. Think of that little one with the curls—I don't believe he is over seventeen, for all his baby moustache—says he's going to build an assembly hall for us to give a dance in next month; and apologizes the next breath to tell us that there isn't any milk to be had nearer than La Grange, and we must do without it, and use syrup in our tea to-morrow."

"And where is all this wealth?" said Christie, forcing herself to smile at her sister's animation.

"Under our very feet, my child, and all along the river. Why, what we thought was pure and simple mud is what they call 'gold-bearing cement.'"

"I suppose that is why they don't brush their boots and trousers, it's so precious," returned Christie drily. "And have they ever translated this precious dirt into actual coin?"

"Bless you, yes. Why, that dirty little gutter, you know, that ran along the side of the road and followed us down the hill all the way here, that cost them—let me see—yes, nearly sixty thousand dollars. And fancy! papa's just condemned it—says it won't do; and they've got to build another."

An impatient sigh from Christie drew Jessie's attention to her troubled eyebrows.

"Don't worry about our disappointment, dear. It isn't so very great. I dare say we'll be able to get along here in some way, until papa is rich again. You know they intend to make him share with them."

"It strikes me that he is sharing with them already," said Christie, glancing bitterly round the cabin; "sharing everything—ourselves, our lives, our tastes."

"Ye-e-s!" said Jessie, with vaguely hesitating assent. "Yes, even these:" she showed two dice in the palm of her little hand. "I found 'em in the drawer of our dressing-table."

"Throw them away," said Christie impatiently.

But Jessie's small fingers closed over the dice. I'll give them to the little Kearney. I dare say they were the poor boy's playthings."

The appearance of these relics of wild dissipation, however, had lifted Christie out of her sublime resignation. "For Heaven's sake, Jessie," she said, "look around and see if there is anything more!"

To make sure, they each began to scrimmage; the broken-spirited Christie exhibiting both alacrity and penetration in searching obscure corners. In the dining-room, behind the dresser, three or four books were discovered: an odd volume of Thackeray, another of Dickens, a memorandum-book or diary. "This seems to be Latin," said Jessie, fishing out a smaller book. "I can't read it."

"It's just as well you shouldn't," said Christie shortly, whose ideas of a general classical impropriety had been gathered from pages of Lemprière's dictionary. "Put it back directly."

Jessie returned certain odes of one Horatius Flaccus

to the corner, and uttered an exclamation. "Oh, Christie! here are some letters tied up with a ribbon."

They were two or three prettily written letters, exhaling a faint odor of refinement and of the pressed flowers that peeped from between the loose leaves. "I see, 'My darling Fairfax.' It's from some woman."

"I don't think much of her, whosoever she is," said Christie, tossing the intact packet back into the corner.

"Nor I," echoed Jessie.

Nevertheless, by some feminine inconsistency, evidently the circumstance did make them think more of *him,* for a minute later, when they had reëntered their own room, Christie remarked, "The idea of petting a man by his family name! Think of mamma ever having called papa 'darling Carr'!"

"Oh, but his family name isn't Fairfax," said Jessie hastily; "that's his *first* name, his Christian name. I forget what's his other name, but nobody ever calls him by it."

"Do you mean," said Christie, with glistening eyes and awful deliberation—"do you mean to say that we're expected to fall in with this insufferable familiarity? I suppose they'll be calling *us* by our Christian names next."

"Oh, but they do!" said Jessie, mischievously.

"What!"

"They call me Miss Jessie; and Kearney, the little one, asked me if Christie played."

"And what did you say?"

"I said that you did," answered Jessie, with an affectation of cherubic simplicity. "You do, dear; don't you? . . . There, don't get angry, darling; I couldn't flare up all of a sudden in the face of that poor little creature; he looked so absurd—and so—so honest."

Christie turned away, relapsing into her old resigned manner, and assuming her household duties in a quiet, temporizing way that was, however, without hope or expectation.

Mr. Carr, who had dined with his friends under the excuse of not adding to the awkwardness of the first

day's housekeeping returned late at night with a mass
of papers and drawings, into which he afterwards withdrew, but not until he had delivered himself of a mysterious package entrusted to him by the young men for
his daughters. It contained a contribution to their board
in the shape of a silver spoon and battered silver mug,
which Jessie chose to facetiously consider as an affecting reminiscence of the youthful Kearney's christening
days—which it probably was.

The young girls retired early to their white snow-
drifts: Jessie not without some hilarious struggles with
hers, in which she was, however, quickly surprised by
the deep and refreshing sleep of youth; Christie to lie
awake and listen to the night wind, that had changed
from the first cool whispers of sunset to the sturdy
breath of the mountain. At times the frail house shook
and trembled. Wandering gusts laden with the deep
resinous odors of the wood found their way through
the imperfect jointure of the two cabins, swept her
cheek and even stirred her long, wide-open lashes. A
broken spray of pine needles rustled along the roof,
or a pine cone dropped with a quick reverberating tap-
tap that for an instant startled her. Lying thus, wide
awake, she fell into a dreamy reminiscence of the past,
hearing snatches of old melody in the moving pines, fragments of sentences, old words, and familiar epithets in the
murmuring wind at her ear, and even the faint breath of
long-forgotten kisses on her cheek. She remembered
her mother—a pallid creature, who had slowly faded
out of one of her father's vague speculations in a vaguer
speculation of her own, beyond his ken—whose place
she had promised to take at her father's side. The
words, "Watch over him, Christie; he needs a woman's
care," again echoed in her ears, as if borne on the night
wind from the lonely grave in the lonelier cemetery by
the distant sea. She had devoted herself to him with
some little sacrifices of self, only remembered now for
their uselessness in saving her father the disappointment
that sprang from his sanguine and one-idea'd temperament. She thought of him lying asleep in the other

room, ready on the morrow to devote those fateful qualities to the new enterprise that with equally fateful disposition she believed would end in failure. It did not
occur to her that the doubts of her own practical nature
were almost as dangerous and illogical as his enthusiasm,
and that for that reason she was fast losing what little
influence she possessed over him. With the example of
her mother's weakness before her eyes, she had become
an unsparing and distrustful critic, with the sole effect
of awakening his distrust and withdrawing his confidence
from her.

He was beginning to deceive her as he had never
deceived her mother. Even Jessie knew more of this last
enterprise than she did herself.

All that did not tend to decrease her utter restlessness.
It was already past midnight when she noticed that the
wind had again abated. The mountain breeze had by
this time possessed the stifling valleys and heated bars
of the river in its strong, cold embraces; the equilibrium
of Nature was restored, and a shadowy mist rose from
the hollow. A stillness, more oppressive and intolerable
than the previous commotion, began to pervade the house
and the surrounding woods. She could hear the regular
breathing of the sleepers; she even fancied she could
detect the faint impulses of the more distant life in the
settlement. The far-off barking of a dog, a lost shout,
the indistinct murmur of some nearer watercourse—mere
phantoms of sound—made the silence more irritating.
With a sudden resolution she arose, dressed herself
quietly and completely, threw a heavy cloak over her
head and shoulders, and opened the door between the
living-room and her own. Her father was sleeping
soundly in his bunk in the corner. She passed noiselessly through the room, opened the lightly fastened
door, and stepped out into the night.

In the irritation and disgust of her walk hither, she
had never noticed the situation of the cabin, as it
nestled on the slope at the fringe of the woods; in the
preoccupation of her disappointment and the mechanical putting away of her things, she had never looked

once from the window of her room, or glanced backward out of the door that she had entered. The view before her was a revelation—a reproach, a surprise that took away her breath. Over her shoulders the newly risen moon poured a flood of silvery light, stretching from her feet across the shining bars of the river to the opposite bank, and on up to the very crest of the Devil's Spur— no longer a huge bulk of crushing shadow, but the steady exaltation of plateau, spur, and terrace clothed with replete and unutterable beauty. In this magical light that beauty seemed to be sustained and carried along by the river winding at its base, lifted again to the broad shoulder of the mountain, and lost only in the distant vista of death-like, overcrowning snow. Behind and above where she stood the towering woods seemed to be waiting with opened ranks to absorb her with the little cabin she had quitted, dwarfed into insignificance in the vast prospect; but nowhere was there another sign or indication of human life and habitation. She looked in vain for the settlement, for the rugged ditches, the scattered cabins, and the unsightly heaps of gravel. In the glamour of the moonlight they had vanished; a veil of silver-gray vapor touched here and there with ebony shadows masked its site. A black strip beyond was the river bank. All else was changed. With a sudden sense of awe and loneliness she turned to the cabin and its sleeping inmates—all that seemed left to her in the vast and stupendous domination of rock and wood and sky.

But in another moment the loneliness passed. A new and delicious sense of an infinite hospitality and friendliness in their silent presence began to possess her. This same slighted, forgotten, uncomprehended, but still foolish and forgiving Nature seemed to be bending over her frightened and listening ear with vague but thrilling murmurings of freedom and independence. She felt her heart expand with its wholesome breath, her soul fill with its sustaining truth.

She felt—

What was that?

An unmistakable outburst of a drunken song at the foot of the slope:—

> " Oh, my name it is Johnny from Pike,
>   I'm h—ll on a spree or a strike " . . .

She stopped as crimson with shame and indignation as if the viewless singer had risen before her.

> " I knew when to bet, and get up and get—"

"Hush! D—n it all. Don't you hear?"

There was the sound of hurried whispers, a "No" and "Yes," and then a dead silence.

Christie crept nearer to the edge of the slope in the shadow of a buckeye. In the clearer view she could distinguish a staggering figure in the trail below who had evidently been stopped by two other expostulating shadows that were approaching from the shelter of a tree.

"Sho!—didn't know!"

The staggering figure endeavored to straighten itself, and then slouched away in the direction of the settlement. The two mysterious shadows retreated again to the tree, and were lost in its deeper shadow. Christie darted back to the cabin, and softly reëntered her room.

"I thought I heard a noise that woke me, and I missed you," said Jessie, rubbing her eyes. "Did you see anything?"

"No," said Christie, beginning to undress.

"You weren't frightened, dear?"

"Not in the least," said Christie, with a strange little laugh. "Go to sleep."

CHAPTER III

THE five impulsive millionaires of Devil's Ford fulfilled not a few of their most extravagant promises. In less than six weeks Mr. Carr and his daughters were installed in a new house, built near the site of the double cabin, which was again transferred to the settlement, in order to give greater seclusion to the fair guests. It was a long, roomy, one-storied villa, with a not unpicturesque combination of deep veranda and trellis work, which relieved the flat monotony of the interior and the barrenness of the freshly-cleared ground. An upright piano, brought from Sacramento, occupied the corner of the parlor. A suite of gorgeous furniture, whose pronounced and extravagant glories the young girls instinctively hid under home-made linen covers, had also been spoils from afar. Elsewhere the house was filled with ornaments and decorations that in their incongruity forcibly recalled the gilded plate-glass mirrors of the bedroom in the old cabin. In the hasty furnishing of this Aladdin's palace, the slaves of the ring had evidently seized upon anything that would add to its glory, without reference always to fitness.

"I wish it didn't look so cussedly like a robber's cave," said George Kearney, when they were taking a quiet preliminary survey of the unclassified treasures, before the Carrs took possession.

"Or a gambling hell," said his brother reflectively.

"It's about the same thing, I reckon," said Dick Mattingly, who was supposed, in his fiery youth, to have encountered the similarity.

Nevertheless, the two girls managed to bestow the heterogeneous collection with tasteful adaptation to their needs. A crystal chandelier, which had once lent a fascinating illusion to the game of *Monte*, hung unlighted in the broad hall, where a few other *bizarre* and public articles were relegated. A long red sofa or bench, which had done duty beside a billiard-table found a place here also. Indeed, it is to be feared that some of the more rustic and bashful youths of Devil's Ford, who had felt it incumbent upon them to pay their respects to the new-comers, were more at ease in this vestibule than in the arcana beyond, whose glories they could see through the open door. To others, it represented a recognized state of probation before their *re-entrée* into civilization again. "I reckon, if you don't mind, miss," said the spokesman of one party, "ez this is our first call, we'll

sorter hang out in the hall yer, until you'r used to us."
On another occasion, one Whiskey Dick, impelled by a
sense of duty, paid a visit to the new house and its fair
occupants, in a fashion frankly recounted by him afterwards at the bar of the Tecumseh Saloon.

"You see, boys, I dropped in there the other night,
when some of you fellers was doin' the high-toned
'thankee, marm' business in the parlor. I just came to
anchor in the corner of the sofy in the hall, without
lettin' on to say that I was there, and took up a Webster's
dictionary that was on the table and laid it open—keerless
like, on my knees, ez if I was sorter consultin' it—and
kinder dozed off there, listenin' to you fellows gassin'
with the young ladies, and that yer Miss Christie just
snakin' music outer that pianner, and I reckon I fell
asleep. Anyhow, I was there nigh on to two hours.
It's mighty soothin', them fashionable calls; sorter knocks
the old camp dust outer a fellow, and sets him up again."

It would have been well if the new life of the Devil's
Ford had shown no other irregularity than the harmless
eccentricities of its original locaters. But the news of
its sudden fortune, magnified by report, began presently
to flood the settlement with another class of adventurers.
A tide of waifs, strays, and malcontents of old camps
along the river began to set towards Devil's Ford, in very
much the same fashion as the *débris,* drift, and alluvium
had been carried down in bygone days and cast upon its
banks. A few immigrant wagons, diverted from the
highways of travel by the fame of the new diggings,
halted upon the slopes of Devil's Spur and on the arid
flats of the Ford, and disgorged their sallow freight of
alkali-poisoned, prematurely-aged women and children
and maimed and fever-stricken men. Against this rude
form of domesticity were opposed the chromo-tinted
dresses and extravagant complexions of a few single unattended women—happily seen more often at night behind gilded bars than in the garish light of day—and an
equal number of pale-faced, dark-moustached, well-
dressed, and suspiciously idle men. A dozen rivals of
Thompson's Saloon had sprung up along the narrow

main street. There were two new hotels—one a "Temperance House," whose ascetic quality was confined only to the abnegation of whiskey—a rival stage office, and a small one-storied building, from which the "Sierran Banner" fluttered weekly, for "ten dollars a year, in advance." Insufferable in the glare of a Sabbath sun, bleak, windy, and flaring in the gloom of a Sabbath night, and hopelessly depressing on all days of the week, the First Presbyterian Church lifted its blunt steeple from the barrenest area of the flats, and was hideous! The civic improvements so enthusiastically contemplated by the five millionaires in the earlier pages of this veracious chronicle— the fountain, reservoir, town-hall, and free library—had not yet been erected. Their sites had been anticipated by more urgent buildings and mining works, unfortunately not considered in the sanguine dreams of the enthusiasts, and, more significant still, their cost and expense had been also anticipated by the enormous outlay of their earnings in the work upon Devil's Ditch.

Nevertheless, the liberal fulfilment of their promise in the new house in the suburbs blinded the young girls' eyes to their shortcomings in the town. Their own remoteness and elevation above its feverish life kept them from the knowledge of much that was strange, and perhaps disturbing to their equanimity. As they did not mix with the immigrant women—Miss Jessie's goodnatured intrusion into one of their half-nomadic camps one day having been met with rudeness and suspicion— they gradually fell into the way of trusting the responsibility of new acquaintances to the hands of their original hosts, and of consulting them in the matter of local recreation. It thus occurred that one day the two girls, on their way to the main street for an hour's shopping at the Villa de Paris and Variety Store, were stopped by Dick Mattingly a few yards from their house, with the remark that, as the county election was then in progress, it would be advisable for them to defer their intention for a few hours. As he did not deem it necessary to add that two citizens, in the exercise of a freeman's franchise, had been supplementing their ballots with bullets, in front of an admiring crowd, they knew nothing of that accident that removed from Devil's Ford an entertaining stranger, who had only the night before partaken of their hospitality.

A week or two later, returning one morning from a stroll in the forest, Christie and Jessie were waylaid by George Kearney and Fairfax, and, under pretext of being shown a new and romantic trail, were diverted from the regular path. This enabled Mattingly and Maryland Joe to cut down the body of a man hanged by the Vigilance Committee a few hours before on the regular trail, and to remonstrate with the committee on the incompatibility of such exhibitions with a maidenly worship of nature.

"With the whole county to hang a man in," expostulated Joe, "you might keep clear of Carr's woods."

It is needless to add that the young girls never knew of this act of violence, or the delicacy that kept them in ignorance of it. Mr. Carr was too absorbed in business to give heed to what he looked upon as a convulsion of society as natural as a geological upheaval, and too prudent to provoke the criticism of his daughters by comment in their presence.

An equally unexpected confidence, however, took its place. Mr. Carr having finished his coffee one morning, lingered a moment over his perfunctory paternal embraces, with the awkwardness of a preoccupied man endeavoring by the assumption of a lighter interest to veil another abstraction.

"And what are we doing to-day, Christie?" he asked, as Jessie left the dining-room.

"Oh, pretty much the usual thing—nothing in particular. If George Kearney gets the horses from the summit, we're going to ride over to Indian Spring to picnic. Fairfax—Mr. Munroe—I always forget that man's real name in this dreadfully familiar country— well, he's coming to escort us, and take me, I suppose— that is, if Kearney takes Jessie."

"A very nice arrangement," returned her father, with a slight nervous contraction of the corners of his mouth and eyelids to indicate mischievousness. "I've no doubt they'll both be here. You know they usually are—ha! ha! And what about the two Mattinglys and Philip Kearney, eh?" he continued; "won't they be jealous?"

"It isn't their turn," said Christie carelessly; "besides, they'll probably be there."

"And I suppose they're beginning to be resigned," said Carr, smiling.

"What on earth are you talking of, father?"

She turned her clear brown eyes upon him, and was regarding him with such manifest unconsciousness of the drift of his speech, and, withal, a little vague impatience of his archness, that Mr. Carr was feebly alarmed. It had the effect of banishing his assumed playfulness, which made his serious explanation the more irritating.

"Well, I rather thought that—that young Kearney was paying considerable attention to—to—to Jessie," replied her father, with hesitating gravity.

"What! that boy?"

"Young Kearney is one of the original locators, and an equal partner in the mine. A very enterprising young fellow. In fact, much more advanced and bolder in his conceptions than the others. I find no difficulty with him."

At another time Christie would have questioned the convincing quality of this proof, but she was too much shocked at her father's first suggestion, to think of anything else.

"You don't mean to say, father, that you are talking seriously of these men—your friends—whom we see every day—and our only company?"

"No, no!" said Mr. Carr hastily; "you misunderstand. I don't suppose that Jessie or you—"

"Or *me!* Am *I* included?"

"You don't let me speak, Christie. I mean, I am not talking seriously," continued Mr. Carr, with his most serious aspect, "of you and Jessie in this matter; but it may be a serious thing to these young men to be thrown continually in the company of two attractive girls."

"I understand—you mean that we should not see so

much of them," said Christie, with a frank expression of
relief so genuine as to utterly discompose her father.
"Perhaps you are right, though I fail to discover anything serious in the attentions of young Kearney to Jessie
—or—whoever it may be—to me. But it will be very
easy to remedy it, and see less of them. Indeed, we
might begin to-day with some excuse."

"Yes—certainly. Of course!" said Mr. Carr, fully
convinced of his utter failure, but, like most weak creatures, consoling himself with the reflection that he had
not shown his hand or committed himself. "Yes; but it
would perhaps be just as well for the present to let
things go on as they were. We'll talk of it again—I'm
in a hurry now," and, edging himself through the door,
he slipped away.

"What do you think is father's last idea?" said Christie,
with, I fear, a slight lack of reverence in her tone, as
her sister reëntered the room. "He thinks George Kearney is paying you too much attention."

"No!" said Jessie, replying to her sister's half-inter-
rogative, half-amused glance with a frank, unconscious
smile.

"Yes, and he says that Fairfax—I think it's Fairfax—
is equally fascinated with *me*."

Jessie's brow slightly contracted as she looked curiously
at her sister.

"Of all things," she said, "I wonder if any one has put
that idea into his dear old head. He couldn't have
thought it himself."

"I don't know," said Christie musingly; "but perhaps
it's just as well if we kept a little more to ourselves for
a while."

"Did father say so?" said Jessie quickly.

"No, but that is evidently what he meant."

"Ye-es," said Jessie slowly, "unless—"

"Unless what?" said Christie sharply. "Jessie, you
don't for a moment mean to say that you could possibly
conceive of anything else?"

"I mean to say," said Jessie, stealing her arm around
her sister's waist demurely, "that you are perfectly right.

We'll keep away from these fascinating Devil's Forders, and particularly the youngest Kearney. I believe there has been some ill-natured gossip. I remember that the other day, when we passed the shanty of that Pike County family on the slope, there were three women at the door, and one of them said something that made poor little Kearney turn white and pink alternately, and dance with suppressed rage. I suppose the old lady—M'Corkle, that's her name—would like to have a share of our cavaliers for her Euphemy and Mamie. I dare say it's only right; I would lend them the cherub occasionally, and you might let them have Mr. Munroe twice a week."

She laughed, but her eyes sought her sister's with a certain watchfulness of expression.

Christie shrugged her shoulders, with a suggestion of disgust.

"Don't joke. We ought to have thought of all this before."

"But when we first knew them, in the dear old cabin, there wasn't any other woman and nobody to gossip, and that's what made it so nice. I don't think so very much of civilization, do you?" said the young lady pertly.

Christie did not reply. Perhaps she was thinking the same thing. It certainly had been very pleasant to enjoy the spontaneous and chivalrous homage of these men, with no further suggestion of recompense or responsibility than the permission to be worshipped; but beyond that she racked her brain in vain to recall any look or act that proclaimed the lover. These men, whom she had found so relapsed into barbarism that they had forgotten the most ordinary forms of civilization; these men, even in whose extravagant admiration there was a certain loss of self-respect, that as a woman she would never forgive; these men, who seemed to belong to another race—impossible! Yet it was so.

"What construction must they have put upon her father's acceptance of their presents—of their company— of her freedom in their presence? No! they must have understood from the beginning that she and her sister had never looked upon them except as transient hosts and chance acquaintances. Any other idea was preposterous. And yet—"

It was the recurrence of this "yet" that alarmed her. For she remembered now that but for their slavish devotion they might claim to be her equal. According to her father's account, they had come from homes as good as their own; they were certainly more than her equal in fortune; and her father had come to them as an employé, until they had taken him into partnership. If there had only been sentiment of any kind connected with any of them! But they were all alike, brave, unselfish, humorous—and often ridiculous. If anything, Dick Mattingly was funniest by nature, and made her laugh more. Maryland Joe, his brother, told better stories (sometimes of Dick), though not so good a mimic as the other Kearney, who had a fairly sympathetic voice in singing. They were all good-looking enough; perhaps they set store on that—men are so vain.

And as for her own rejected suitor, Fairfax Munroe, except for a kind of grave and proper motherliness about his protecting manner, he absolutely was the most indistinctive of them all. He had once brought her some rare tea from the Chinese camp, and had taught her how to make it; he had cautioned her against sitting under the trees at nightfall; he had once taken off his coat to wrap around her. Really, if this were the only evidence of devotion that could be shown, she was safe!

"Well," said Jessie, "it amuses you, I see."

Christie checked the smile that had been dimpling the cheek nearest Jessie, and turned upon her the face of an elder sister.

"Tell me, have *you* noticed this extraordinary attention of Mr. Munroe to me?"

"Candidly?" asked Jessie, seating herself comfortably on the table sideways, and endeavoring to pull her skirt over her little feet. "Honest Injun?"

"Don't be idiotic, and, above all, don't be slangy! Of course, candidly."

"Well, no. I can't say that I have."

"Then," said Christie, "why in the name of all that's

preposterous, do they persist in pairing me off with the
least interesting man of the lot?"

Jessie leaped from the table.

"Come now," she said, with a little nervous laugh, "he's
not so bad as all that. You don't know him. But what
does it matter now, as long as we're not going to see
them any more?"

"They're coming here for the ride to-day," said Christie
resignedly. "Father thought it better not to break it off
at once."

"Father thought so!" echoed Jessie, stopping with her
hand on the door.

"Yes; why do you ask?"

But Jessie had already left the room, and was singing
in the hall.

CHAPTER IV

THE afternoon did not, however, bring their expected
visitors. It brought, instead, a brief note by the hands
of Whiskey Dick from Fairfax, apologizing for some
business that kept him and George Kearney from accompanying the ladies. It added that the horses were
at the disposal of themselves and any escort they might
select, if they would kindly give the message to Whiskey
Dick.

The two girls looked at each other awkwardly; Jessie
did not attempt to conceal a slight pout.

"It looks as if they were anticipating us," she said,
with a half-forced smile. "I wonder, now, if there
really has been any gossip? But no! They wouldn't have
stopped for that, unless—" She looked curiously at her
sister.

"Unless what?" repeated Christie; "you are horribly
mysterious this morning."

"Am I? It's nothing. But they're wanting an answer.
Of course you'll decline."

"And intimate we only care for their company! No!
We'll say we're sorry they can't come, and—accept their
horses. We can do without an escort, we two."

"Capital!" said Jessie, clapping her hands. "We'll show them—"

"We'll show them nothing," interrupted Christie decidedly. "In our place there's only the one thing to do. Where is this—Whiskey Dick?"

"In the parlor."

"The parlor!" echoed Christie. "Whiskey Dick? What—is he—"

"Yes; he's all right," said Jessie confidently. "He's been here before, but he stayed in the hall; he was so shy. I don't think you saw him."

"I should think not—Whiskey Dick!"

"Oh, you can call him Mr. Hall, if you like," said Jessie, laughing. "His real name is Dick Hall. If you want to be funny, you can say Alky Hall, as the others do."

Christie's only reply to this levity was a look of superior resignation as she crossed the hall and entered the parlor.

Then ensued one of those surprising, mystifying, and utterly inexplicable changes that leave the masculine being so helpless in the hands of his feminine master. Before Christie opened the door her face underwent a rapid transformation: the gentle glow of a refined woman's welcome suddenly beamed in her interested eyes; the impulsive courtesy of an expectant hostess eagerly seizing a long-looked-for opportunity broke in a smile upon her lips as she swept across the room, and stopped with her two white outstretched hands before Whiskey Dick.

It needed only the extravagant contrast presented by that gentleman to complete the tableau. Attired in a suit of shining black alpaca, the visitor had evidently prepared himself with some care for a possible interview. He was seated by the French window opening upon the veranda, as if to secure a retreat in case of an emergency. Scrupulously washed and shaven, some of the soap appeared to have lingered in his eyes and inflamed the lids, even while it lent a sleek and shining lustre, not unlike his coat, to his smooth black hair.

Nevertheless, leaning back in his chair, he had allowed a large white handkerchief to depend gracefully from his fingers—a pose at once suggesting easy and elegant langour.

"How kind of you to give me an opportunity to make up for my misfortune when you last called! I was so sorry to have missed you. But it was entirely my fault! You were hurried, I think—you conversed with others in the hall—you—"

She stopped to assist him to pick up the handkerchief that had fallen, and the Panama hat that had rolled from his lap towards the window when he had started suddenly to his feet at the apparition of grace and beauty. As he still nervously retained the two hands he had grasped, this would have been a difficult feat, even had he not endeavored at the same moment, by a backward furtive kick, to propel the hat out of the window, at which she laughingly broke from his grasp and flew to the rescue.

"Don't mind it, miss," he said hurriedly. "It is not worth your demeaning yourself to touch it. Leave it outside thar, miss. I wouldn't have toted it in, anyhow, if some of those high-falutin' fellows hadn't allowed, the other night, ez it were the reg'lar thing to do; as if, miss, any gentleman kalkilated to ever put on his hat in the house afore a lady!"

But Christie had already possessed herself of the unlucky object, and had placed it upon the table. This compelled Whiskey Dick to rise again, and as an act of careless good breeding to drop his handkerchief in it. He then leaned one elbow upon the piano, and, crossing one foot over the other, remained standing in an attitude he remembered to have seen in the pages of an illustrated paper as portraying the hero in some drawing-room scene. It was easy and effective, but seemed to be more favorable to revery than conversation. Indeed, he remembered that he had forgotten to consult the letterpress as to which it represented.

"I see you agree with me, that politeness is quite a matter of intention," said Christie, "and not of mere fashion and rules. Now, for instance," she continued, with a dazzling smile, "I suppose, according to the rules, I ought to give you a note to Mr. Munroe, accepting his offer. That is all that is required; but it seems so much nicer, don't you think, to tell it to *you* for *him,* and have the pleasure of your company and a little chat at the same time."

"That's it, that's just it, Miss Carr; you've hit it in the centre this time," said Whiskey Dick, now quite convinced that his attitude was not intended for eloquence, and shifting back to his own seat, hat and all; "that's tantamount to what I said to the boys just now. 'You want an excuse,' sez I, 'for not goin' out with the young ladies. So, accorden' to rules, you writes a letter allowin' buzziness and that sorter thing detains you. But wot's the facts? You're a gentleman, and as gentlemen you and George comes to the opinion that you're rather playin' it for all it's worth in this yer house, you know—comin' here night and day, off and on, reg'lar sociable and fam'ly like, and makin' people talk about things they ain't any call to talk about, and, what's a darned sight more, *you fellows* ain't got any right *yet* to allow 'em to talk about, d'ye see?" He paused, out of breath.

It was Miss Christie's turn to move about. In changing her seat to the piano-stool, so as to be nearer her visitor, she brushed down some loose music, which Whiskey Dick hastened to pick up.

"Pray don't mind it," she said, "pray don't, really—let it be—" But Whiskey Dick, feeling himself on safe ground in this attention, persisted to the bitter end of a disintegrated and well-worn "Travatore." "So that is what Mr. Munroe said," she remarked quietly.

"Not just then, in course, but it's what's bin on his mind and in his talk for days off and on," returned Dick, with a knowing smile and a nod of mysterious confidence. "Bless your soul, Miss Carr, folks like you and me don't need to have them things explained. That's what I said to him, sez I. 'Don't send no note, but just go up there and hev it out fair and square, and say what you do mean.' But they would hev the note, and I kalkilated to bring it. But when I set my eyes on you, and heard you express yourself as you did just now, I sez to my-self, sez I, 'Dick, yer's a young lady, and a fash'nable lady at that, ez don't go foolin' round on rules and etiketts'—excuse my freedom, Miss Carr—'and you and her, sez I, 'kin just discuss this yer matter in a sociable, off-hand, fash'nable way.' They're a good lot o' boys, Miss Carr, a square lot—white men all of 'em; but they're a little soft and green, may be, from livin' in these yer pine woods along o' the other sap. They just worship the ground you and your sister tread on—cer-tain! of course! of course!" he added hurriedly, recog-nizing Christie's half-conscious, deprecating gesture with more exaggerated deprecation. "I understand. But what I wanter say is that they'd be willin' to be that ground, and lie down and let you walk over them—so to speak, Miss Carr, so to speak—if it would keep the hem of your gown from gettin' soiled in the mud o' the camp. But it wouldn't do for them to make a reg'lar curderoy road o' themselves for the houl camp to trapse over, on the mere chance of your some time passin' that way, would it now?"

"Won't you let me offer you some refreshment, Mr. Hall?" said Christie, rising, with a slight color. "I'm really ashamed of my forgetfulness again, but I'm afraid it's partly *your* fault for entertaining me to the exclu-sion of yourself. No, thank you, let me fetch it for you."

She turned to a handsome sideboard near the door, and presently faced him again with a decanter of whiskey and a glass in her hand, and a return of the bewitching smile she had worn on entering.

"But perhaps you don't take whiskey?" suggested the arch deceiver, with a sudden affected but pretty per-plexity of eye, brow, and lips.

For the first time in his life Whiskey Dick hesitated between two forms of intoxication. But he was still nervous and uneasy; habit triumphed, and he took the whiskey. He, however, wiped his lips with a slight wave of his handkerchief, to support a certain easy elegance which he firmly believed relieved the act of any vulgar quality.

"Yes, ma'am," he continued, after an exhilarated pause. "Ez I said afore, this yer's a matter you and me can discuss after the fashion o' society. My idea is that these yer boys should kinder let up on you and Miss Jessie for a while, and do a little more permiskus attention round the Ford. There's one or two families yer with grown-up gals ez oughter be squared; that is—the boys mighter put in a few fancy touches among them—kinder take 'em buggy riding—or to church—once in a while— just to take the pizen outer their tongues, and make a kind o' bluff to the parents, d'ye see? That would sorter divert their own minds; and even if it didn't, it would kinder get 'em accustomed agin to the old style and their own kind. I want to warn ye agin an idea that might occur to you in a giniral way. I don't say you hev the idea, but it's kind o' nat'ral you might be thinkin' of it some time, and I thought I'd warn you agin it."

"I think we understand each other too well to differ much, Mr. Hall," said Christie, still smiling; "but what is the idea?"

The delicate compliment to their confidential relations and the slight stimulus of liquor had tremulously exalted Whiskey Dick. Affecting to look cautiously out of the window and around the room, he ventured to draw nearer the young woman with a half-paternal, half-timid familiarity.

"It might have occurred to you," he said, laying his handkerchief as if to veil mere vulgar contact, on Christie's shoulder, "that it would be a good thing on *your* side to invite down some of your high-toned gentlemen friends from 'Frisco to visit you and escort you round. It seems quite nat'ral like, and I don't say it ain't, but—the boys wouldn't stand for it."

In spite of her self-possession, Christie's eyes suddenly darkened, and she involuntarily drew herself up. But Whiskey Dick, guiltily attributing the movement to his own indiscreet gesture, said, "Excuse me, miss," recovered himself by lightly dusting her shoulder with his handkerchief, as if to remove the impression, and her smile returned.

"They wouldn't stand for it," said Dick, "and there'd be some shooting! Not afore you, miss—not afore you, in course! But they'd adjourn to the woods some morning with them city folks, and hev it out with rifles at a hundred yards. Or, seein' ez they're city folks, the boys would do the square thing with pistols at twelve paces. They're good boys, as I said afore; but they're quick and tetchy—George, being the youngest, nat'rally is the tetchiest. You know how it is, Miss Carr; his pretty, gal-like face and little moustaches haz cost him half a dozen scrimmages already. He'z had a fight for every hair that's growed in his moustache since he kem here."

"Say no more, Mr. Hall!" said Christie, rising and pressing her hands lightly on Dick's tremulous fingers. "If I ever had any such idea, I should abandon it now; you are quite right in this as in your other opinions. I shall never cease to be thankful to Mr. Munroe and Mr. Kearney that they intrusted this delicate matter to your hands."

"Well," said the gratified and reddening visitor, "it ain't perhaps the square thing to them or myself to say that they reckon⌐d to have me discuss their delicate affairs for them, but—"

"I understand," interrupted Christie. "They simply gave you the letter as a friend. It was my good fortune to find you a sympathizing and liberal man of the world." The delighted Dick, with conscious vanity beaming from every feature of his shining face, lightly waved the compliment aside with his handkerchief, as she continued, "But I am forgetting the message. We accept the horses. Of course we *could* do without an escort; but forgive my speaking so frankly, are *you* engaged this afternoon?"

"Excuse me, miss, I don't take—" stammered Dick, scarcely believing his ears.

"Could you give us your company as an escort?" repeated Christie with a smile.

Was he awake or dreaming, or was this some trick of liquor in his often distorted fancy? He, Whiskey Dick! the butt of his friends, the chartered oracle of the barrooms, even in whose wretched vanity there was always the haunting suspicion that he was despised and scorned; he, who had dared so much in speech, and achieved so little in fact! he, whose habitual weakness had even led him into the wildest indiscretion here; he— now offered a reward for that indiscretion! He, Whiskey Dick, the solicited escort of these two beautiful and peerless girls! What would they say at the Ford? What would his friends think? It would be all over the Ford the next day. His past would be vindicated, his future secured. He grew erect at the thought. It was almost in other voice, and with no trace of his previous exaggeration, that he said, "With pleasure."

"Then, if you will bring the horses at once, we shall be ready when you return."

In another instant he had vanished, as if afraid to trust the reality of his good fortune to the dangers of delay. At the end of half an hour he reappeared, leading the two horses, himself mounted on a half-broken mustang. A pair of large, jingling silver spurs and a stiff *sombrero,* borrowed with the mustang from some mysterious source, were donned to do honor to the occasion.

The young girls were not yet ready, but he was shown by the Chinese servant into the parlor to wait for them. The decanter of whiskey and glasses were still invitingly there. He was hot, trembling, and flushed with triumph. He walked to the table and laid his hand on the decanter, when an odd thought flashed upon him. He would not drink this time. No, it should not be said that he, the selected escort of the *élite* of Devil's Ford, had to fill himself up with whiskey before they started. The boys might turn to each other in their astonishment, as he proudly passed with his fair companions, and say, "It's Whiskey Dick," but he'd be d——d if they should add, "and full as ever." No, sir! Nor when he was riding beside these real ladies, and leaning over them at some confidential moment, should they even know it from his breath! No. . . . Yet a thimbleful, taken straight, only a thimbleful, wouldn't be much, and might help to pull him together. He again reached his trembling hand for the decanter, hesitated, and then, turning his back upon it, resolutely walked to the open window. Almost at the same instant he found himself face to face with Christie on the veranda.

She looked into his bloodshot eyes, and cast a swift glance at the decanter.

"Won't you take something before you go?" she said sweetly.

"I—reckon—not, jest now," stammered Whiskey Dick, with a heroic effort.

"You're right," said Christie. "I see you are like me. It's too hot for anything fiery. Come with me."

She led him into the dining-room, and pouring out a glass of iced tea handed it to him. Poor Dick was not prepared for this terrible culmination. Whiskey Dick and iced tea! But under pretence of seeing if it was properly flavored, Christie raised it to her own lips.

"Try it, to please me."

He drained the goblet.

"Now, then," said Christie gayly, "let's find Jessie, and be off!"

CHAPTER V

WHATEVER might have been his other deficiencies as an escort, Whiskey Dick was a good horseman, and, in spite of his fractious brute, exhibited such skill and confidence as to at once satisfy the young girls of his value to them in the management of their own horses, to whom side-saddles were still an alarming novelty. Jessie, who had probably already learned from her sister the purport of Dick's confidences, had received him with equal cordiality and perhaps a more unqualified amusement; and now, when fairly lifted into the saddle by his tremulous but respectful hands, made a very charming picture of youthful and rosy satisfaction. And when Christie, more fascinating than ever in her riding-habit, took her place on the

other side of Dick, as they sallied from the gate, that
gentleman felt his cup of happiness complete. His tri-
umphal *entrée* into the world of civilization and fashion
was secure. He did not regret the untasted liquor; here
was an experience in after years to lean his back against
comfortably in bar-rooms, to entrance or defy mankind.
He had even got so far as to formulate in fancy the
sentence: "I remember, gentlemen, that one afternoon,
being on a *pasear* with two fash'nable young ladies," etc.,
etc.

At present, however, he was obliged to confine himself
to the functions of an elegant guide and *cicerone*—when
not engaged in "having it out" with his horse. Their way
lay along the slope, crossing the high-road at right angles,
to reach the deeper woods beyond. Dick would have
lingered on the highway—ostensibly to point out to his
companions the new flume that had taken the place of the
condemned ditch, but really in the hope of exposing himself in his glory to the curious eyes of the wayfaring
world.

Unhappily the road was deserted in the still powerful
sunlight, and he was obliged to seek the cover of the
woods, with a passing compliment to the parent of his
charges. Waving his hands towards the flume, he said,
"Look at that work of your father's; there ain't no other
man in Californy but Philip Carr ez would hev the grit
to hold up such a bluff agin natur and agin luck ez that
yer flume stands for. I don't say it 'cause you're his
daughters, ladies! That ain't the style, ez *you* know, in
sassiety, Miss Carr," he added, turning to Christie as the
more socially experienced. "No! but there ain't another
man to be found ez could do it. It cost already two hundred thousand; it'll cost five hundred thousand afore it's
done; and every cent of it is got out of the yearth beneath it, or *hez* got to be out of it. 'Tain't ev'ry man,
Miss Carr, ez hev got the pluck to pledge not only what
he's got, but what he reckons to git."

"But suppose he don't get it?" said Christie, slightly
contracting her brows.

"Then there's the flume to show for it," said Dick.

"But of what use is the flume, if there isn't any more gold?" continued Christie, almost angrily.

"That's good from *you*, miss," said Dick, giving way to a fit of hilarity. "That's good for a fash'nable young lady —own daughter of Philip Carr. She sez, says she," continued Dick, appealing to the sedate pines for appreciation of Christie's rare humor, " 'Wot's the use of a flume, when gold ain't there?' I must tell that to the boys."

"And what's the use of the gold in the ground when the flume isn't there to work it out?" said Jessie to her sister, with a cautioning glance towards Dick.

But Dick did not notice the look that passed between the sisters. The richer humor of Jessie's retort had thrown him into convulsions of laughter.

"And now *she* says, wot's the use o' the gold without the flume? 'Xcuse me, ladies, but that's just puttin' the hull question that's agitatin' this yer camp inter two speeches as clear as crystal. There's the hull crowd outside—and some on 'em inside, like Fairfax, hez their doubts—ez says with Miss Christie; and there's all of us inside, ez holds Miss Jessie's views."

"I never heard Mr. Munroe say that the flume was wrong," said Jessie quickly.

"Not to you, nat'rally," said Dick, with a confidential look at Christie; "but I reckon he'd like some of the money it cost laid out for suthin' else. But what's the odds? The gold is there, and *we're* bound to get it."

Dick was the foreman of a gang of paid workmen, who had replaced the millionaires in mere manual labor, and the *we* was a polite figure of speech.

The conversation seemed to have taken an unfortunate turn, and both the girls experienced a feeling of relief when they entered the long gulch or defile that led to Indian Spring. The track now becoming narrow, they were obliged to pass in single file along the precipitous hillside, led by this escort. This effectually precluded any further speech, and Christie at once surrendered herself to the calm, obliterating influences of the forest. The settlement and its gossip were far behind and forgotten. In the absorption of nature, her companions passed out of her mind, even as they sometimes passed out of her sight in the windings of the shadowy trail. As she rode alone, the fronds of breast-high ferns seemed to caress her with outstretched and gently-detaining hands; strange wild-flowers sprang up through the parting underbrush; even the granite rocks that at times pressed closely upon the trail appeared as if cushioned to her contact with star-rayed mosses, or lightly flung after her long lassoes of delicate vines. She recalled the absolute freedom of their *al-fresco* life in the old double cabin, when she spent the greater part of her waking hours under the mute trees in the encompassing solitude, and, half regretting the more civilized restraints of this newer and more ambitious abode, forgot that she had ever rebelled against it. The social complication that threatened her now seemed to her rather the outcome of her half-civilized parlor than of the sylvan glade. How easy it would have been to have kept the cabin, and then to have gone away en-tirely, than for her father to have allowed them to be compromised with the growing fortunes of the settle-ment! The suspicions and distrust that she had always felt of their fortunes seemed to grow with the involun-tary admission of Whiskey Dick that they were shared by others who were practical men. She was fain to have recourse to the prospect again to banish these thoughts, and this opened her eyes to the fact that her companions had been missing from the trail ahead of her for some time. She quickened her pace slightly to reach a pro-jecting point of rock that gave her a more extended prospect. But they had evidently disappeared.

She was neither alarmed nor annoyed. She could easily overtake them soon, for they would miss her, and return or wait for her at the spring. At the worst she would have no difficulty in retracing her steps home. In her present mood, she could readily spare their company; indeed she was not sorry that no other being should interrupt that sympathy with the free woods which was beginning to possess her.

She was destined, however, to be disappointed. She had not proceeded a hundred yards before she noticed the moving figure of a man beyond her in the hillside chaparral above the trail. He seemed to be going in the same direction as herself, and, as she fancied, endeavoring to avoid her. This excited her curiosity to the point of urging her horse forward until the trail broadened into the level forest again, which she now remembered was a part of the environs of Indian Spring. The stranger hesitated, pausing once or twice with his back towards her, as if engaged in carefully examining the dwarf willows to select a switch. Christie slightly checked her speed as she drew nearer; when, as if obedient to a sudden resolution, he turned and advanced towards her. She was relieved and yet surprised to recognize the boyish face and figure of George Kearney. He was quite pale and agitated, although attempting, by a jaunty swinging of the switch he had just cut, to assume the appearance of ease and confidence.

Here was an opportunity. Christie resolved to profit by it. She did not doubt that the young fellow had already passed her sister on the trail, but, from bashfulness, had not dared to approach her. By inviting his confidence, she would doubtless draw something from him that would deny or corroborate her father's opinion of his sentiments. If he was really in love with Jessie, she would learn what reasons he had for expecting a serious culmination of his suit, and perhaps she might be able delicately to open his eyes to the truth. If, as she believed, it was only a boyish fancy, she would laugh him out of it with that *camaraderie* which had always existed between them. A half motherly sympathy, albeit born quite as much from a contemplation of his beautiful yearning eyes as from his interesting position, lightened the smile with which she greeted him.

"So you contrived to throw over your stupid business and join us, after all," she said; "or was it that you changed your mind at the last moment?" she added mischievously. "I thought only we women were permitted that!" Indeed, she could not help noticing that there was really a strong feminine suggestion in the shifting color and slightly conscious eyelids of the young fellow.

"Do young girls always change their minds?" asked George, with an embarrassed smile.

"Not, always; but sometimes they don't know their own mind—particularly if they are very young; and when they do at last, you clever creatures of men, who have interpreted their ignorance to please yourselves, abuse them for being fickle." She stopped to observe the effect of what she believed a rather clear and significant exposition of Jessie's and George's possible situation. But she was not prepared for the look of blank resignation that seemed to drive the color from his face and moisten the fire of his dark eyes.

"I reckon you're right," he said, looking down.

"Oh! we're not accusing you of fickleness," said Christie gayly; "although you didn't come, and we were obliged to ask Mr. Hall to join us. I suppose you found him and Jessie just now?"

But George made no reply. The color was slowly coming back to his face, which, as she glanced covertly at him, seemed to have grown so much older that his returning blood might have brought two or three years with it.

"Really, Mr. Kearney," she said dryly, "one would think that some silly, conceited girl" — she was quite earnest in her epithets, for a sudden, angry conviction of some coquetry and disingenuousness in Jessie had come to her in contemplating its effects upon the young fellow at her side — "some country jilt, had been trying her rustic hand upon you."

"She is not silly, conceited, nor countrified," said George, slowly raising his beautiful eyes to the young girl half reproachfully. "It is I who am all that. No, she is right, and you know it."

Much as Christie admired and valued her sister's charms, she thought this was really going too far. What had Jessie ever done—what was Jessie—to provoke and remain insensible to such a blind devotion as this? And really, looking at him now, he was not so *very young* for Jessie; whether his unfortunate passion had brought out all his latent manliness, or whether he had hitherto

kept his serious nature in the background, certainly he
was not a boy. And certainly his was not a passion that
he could be laughed out of. It was getting very tire-
some. She wished she had not met him—at least until
she had had some clearer understanding with her sister.
He was still walking beside her, with his hand on her
bridle rein, partly to lead her horse over some boulders
in the trail, and partly to conceal his first embarrassment.
When they had fairly reached the woods, he stopped.

"I am going to say good-by, Miss Carr."

"Are you not coming further? We must be near
Indian Spring, now; Mr. Hall and—and Jessie—cannot
be far away. You will keep me company until we meet
them?"

"No," he replied quietly. "I only stopped you to say
good-by. I am going away."

"Not from Devil's Ford?" she asked, in half-incredu-
lous astonishment. "At least, not for long?"

"I am not coming back," he replied.

"But this is very abrupt," she said hurriedly, feeling
that in some ridiculous way she had precipitated an
equally ridiculous catastrophe. "Surely you are not going away in this fashion, without saying good-by to
Jessie and—and father?"

"I shall see your father, of course—and you will give
my regards to Miss Jessie."

He evidently was in earnest. Was there ever anything so perfectly preposterous? She became indignant.

"Of course," she said coldly, "I won't detain you; your
business must be urgent, and I forgot—at least I had
forgotten until to-day—that you have other duties more
important than that of squire of dames. I am afraid this
forgetfulness made me think you would not part from us
in quite such a business fashion. I presume, if you had
not met me just now, we should none of us have seen
you again?"

He did not reply.

"Will you say good-by, Miss Carr?"

He held out his hand.

"One moment, Mr. Kearney. If I have said any-thing which you think justifies this very abrupt leave-taking, I beg you will forgive and forget it—or, at least, let it have no more weight with you than the idle words of any woman. I only spoke generally. You know—I—I might be mistaken."

His eyes, which had dilated when she began to speak, darkened; his color, which had quickly come, as quickly sank when she had ended.

"Don't say that, Miss Carr. It is not like you, and—it is useless. You know what I meant a moment ago. I read it in your reply. You meant that I, like others, had deceived myself. Did you not?"

She could not meet those honest eyes with less than equal honesty. She knew that Jessie did not love him—would not marry him—whatever coquetry she might have shown.

"I did not mean to offend you," she said hesitatingly; "I only half suspected it when I spoke."

"And you wish to spare me the avowal?" he said bitterly.

"To me, perhaps, yes, by anticipating it. I could not tell what ideas you might have gathered from some in-discreet frankness of Jessie—or my father," she added, with almost equal bitterness.

"I have never spoken to either," he replied quickly. He stopped, and added, after a moment's mortifying reflection, "I've been brought up in the woods, Miss Carr, and I suppose I have followed my feelings, instead of the etiquette of society."

Christie was too relieved at the rehabilitation of Jessie's truthfulness to notice the full significance of his speech.

"Good-by," he said again, holding out his hand.

"Good-by!"

She extended her own, ungloved, with a frank smile. He held it for a moment, with his eyes fixed upon hers. Then suddenly, as if obeying an uncontrollable impulse, he crushed it like a flower again and again against his burning lips, and darted away.

Christie sank back in her saddle with a little cry, half of pain and half of frightened surprise. Had the poor boy suddenly gone mad, or was this vicarious farewell a part of the courtship of Devil's Ford? She looked at her little hand, which had reddened under the pressure, and suddenly felt the flush extending to her cheeks and the roots of her hair. This was intolerable.

"Christie!"

It was her sister emerging from the wood to seek her. In another moment she was at her side.

"We thought you were following," said Jessie. "Good heavens! how you look! What has happened?"

"Nothing. I met Mr. Kearney a moment ago on the trail. He is going away, and—and—" She stopped, furious and flushing.

"And," said Jessie, with a burst of merriment, "he told you at last he loved you. Oh, Christie!"

CHAPTER VI

THE abrupt departure of George Kearney from Devil's Ford excited but little interest in the community, and was soon forgotten. It was generally attributed to differences between himself and his partners on the question of further outlay of their earnings on mining improvements—he and Philip Carr alone representing a sanguine minority whose faith in the future of the mine accepted any risks. It was alleged by some that he had sold out to his brother; it was believed by others that he had simply gone to Sacramento to borrow money on his share, in order to continue the improvements on his own responsibility. The partners themselves were uncommunicative; even Whiskey Dick, who since his remarkable social elevation had become less oracular, much to his own astonishment, contributed nothing to the gossip except a suggestion that as the fiery temper of George Kearney brooked no opposition, even from his brother, it was better they should separate before the estrangement became serious.

Mr. Carr did not disguise his annoyance at the loss of his young disciple and firm ally. But an unlucky allusion to his previous remarks on Kearney's attentions to Jessie, and a querulous regret that he had permitted a disruption of their social intimacy, brought such an ominous and frigid opposition, not only from Christie, but even the frivolous Jessie herself, that Carr sank back in a crushed and terrified silence. "I only meant to say," he stammered after a pause, in which he, however, resumed his aggrieved manner, "that *Fairfax* seems to come here still, and *he* is not such a particular friend of mine."

"But she is—and has your interest entirely at heart," said Jessie, stoutly, "and he only comes here to tell us how things are going on at the works."

"And criticise your father, I suppose," said Mr. Carr, with an attempt at jocularity that did not, however, disguise an irritated suspiciousness. "He really seems to have supplanted *me* as he has poor Kearney in your estimation."

"Now, father," said Jessie, suddenly seizing him by the shoulders in affected indignation, but really to conceal a certain embarrassment that sprang quite as much from her sister's quietly observant eye as her father's speech, "you promised to let this ridiculous discussion drop. You will make me and Christie so nervous that we will not dare to open the door to a visitor, until he declares his innocence of any matrimonial intentions. You don't want to give color to the gossip that agreement with your views about the improvements is necessary to getting on with us."

"Who dares talk such rubbish?" said Carr, reddening; "is that the kind of gossip that Fairfax brings here?"

"Hardly, when it's known that he don't quite agree with you, and *does* come here. That's the best denial of the gossip."

Christie, who had of late loftily ignored these discussions, waited until her father had taken his departure.

"Then that is the reason why you still see Mr. Munroe, after what you said," she remarked quietly to Jessie.

Jessie, who would have liked to escape with her father, was obliged to pause on the threshold of the door, with a pretty assumption of blank forgetfulness in her blue eyes and lifted eyebrows.

"Said what? when?" she asked vacantly.

"When—when Mr. Kearney that day—in the woods—went away," said Christie, faintly coloring.

"Oh! *that* day," said Jessie briskly; "the day he just gloved your hand with kisses, and then fled wildly into the forest to conceal his emotion."

"The day he behaved very foolishly," said Christie, with reproachful calmness, that did not, however, prevent a suspicion of indignant moisture in her eyes—"when you explained"—

"That it wasn't meant for *me*," interrupted Jessie.

"That it was to you that *Mr. Munroe's* attentions were directed. And then we agreed that it was better to prevent any further advances of this kind by avoiding any familiar relations with either of them."

"Yes," said Jessie, "I remember; but you're not confounding my seeing Fairfax occasionally now with that sort of thing. *He* doesn't kiss my hand like anything," she added, as if in abstract reflection.

"Nor run away, either," suggested the trodden worm, turning.

There was an ominous silence.

"Do you know we are nearly out of coffee?" said Jessie choking, but moving towards the door with Spartan-like calmness.

"Yes. And something must be done this very day about the washing," said Christie, with suppressed emotion, going towards the opposite entrance.

Tears stood in each other's eyes with this terrible exchange of domestic confidences. Nevertheless, after a moment's pause, they deliberately turned again, and, facing each other with frightful calmness, left the room by purposeless and deliberate exits other than those they had contemplated—a crushing abnegation of self, that, to some extent, relieved their surcharged feelings.

Meantime the material prosperity of Devil's Ford increased, if a prosperity based upon no visible foundation but the confidences and hopes of its inhabitants could be called material. Few, if any, stopped to consider that the improvements, buildings, and business were simply the outlay of capital brought from elsewhere, and as yet the settlement or town, as it was now called, had neither produced nor exported capital of itself equal to half the amount expended. It was true that some land was cultivated on the further slope, some mills erected and lumber furnished from the inexhaustible forest; but the consumers were the inhabitants themselves, who paid for their produce in borrowed capital or unlimited credit. It was never discovered that while all roads led to Devil's Ford, Devil's Ford led to nowhere. The difficulties overcome in getting things into the settlement were never surmounted for getting things out of it. The lumber was practically valueless for export to other settlements across the mountain roads, which were equally rich in timber. The theory so enthusiastically held by the original locators, that Devil's Ford was a vast sink that had, through ages, exhausted and absorbed the trickling wealth of the adjacent hills and valleys, was suffering an ironical corroboration.

One morning it was known that work was stopped at the Devil's Ford Ditch—temporarily only, it was alleged, and many of the old workmen simply had their labor for the present transferred to excavating the river banks, and the collection of vast heaps of "pay gravel." Specimens from these mounds, taken from different localities, and at different levels, were sent to San Francisco for more rigid assay and analysis. It was believed that this would establish the fact of the permanent richness of the drifts, and not only justify past expenditure, but a renewed outlay of credit and capital. The suspension of engineering work gave Mr. Carr an opportunity to visit San Francisco on general business of the mine, which could not, however, prevent him from arranging further combinations with capital. His two daughters accompanied him. It offered an admirable opportunity for a shopping expedition, a change of scene, and a peaceful solution of their perplexing and anomalous social relations with Devil's Ford. In the first flush of gratitude to their father for this opportune holiday, something of harmony had been restored to the family circle that had of late been shaken by discord.

But their sanguine hopes of enjoyment were not entirely fulfilled. Both Jessie and Christie were obliged to confess to a certain disappointment in the aspect of the civilization they were now reëntering. They at first attributed it to the change in their own habits during the last three months, and their having become barbarous and countrified in their seclusion. Certainly in the matter of dress they were behind the fashions as revealed in Montgomery Street. But when the brief solace afforded them by the *modiste* and dressmaker was past, there seemed little else to be gained. They missed at first, I fear, the chivalrous and loyal devotion that had only amused them at Devil's Ford, and were the more inclined, I think, to distrust the conscious and more civilized gallantry of the better dressed and more carefully presented men they met. For it must be admitted that, for obvious reasons, their criticisms were at first confined to the sex they had been most in contact with. They could not help noticing that the men were more eager, annoyingly feverish, and self-asserting in their superior elegance and external show than their old associates were in their frank, unrestrained habits. It seemed to them that the five millionaires of Devil's Ford, in their radical simplicity and thoroughness, were perhaps nearer the type of true gentlemanhood than these citizens who imitated a civilization they were unable yet to reach.

The women simply frightened them, as being, even more than the men, demonstrative and excessive in their fine looks, their fine dresses, their extravagant demand for excitement. In less than a week they found themselves regretting—not the new villa on the slope of Devil's Ford, which even in its own *bizarre* fashion was exceeded by the barbarous ostentation of the villas and private houses around them—but the double cabin under the trees, which now seemed to them almost aristocratic in its grave simplicity and abstention. In the mysterious forests of masts that thronged the city's quays they recalled the straight shafts of the pines on Devil's slopes, only to miss the sedate repose and infinite calm that used to environ them. In the feverish, pulsating life of the young metropolis they often stopped oppressed, giddy, and choking; the roar of the streets and thoroughfares was meaningless to them, except to revive strange memories of the deep, unvarying monotone of the evening wind over their humbler roof on the Sierran hillside. Civic bred and nurtured as they were, the recurrence of these sensations perplexed and alarmed them.

"It seems so perfectly ridiculous," said Jessie, "for us to feel as out of place here as that Pike County servant girl in Sacramento who had never seen a steamboat before; do you know, I quite had a turn the other day at seeing a man on the Stockton wharf in a red shirt, with a rifle on his shoulder."

"And you wanted to go and speak to him?" said Christie, with a sad smile.

"No, that's just it; I felt awfully hurt and injured that he did not come up and speak to *me!* I wonder if we got any fever or that sort of thing up there; it makes one quite superstitious."

Christie did not reply; more than once before she had felt that inexplicable misgiving. It had sometimes seemed to her that she had never been quite herself since that memorable night when she had slipped out of their sleeping-cabin, and stood alone in the gracious and commanding presence of the woods and hills. In the solitude of night, with the hum of the great city rising below her—at times even in theatres or crowded assemblies of men and women—she forgot herself, and again stood in the weird brilliancy of that moonlight night in mute worship at the foot of that slowly-rising mystic altar of piled terraces, hanging forests, and lifted plateaus that climber forever to the lonely skies. Again she felt before her the expanding and opening arms of the protecting woods. Had they really closed upon her in some pantheistic embrace that made her a part of them? Had she been baptized in that moonlight as a child of the great forest? It was easy to believe in the myths of the poets of an idyllic life under those trees, where, free from conventional restrictions, one loved and was loved. If she, with her own worldly experience, could think of this now, why might not George Kearney have thought? . . . She stopped, and found herself blushing even in the darkness. As the thought and blush were the usual sequel of her reflections, it is to be feared that they may have been at times the impelling cause.

Mr. Carr, however, made up for his daughters' want of sympathy with metropolitan life. To their astonishment, he not only plunged into the fashionable gayeties and amusements of the town, but in dress and manner assumed the *rôle* of a leader of society. The invariable answer to their half-humorous comment was the necessities of the mine, and the policy of frequenting the company of capitalists, to enlist their support and confidence. There was something in this so unlike their father, that what at any other time they would have hailed as a relief to his habitual abstraction now half alarmed them. Yet he was not dissipated—he did not drink nor gamble. There certainly did not seem any harm in his frequenting the society of ladies, with a gallantry that appeared to be forced and a pleasure that to their critical eyes was certainly apocryphal. He did not drag his daughters into the mixed society of that period; he did not press upon them the company of those he most frequented, and whose accepted position in that little world of fashion was considered equal to their own. When Jessie strongly objected to the pronounced manners of a certain widow, whose actual present wealth and pecuniary influence condoned for a more uncertain prehistoric past, Mr. Carr did not urge a further acquaintance. "As long as you're not thinking of marrying again, papa," Jessie had said finally, "I don't see the necessity of our knowing her." "But suppose I were," had replied Mr. Carr. with affected humor. "Then you certainly wouldn't care for any one like her," his daughter had responded trium-ﾑphantly. Mr. Carr smiled, and dropped the subject, but it is probable that his daughters' want of sympathy with his acquaintances did not in the least interfere with his social prestige. A gentleman in all his relations and under all circumstances, even his cold scientific abstraction was provocative; rich men envied his lofty ignorance of the smaller details of money-making, even while they mistrusted his judgment. A man still well preserved, and free from weakening vices, he was a dangerous rival to younger and faster San Francisco, in the eyes of the sex, who knew how to value a repose they did not themselves possess.

Suddenly Mr. Carr announced his intention of proceeding to Sacramento, on further business of the mine, leaving his two daughters in the family of a wealthy friend until he should return for them. He opposed their ready suggestion to return to Devil's Ford with a new and unnecessary inflexibility: he even met their compromise to accompany him to Sacramento with equal decision.

"You will be only in my way," he said curtly. "Enjoy yourselves here while you can."

Thus left to themselves, they tried to accept his advice. Possibly some slight reaction to their previous disappointment may have already set in; perhaps they felt any distraction to be a relief to their anxiety about their father. They went out more; they frequented concerts and parties; they accepted, with their host and his family, an invitation to one of those opulent and barbaric entertainments with which a noted San Francisco millionaire distracted his rare moments of reflection in his gorgeous palace on the hills. Here they could at least be once more in the country they loved, albeit of a milder and less heroic type, and a little degraded by the overlapping tinsel and scattered spangles of the palace.

It was a three days' *fête;* the style and choice of

amusements left to the guests, and an equal and active
participation by no means necessary or indispensable.
Consequently, when Christie and Jessie Carr proposed
a ride through the adjacent cañon on the second morning, they had no difficulty in finding horses in the well-
furnished stables of their opulent entertainers, nor
cavaliers among the other guests, who were too happy
to find favor in the eyes of the two pretty girls who
were supposed to be abnormally fastidious and refined.
Christie's escort was a good-natured young banker,
shrewd enough to avoid demonstrative attentions, and
lucky enough to interest her during the ride with his
clear and half-humorous reflections on some of the business speculations of the day. If his ideas were occasionally too clever, and not always consistent with a
high sense of honor, she was none the less interested
to know the ethics of that world of speculation into
which her father had plunged, and the more convinced,
with mingled sense of pride and anxiety, that his still
dominant gentlemanhood would prevent his coping with
it on equal terms. Nor could she help contrasting
the conversation of the sharp-witted man at her side
with what she still remembered of the vague, touching,
boyish enthusiasm of the millionaires of Devil's Ford.
Had her escort guessed the result of this contrast, he
would hardly have been as gratified as he was with the
grave attention of her beautiful eyes.

The fascination of a gracious day and the leafy solitude of the cañon led them to prolong their ride beyond
the proposed limit, and it became necessary towards
sunset for them to seek some shorter cut home.

"There's a *vaquero* in yonder field," said Christie's
escort, who was riding with her a little in advance of the
others, "and those fellows know every trail that a horse
can follow. I'll ride on, intercept him, and try my Spanish on him. If I miss him, as he's galloping on, you
might try your hand on him yourself. He'll understand
your eyes, Miss Carr, in any language."

As he dashed away, to cover his first audacity of compliment, Christie lifted the eyes thus apostrophized to

the opposite field. The *vaquero,* who was chasing some
cattle, was evidently too preoccupied to heed the shouts
of her companion, and wheeling round suddenly to intercept one of the deviating fugitives, permitted Christie's
escort to dash past him before that gentleman
could rein in his excited steed. This brought the
vaquero directly in her path. Perceiving her, he threw
his horse back on its haunches, to prevent a collision.
Christie rode up to him, suddenly uttered a cry, and
halted. For before her, sunburnt in cheek and throat,
darker in the free growth of moustache and curling hair,
clad in the coarse, picturesque finery of his class, undisguised only in his boyish beauty, sat George Kearney.

The blood, that had forsaken her astonished face,
rushed as quickly back. His eyes, which had suddenly
sparkled with an electrical glow, sank before hers. His
hand dropped, and his cheek flushed with a dark embarrassment.

"You here, Mr. Kearney? How strange!—but how
glad I am to meet you again!"

She tried to smile; her voice trembled, and her little
hand shook as she extended it to him.

He raised his dark eyes quickly, and impulsively
urged his horse to her side. But, as if suddenly awakening to the reality of the situation, he glanced at her
hurriedly, down at his barbaric finery, and threw a
searching look towards her escort.

In an instant Christie saw the infelicity of her position, and its dangers. The words of Whiskey Dick,
"He wouldn't stand that," flashed across her mind.
There was no time to lose. The banker had already
gained control over his horse, and was approaching
them, all unconscious of the fixed stare with which
George was regarding him. Christie hastily seized the
hand which he had allowed to fall at his side, and said
quickly.—

"Will you ride with me a little way, Mr. Kearney?"

He turned the same searching look upon her. She met
it clearly and steadily; he even thought reproachfully.

"Do!" she said hurriedly. "I ask it as a favor. I

want to speak to you. Jessie and I are here alone. Father is away. *You* are one of our oldest friends."

He hesitated. She turned to the astonished young banker, who rode up.

"I have just met an old friend. Will you please ride back as quickly as you can, and tell Jessie that Mr. Kearney is here, and ask her to join us?"

She watched her dazed escort, still speechless from the spectacle of the fastidious Miss Carr *tête-à-tete* with a common Mexican *vaquero,* gallop off in the direction of the cañon, and then turned to George.

"Now take me home, the shortest way, as quick as you can."

"Home?" echoed George.

"I mean to Mr. Prince's house. Quick! before they can come up to us."

He mechanically put spurs to his horse; she followed. They presently struck into a trail that soon diverged again into a disused logging track through the woods.

"This is the short cut to Prince's, by two miles," he said, as they entered the woods.

As they were still galloping, without exchanging a word, Christie began to slacken her speed; George did the same. They were safe from intrusion at the present, even if the others had found the short cut. Christie, bold and self-reliant a moment ago, suddenly found herself growing weak and embarrassed. What had she done?

She checked her horse suddenly.

"Perhaps we had better wait for them," she said timidly.

George had not raised his eyes to hers.

"You said you wanted to hurry home," he replied gently, passing his hand along his mustang's velvety neck, "and—and you had something to say to me."

"Certainly," she answered, with a faint laugh. "I'm so astonished at meeting you here. I'm quite bewildered. You are living here; you have forsaken us to buy a ranche?" she continued, looking at him attentively.

His brow colored slightly.

"No, I'm living here, but I have bought no ranche.
I'm only a hired man on somebody else's ranche, to
look after the cattle."

He saw her beautiful eyes fill with astonishment and—
something else. His brow cleared; he went on, with his
old boyish laugh:

"No, Miss Carr. The fact is, I'm dead broke. I've
lost everything since I saw you last. But as I know how
to ride, and I'm not afraid of work, I manage to keep
along."

"You have lost money in—in the mines?" said Christie
suddenly.

"No"—he replied quickly, evading her eyes. "My
brother has my interest, you know. I've been foolish
on my own account solely. You know I'm rather inclined to that sort of thing. But as long as my folly
don't affect others, I can stand it."

"But it may affect others—and *they* may not think
of it as folly—" She stopped short, confused by his
brightening color and eyes. "I mean— Oh, Mr.
Kearney, I want you to be frank with me. I know nothing of business, but I know there has been trouble about
the mine at Devil's Ford. Tell me honestly, has my
father anything to do with it? If I thought that through
any imprudence of his, you had suffered—if I believed
that you could trace any misfortune of yours to him—to
us—I should never forgive myself"—she stopped and
flashed a single look at him—"I should never forgive
you for abandoning us."

The look of pain which had at first shown itself in his
face, which never concealed anything, passed, and a
quick smile followed her feminine anticlimax.

"Miss Carr," he said, with boyish eagerness, "if any
man suggested to me that your father wasn't the brightest and best of his kind—too wise and clever for the
fools about him to understand—I'd—I'd shoot him."

Confused by his ready and gracious disclaimer of what
she had *not* intended to say, there was nothing left for
her but to rush upon what she really intended to say,
with what she felt was shameful precipitation.

"One word more, Mr. Kearney," she began, looking down, but feeling the color come to her face as she spoke. "When you spoke to me the day you left, you must have thought me hard and cruel. When I tell you that I thought you were alluding to Jessie and some feeling you had for her—"

"For Jessie!" echoed George.

"You will understand that—that—"

"That what?" said George, drawing nearer to her.

"That I was only speaking as she might have spoken had you talked to her of me," added Christie hurriedly, slightly backing her horse away from him.

But this was not so easy, as George was the better rider, and by an imperceptible movement of his wrist and foot had glued his horse to her side. "He will go now," she had thought, but he didn't.

"We must ride on," she suggested faintly.

"No," he said with a sudden dropping of his boyish manner and a slight lifting of his head. "We must ride together no further, Miss Carr. I must go back to the work I am hired to do, and you must go on with your party, whom I hear coming. But when we part here you must bid me good-by—not as Jessie's sister—but as Christie—the one—the only woman that I love, or that I ever have loved."

He held out his hand. With the recollection of their previous parting, she tremblingly advanced her own. He took it, but did not raise it to his lips. And it was she who found herself half confusedly retaining his hand in hers, until she dropped it with a blush.

"Then is this the reason you give for deserting us as you have deserted Devil's Ford?" she said coldly.

He lifted his eyes to her with a strange smile, and said, "Yes," wheeled his horse, and disappeared in the forest.

He had left her thus abruptly once before, kissed, blushing, and indignant. He was leaving her now, un-kissed, but white and indignant. Yet she was so self-possessed when the party joined her, that the singular rencontre and her explanation of the stranger's sudden departure excited no further comment. Only Jessie managed to whisper in her ear,—

"I hope you are satisfied now that it wasn't me he meant?"

"Not at all," said Christie coldly.

CHAPTER VII

A few days after the girls had returned to San Francisco, they received a letter from their father. His business, he wrote, would detain him in Sacramento some days longer. There was no reason why they should return to Devil's Ford in the heat of the summer; their host had written to beg him to allow them a more extended visit, and, if they were enjoying themselves, he thought it would be well not to disoblige an old friend. He had heard they had a pleasant visit to Mr. Prince's place, and that a certain young banker had been very attentive to Christie.

"Do you know what all this means, dear?" asked Jessie, who had been watching her sister with an unusually grave face.

Christie whose thoughts had wandered from the letter, replied carelessly,—

"I suppose it means that we are to wait here until father sends for us."

"It means a good deal more. It means that papa has had another reverse; it means that the assay has turned out badly for the mine—that the further they go from the flat the worse it gets—that all the gold they will probably ever see at Devil's Ford is what they have already found or will find on the flat; it means that all Devil's Ford is only a 'pocket,' and not a 'lead.'" She stopped, with unexpected tears in her eyes.

"Who told you this?" asked Christie breathlessly.

"Fairfax—Mr. Munroe," stammered her sister, "writes to me as if we already knew it—tells me not to be alarmed, that it isn't so bad—and all that."

"How long has this happened, Jessie?" said Christie, taking her hand, with a white but calm face.

"Nearly ever since we've been here, I suppose. It must be so, for he says poor papa is still hopeful of doing something yet."

"And Mr. Munroe writes to you?" said Christie abstractedly.

"Of course," said Jessie quickly. "He feels interested in—us."

"Nobody tells *me* anything," said Christie.

"Didn't—"

"No," said Christie bitterly.

"What on earth *did* you talk about? But people don't confide in you because they're afraid of you. You're so—"

"So what?"

"So gently patronizing, and so 'I-don't-suppose-you-can-help-it,-poor-thing,' in your general style," said Jessie, kissing her. "There! I only wish I was like you. What do you say if we write to father that we'll go back to Devil's Ford? Mr. Munroe thinks we will be of service there just now. If the men are dissatisfied, and think we're spending money—"

"I'm afraid Mr. Munroe is hardly a disinterested adviser. At least, I don't think it would look quite decent for you to fly back without your father, at his suggestion," said Christie coldly. "He is not the only partner. We are spending no money. Besides, we have engaged to go to Mr. Prince's again next week."

"As you like, dear," said Jessie, turning away to hide a faint smile.

Nevertheless, when they returned from their visit to Mr. Prince's, and one or two uneventful rides, Christie looked grave. It was only a few days later that Jessie burst upon her one morning.

"You were saying that nobody ever tells you anything. Well, here's your chance. Whiskey Dick is below."

"Whiskey Dick?" repeated Christie. "What does he want?"

"*You,* love. Who else? You know he always scorns me as not being high-toned and elegant enough for his social confidences. He asked for you only."

With an uneasy sense of some impending revelation, Christie descended to the drawing-room. As she opened the door, a strong flavor of that toilet soap and eau de Cologne with which Whiskey Dick was in the habit of gracefully effacing the traces of dissipation made known his presence. In spite of a new suit of clothes, whose pristine folds refused to adapt themselves entirely to the contour of his figure, he was somewhat subdued by the unexpected elegance of the drawing-room of Christie's host. But a glance at Christie's sad but gracious face quickly reassured him. Taking from his hat a three-cornered parcel, he unfolded a handsome *saffrona* rose, which he gravely presented to her. Having thus reëstablished his position, he sank elegantly into a *tête-à-tete* ottoman. Finding the position inconvenient to face Christie, who had seated herself on a chair, he transferred himself to the other side of the ottoman, and addressed her over its back as from a pulpit.

"Is this really a fortunate accident, Mr. Hall, or did you try to find us?" said Christie pleasantly.

"Partly promiskuss, and partly coincident, Miss Christie, one up and t'other down," said Dick lightly. "Work being slack at present at Devil's Ford, I reck'ned I'd take a *pasear* down to 'Frisco, and dip into the vortex o' fash'nable society and out again." He lightly waved a new handkerchief to illustrate his swallow-like intrusion. "This yer minglin' with the *bo-tong* is apt to be wearisome, ez you and me knows, unless combined with experience and judgment. So when them boys up there allows that there's a little too much fash'nable society and San Francisco capital and high-falutin' about the future goin' on fer square surface mining, I sez, 'Look yere, gentlemen,' sez I, 'you don't see the pint. The pint is to get the pop'lar eye fixed, so to speak, on Devil's Ford. When a fash'nable star rises above the 'Frisco horizon—like Miss Carr—and, so to speak, dazzles the gineral eye, people want to know who she is.

'And when people say that's the accomplished daughter
o' the accomplished superintendent of the Devil's Ford
claim—otherwise known as the Star-eyed Goddess o'
Devil's Ford—every eye is fixed on the mine, and Capital,
so to speak, tumbles to her.' And when they sez that
the old man—excuse my freedom, but that's the way the
boys talk of your father, meaning no harm—the old man,
instead o' trying to corral rich widders—grass or otherwise—to spend their money on the big works for the
gold that ain't there yet—should stay in Devil's Ford
and put all his *sabe* and genius into grindin' out the
little gold that is there, I sez to them that it ain't your
father's style. 'His style,' sez I, 'ez to go in and build
them works.' When they're done he turns round to
Capital, and sez he—'Look yer,' sez he, 'thar's all the
works you want, first quality—cost a million; thar's all
the water you want, onlimited—cost another million;
thar's all the pay gravel you want in and outer the
ground—call it two millions more. Now my time's too
vally'ble; my professhun's too high-toned to *work* mines.
I *make* 'em. Hand me over a check for ten millions and
call it square, and work it for yourself.' So Capital
hands over the money and waltzes down to run the
mine, and you original locators walks round with yer
hands in yer pockets a-top of your six million profit,
and you let's Capital take the work and the responsibility."

Preposterous as this seemed from the lips of Whiskey
Dick, Christie had a haunting suspicion that it was not
greatly unlike the theories expounded by the clever young
banker who had been her escort. She did not interrupt
his flow of reminiscent criticism; when he paused for
breath, she said, quietly:

"I met Mr. George Kearney the other day in the
country."

Whiskey Dick stopped awkwardly, glanced hurriedly
at Christie, and coughed behind his handkerchief.

"Mr. Kearney—eh—er—certengly—yes—er—met him,
you say. Was he—er—er—well?"

"In health, yes; but otherwise he has lost everything," said Christie, fixing her eyes on the embarrassed Dick.

"Yes—er—in course—in course—" continued Dick, nervously glancing round the apartment as if endeavoring to find an opening to some less abrupt statement of the fact.

"And actually reduced to take some menial employment," added Christie, still regarding Dick with her clear glance.

"That's it—that's just it," said Dick, beaming as he suddenly found his delicate and confidential opportunity. "That's it, Miss Christie; that's just what I was sayin' to the boys. 'Ez it the square thing,' sez I, 'jest because George hez happened to hypothecate every dollar he has, or expects to hev, to put into them works, only to please Mr. Carr, and just because he don't want to distress that intelligent gentleman by letting him see he's dead broke —for him to go and demean himself and Devil's Ford by rushing away and hiring out as a Mexican *vaquero* on Mexican wages? Look,' sez I, 'at the disgrace he brings upon a high-toned, fash'nable girl, at whose side he's walked and danced, and passed rings, and sentiments, and bokays in the changes o' the cotillion and the mizzourka. And wot,' sez I, 'if some day, prancing along in a fash'nable cavalcade, she all of a suddents comes across him drivin' a Mexican steer?' That's what I said to the boys. And so you met him, Miss Christie, as usual," continued Dick, endeavoring under the appearance of a large social experience to conceal an eager anxiety to know the details—"so you met him; and, in course, you didn't let on yer knew him, so to speak, nat'rally, or p'raps you kinder like asked him to fix your saddle-girth, and give him a five-dollar piece—eh?"

Christie, who had risen and gone to the window, suddenly turned a very pale face and shining eyes on Dick.

"Mr. Hall," she said, with a faint attempt at a smile, "we are old friends, and I feel I can ask you a favor. You once before acted as our escort—it was for a short but a happy time—will you accept a larger trust? My father is busy in Sacramento for the mine: will you, without saying anything to anybody, take Jessie and me back at once to Devil's Ford?"

"Will I? Miss Christie," said Dick, choking between an intense gratification and a desire to keep back its vulgar exhibition, "I shall be proud!"

"When I say keep it a secret"—she hesitated—"I don't mean that I object to your letting Mr. Kearney, if you happen to know where he is, understand that we are going back to Devil's Ford."

"Cert'nly—nat'rally," said Dick, waving his hand gracefully; "sorter drop him a line, saying that bizness of a social and delicate nature—being the escort of Miss Christie and Jessie Carr to Devil's Ford—prevents my having the pleasure of calling."

"That will do very well, Mr. Hall," said Christie, faintly smiling through her moist eyelashes. "Then will you go at once and secure tickets for to-night's boat, and bring them here? Jessie and I will arrange everything else."

"Cert'nly," said Dick impulsively, and preparing to take a graceful leave.

"We'll be impatient until you return with the tickets," said Christie graciously.

Dick shook hands gravely, got as far as the door, and paused.

"You think it better to take the tickets now?" he said dubiously.

"By all means," said Christie impetuously. "I've set my heart on going to-night—and unless you secure berths early—"

"In course—in course," interrupted Dick nervously. "But—"

"But what?" said Christie impatiently.

Dick hesitated, shut the door carefully, and, looking round the room, lightly shook out his handkerchief, apparently flicked away an embarrassing suggestion, and said, with a little laugh:

"It's ridiklous, perfectly ridiklous, Miss Christie; but not bein' in the habit of carryin' ready money, and havin' omitted to cash a draft on Wells, Fargo & Co.—"

"Of course," said Christie rapidly. "How forgetful I am! Pray forgive me, Mr. Hall. I didn't think. I'll run up and get it from our host; he will be glad to be our banker."

"One moment, Miss Christie," said Dick lightly, as his thumb and finger relaxed in his waistcoat pocket over the only piece of money in the world that had remained to him after his extravagant purchase of Christie's *saffrona* rose, "one moment: in this yer monetary transaction, if you like, you are at liberty to use *my* name."

CHAPTER VIII

As Christie and Jessie Carr looked from the windows of the coach, whose dust-clogged wheels were slowly dragging them, as if reluctant, nearer the last stage of their journey to Devil's Ford, they were conscious of a change in the landscape, which they could not entirely charge upon their changed feelings. The few bared open spaces on the upland, the long stretch of rocky ridge near the summit, so vivid and so velvety during their first journey, were now burnt and yellow; even the brief openings in the forest were seared as if by a hot iron in the scorching rays of a half year's sun. The pastoral slopes of the valley below were cloaked in lustreleather: the rare watercourses along the road had faded from the waiting eye and ear; it seemed as if the long and dry summer had even invaded the close-set ranks of pines, and had blown a simoom breath through the densest woods, leaving its charred red ashes on every leaf and spray along the tunnelled shade. As they leaned out of the window and inhaled the half-dead spices of the evergreens, they seemed to have entered the atmosphere of some exhausted passion—of some fierce excitement that was even now slowly burning itself out.

It was a relief at last to see the straggling houses of Devil's Ford far below come once more into view, as they rounded the shoulder of Devil's Spur and began the long descent. But as they entered the town a change more ominous and startling than the desiccation of the landscape forced itself upon them. The town was still there, but where were the inhabitants? Four months ago they had left the straggling street thronged with busy citizens—groups at every corner, and a chaos of merchandise and traders in the open *plaza* or square beside the Presbyterian church. Now all was changed. Only a few wayfarers lifted their heads lazily as the coach rattled by, crossing the deserted square littered with empty boxes, and gliding past empty cabins or vacant shop windows, from which not only familiar faces, but even the window sashes themselves, were gone. The great unfinished serpent-like flume, crossing the river on gigantic trestles, had advanced as far as the town, stooping over it like some enormous reptile that had sucked its life blood and was gorged with its prey.

Whiskey Dick, who had left the stage on the summit to avail himself of a shorter foot trail to the house, that would give him half an hour's grace to make preparations, met them at the stage office with a buggy. A glance at the young girls, perhaps, convinced him that the graces of elegant worldly conversation were out of place with the revelation he read on their faces. Perhaps, he, too, was a trifle indisposed. The short journey to the house was made in profound silence.

The villa had been repainted and decorated, and it looked fresher, and even, to their preoccupied minds, appeared more attractive than ever. Thoughtful hands had taken care of the vines and rose-bushes on the trellises; water—that precious element in Devil's Ford —had not been spared in keeping green through the long drought the plants which the girls had so tenderly nurtured. It was the one oasis in which the summer still lingered; and yet a singular sense of loss came over the girls as they once more crossed its threshold. It seemed no longer their own.

"Ef I was you, Miss Christie, I'd keep close to the house for a day or two, until—until—things is settled," said Dick; "there's a heap o' tramps and sich cattle trapsin' round. P'raps you wouldn't feel so lonesome if you was nearer town—for instance, 'bout wher' you useter live."

"In the dear old cabin," said Christie quickly; "I remember it; I wish we were there now."

"Do you really? Do you?" said Whiskey Dick, with suddenly twinkling eyes. "That's like you to say it. That's what I allus said," continued Dick, addressing space generally; "if there's any one ez knows how to come square down to the bottom rock without flinchin', it's your high-toned, fash'nable gals. But I must meander back to town, and let the boys know you're in possession, safe and sound. It's right mean that Fairfax and Mattingly had to go down to Lagrange on some low business yesterday, but they'll be back to-morrow. So long."

Left alone, the girls began to realize their strange position. They had conceived no settled plan. The night they left San Francisco they had written an earnest letter to their father, telling him that on learning the truth about the reverses of Devil's Ford, they thought it their duty to return and share them with others, without obliging him to prefer the request, and with as little worry to him as possible. He would find them ready to share his trials, and in what must be the scene of their work hereafter.

"It will bring father back," said Christie; "he won't leave us here alone; and then together we must come to some understanding with him—with *them*— for somehow I feel as if this house belonged to us no longer."

Her surmise was not far wrong. When Mr. Carr arrived hurriedly from Sacramento the next evening, he found the house deserted. His daughters were gone; there were indications that they had arrived, and, for some reason, suddenly departed. The vague fear that had haunted his guilty soul after receiving their letter, and during his breathless journey, now seemed to be realized. He was turning from the empty house, whose reproachful solitude frightened him, when he was confronted on the threshold by the figure of Fairfax Munroe.

"I came to the stage office to meet you," he said; "you must have left the stage at the summit."

"I did," said Carr angrily. "I was anxious to meet my daughters quickly, to know the reason of their foolish alarm, and to know also who had been frightening them. Where are they?"

"They are safe in the old cabin beyond, that has been put up ready to receive them again," said Fairfax quietly.

"But what is the meaning of this? Why are they not here?" demanded Carr, hiding his agitation in a burst of querulous rage.

"Do *you* ask, Mr. Carr?" said Fairfax sadly. "Did you expect them to remain here until the sheriff took possession? No one knows better than yourself that the money advanced you on the deeds of this homestead has never been repaid."

Carr staggered, but recovered himself with feeble violence.

"Since you know so much of my affairs, how do you know that this claim will ever be pressed for payment? How do you know it is not the advance of a—a— friend?"

"Because I have seen the woman who advanced it," said Fairfax hopelessly. "She was here to look at the property before your daughters came."

"Well?" said Carr nervously.

"Well! You force me to tell you something I should like to forget. You force me to anticipate a disclosure I expected to make to you only when I came to ask permission to woo your daughter Jessie; and when I tell you what it is, you will understand that I have no right to criticise your conduct. I am only explaining my own."

"Go on," said Carr impatiently.

"When I first came to this country, there was a woman I loved passionately. She treated me as women of her kind only treat men like me; she ruined me, and left me. That was four years ago. I love your daughter, Mr. Carr, but she has never heard it from my lips. I would not woo her until I had told you all. I have tried to do it ere this, and failed. Perhaps I should not now, but—"

"But what?" said Carr furiously; "speak out!"

"But this. Look!" said Fairfax, producing from his pocket the packet of letters Jessie had found; "perhaps you know the handwriting?"

"What do you mean?" gasped Carr.

"That woman—my mistress—is the woman who advanced you money, and who claims this house."

. . . .

The interview, and whatever came of it, remained a secret with the two men. When Mr. Carr accepted the hospitality of the old cabin again, it was understood that he had sacrificed the new house and its furniture to some of the more pressing debts of the mine, and the act went far to restore his waning popularity. But a more genuine feeling of relief was experienced by Devil's Ford when it was rumored that Fairfax Munroe had asked for the hand of Jessie Carr, and that some promise contingent upon the equitable adjustment of the affairs of the mine had been given by Mr. Carr. To the superstitious mind of Devil's Ford and its few remaining locators, this new partnership seemed to promise that unity of interest and stability of fortune that Devil's Ford had lacked. But nothing could be done until the rainy season had fairly set in; until the long-looked-for element that was to magically separate the gold from the dross in those dull mounds of dust and gravel had come of its own free will, and in its own appointed channels, independent of the feeble auxiliaries that had hopelessly riven the rocks on the hillside, or hung incomplete and unfinished in lofty scaffoldings above the settlement.

The rainy season came early. At first in gathered mists on the higher peaks that were lifted in the morning sun only to show a fresher field of dazzling white below; in white clouds that at first seemed to be mere drifts blown across from those fresh snowfields, and obscuring the clear blue above; in far-off murmurs in the hollow hills and gulches; in nearer tinkling melody and baby prattling in the leaves. It came with bright flashes of sunlight by day, with deep, monotonous shadow at night; with the onset of heavy winds, the roar of turbulent woods, the tumultuous tossing of leafy arms, and with what seemed the silent dissolution of the whole landscape in days of steady and uninterrupted downfall. It came extravagantly, for every cañon had grown into a torrent, every gulch a waterspout, every watercourse a river, and all pouring into the North Fork, that, rushing past the settlement, seemed to threaten it with lifted crest and flying mane. It came dangerously, for one night the river, leaping the feeble barrier of Devil's Ford, swept away houses and banks, scattered with unconscious irony the laboriously collected heaps of gravel left for hydraulic machinery, and spread out a vast and silent lake across the submerged flat.

In the hurry and confusion of that night the girls had thrown open their cabin to the escaping miners, who hurried along the slope that was now the bank of the river. Suddenly Christie felt her arm grasped, and she was half-led, half-dragged, into the inner room. Her father stood before her.

"Where is George Kearney?" he asked tremulously.

"George Kearney!" echoed Christie, for a moment believing the excitement had turned her father's brain. "You know he is not here; he is in San Francisco."

"He is here—I tell you," said Carr impatiently; "he has been here ever since the high water, trying to save the flume and reservoir."

"George—here!" Christie could only gasp.

"Yes! He passed here a few moments ago, to see if you were all safe, and he has gone on towards the flume. But what he is trying to do is madness. If you see him, implore him to do no more. Let him abandon the accursed flume to its fate. It has worked already too much woe upon us all; why should it carry his brave and youthful soul down with it?"

The words were still ringing in her ears, when he suddenly passed away, with the hurrying crowd. Scarcely knowing what she did, she ran out, vaguely intent only on one thought, seeking only the one face, lately so

dear in recollection that she felt she would die if she
never saw it again. Perplexed by confused voices in the
woods, she lost track of the crowd, until the voices suddenly were raised in one loud outcry, followed by the
crashing of timber, the splashing of water, a silence, and
then a dull, continuous roar. She ran vaguely on in the
direction of the reservoir, with her father's injunction
still in her mind, until a terrible idea displaced it, and
she turned at right angles suddenly, and ran towards
the slope leading down to the submerged flat. She had
barely left the shelter of the trees behind her before the
roar of water seemed to rise at her very feet. She
stopped, dazed, bewildered, and horror-stricken, on the
edge of the slope. It was the slope no longer, but the
bank of the river itself!

Even in the gray light of early morning, and with inexperienced eyes, she saw all too clearly now. The
trestle-work had given way; the curving mile of flume,
fallen into the stream, and, crushed and dammed against
the opposite shore, had absolutely turned the whole
river through the half-finished ditch and partly excavated
mine in its way, a few rods further on to join the old
familiar channel. The bank of the river was changed;
the flat had become an island, between which and the
slope where she stood the North Fork was rolling its
resistless yellow torrent. As she gazed spellbound, a
portion of the slope beneath her suddenly seemed to
sink and crumble, and was swallowed up in the rushing
stream. She heard a cry of warning behind her, but,
rooted to the spot by a fearful fascination, she heeded
it not.

Again there was a sudden disruption, and another part
of the slope sank to rise no more; but this time she felt
herself seized by the waist and dragged back. It was
her father standing by her side.

He was flushed and excited, gazing at the water with
a strange exultation.

"Do you see it? Do you know what has happened?"
he asked quickly.

"The flume has fallen and turned the river," said

Christie hurriedly. "But—have you seen him—is he safe?"

"He—who?" he answered vacantly.

"George Kearney!"

"He is safe," he said impatiently. "But, do you see, Christie? Do you know what this means?"

He pointed with his tremulous hand to the stream before them.

"It means we are ruined," said Christie coldly.

"Nothing of the kind! It means that the river is doing the work of the flume. It is sluicing off the gravel, deepening the ditch, and altering the slope which was the old bend of the river. It will do in ten minutes the work that would take us a year. If we can stop it in time, or control it, we are safe; but if we can not, it will carry away the bed and deposit with the rest, and we are ruined again."

With a gesture of impotent fury, he dashed away in the direction of an equally excited crowd, that on a point of the slope nearer the island were gesticulating and shouting to a second group of men, who on the opposite shore were clambering on over the choked *débris* of the flume that had dammed and diverted the current. It was evident that the same idea had occurred to them, and they were risking their lives in the attempt to set free the impediments. Shocked and indignant as Christie had been at the degrading absorption of material interests at such a moment, the element of danger lifted the labors of these men into heroism, and she began to feel a strange exultation as she watched them. Under the skilful blows of their axes, in a few moments the vast body of drift began to disintegrate, and then to swing round and move towards the old channel. A cheer went up, but as suddenly died away again. An overlapping fringe of wreckage had caught on the point of the island and arrested the whole mass.

The men, who had gained the shore with difficulty, looked back with a cry of despair. But the next moment from among them leaped a figure, alert, buoyant, invincible, and, axe in hand, once more essayed the passage.

Springing from timber to timber, he at last reached the point of obstruction. A few strokes of the axe were sufficient to clear it; but at the first stroke it was apparent that the striker was also losing his hold upon the shore, and that he must inevitably be carried away with the tossing *débris*. But this consideration did not seem to affect him; the last blow was struck, and as the freed timbers rolled on, over and over, he boldly plunged into the flood. Christie gave a little cry—her heart had bounded with him; it seemed as if his plunge had splashed the water in her eyes. He did not come to the surface until he had passed the point below where her father stood, and then struggling feebly, as if stunned or disabled by a blow. It seemed to her that he was trying to approach the side of the river where she was. Would he do it? Could she help him? She was alone; he was hidden from the view of the men on the point, and no succor could come from them. There was a fringe of alder nearly opposite their cabin that almost overhung the stream. She ran to it, clutched it with a frantic hand, and, leaning over the boiling water, uttered for the first time his name:

"George!"

As if called to the surface by the magic of her voice, he rose a few yards from her in mid-current, and turned his fading eyes towards the bank. In another moment he would have been swept beyond her reach, but with a supreme effort he turned on one side; the current, striking him sideways, threw him towards the bank, and she caught him by his sleeve. For an instant it seemed as if she would be dragged down with him. For one dangerous moment she did not care, and almost yielded to the spell; but as the rush of water pressed him against the bank, she recovered herself, and managed to lift him beyond its reach.. And then she sat down, half-fainting, with his white face and damp curls upon her breast.

"George, darling, speak to me! Only one word! Tell me, have I saved you?"

His eyes opened. A faint twinkle of the old days came to them—a boyish smile played upon his lips.

"For yourself—or Jessie?"

She looked around her with a little frightened air. They were alone. There was but one way of sealing those mischievous lips, and she found it!

.   .   .   .

"That's what I allus said, gentlemen," lazily remarked Whiskey Dick, a few weeks later, leaning back against the bar, with his glass in his hand. " 'George,' sez I, 'it ain't what you *say* to a fash'nable, high-toned young lady; it's what you *does* ez makes or breaks you.' And that's what I sez gin'rally o' things in the Ford. It ain't what Carr and you boys allows to do; it's the gin'- ral average o' things ez *is* done that gives tone to the hull, and hez brought this yer new luck to you all!"

A WAIF OF THE PLAINS

A WAIF OF THE PLAINS

CHAPTER I

A LONG level of dull gray that further away became a faint blue, with here and there darker patches that looked like water. At times an open space, blackened and burnt in an irregular circle, with a shred of newspaper, an old rag, or broken tin can lying in the ashes. Beyond these always a low dark line that seemed to sink into the ground at night, and rose again in the morning with the first light, but never otherwise changed its height and distance. A sense of always moving with some indefinite purpose, but of always returning at night to the same place—with the same surroundings, the same people, the same bedclothes, and the same awful black canopy dropped down from above. A chalky taste of dust on the mouth and lips, a gritty sense of earth on the fingers, and an all-pervading heat and smell of cattle.

This was "The Great Plains" as they seemed to two children from the hooded depth of an emigrant wagon, above the swaying heads of toiling oxen, in the summer of 1852.

It had appeared so to them for two weeks, always the same and always without the least sense to them of wonder or monotony. When they viewed it from the road, walking beside the wagon, there was only the team itself added to the unvarying picture. One of the wagons bore on its canvas hood the inscription, in large black letters, "Off to California!" on the other "Root, Hog, or Die," but neither of them awoke in the minds of the children the faintest idea of playfulness or jocularity. Perhaps it was difficult to connect the serious men, who occasionally walked beside them and seemed to grow more taciturn and depressed as the day wore on, with this past effusive pleasantry.

Yet the impressions of the two children differed slightly. The eldest, a boy of eleven, was apparently new to the domestic habits and customs of a life to which the younger, a girl of seven, was evidently native and familiar. The food was coarse and less skillfully prepared than that to which he had been accustomed. There was a certain freedom and roughness in their intercourse, a simplicity that bordered almost on rudeness in their domestic arrangements, and a speech that was at times almost untranslatable to him. He slept in his clothes, wrapped up in blankets; he was conscious that in the matter of cleanliness he was left to himself to overcome the difficulties of finding water and towels. But it is doubtful if in his youthfulness it affected him more than a novelty. He ate and slept well, and found his life amusing. Only at times the rudeness of his companions, or, worse, an indifference that made him feel his dependency upon them, awoke a vague sense of some wrong that had been done to him which while it was voiceless to all others and even uneasily put aside by himself, was still always slumbering in his childish consciousness.

To the party he was known as an orphan put on the train at "St. Jo" by some relative of his stepmother, to be delivered to another relative at Sacramento. As his stepmother had not even taken leave of him, but had entrusted his departure to the relative with whom he had been lately living, it was considered as an act of "riddance," and accepted as such by her party, and even vaguely acquiesced in by the boy himself. What consideration had been offered for his passage he did not know; he only remembered that he had been told "to make himself handy." This he had done cheerfully. if at times with the unskillfulness of a novice; but it was not a peculiar or a menial task in a company where all took part in manual labor, and where existence seemed to him to bear the charm of a prolonged picnic.

Neither was he subjected to any difference of affection or treatment from Mrs. Silsbee, the mother of his little companion, and the wife of the leader of the train. Prematurely old, of ill-health, and harassed with cares, she had no time to waste in discriminating maternal tenderness for her daughter, but treated the children with equal and unbiased querulousness.

The rear wagon creaked, swayed, and rolled on slowly and heavily. The hoofs of the draft-oxen, occasionally striking in the dust with a dull report, sent little puffs like smoke on either side of the track. Within, the children were playing "keeping store." The little girl, as an opulent and extravagant customer, was purchasing of the boy, who sat behind a counter improvised from a nail-keg and the front seat, most of the available contents of the wagon, either under their own names or an imaginary one as the moment suggested, and paying for them in the easy and liberal currency of dried beans and bits of paper. Change was given by the expeditious method of tearing the paper into smaller fragments. The diminution of stock was remedied by buying the same article over again under a different name. Nevertheless, in spite of these favorable commercial conditions, the market seemed dull.

"I can show you a fine quality of sheeting at four cents a yard, double width," said the boy, rising and leaning on his fingers on the counter as he had seen the shopmen do. "All wool and will wash," he added, with easy gravity.

"I can buy it cheaper at Jackson's," said the girl, with the intuitive duplicity of her bargaining sex.

"Very well," said the boy. "I won't play any more."

"Who cares?" said the girl indifferently. The boy here promptly upset the counter; the rolled-up blanket which had deceitfully represented the desirable sheeting falling on the wagon floor. It apparently suggested a new idea to the former salesman. "I say! let's play 'damaged stock.' See, I'll tumble all the things down here right on top o' the others, and sell 'em for less than cost."

The girl looked up. The suggestion was bold, bad, and momentarily attractive. But she only said "No," apparently from habit, picked up her doll, and the boy clambered to the front of the wagon. The incomplete episode terminated at once with that perfect forgetfulness, indifference, and irresponsibility common to all young animals. If either could have flown away or bounded off finally at that moment, they would have done so with no more concern for preliminary detail than a bird or squirrel. The wagon rolled steadily on. The boy could see that one of the teamsters had climbed up on the tail-board of the preceding vehicle. The other seemed to be walking in a dusty sleep.

"Kla'uns," said the girl.

The boy, without turning his head, responded, "Susy."

"Wot are you going to be?" said the girl.

"Goin' to be?" repeated Clarence.

"When you is growed," explained Susy.

Clarence hesitated. His settled determination had been to become a pirate, merciless yet discriminating. But reading in a bethumbed "Guide to the Plains" that morning of Fort Lamarie and Kit Carson, he had decided upon the career of a "scout," as being more accessible and requiring less water. Yet, out of compassion for Susy's possible ignorance, he said neither, and responded with the American boy's modest conventionality, "President." It was safe, required no embarrassing description, and had been approved by benevolent old gentlemen with their hands on his head.

"I'm goin' to be a parson's wife," said Susy, "and keep hens, and have things giv' to me. Baby clothes, and apples, and apple sass—and melasses! and more baby clothes! and pork when you kill."

She had thrown herself at the bottom of the wagon, with her back towards him and her doll in her lap. He could see the curve of her curly head, and beyond, her bare dimpled knees, which were raised, and over which she was trying to fold the hem of her brief skirt.

"I wouldn't be a President's wife," she said presently.

"You couldn't!"

"Could if I wanted to!"

"Couldn't!"

"Could now!"

"Couldn't!"

"Why?"

Finding it difficult to explain his convictions of her ineligibility, Clarence thought it equally crushing not to give any. There was a long silence. It was very hot and dusty. The wagon scarcely seemed to move. Clarence gazed at the vignette of the track behind them formed by the hood of the rear. Presently he rose and walked past her to the tail-board. "Goin' to get down," he said, putting his legs over.

"Maw says 'No,'" said Susy.

Clarence did not reply, but dropped to the ground beside the slowly turning wheels. Without quickening his pace he could easily keep his hand on the tail-board.

"Kla'uns."

He looked up.

"Take me."

She had already clapped on her sun-bonnet and was standing at the edge of the tail-board, her little arms extended in such perfect confidence of being caught that the boy could not resist. He caught her cleverly. They halted a moment and let the lumbering vehicle move away from them, as it swayed from side to side as if laboring in a heavy sea. They remained motionless until it had reached nearly a hundred yards, and then, with a sudden half-real, half-assumed, but altogether delightful trepidation, ran forward and caught up with it again. This they repeated two or three times until both themselves and the excitement were exhausted, and they again plodded on hand in hand. Presently Clarence uttered a cry.

"My! Susy—look there!"

The rear wagon had once more slipped away from them a considerable distance. Between it and them, crossing its track, a most extraordinary creature had halted.

At first glance it seemed a dog—a discomfited, shameless, ownerless outcast of streets and byways, rather than an honest stray of some drover's train. It was so gaunt, so dusty, so greasy, so slouching, and so lazy! But as they looked at it more intently they saw that the grayish hair of its back had a bristly ridge, and there were great poisonous-looking dark blotches on its flanks, and that the slouch of its haunches was a peculiarity of its figure, and not the cowering of fear. As it lifted its suspicious head towards them they could see that its thin lips, too short to cover its white teeth, were curled in a perpetual sneer.

"Here, doggie!" said Clarence excitedly. "Good dog! Come."

Susy burst into a triumphant laugh. "Et tain't no dog, silly; it's er coyote."

Clarence blushed. It wasn't the first time the pioneer's daughter had shown her superior knowledge. He said quickly, to hide his discomfiture, "I'll ketch him, any way; he's nothin' mor'n a ki yi."

"Ye can't, tho," said Susy, shaking her sun-bonnet. "He's faster nor a hoss!"

Nevertheless, Clarence ran towards him, followed by Susy. When they had come within twenty feet of him, the lazy creature, without apparently the least effort, took two or three limping bounds to one side, and remained at the same distance as before. They repeated this onset three or four times with more or less excitement and hilarity, the animal evading them to one side, but never actually retreating before them. Finally, it occurred to them both that although they were not catching him they were not driving him away. The consequences of that thought were put into shape by Susy with round-eyed significance.

"Kla'uns, he bites."

Clarence picked up a hard sun-baked clod, and, running forward, threw it at the coyote. It was a clever shot, and struck him on his slouching haunches. He snapped and gave a short snarling yelp, and vanished. Clarence returned with a victorious air to his companion. But she was gazing intently in the opposite direction, and for the first time he discovered that the coyote had been leading them half round a circle.

"Kla'uns," said Susy, with a hysterical little laugh.

"Well?"

"The wagon's gone."

Clarence started. It was true. Not only their wagon, but the whole train of oxen and teamsters had utterly disappeared, vanishing as completely as if they had been caught up in a whirlwind or engulfed in the earth! Even the low cloud of dust that usually marked their distant course by day was nowhere to be seen. The long level plain stretched before them to the setting sun, without a sign or trace of moving life or animation. That great blue crystal bowl, filled with dust and fire by day, with stars and darkness by night, which had always seemed to drop its rim round them everywhere and shut them in, seemed to them now to have been lifted to let the train pass out, and then closed down upon them forever.

CHAPTER II

THEIR first sensation was one of purely animal freedom.

They looked at each other with sparkling eyes and long silent breaths. But this spontaneous outburst of savage nature soon passed. Susy's little hand presently reached forward and clutched Clarence's jacket. The boy understood it, and said quickly,—

"They ain't gone far, and they'll stop as soon as they find us gone."

They trotted on a little faster; the sun they had followed every day and the fresh wagon tracks being their unfailing guides; the keen, cool air of the plains, taking the place of that all-pervading dust and smell of the perspiring oxen, invigorating them with its breath.

"We ain't skeered a bit, are we?" said Susy.

"What's there to be afraid of?" said Clarence scornfully. He said this none the less strongly because he suddenly remembered that they had been often left alone in the wagon for hours without being looked after, and that their absence might not be noticed until the train stopped to encamp at dusk, two hours later. They were not running very fast, yet either they were more tired than they knew, or the air was thinner, for they both seemed to breathe quickly. Suddenly Clarence stopped.

"There they are now."

He was pointing to a light cloud of dust in the far-off horizon, from which the black hulk of a wagon emerged for a moment and was lost. But even as they gazed the cloud seemed to sink like a fairy mirage to the earth again, the whole train disappeared, and only the empty stretching track returned. They did not know that this seemingly flat and level plain was really undulatory, and that the vanished train had simply dipped below their view on some further slope even as it had once before. But they knew they were disappointed, and that disappointment revealed to them the fact that they had concealed it from each other. The girl was the first to succumb, and burst into a quick spasm of angry tears. That single act of weakness called out the boy's pride and strength. There was no longer an equality of suffering; he had become her protector; he felt himself responsible for both. Considering her no longer his equal, he was no longer frank with her.

"There's nothin' to boo-hoo for," he said, with a half-affected brusqueness. "So quit, now! They'll stop in a minit, and send some one back for us. Shouldn't wonder if they're doin' it now."

But Susy, with feminine discrimination detecting the hollow ring in his voice, here threw herself upon him and began to beat him violently with her little fists. "They ain't! They ain't! They ain't. You know it! How dare you?" Then, exhausted with her struggles, she suddenly threw herself flat on the dry grass, shut her eyes tightly, and clutched at the stubble.

"Get up," said the boy, with a pale, determined face that seemed to have got much older.

"You leave me be," said Susy.

"Do you want me to go away and leave you?" asked the boy.

Susy opened one blue eye furtively in the secure depths of her sun-bonnet, and gazed at his changed face. "Ye-e-s."

He pretended to turn away, but really to look at the height of the sinking sun.

"Kla'uns!"

"Well?"

"Take me."

She was holding up her hands. He lifted her gently in his arms, dropping her head over his shoulder. "Now," he said cheerfully, "you keep a good lookout that way, and I this, and we'll soon be there."

The idea seemed to please her. After Clarence had stumbled on for a few moments, she said, "Do you see anything, Kla'uns?"

"Not yet."

"No more don't I." This equality of perception apparently satisfied her. Presently she lay more limp in his arms. She was asleep.

The sun was sinking lower; it had already touched the edge of the horizon, and was level with his dazzled and straining eyes. At times it seemed to impede his eager search and task his vision. Haze and black spots floated across the horizon, and round wafers, like duplicates of the sun, glittered back from the dull surface of the plains. Then he resolved to look no more until he had counted fifty, a hundred, but always with the same result, the return of the empty, unending plains—the disk growing redder as it neared the horizon, the fire it seemed to kindle as it sank, but nothing more.

Staggering under his burden, he tried to distract himself by fancying how the discovery of their absence would be made. He heard the listless, half-querulous discussion about the locality that regularly pervaded the nightly camp. He heard the discontented voice of Jake Silsbee as he halted beside the wagon, and said, "Come out o' that now, you two, and mighty quick about it." He heard the command harshly repeated. He saw the look of irritation on Silsbee's dusty, bearded face, that followed his hurried glance into the empty wagon. He heard the query, "What's gone o' them limbs now?" handed from wagon to wagon. He heard a few oaths; Mrs. Silsbee's high rasping voice, abuse of himself, the hurried and discontented detachment of a search party, Silsbee and one of the hired men, and vociferation and blame. Blame always for himself, the elder, who might have "known better!" A little fear, perhaps, but he could not fancy either pity or commiseration. Perhaps the thought upheld his pride; under the prospect of sympathy he might have broken down.

At last he stumbled, and stopped to keep himself from falling forward on his face. He could go no further; his breath was spent; he was dripping with perspiration; his legs were trembling under him; there was a roaring in his ears; round red disks of the sun were scattered everywhere around him like spots of blood. To the right of the trail there seemed to be a slight mound where he could rest awhile, and yet keep his watchful survey of the horizon. But on reaching it he found that it was only a tangle of taller mesquite grass, into which he sank with his burden. Nevertheless, if useless as a point of vantage, it offered a soft couch for Susy, who seemed to have fallen quite naturally into her usual afternoon siesta, and in a measure it shielded her from a cold breeze that had sprung up from the west. Utterly exhausted himself, but not daring to yield to the torpor that seemed to be creeping over him, Clarence half sat, half knelt down beside her, supporting himself with one hand, and, partly hidden in the long grass, kept his straining eyes fixed on the lonely track.

The red disk was sinking lower. It seemed to have already crumbled away a part of the distance with its eating fires. As it sank still lower, it shot out long, luminous rays, diverging fan-like across the plain, as if, in the boy's excited fancy, it too were searching for the lost estrays. And as one long beam seemed to linger over his hiding-place, he even thought that it might serve as a guide to Silsbee and the other seekers, and was constrained to stagger to his feet, erect in its light. But it soon sank, and with it Clarence dropped back again to his crouching watch. Yet he knew that the daylight was still good for an hour, and with the withdrawal of that mystic sunset glory objects became even more distinct and sharply defined than at any other time. And with the merciful sheathing of that flaming sword which seemed to have swayed between him and the vanished train, his eyes already felt a blessed relief.

CHAPTER III

WITH the setting of the sun an ominous silence fell. He could hear the low breathing of Susy, and even fancied he could hear the beating of his own heart in that oppressive hush of all nature. For the day's march had always been accompanied by the monotonous creaking of wheels and axles, and even the quiet of the night encampment had been always more or less broken by the movement of unquiet sleepers on the wagon beds, or the breathing of the cattle. But here there was neither sound nor motion. Susy's prattle, and even the sound of his own voice, would have broken the benumbing spell, but it was a part of his growing self-denial now that he refrained from waking her even by a whisper. She would awaken soon enough to thirst and hunger, perhaps, and then what was he to do? If that looked-for help would only come now—while she still slept. For it was part of his boyish fancy that if he could deliver her asleep and undemonstrative of fear and suffering, he would be less blameful, and she less mindful of her trouble. If it did not come—but he would not think of that yet! If she was thirsty meantime—well, it might rain, and there was always the dew which they used to brush off the morning grass; he would take off his shirt and catch it in that, like a shipwrecked mariner. It would be funny, and make her laugh. For himself he would not laugh; he felt he was getting very old and grown up in this loneliness.

It was getting darker—they should be looking into the wagons now. A new doubt began to assail him. Ought he not, now that he was rested, make the most of the remaining moments of daylight, and before the glow faded from the west, when he would no longer have any bearings to guide him? But there was always the risk of waking her!—to what? The fear of being confronted again with *her* fear and of being unable to pacify her, at last decided him to remain. But he crept softly through the grass, and in the dust of the track traced the four points of the compass, as he could still determine them by the sunset light, with a large printed W to indicate the west! This boyish contrivance particularly pleased him. If he had only had a pole, a stick, or even a twig, on which to tie his handkerchief and erect it above the clump of mesquite as a signal to the searchers in case they should be overcome by fatigue or sleep, he would have been happy. But the plain was barren of brush or timber; he did not dream that this omission and the very unobtrusiveness of his hiding-place would be his salvation from a greater danger.

With the coming darkness the wind arose and swept the plain with a long-drawn sigh. This increased to a murmur, till presently the whole expanse—before sunk in awful silence—seemed to awake with vague complaints, incessant sounds, and low moanings. At times he thought he heard the halloaing of distant voices, at times it seemed as a whisper in his own ear. In the silence that followed each blast he fancied he could detect the creaking of the wagon, the dull thud of the oxen's hoofs, or broken fragments of speech, blown and scattered even as he strained his ears to listen by the next gust. This tension of the ear began to confuse his brain, as his eyes had been previously dazzled by the sunlight, and a strange torpor began to steal over his faculties. Once or twice his head dropped.

He awoke with a start. A moving figure had suddenly uplifted itself between him and the horizon! It was not twenty yards away, so clearly outlined against the still luminous sky that it seemed even nearer. A human figure, but so disheveled, so fantastic, and yet so mean and puerile in its extravagance, that it seemed the outcome of a childish dream. It was a mounted figure, but so ludicrously disproportionate to the pony it bestrode, whose slim legs were stiffly buried in the dust in a breathless halt, that it might have been a straggler from some vulgar wandering circus. A tall hat, crownless and rimless, a castaway of civilization, surmounted by a turkey's feather, was on its head; over its shoulders hung a dirty tattered blanket that scarcely covered the two painted legs which seemed clothed in soiled yellow hose. In one hand it held a gun; the other was bent above its eyes in eager scrutiny of some distant point beyond and east of the spot where the children lay concealed. Presently, with a dozen quick noiseless strides of the pony's legs, the apparition moved to the right, its gaze still fixed on that mysterious part of the horizon. There was no mistaking it now! The painted Hebraic face, the large curved nose, the bony cheek, the broad mouth, the shadowed eyes, the straight long matted locks! It was an Indian! Not the picturesque creature of Clarence's imagination, but still an Indian! The boy was uneasy, suspicious, antagonistic, but not afraid. He looked at the heavy animal face with the superiority of intelligence, at the half-naked figure with the conscious supremacy of dress, at the lower individuality with the contempt of a higher race. Yet a moment after, when the figure wheeled and disappeared towards the undulating west, a strange chill crept over him. Yet he did not know that in this puerile phantom and painted pigmy the awful majesty of Death had passed him by.

"Mamma!"

It was Susy's voice, struggling into consciousness. Perhaps she had been instinctively conscious of the boy's sudden fears.

"Hush!"

He had just turned to the objective point of the Indian's gaze. There *was* something! A dark line was moving along with the gathering darkness. For a moment he hardly dared to voice his thoughts even to himself. It was a following train overtaking them from the rear! And from the rapidity of its movements a train with horses, hurrying forward to evening camp. He had never dreamt of help from that quarter. This was what the Indian's keen eyes had been watching, and why he had so precipitately fled.

The strange train was now coming up at a round trot. It was evidently well appointed with five or six large wagons and several outriders. In half an hour it would be here. Yet he refrained from waking Susy, who had fallen asleep again; his old superstition of securing her safety first being still uppermost. He took off his jacket to cover her shoulders, and rearranged her nest. Then he glanced again at the coming train. But for some unaccountable reason it had changed its direction, and instead of following the track that should have brought it to his side it had turned off to the left! In ten minutes it would pass abreast of him a mile and a half away! If he woke Susy now, he knew she would he helpless in her terror, and he could not carry her half that distance. He might rush to the train himself and return with help, but he would never leave her alone—in the darkness. Never! If she woke she would die of fright, perhaps, or wander blindly and aimlessly away. No! The train would pass and with it that hope of rescue. Something was in his throat, but he gulped it down and was quiet again albeit he shivered in the night wind.

The train was nearly abreast of him now. He ran out of the tall grass, waving his straw hat above his head in the faint hope of attracting attention. But he did not go far, for he found to his alarm that when he turned back again the clump of mesquite was scarcely distinguishable from the rest of the plain. This settled all question of his going. Even if he reached the train and returned with some one, how would he ever find her again in this desolate expanse?

He watched the train slowly pass—still mechanically, almost hopelessly, waving his hat as he ran up and down before the mesquite, as if he were waving a last fare-

well to his departing hope. Suddenly it appeared to him
that three of the outriders who were preceding the first
wagon had changed their shape. They were no longer
sharp, oblong, black blocks against the horizon but had
become at first blurred and indistinct, then taller and
narrower, until at last they stood out like exclamation
points against the sky. He continued to wave his hat,
they continued to grow taller and narrower. He understood it now—the three transformed blocks were the outriders coming towards him.

This is what he had seen—
■ ■ ■
This is what he saw now—
! ! !

He ran back to Susy to see if she still slept, for his
foolish desire to have her saved unconsciously was
stronger than ever now that safety seemed so near. She
was still sleeping, although she had moved slightly. He
ran to the front again.

The outriders had apparently halted. What were they
doing? Why wouldn't they come on?

Suddenly a blinding flash of light seemed to burst from
one of them. Away over his head something whistled
like a rushing bird, and sped off invisible. They had
fired a gun; they were signaling to him—Clarence—like
a grown-up man. He would have given his life at
that moment to have had a gun. But he could only
wave his hat frantically.

One of the figures here bore away and impetuously
darted forward again. He was coming nearer, powerful,
gigantic, formidable, as he loomed through the darkness.
All at once he threw up his arm with a wild gesture to
the others; and his voice, manly, frank, and assuring,
came ringing before him.

"Hold up! Good God! It's no Injun—it's a child!"

In another moment he had reined up beside Clarence
and leaned over him, bearded, handsome, powerful and
protecting.

"Hallo! What's all this? What are you doing
here?"

"Lost from Mr. Silsbee's train," said Clarence, pointing to the darkened west.

"Lost?—how long?"

"About three hours. I thought they'd come back for us," said Clarence apologetically to this big, kindly man.

"And you kalkilated to wait here for 'em?"

"Yes, yes—I did—till I saw you."

"Then why in thunder didn't you light out straight for us, instead of hanging round here and drawing us out?"

The boy hung his head. He knew his reasons were unchanged, but all at once they seemed very foolish and unmanly to speak out.

"Only that we were on the keen jump for Injins," continued the stranger, "we wouldn't have seen you at all, and might hev shot you when we did. What possessed you to stay here?"

The boy was still silent. "Kla'uns," said a faint, sleepy voice from the mesquite, "take me." The rifle-shot had awakened Susy.

The stranger turned quickly towards the sound. Clarence started and recalled himself. "There," he said bitterly, "you've done it now, you've wakened her! *That's* why I stayed. I couldn't carry her over there to you. I couldn't let her walk, for she'd be frightened. I wouldn't wake her up, for she'd be frightened, and I mightn't find her again. There! He had made up his mind to be abused, but he was reckless now that she was safe.

The men glanced at each other. "Then," said the spokesman quietly, "you didn't strike out for us on account of your sister?"

"She ain't my sister," said Clarence quickly. "She's a little girl. She's Mrs. Silsbee's little girl. We were in the wagon and got down. It's my fault. I helped her down."

The three men reined their horses closely round him, leaning forward from their saddles, with their hands on their knees and their heads on one side. "Then," said the spokesman gravely, "you just reckoned to stay here, old man, and take your chances with her rather than run the risk of frightening or leaving her—though it was your one chance of life!"

"Yes," said the boy, scornful of this feeble, grown-up repetition.

"Come here."

The boy came doggedly forward. The man pushed back the well-worn straw hat from Clarence's forehead and looked into his lowering face. With his hand still on the boy's head he turned him round to the others, and said quietly,—

"Suthin of a pup, eh?"

"You bet," they responded.

The voice was not unkindly, although the speaker had thrown his lower jaw forward as if to pronounce the word "pup" with a humorous suggestion of a mastiff. Before Clarence could make up his mind if the epithet was insulting or not, the man put out his stirruped foot, and, with a gesture of invitation, said, "Jump up."

"But Susy," said Clarence, drawing back.

"Look; she's making up to Phil already."

Clarence looked. Susy had crawled out of the mesquite, and with her sun-bonnet hanging down her back, her curls tossed around her face, still flushed with sleep, and Clarence's jacket over her shoulders, was gazing up with grave satisfaction in the laughing eyes of one of the men who was with outstretched hands bending over her. Could he believe his senses? The terror-stricken, willful, unmanageable Susy, whom he would have translated unconsciously to safety without this terrible ordeal of being awakened to the loss of her home and parents at any sacrifice to himself—this ingenuous infant was absolutely throwing herself with every appearance of forgetfulness into the arms of the first new-comer! Yet his perception of this fact was accompanied by no sense of ingratitude. For her sake he felt relieved, and with a boyish smile of satisfaction and encouragement vaulted into the saddle before the stranger.

CHAPTER IV

THE dash forward to the train, securely held in the saddle by the arms of their deliverers, was a secret joy to the children that seemed only too quickly over. The resistless gallop of the fiery mustangs, the rush of the night wind, the gathering darkness in which the distant wagons, now halted and facing them, looked like domed huts in the horizon—all these seemed but a delightful and fitting climax to the events of the day. In the sublime forgetfulness of youth, all they had gone through had left no embarrassing record behind it; they were willing to repeat their experiences on the morrow, confident of some equally happy end. And when Clarence, timidly reaching his hand towards the horse-hair reins lightly held by his companion, had them playfully yielded up to him by that bold and confident rider, the boy felt himself indeed a man.

But a greater surprise was in store for them. As they neared the wagons, now formed into a circle with a certain degree of military formality, they could see that the appointments of the strange party were larger and more liberal than their own, or indeed anything they had ever known of the kind. Forty or fifty horses were tethered within the circle, and the camp fires were already blazing. Before one of them a large tent was erected, and through the parted flaps could be seen a table actually spread with a white cloth. Was it a school feast, or was this their ordinary household arrangement? Clarence and Susy thought of their own dinners, usually laid on bare boards beneath the sky, or under the low hood of the wagon in rainy weather, and marveled. And when they finally halted, and were lifted from their horses, and passed one wagon fitted up as a bedroom and another as a kitchen, they could only nudge each other with silent appreciation. But here again the difference already noted in the quality of the sensations of the two children was observable. Both were equally and agreeably surprised. But Susy's wonder was merely the sense of novelty and inexperience, and a slight disbelief in the actual necessity of what she saw; while Clarence, whether from some previous general experience or peculiar temperament, had the conviction that what he saw here was the usual custom, and what he had known with the Silsbees was the novelty. The feeling was attended with a slight sense of wounded pride for Susy, as if her enthusiasm had exposed her to ridicule.

The man who had carried him, and seemed to be the head of the party, had already preceded them to the tent, and presently reappeared with a lady with whom he had exchanged a dozen hurried words. They seemed to refer to him and Susy; but Clarence was too much preoccupied with the fact that the lady was pretty, that her clothes were neat and thoroughly clean, that her hair was tidy and not rumpled, and that, although she wore an apron, it was as clean as her gown, and even had ribbons on it, to listen to what was said. And when she ran eagerly forward, and with a fascinating smile lifted the astonished Susy in her arms, Clarence, in his delight for his young charge, quite forgot that she had not noticed him. The bearded man, who seemed to be the lady's husband, evidently pointed out the omission, with some additions that Clarence could not catch; for after saying, with a pretty pout, "Well, why shouldn't he?" she came forward with the same dazzling smile, and laid her small and clean white hand upon his shoulder.

"And so you took good care of the dear little thing? She's such an angel, isn't she? and you must love her very much."

Clarence colored with delight. It was true it had never occurred to him to look at Susy in the light of a celestial visitant, and I fear he was just then more struck with the fair complimenter than the compliment to his companion, but he was pleased for her sake. He was not yet old enough to be conscious of the sex's belief in its irresistible domination over mankind at all ages, and that Johnny in his check apron would be always a hopeless conquest of Jeannette in her pinafore, and that he ought to have been in love with Susy.

Howbeit, the lady suddenly whisked her away to the recesses of her own wagon, to reappear later, washed, curled, and beribboned like a new doll, and Clarence was left alone with the husband and another of the party.

"Well, my boy, you haven't told me your name yet."

"Clarence, sir."

"So Susy calls you, but what else?"

"Clarence Brant."

"Any relation to Colonel Brant?" asked the second man carelessly.

"He was my father," said the boy, brightening under this faint prospect of recognition in his loneliness.

The two men glanced at each other. The leader looked at the boy curiously, and said,—

"Are you the son of Colonel Brant, of Louisville?"

"Yes, sir," said the boy, with a dim stirring of uneasiness in his heart. "But he's dead now," he added finally.

"Ah, when did he die?" said the man quickly.

"Oh, a long time ago. I don't remember him much. I was very little," said the boy, half apologetically.

"Ah, you don't remember him?"

"No," said Clarence shortly. He was beginning to fall back upon that certain dogged repetition which in sensitive children arises from their hopeless inability to express their deeper feelings. He also had an instinctive consciousness that this want of a knowledge of his father was part of that vague wrong that had been done him. It did not help his uneasiness that he could see that one of the two men, who turned away with a half-laugh, misunderstood or did not believe him.

"How did you come with the Silsbees?" asked the first man.

Clarence repeated mechanically, with a child's distaste of practical details, how he had lived with an aunt at St. Jo, and how his stepmother had procured his passage with the Silsbees to California, where he was to meet his cousin. All this with a lack of interest and abstraction that he was miserably conscious told against him, but he was yet helpless to resist.

The first man remained thoughtful, and then glanced

at Clarence's sunburnt hands. Presently his large, good-humored smile returned.

"Well, I suppose you are hungry?"

"Yes," said Clarence shyly. "But—"

"But what?"

"I should like to wash myself a little," he returned hesitatingly, thinking of the clean tent, the clean lady, and Susy's ribbons.

"Certainly," said his friend, with a pleased look. "Come with me." Instead of leading Clarence to the battered tin basin and bar of yellow soap which had formed the toilet service of the Silsbee party, he brought the boy into one of the wagons, where there was a washstand, a china basin, and a cake of scented soap. Standing beside Clarence, he watched him perform his ablutions with an approving air which rather embarrassed his *protégé*. Presently he said, almost abruptly,—

"Do you remember your father's house at Louisville?"

"Yes, sir; but it was a long time ago."

Clarence remembered it as being very different from his home at St. Joseph's, but from some innate feeling of diffidence he would have shrunk from describing it in that way. He, however, said he thought it was a large house. Yet the modest answer only made his new friend look at him the more keenly.

"Your father was Colonel Hamilton Brant, of Louisville, wasn't he?" he said, half-confidentially.

"Yes," said Clarence hopelessly.

"Well," said his friend cheerfully, as if dismissing an abstruse problem from his mind, "Let's go to supper."

When they reached the tent again, Clarence noticed that the supper was laid only for his host and wife and the second man—who was familiarly called "Harry," but who spoke of the former always as "Mr. and Mrs. Peyton"—while the remainder of the party, a dozen men, were at a second camp fire, and evidently enjoying themselves in a picturesque fashion. Had the boy been allowed to choose, he would have joined them, partly because it seemed more "manly," and partly that he dreaded a renewal of the questioning.

But here, Susy, sitting bolt upright on an extemporized high stool, happily diverted his attention by pointing to the empty chair beside her.

"Kla'uns," she said suddenly, with her usual clear and appalling frankness, "they is chickens, and hamanaigs, and hot biksquits, and lasses, and Mister Peyton says I kin have 'em all."

Clarence, who had begun suddenly to feel that he was responsible for Susy's deportment, and was balefully conscious that she was holding her plated fork in her chubby fist by its middle, and, from his previous knowledge of her, was likely at any moment to plunge it into the dish before her, said softly,—

"Hush!"

"Yes, you shall, dear," said Mrs. Peyton, with tenderly beaming assurance to Susy and a half-reproachful glance at the boy. "Eat what you like, darling."

"It's a fork," whispered the still uneasy Clarence, as Susy now seemed inclined to stir her bowl of milk with it.

"'Tain't, now, Kla'uns, it's only a split spoon," said Susy.

But Mrs. Peyton, in her rapt admiration, took small note of these irregularities, plying the child with food, forgetting her own meal, and only stopping at times to lift back the forward straying curls on Susy's shoulders. Mr. Peyton looked on gravely and contentedly. Suddenly the eyes of husband and wife met.

"She'd have been nearly as old as this, John," said Mrs. Peyton, in a faint voice.

John Peyton nodded without speaking, and turned his eyes away into the gathering darkness. The man "Harry" also looked abstractedly at his plate, as if he was saying grace. Clarence wondered who "she" was, and why two little tears dropped from Mrs. Peyton's lashes into Susy's milk, and whether Susy might not violently object to it. He did not know until later that the Peytons had lost their only child, and Susy comfortably drained this mingled cup of a mother's grief and tenderness without suspicion.

"I suppose we'll come up with their train early to-morrow, if some of them don't find us to-night," said Mrs. Peyton, with a long sigh and a regretful glance at Susy. "Perhaps we might travel together for a little while," she added timidly.

Harry laughed, and Mr. Peyton replied gravely, "I am afraid we wouldn't travel with them, even for company's sake; and," he added, in a lower and graver voice, "it's rather odd the search party hasn't come upon us yet, though I'm keeping Pete and Hank patrolling the trail to meet them."

"It's heartless—so it is!" said Mrs. Peyton, with sudden indignation. "It would be all very well if it was only this boy, who can take care of himself; but to be so careless of a mere baby like this, it's shameful!"

For the first time Clarence tasted the cruelty of discrimination. All the more keenly that he was beginning to worship, after his boyish fashion, this sweet-faced, clean, and tender-hearted woman. Perhaps Mr. Peyton noticed it, for he came quietly to his aid.

"Maybe they knew better than we in what careful hands they had left her," he said, with a cheerful nod towards Clarence. "And, again, they may have been fooled as we were by Injin signs and left the straight road."

This suggestion instantly recalled to Clarence his vision in the mesquite. Should he dare tell them? Would they believe him, or would they laugh at him before her? He hesitated, and at last resolved to tell it privately to the husband. When the meal was ended, and he was made happy by Mrs. Peyton's laughing acceptance of his offer to help her clear the table and wash the dishes, they all gathered comfortably in front of the tent before the large camp fire. At the other fire the rest of the party were playing cards and laughing, but Clarence no longer cared to join them. He was quite tranquil in the maternal propinquity of his hostess, albeit a little uneasy as to his reticence about the Indian.

"Kla'uns," said Susy, relieving a momentary pause,

in her highest voice, "knows how to speak. Speak, Kla'uns!"

It appearing from Clarence's blushing explanation that this gift was not the ordinary faculty of speech, but a capacity to recite verse, he was politely pressed by the company for a performance.

"Speak 'em, Kla'uns, the boy what stood unto the burnin' deck, and said, 'The boy, oh, where was he?'" said Susy, comfortably lying down on Mrs. Peyton's lap, and contemplating her bare knees in the air. "It's 'bout a boy," she added confidentially to Mrs. Peyton, "whose father wouldn't never, never stay with him on a burnin' ship, though he said, 'Stay, father, stay,' ever so much."

With this clear, lucid, and perfectly satisfactory explanation of Mrs. Hemans's "Casabianca," Clarence began. Unfortunately, his actual rendering of this popular school performance was more an effort of memory than anything else, and was illustrated by those wooden gestures which a Western schoolmaster had taught him. He described the flames that "roared around him," by indicating with his hand a perfect circle, of which he was the axis; he adjured his father, the late Admiral Casabianca, by clasping his hands before his chin, as if wanting to be manacled in an attitude which he was miserably conscious was unlike anything he himself had ever felt or seen before; he described that father "faint in death below," and "the flag on high," with one single motion. Yet something that the verses had kindled in his active imagination, perhaps, rather than an illustration of the verses themselves, at times brightened his gray eyes, became tremulous in his youthful voice, and I fear occasionally incoherent on his lips. At times, when not conscious of his affected art, the plain and all upon it seemed to him to slip away into the night, the blazing camp fire at his feet to wrap him in a fateful glory, and a vague devotion to something—he knew not what—so possessed him that he communicated it, and probably some of his own youthful delight in extravagant voice, to his hearers, until, when he ceased with a glowing face, he was surprised to find that the card players had deserted their camp fires and gathered round the tent.

CHAPTER V

"You didn't say 'Stay, father, stay,' enough, Kla'uns," said Susy critically. Then suddenly starting upright in Mrs. Peyton's lap, she continued rapidly, "I kin dance. And sing. I kin dance High Jamboree."

"What's High Jamboree, dear?" asked Mrs. Peyton.

"You'll see. Lemme down." And Susy slipped to the ground.

The dance of High Jamboree, evidently of remote mystical African origin, appeared to consist of three small skips to the right and then to the left, accompanied by the holding up of very short skirts, incessant "teetering" on the toes of small feet, the exhibition of much bare knee and stocking, and a gurgling accompaniment of childish laughter. Vehemently applauded, it left the little performer breathless, but invincible and ready for fresh conquest.

"I kin sing, too," she gasped hurriedly, as if unwilling that the applause should lapse. "I kin sing. Oh, dear! Kla'uns," piteously, *"what* is it I sing?"

"Ben Bolt," suggested Clarence.

"Oh, yes. Oh, don't you remember sweet Alers Ben Bolt?" began Susy, in the same breath and the wrong key. "Sweet Alers, with hair so brown, who wept with delight when you giv'd her a smile, and—" with knitted brows and appealing recitative, "what's er rest of it, Kla'uns?"

"Who trembled with fear at your frown?" prompted Clarence.

"Who trembled with fear at my frown?" shrilled Susy. "I forget er rest. Wait! I kin sing—"

"Praise God," suggested Clarence.

"Yes." Here Susy, a regular attendant in camp and prayer-meetings, was on firmer ground.

Promptly lifting her high treble, yet with a certain acquired deliberation, she began, "Praise God, from whom all blessings flow." At the end of the second line the whispering and laughing ceased. A deep voice to the right, that of the champion poker player, suddenly rose on the swell of the third line. He was instantly followed by a dozen ringing voices, and by the time the last line was reached it was given with a full chorus, in which the dull chant of teamsters and drivers mingled with the soprano of Mrs. Peyton and Susy's childish treble. Again and again it was repeated, with forgetful eyes and abstracted faces, rising and falling with the night wind and the leap and gleam of the camp fires, and fading again like them in the immeasurable mystery of the darkened plain.

In the deep and embarrassing silence that followed, at last the party hesitatingly broke up, Mrs. Peyton retiring with Susy after offering the child to Clarence for a perfunctory "good-night" kiss, an unusual proceeding, which somewhat astonished them both—and Clarence found himself near Mr. Peyton.

"I think," said Clarence timidly, "I saw an Injin to-day."

Mr. Peyton bent down towards him. "An Injin— where?" he asked quickly, with the same look of doubting interrogatory with which he had received Clarence's name and parentage.

The boy for a moment regretted having spoken. But with his old doggedness he particularized his statement. Fortunately, being gifted with a keen perception, he was able to describe the stranger accurately, and to impart with his description that contempt for its subject which he had felt, and which to his frontier auditor established its truthfulness. Peyton turned abruptly away, but presently returned with Harry and another man.

"You are sure of this?" said Peyton, half-encouragingly.

"Yes, sir."

"As sure as you are that your father is Colonel Brant and is dead?" said Harry, with a light laugh.

Tears sprang into the boy's lowering eyes. "I don't lie," he said doggedly.

"I believe you, Clarence," said Peyton quietly. "But why didn't you say it before?"

"I didn't like to say it before Susy and—her!" stammered the boy.

"Her?"

"Yes, sir—Mrs. Peyton," said Clarence blushingly.

"Oh," said Harry sarcastically, "how blessed polite we are!"

"That'll do. Let up on him, will you?" said Peyton, roughly, to his subordinate. "The boy knows what he's about. But," he continued, addressing Clarence, "how was it the Injin didn't see you?"

"I was very still on account of not waking Susy," said Clarence, "and—" He hesitated.

"And what?"

"He seemed more keen watching what *you* were doing," said the boy boldly.

"That's so," broke in the second man, who happened to be experienced, "and as he was to wind'ard o' the boy he was off *his* scent and bearings. He was one of their rear scouts; the rest o' them's ahead crossing our track to cut us off. Ye didn't see anything else?"

"I saw a coyote first," said Clarence, greatly encouraged.

"Hold on!" said the expert, as Harry turned away with a sneer. "That's a sign, too. Wolf don't go where wolf hez been, and coyote don't foller Injins—there's no pickin's! How long afore did you see the coyote?"

"Just after we left the wagon," said Clarence.

"That's it," said the man, thoughtfully. "He was driven on ahead, or hanging on their flanks. These Injins are betwixt us and that ar train, or following it."

Peyton made a hurried gesture of warning, as if reminding the speaker of Clarence's presence—a gesture which the boy noticed and wondered at. Then the conversation of the three men took a lower tone, although Clarence distinctly heard the concluding opinion of the expert.

"It ain't no good now, Mr. Peyton, and you'd be only exposing yourself on their ground by breakin' camp agin to-night. And you don't know that it ain't *us* they're watchin'. You see, if we hadn't turned off the straight road when we got that first scare from these yer lost children, we might hev gone on and walked plump into some cursed trap of those devils. To my mind, we're just in nigger luck, and with a good watch and my patrol we're all right to be fixed where we be till daylight."

Mr. Peyton presently turned away, taking Clarence with him. "As we'll be up early and on the track of your train to-morrow, my boy, you had better turn in now. I've put you up in my wagon, and as I expect to be in the saddle most of the night, I reckon I won't trouble you much." He led the way to a second wagon—drawn up beside the one where Susy and Mrs. Peyton had retired—which Clarence was surprised to find fitted with a writing table and desk, a chair, and even a bookshelf containing some volumes. A long locker, fitted like a lounge, had been made up as a couch for him, with the unwonted luxury of clean white sheets and pillow-cases. A soft matting covered the floor of the heavy wagon bed, which, Mr. Peyton explained, was hung on centre springs to prevent jarring. The sides and roof of the vehicle were of lightly paneled wood, instead of the usual hooked canvas frame of the ordinary emigrant wagon, and fitted with a glazed door and movable window for light and air. Clarence wondered why the big, powerful man, who seemed at home on horseback, should ever care to sit in this office like a merchant or a lawyer; and if this train sold things to the other trains, or took goods, like the peddlers, to towns on the route; but there seemed to be nothing to sell, and the other wagons were filled with only the goods required by the party. He would have liked to ask Mr. Peyton who *he* was, and have questioned *him* as freely as he himself had been questioned. But as the average adult man never takes into consideration the injustice of denying to the natural and even necessary curiosity of childhood that questioning which he himself is so apt to assume without right, and almost always without delicacy, Clarence had no recourse. Yet the boy, like all children, was con-

scious that if he had been afterwards questioned about
this inexplicable experience, he would have been blamed
for his ignorance concerning it. Left to himself presently, and ensconced between the sheets, he lay for some
moments staring about him. The unwonted comfort of
his couch, so different from the stuffy blanket ¡ the hard
wagon bed which he had shared with one of the teamsters, and the novelty, order, and cleanliness of his surroundings, while they were grateful to his instincts, began
in some vague way to depress him. To his loyal nature
it seemed a tacit infidelity to his former rough companions
to be lying here; he had a dim idea that he had lost that
independence which equal discomfort and equal pleasure
among them had given him. There seemed a sense of
servitude in accepting this luxury which was not his.
This set him endeavoring to remember something of his
father's house, of the large rooms, drafty staircases, and
far-off ceilings, and the cold formality of a life that
seemed made up of strange faces; some stranger—his
parents; some kinder—the servants; particularly the black
nurse who had him in charge. Why did Mr. Peyton ask
him about it? Why, if it were so important to strangers,
had not his mother told him more of it? And why was
she not like this good woman with the gentle voice who
was so kind to—to Susy? And what did they mean by
making *him* so miserable? Something rose in his throat,
but with an effort he choked it back, and, creeping from
the lounge, went softly to the window, opened it to see
if it "would work," and looked out. The shrouded camp
fires, the stars that glittered but gave no light, the dim
moving bulk of a patrol beyond the circle, all seemed to
intensify the darkness, and changed the current of his
thoughts. He remembered what Mr. Peyton had said of
him when they first met. "Suthin of a pup, ain't he?"
Surely that meant something that was not bad! He
crept back to the couch again.

Lying there, still awake, he reflected that he wouldn't
be a scout when he grew up, but would be something like
Mr. Peyton, and have a train like this, and invite the
Silsbees and Susy to accompany him. For this purpose,

he and Susy, early to-morrow morning, would get permission to come in here and play at that game. This
would familiarize him with the details, so that he would
be able at any time to take charge of it. He was already
an authority on the subject of Indians! He had once
been fired at—as an Indian. He would always carry a
rifle like that hanging from the hooks at the end of the
wagon before him, and would eventually slay many Indians and keep an account of them in a big book like that
on the desk. Susy would help him, having grown up a
lady, and they would both together issue provisions and
rations from the door of the wagon to the gathered crowds.
He would be known as the "White Chief," his Indian
name being "Suthin of a Pup." He would have a circus
van attached to the train, in which he would occasionally perform. He would also have artillery for protection.
There would be a terrific engagement, and he would rush
into the wagon, heated and blackened with gunpowder;
and Susy would put down an account of it in a book, and
Mrs. Peyton—for she would be there in some vague
capacity—would say, "Really, now, I don't see but what
we were very lucky in having such a boy as Clarence
with us. I begin to understand him better." And Harry,
who, for purposes of vague poetical retaliation, would
also drop in at that moment, would mutter and say, "He
is certainly the son of Colonel Brant; dear me!" and
apologize. And his mother would come in also, in her
coldest and most indifferent manner, in a white ball dress,
and start and say, "Good gracious, how that boy has
grown! I am sorry I did not see more of him when he
was young." Yet even in the midst of this came a con-
fusing numbness, and then the side of the wagon seemed
to melt away, and he drifted out again alone into the
empty desolate plain from which even the sleeping Susy
had vanished, and he was left deserted and forgotten.
Then all was quiet in the wagon, and only the night wind
moving round it. But lo! the lashes of the sleeping
White Chief—the dauntless leader, the ruthless destroyer
of Indians—were wet with glittering tears!

Yet it seemed only a moment afterwards that he awoke

with a faint consciousness of some arrested motion. To his utter consternation, the sun, three hours high, was shining in the wagon, already hot and stifling in its beams. There was the familiar smell and taste of the dirty road in the air about him. There was a faint creaking of boards and springs, a slight oscillation, and beyond the audible rattle of harness, as if the train had been under way, the wagon moving, and then there had been a sudden halt. They had probably come up with the Silsbee train; in a few moments the change would be effected and all of his strange experience would be over. He must get up now. Yet, with the morning laziness of the healthy young animal, he curled up a noment longer in his luxurious couch.

How quiet it was! There were far-off voices, but they seemed suppressed and hurried. Through the window he saw one of the teamsters run rapidly past him with a strange, breathless, preoccupied face, halt a moment at one of the following wagons, and then run back again to the front.

Then two of the voices came nearer, with the dull beating of hoofs in the dust.

"Rout out the boy and ask him," said a half-suppressed, impatient voice, which Clarence at once recognized as the man Harry's.

"Hold on till Peyton comes up," said the second voice, in a low tone; "leave it to him."

"Better find out what they were like, at once," grumbled Harry.

"Wait, stand back," said Peyton's voice, joining the others; "*I'll* ask him."

Clarence looked wonderingly at the door. It opened on Mr. Peyton, dusty and dismounted, with a strange, abstracted look in his face.

"How many wagons are in your train, Clarence?"

"Three, sir."

"Any marks on them?"

"Yes, sir," said Clarence, eagerly: "'Off to California' and 'Root, Hog, or Die.'"

Mr. Peyton's eye seemed to leap up and hold Clarence's

with a sudden, strange significance, and then looked down.

"How many were you in all?" he continued.

"Five, and there was Mrs. Silsbee."

"No other woman?"

"No."

"Get up and dress yourself," he said gravely, "and wait here till I come back. Keep cool and have your wits about you." He dropped his voice slightly. "Perhaps something's happened that you'll have to show yourself a little man again for, Clarence!"

The door closed, and the boy heard the same muffled hoofs and voices die away towards the front. He began to dress himself mechanically, almost vacantly, yet conscious always of a vague undercurrent of thrilling excitement. When he had finished he waited almost breathlessly, feeling the same beating of his heart that he had felt when he was following the vanished train the day before. At last he could stand the suspense no longer, and opened the door. Everything was still in the motionless caravan, except—it struck him oddly even then—the unconcerned prattling voice of Susy from one of the nearer wagons. Perhaps a sudden feeling that this was something that concerned *her*, perhaps an irresistible impulse overcame him, but the next moment he had leaped to the ground, faced about, and was running feverishly to the front.

The first thing that met his eyes was the helpless and desolate bulk of one of the Silsbee wagons a hundred rods away, bereft of oxen and pole, standing alone and motionless against the dazzling sky! Near it was the broken frame of another wagon, its fore wheels and axles gone, pitched forward on its knees like an ox under the butcher's sledge. Not far away there were the burnt and blackened ruins of a third, around which the whole party on foot and horseback seemed to be gathered. As the boy ran violently on, the group opened to make way for two men carrying some helpless but awful object between them. A terrible instinct made Clarence swerve from it in his headlong course, but he was at the same moment

discovered by the others, and a cry arose of "Go back!"
"Stop!" "Keep him back!" Heeding it no more than
the wind that whistled by him, Clarence made directly
for the foremost wagon—the one in which he and Susy
had played. A powerful hand caught his shoulder; it was
Mr. Peyton's.

"Mrs. Silsbee's wagon," said the boy, with white lips,
pointing to it. "Where is she?"

"She's missing," said Peyton, "and one other—the rest
are dead."

"She must be there," said the boy, struggling, and
pointing to the wagon; "let me go."

"Clarence," said Peyton sternly, accenting his grasp
upon the boy's arm, "be a man! Look around you. Try
and tell us who these are."

There seemed to be one or two heaps of old clothes
lying on the ground, and further on, where the men at
a command from Peyton had laid down their burden,
another. In those ragged, dusty heaps of clothes, from
which all the majesty of life seemed to have been ruth-
lessly stamped out, only what was ignoble and grotesque
appeared to be left. There was nothing terrible in this.
The boy moved slowly towards them; and, incredible even
to himself, the overpowering fear of them that a moment
before had overcome him left him as suddenly. He
walked from the one to the other, recognizing them by
certain marks and signs, and mentioning name after
name. The groups gazed at him curiously; he was conscious that he scarcely understood himself, still less the
same quiet purpose that made him turn towards the
furthest wagon.

"There's nothing there," said Peyton; "we've searched
it." But the boy, without replying, continued his way,
and the crowd followed him.

The deserted wagon, more rude, disorderly, and slovenly
than it had ever seemed to him before, was now heaped
and tumbled with broken bones, cans, scattered provisions,
pots, pans, blankets, and clothing in the foul confusion of
a dust-heap. But in this heterogeneous mingling the boy's
quick eye caught sight of a draggled edge of calico.

"That's Mrs. Silsbee's dress!" he cried, and leapt into the wagon.

At first the men stared at each other, but an instant later a dozen hands were helping him, nervously digging and clearing away the rubbish. Then one man uttered a sudden cry, and fell back with frantic but furious eyes uplifted against the pitiless, smiling sky above him.

"Great God! look here!"

It was the yellowish, waxen face of Mrs. Silsbee that had been uncovered. But to the fancy of the boy it had changed; the old familiar lines of worry, care, and querulousness had given way to a look of remote peace and statue-like repose. He had often vexed her in her aggressive life; he was touched with remorse at her cold, passionless apathy now, and pressed timidly forward. Even as he did so, the man, with a quick but warning gesture, hurriedly threw his handkerchief over the matted locks, as if to shut out something awful from his view. Clarence felt himself drawn back; but not before the white lips of a bystander had whispered a single word—

"Scalped, too! by God!"

CHAPTER VI

THEN followed days and weeks that seemed to Clarence as a dream. At first, an interval of hushed and awed restraint when he and Susy were kept apart, a strange and artificial interest taken little note of by him, but afterwards remembered when others had forgotten it; the burial of Mrs. Silsbee beneath a cairn of stones, with some ceremonies that, simple though they were, seemed to usurp the sacred rights of grief from him and Susy, and leave them cold and frightened; days of frequent and incoherent childish outbursts from Susy, growing fainter and rarer as time went on, until they ceased, he knew not when; the haunting by night of that morning vision of the three or four heaps of ragged clothes on the ground and a half regret that he had not examined them more closely; a recollection of the awful loneliness and desolation of the broken and abandoned wagon left behind on its knees as if praying mutely when the train went on and left it; the trundling behind of the fateful wagon in which Mrs. Silsbee's body had been found, superstitiously shunned by every one, and when at last turned over to the authorities at an outpost garrison, seeming to drop the last link from the dragging chain of the past. The revelation to the children of a new experience in that brief glimpse of the frontier garrison; the handsome officer in uniform and belted sword, an heroic, vengeful figure to be admired and imitated hereafter; the sudden importance and respect given to Susy and himself as "survivors"; the sympathetic questioning and kindly exaggerations of their experiences, quickly accepted by Susy—all these, looking back upon them afterwards, seemed to have passed in a dream.

No less strange and visionary to them seemed the real transitions they noted from the moving train. How one morning they missed the changeless, motionless, low, dark line along the horizon, and before noon found themselves among the rocks and trees and a swiftly rushing river. How there suddenly appeared beside them a few days later a great gray cloud-covered ridge of mountains that they were convinced was that same dark line that they had seen so often. How the men laughed at them, and said that for the last three days they had been *crossing* that dark line, and that it was *higher* than the great gray-clouded range before them, which it had always hidden from their view! How Susy firmly believed that these changes took place in her sleep, when she always "kinder felt they were crawlin' up," and how Clarence, in the happy depreciation of extreme youth, expressed his conviction that they "weren't a bit high, after all." How the weather became cold, though it was already summer, and at night the camp fire was a necessity, and there was a stove in the tent with Susy; and yet how all this faded away, and they were again upon a dazzling, burnt, and sun-dried plain! But always as in a dream!

More real were the persons who composed the party—
whom they seemed to have always known—and who,
in the innocent caprice of children, had become to them
more actual than the dead had even been. There was
Mr. Peyton, who they now knew owned the train, and
who was so rich that he "needn't go to California if he
didn't want to, and was going to buy a great deal of it
if he liked it," and who was also a lawyer and "police-
man"—which was Susy's rendering of "politician"—
and was called "Squire" and "Judge" at the frontier
outpost, and could order anybody to be "took up if he
wanted to," and who knew everybody by their Christian
names; and Mrs. Peyton, who had been delicate and was
ordered by the doctor to live in the open air for six
months, and "never go into a house or a town agin,"
and who was going to adopt Susy as soon as her husband could arrange with Susy's relatives, and draw up
the papers! How "Harry" was Henry Benham, Mrs.
Peyton's brother, and a kind of partner of Mr. Peyton.
And how the scout's name was Gus Gildersleeve, or
the "White Crow," and how, through his recognized
intrepidity, an attack upon their train was no doubt
averted. Then there was "Bill," the stock herder, and
"Texas Jim," the *vaquero*—the latter marvelous and
unprecedented in horsemanship. Such were their companions, as appeared through the gossip of the train
and their own inexperienced consciousness. To them,
they were all astounding and important personages.
But, either from boyish curiosity or some sense of being
misunderstood, Clarence was more attracted by the two
individuals of the party who were least kind to him—
namely, Mrs. Peyton and her brother Harry. I fear that,
after the fashion of most children, and some grown-up
people, he thought less of the steady kindness of Mr.
Peyton and the others than of the rare tolerance of
Harry or the polite concessions of his sister. Miserably
conscious of this at times, he quite convinced himself
that if he could only win a word of approbation from
Harry, or a smile from Mrs. Peyton, he would afterwards revenge himself by "running away." Whether

he would or not, I cannot say. I am writing of a foolish, growing, impressionable boy of eleven, of whose sentiments nothing could be safely predicted but uncertainty.

It was at this time that he became fascinated by another member of the party whose position had been too humble and unimportant to be included in the group already noted. Of the same appearance as the other teamsters in size, habits, and apparel, he had not at first exhibited to Clarence any claim to sympathy. But it appeared that he was actually a youth of only sixteen— a hopeless incorrigible of St. Joseph, whose parents had prevailed on Peyton to allow him to join the party, by way of removing him from evil associations and as a method of reform. Of this Clarence was at first ignorant, not from any want of frankness on the part of the youth, for that ingenious young gentleman later informed him that he had killed three men in St. Louis, two in St. Jo, and that the officers of justice were after him. But it was evident that to precocious habits of drinking, smoking, chewing, and card-playing this overgrown youth added a strong tendency to exaggeration of statement. Indeed, he was known as "Lying Jim Hooker," and his various qualities presented a problem to Clarence that was attractive and inspiring, doubtful, but always fascinating. With the hoarse voice of early wickedness and a contempt for ordinary courtesy, he had a round, perfectly good-humored face, and a disposition that when not called upon to act up to his self-imposed *rôle* of reckless wickedness, was not unkindly.

It was only a few days after the massacre, and while the children were still wrapped in the gloomy interest and frightened reticence which followed it, that "Jim Hooker" first characteristically flashed upon Clarence's perceptions. Hanging half on and half off the saddle of an Indian pony, the lank Jim suddenly made his appearance, dashing violently up and down the track, and around the wagon in which Clarence was sitting, tugging desperately at the reins, with every indication of being furiously run away with, and retaining his seat only with the most dauntless courage and skill. Round and round they went, the helpless rider at times hanging by a single stirrup near the ground, and again recovering himself by—as it seemed to Clarence—almost superhuman effort. Clarence sat open-mouthed with anxiety and excitement, and yet a few of the other teamsters laughed. Then the voice of Mr. Peyton, from the window of his car, said quietly,—

"There, that will do, Jim. Quit it!"

The furious horse and rider instantly disappeared. A few moments after, the bewildered Clarence saw the redoubted horseman trotting along quietly in the dust of the rear, on the same fiery steed, who in that prosaic light bore an astounding resemblance to an ordinary team horse. Later in the day he sought an explanation from the rider.

"You see," answered Jim gloomily, "thar ain't a galoot in this yer crowd ez knows jist *what's* in that hoss! And them ez suspecks daren't say! It wouldn't do for to hev it let out that the Judge hez a Morgan-Mexican plug that's killed two men afore he got him, and is bound to kill another afore he gets through! Why, on'y the week afore we kem up to you, that thar hoss bolted with me at camping! Bucked and throwed me, but I kept my holt o' the stirrups with my foot— so! Dragged me a matter of two miles, head down, and me keepin' away rocks with my hand—so!"

"Why didn't you loose your foot and let go?" asked Clarence breathlessly.

"*You* might," said Jim, with deep scorn; "that ain't *my* style. I just laid low till we kem to a steep pitched hill, and goin' down when the hoss was, so to speak, kinder *below* me, I just turned a hand spring, so, and that landed me onter his back again."

This action, though vividly illustrated by Jim's throwing his hands down like feet beneath him, and indicating the parabola of a spring in the air, proving altogether too much for Clarence's mind to grasp, he timidly turned to a less difficult detail.

"What made the horse bolt first, Mr. Hooker?"

"Smelt Injins!" said Jim, carelessly expectorating tobacco juice in a curving jet from the side of his mouth—a singularly fascinating accomplishment, peculiarly his own, " 'n' likely *your* Injins."

"But," argued Clarence hesitatingly, "you said it was a week before—and—"

"Er Mexican plug kin smell Injins fifty, yes, a hundred miles away," said Jim, with scornful deliberation; " 'n' if Judge Peyton had took my advice, and hadn't been so mighty feared about the character of his hoss gettin' out he'd hev played roots on them Injins afore they tetched ye. But," he added, with gloomy dejection, "there ain't no sand in this yer crowd, thar ain't no vim, thar ain't nothin'; and thar kan't be ez long ez thar's women and babies, and women and baby fixin's, mixed up with it. I'd hev cut the whole blamed gang ef it weren't for one or two things," he added darkly.

Clarence, impressed by Jim's mysterious manner, for the moment forgot his contemptuous allusion to Mr. Peyton, and the evident implication of Susy and himself, and asked hurriedly, "What things?"

Jim, as if forgetful of the boy's presence in his fitful mood, abstractedly half drew a glittering bowie knife from his bootleg, and then slowly put it back again. "Thar's one or two old scores," he continued, in a low voice, although no one was in hearing distance of them, "one or two private accounts," he went on tragically, averting his eyes as if watched by some one, "thet hev to be wiped out with blood afore *I* leave. Thar's one or two men *too many* alive and breathin' in this yer crowd. Mebbee it's Gus Gildersleeve; mebbee it's Harry Benham; mebbee," he added, with a dark yet noble disinterestedness, "it's *me*."

"Oh, no," said Clarence, with polite deprecation.

Far from placating the gloomy Jim, this seemed only to awake his suspicions. "Mebbee," he said, dancing suddenly away from Clarence, "mebbee you think I'm lyin'. Mebbee you think, because you're Colonel Brant's son, yer kin run *me* with this yer train. Mebbee," he continued, dancing violently back again, "ye kalkilate, because ye run off'n' stampeded a baby, ye kin tote me round too, sonny. Mebbee," he went on, executing a double shuffle in the dust and alternately striking his hands on the sides of his boots, "mebbee you're spyin' round and reportin' to the Judge."

Firmly convinced that Jim was working himself up by an Indian war-dance to some desperate assault on himself, but resenting the last unjust accusation, Clarence had recourse to one of his old dogged silences. Happily at this moment an authoritative voice called out, "Now, then, you Jim Hooker!" and the desperate Hooker, as usual, vanished instantly. Nevertheless, he appeared an hour or two later beside the wagon in which Susy and Clarence were seated, with an expression of satiated vengeance and remorseful bloodguiltiness in his face, and his hair combed Indian fashion over his eyes. As he generously contented himself with only passing a gloomy and disparaging criticism on the game of cards that the children were playing, it struck Clarence for the first time that a great deal of his real wickedness resided in his hair. This set him to thinking that it was strange that Mr. Peyton did not try to reform him with a pair of scissors, but not until Clarence himself had for at least four days attempted to imitate Jim by combing his own hair in that fashion.

A few days later, Jim again casually favored him with a confidential interview. Clarence had been allowed to bestride one of the team leaders postillionwise, and was correspondingly elevated, when Jim joined him, on the Mexican plug, which appeared—no doubt a part of its wicked art—heavily docile, and even slightly lame.

"How much," said Jim, in a tone of gloomy confidence,—"how much did you reckon to make by stealin' that gal-baby, sonny?"

"Nothing," replied Clarence with a smile. Perhaps it was an evidence of the marked influence that Jim was beginning to exert over him that he already did not attempt to resent this fascinating implication of grown-up guilt.

"It orter bin a good job, if it warn't revenge," continued Jim moodily.

"No, it wasn't revenge," said Clarence hurriedly.

"Then ye kalkilated ter get er hundred dollars reward ef the old man and old woman hadn't bin scelped afore yet got up to 'em?" said Jim. "That's your blamed dodgasted luck, eh! Enyhow, you'll make Mrs. Peyton plank down suthin' if she adopts the babby. Look yer, young feller," he said, starting suddenly and throwing his face forward, glaring fiendishly through his matted side-locks, "d'ye mean ter tell me it wasn't a plant—a skin game—the hull thing?"

"A what?" said Clarence.

"D'ye mean to say"—it was wonderful how gratuitously husky his voice became at this moment—"d'ye mean ter tell me ye didn't set on them Injins to wipe out the Silsbees, so that ye could hev an out-an'-out gal *orfen* on hand fer Mrs. Peyton ter adopt—eh?"

But here Clarence was forced to protest, and strongly, although Jim contemptuously ignored it. "Don't lie ter me," he repeated mysteriously, "I'm fly. I'm dark, young fel. We're cahoots in this thing?" And with this artful suggestion of being in possession of Clarence's guilty secret he departed in time to elude the usual objurgation of his superior, "Phil," the head teamster.

Nor was his baleful fascination exercised entirely on Clarence. In spite of Mrs. Peyton's jealously affectionate care, Clarence's frequent companionship, and the little circle of admiring courtiers that always surrounded Susy, it became evident that this small Eve had been secretly approached and tempted by the Satanic Jim. She was found one day to have a few heron's feathers in her possession with which she adorned her curls, and at another time was discovered to have rubbed her face and arms with yellow and red ochre, confessedly the free gift of Jim Hooker. It was to Clarence alone that she admitted the significance and purport of these offerings. "Jim gived 'em to me," she said, "and Jim's a kind of Injin hisself that won't hurt me; and when bad Injins come, they'll think I'm his Injin baby and run away.

And Jim said if I'd just told the Injins when they came to kill papa and mamma, that I b'longed to him, they'd hev runned away."

"But," said the practical Clarence, "you could not; you know you were with Mrs. Peyton all the time."

"Kla'uns," said Susy, shaking her head and fixing her round blue eyes with calm mendacity on the boy, "don't you tell me. *I was there!*"

Clarence started back, and nearly fell over the wagon in hopeless dismay at this dreadful revelation of Susy's powers of exaggeration. "But," he gasped, "you know, Susy, you and me left before—".

"Kla'uns," said Susy calmly, making a little pleat in the skirt of her dress with her small thumb and fingers, "don't you talk to me. I was there. I'se a *seriver!* The men at the fort said so! The *serivers* is allus, allus there, and allus allus knows everythin'."

Clarence was too dumfounded to reply. He had a vague recollection of having noticed before that Susy was very much fascinated by the reputation given to her at Fort Ridge as a "survivor," and was trying in an infantile way to live up to it. This the wicked Jim had evidently encouraged. For a day or two Clarence felt a little afraid of her, and more lonely than ever.

It was in this state, and while he was doggedly conscious that his association with Jim did not prepossess Mrs. Peyton or her brother in his favor, and that the former even believed him responsible for Susy's unhallowed acquaintance with Jim, that he drifted into one of those youthful escapades on which elders are apt to sit in severe but not always considerate judgment. Believing, like many other children, that nobody cared particularly for him, except to *restrain* him, discovering, as children do, much sooner than we complacently imagine, that love and preference have no logical connection with desert or character, Clarence became boyishly reckless. But when, one day, it was rumored that a herd of buffalo was in the vicinity, and that the train would be delayed the next morning in order that a hunt might be organized, by Gildersleeve, Benham, and a few others, Clarence listened willingly to Jim's proposition that they should secretly follow it.

To effect their unhallowed purpose required boldness and duplicity. It was arranged that shortly after the departure of the hunting party Clarence should ask permission to mount and exercise one of the team horses— a favor that had been frequently granted him; that in the outskirts of the camp he should pretend that the horse ran away with him, and Jim would start in pursuit. The absence of the shooting party with so large a contingent of horses and men would preclude any further detachment from the camp to assist them. Once clear, they would follow the track of the hunters, and, if discovered by them, would offer the same excuse, with the addition that they had lost their way to the camp. The plan was successful. The details were carried out with almost too perfect effect; as it appeared that Jim, in order to give dramatic intensity to the fractiousness of Clarence's horse, had inserted a thorn apple under the neck of his saddle, which Clarence only discovered in time to prevent himself from being unseated. Urged forward by ostentatious "Whoas!" and surreptitious cuts in the rear from Jim, pursuer and pursued presently found themselves safely beyond the half-dry stream and fringe of alder bushes that skirted the camp. They were not followed. Whether the teamsters suspected and winked at this design, or believed that the boys could take care of themselves, and ran no risk of being lost in the proximity of the hunting party, there was no general alarm.

Thus reassured, and having a general idea of the direction of the hunt, the boys pushed hilariously forward. Before them opened a vast expanse of bottom land, slightly sloping on the right to a distant half-filled lagoon, formed by the main river overflow, on whose tributary they had encamped. The lagoon was partly hidden by straggling timber and "brush," and beyond that again stretched the unlimitable plains—the pasture of their mighty game. Hither, Jim hoarsely informed his companion, the buffaloes came to water. A few rods further on, he started dramatically, and, alighting, proceeded to slowly examine the ground. It seemed to be scattered over with half-circular patches, which he pointed out mysteriously as "buffalo chip." To Clarence's inexperienced perception the plain bore a singular resemblance to the surface of an ordinary unromantic cattle pasture that somewhat chilled his heroic fancy. However, the two companions halted and professionally examined their arms and equipments.

These, I grieve to say, though varied, were scarcely full or satisfactory. The necessities of their flight had restricted Jim to an old double-barreled fowling-piece, which he usually carried slung across his shoulders; an old-fashioned "six-shooter," whose barrels revolved occasionally and unexpectedly, known as "Allen's Pepper Box" on account of its culinary resemblance; and a bowie-knife. Clarence carried an Indian bow and arrow with which he had been exercising, and a hatchet which he had concealed under the flanks of his saddle. To this Jim generously added the six-shooter, taking the hatchet in exchange—a transfer that at first delighted Clarence, until, seeing the warlike and picturesque effect of the hatchet in Jim's belt, he regretted the transfer. The gun, Jim meantime explained, "extry charged," "chuck up" to the middle with slugs and revolver bullets, could only be fired by himself, and even then, he darkly added, not without danger. This poverty of equipment was, however, compensated by opposite statements from Jim of the extraordinary results obtained by these simple weapons from "fellers I knew:" how *he* himself had once brought down a "bull" by a bold shot with a revolver through its open bellowing mouth that pierced his "innards;" how a friend of his—an intimate in fact—now in jail at Louisville for killing a sheriff's deputy, had once found himself alone and dismounted with a simple clasp-knife and a lariat among a herd of buffaloes; how, leaping calmly upon the shaggy shoulders of the biggest bull, he lashed himself with the lariat firmly to its horns, goading it onward with his clasp-knife, and subsisting for days upon the flesh cut from its living body, until, abandoned by its fellows and exhausted by the loss of blood, it finally succumbed to its victor at the very outskirts of the camp to which he had artfully driven it! It must be confessed that this recital somewhat took away Clarence's breath, and he would have liked to ask a few questions. But they were alone on the prairie, and linked by a common transgression; the glorious sun was coming up victoriously, the pure, crisp air was intoxicating their nerves; in the bright forecast of youth everything *was* possible!

The surface of the bottom land that they were crossing was here and there broken up by fissures and "potholes," and some circumspection in their progress became necessary. In one of these halts, Clarence was struck by a dull, monotonous jarring that sounded like the heavy regular fall of water over a dam. Each time that they slackened their pace the sound would become more audible, and was at last accompanied by that slight but unmistakable tremor of the earth that betrayed the vicinity of a waterfall. Hesitating over the phenomenon, which seemed to imply that their topography was wrong and that they had blundered from the track, they were presently startled by the fact that the sound was actually *approaching* them! With a sudden instinct they both galloped towards the lagoon. As the timber opened before them Jim uttered a long ecstatic shout. "Why, it's *them!*"

At a first glance it seemed to Clarence as if the whole plain beyond was broken up and rolling in tumbling waves or furrows towards them. A second glance showed the tossing fronts of a vast herd of buffaloes, and here and there, darting in and out and among them, or emerging from the cloud of dust behind, wild figures and flashes of fire. With the idea of water still in his mind, it seemed as if some tumultuous tidal wave were sweeping unseen towards the lagoon, carrying everything before it. He turned with eager eyes, in speechless expectancy, to his companion.

Alack! that redoubtable hero and mighty hunter was, to all appearances, equally speechless and astonished. It was true that he remained rooted to the saddle, a lank, still heroic figure, alternately grasping his hatchet and gun with a kind of spasmodic regularity. How long he would have continued this would never be known, for the next moment, with a deafening crash, the herd broke through the brush, and, swerving at the right of the lagoon, bore down directly upon them. All further doubt or hesitation on their part was stopped. The far-seeing, sagacious Mexican plug with a terrific snort wheeled and fled furiously with his rider. Moved, no doubt, by touching fidelity, Clarence's humbler team-horse instantly followed. In a few moments those devoted animals struggled neck to neck in noble emulation.

"What are we goin' off this way for?" gasped the simple Clarence.

"Peyton and Gildersleeve are back there—and they'll see us," gasped Jim in reply. It struck Clarence that the buffaloes were much nearer them than the hunting party, and that the trampling hoofs of a dozen bulls were close behind them, but with another gasp he shouted,

"When are we going to hunt 'em?"

"Hunt *them!*" screamed Jim, with a hysterical outburst of truth; "why, they're huntin' *us*—dash it!"

Indeed, there was no doubt that their frenzied horses were flying before the equally frenzied herd behind them. They gained a momentary advantage by riding into one of the fissures, and out again on the other side, while their pursuers were obliged to make a detour. But in a few minutes they were overtaken by that part of the herd who had taken the other and nearer side of the lagoon, and were now fairly in the midst of them. The ground shook with their trampling hoofs; their steaming breath, mingling with the stinging dust that filled the air, half choked and blinded Clarence. He was dimly conscious that Jim had wildly thrown his hatchet at a cow buffalo pressing close upon his flanks. As they swept down into another gully he saw him raise his fateful gun with utter desperation. Clarence crouched low on his horse's outstretched neck. There was a blinding flash, a single stunning report of both barrels; Jim reeled in one way half out of the saddle, while the smoking gun seemed to leap in another over his head, and then rider and horse vanished in a choking cloud of dust and gunpowder. A moment after Clarence's horse stopped with a sudden check, and the boy felt himself hurled over its head into the gully, alighting on something that seemed to be a bounding cushion of curled and twisted hair. It was the shaggy shoulder of an enormous buffalo! For Jim's desperate random shot and double charge had taken effect on the near hind leg of a preceding bull, tearing away the flesh and ham-stringing the animal, who had dropped in the gully just in front of Clarence's horse.

Dazed but unhurt, the boy rolled from the lifted fore-quarters of the struggling brute to the ground. When he staggered to his feet again, not only his horse was gone but the whole herd of buffaloes seemed to have passed too, and he could hear the shouts of unseen hunters now ahead of him. They had evidently over-looked his fall, and the gully had concealed him. The sides before him were too steep for his aching limbs to climb; the slope by which he and the bull had descended when the collision occurred was behind the wounded animal. Clarence was staggering towards it when the bull, by a supreme effort, lifted itself on three legs, half turned, and faced him.

These events had passed too quickly for the inexperi-enced boy to have felt any active fear, or indeed any-thing but wild excitement and confusion. But the spec-tacle of that shaggy and enormous front, that seemed to fill the whole gully, rising with awful deliberation between him and escape, sent a thrill of terror through his frame. The great, dull, bloodshot eyes glared at him with a dumb, wondering fury; the large wet nostrils were so near that their first snort of inarticulate rage made him reel backwards as from a blow. The gully was only a narrow and short fissure or subsidence of the plain; a few paces more of retreat and he would be at

its end, against an almost perpendicular bank fifteen feet
high. If he attempted to climb its crumbling sides and
fell, there would be those short but terrible horns waiting to impale him! It seemed too terrible, too cruel!
He was so small beside this overgrown monster. It
wasn't fair! The tears started to his eyes, and then,
in a rage at the injustice of Fate, he stood doggedly
still with clenched fists. He fixed his gaze with half-
hysterical, childish fury on those lurid eyes; he did not
know that, owing to the strange magnifying power of
the bull's convex pupils, he, Clarence, appeared much
bigger than he really was to the brute's heavy consciousness, the distance from him most deceptive, and that it
was to this fact that hunters so often owed their escape.
He only thought of some desperate means of attack.
Ah! the six-shooter. It was still in his pocket. He drew
it nervously, hopelessly—it looked so small compared
with his large enemy!

He presented it with flashing eyes, and pulled the
trigger. A feeble click followed, another, and again!
Even *this* had mocked him. He pulled the trigger once
more, wildly; there was a sudden explosion, and another.
He stepped back; the balls had apparently flattened
themselves harmlessly on the bull's forehead. He pulled
again, hopelessly; there was another report, a sudden
furious bellow, and the enormous brute threw his head
savagely to one side, burying his left horn deep in the
crumbling bank beside him. Again and again he charged
the bank, driving his left horn home, and bringing down
the stones and earth in showers. It was some seconds
before Clarence saw in a single glimpse of that wildly
tossing crest the reason of this fury. The blood was
pouring from his left eye, penetrated by the last bullet;
the bull was blinded! A terrible revulsion of feeling, a
sudden sense of remorse that was for the moment more
awful than even his previous fear, overcame him. *He*
had done *that thing!* As much to fly from the dreadful
spectacle as any instinct of self-preservation, he took
advantage of the next mad paroxysms of pain and blind-
ness, that always impelled the suffering beast towards

the left, to slip past him on the right, reach the incline, and scramble wildly up to the plain again. Here he ran confusedly forward, not knowing whither—only caring to escape that agonized bellowing, to shut out forever the accusing look of that huge blood-weltering eye.

Suddenly he heard a distant angry shout. To his first hurried glance the plain had seemed empty, but, looking up, he saw two horsemen rapidly advancing with a led horse behind them—his own. With the blessed sense of relief that overtook him now came the fevered desire for sympathy and to tell them all. But as they came nearer he saw that they were Gildersleeve, the scout, and Henry Benham, and that, far from sharing any delight in his deliverance, their faces only exhibited irascible impatience. Overcome by this new defeat, the boy stopped, again dumb and dogged.

"Now, then, blank it all, *will* you get up and come along, or do you reckon to keep the train waiting another hour over your blanked foolishness?" said Gildersleeve savagely.

The boy hesitated, and then mounted mechanically, without a word.

" 'Twould have served 'em right to have gone and left 'em," muttered Benham vindictively.

For one wild instant Clarence thought of throwing himself from his horse and bidding them go on and leave him. But before he could put his thought into action the two men were galloping forward, with his horse led by a lariat fastened to the horn of Gildersleeve's saddle.

In two hours more they had overtaken the train, already on the march, and were in the midst of the group of outriders. Judge Peyton's face, albeit a trifle perplexed, turned towards Clarence with a kindly, half-tolerant look of welcome. The boy's heart instantly melted with forgiveness.

"Well, my boy, let's hear *your* story. What happened?"

Clarence cast a hurried glance around, and saw Jim, with face averted, riding gloomily behind. Then nervously and hurriedly he told how he had been thrown into the gully on the back of the wounded buffalo, and the manner of his escape. An audible titter ran through the cavalcade. Mr. Peyton regarded him gravely. "But how did the buffalo get so conveniently into the gully?" he asked.

"Jim Hooker lamed him with a shotgun, and he fell over," said Clarence timidly.

A roar of Homeric laughter went up from the party. Clarence looked up, stung and startled, but caught a single glimpse of Jim Hooker's face that made him forget his own mortification. In its hopeless, heart-sick, and utterly beaten dejection—the first and only real expression he had seen on it—he read the dreadful truth. Jim's *reputation* had ruined him! The one genuine and striking episode of his life, the one trustworthy account he had given of it, had been unanimously accepted as the biggest and most consummate lie of his record!

CHAPTER VII

WITH this incident of the hunt closed, to Clarence, the last remembered episode of his journey. But he did not know until long after that it had also closed to him what might have been the opening of a new career. For it had been Judge Peyton's intention in adopting Susy to include a certain guardianship and protection of the boy, provided he could get the consent of that vague relation to whom he was consigned. But it had been pointed out by Mrs. Peyton and her brother that Clarence's association with Jim Hooker had made him a doubtful companion for Susy, and even the Judge himself was forced to admit that the boy's apparent taste for evil company was inconsistent with his alleged birth and breeding. Unfortunately, Clarence, in the conviction of being hopelessly misunderstood, and that dogged acquiescence to fate which was one of his characteristics, was too proud to correct the impression by any of the hypocracies of childhood. He had also a cloudy instinct of loyalty to Jim in his disgrace, without, however, experiencing either the sympathy of an equal or the zeal of a partisan, but rather —if it could be said of a boy of his years—with the patronage and protection of a superior. So he accepted without demur the intimation that when the train reached California he would be forwarded from Stockton with an outfit and a letter of explanation to Sacramento, it being understood that in the event of not finding his relative he would return to the Peytons in one of the southern valleys, where they elected to purchase a tract of land.

With this outlook, and the prospect of change, independence, and all the rich possibilities that to the imagination of youth are included in them, Clarence had found the days dragging. The halt at Salt Lake, the transit of the dreary Alkali desert, even the wild passage of the Sierras, were but a blurred picture in his memory. The sight of eternal snows and the rolling of endless ranks of pines, the first glimpse of a hillside of wild oats, the spectacle of a rushing yellow river that to his fancy seemed tinged with gold, were momentary excitements, quickly forgotten. But when, one morning, halting at the outskirts of a struggling settlement, he found the entire party eagerly gathered around a passing stranger, who had taken from his saddle-bags a small buckskin pouch to show them a double handful of shining scales of metal, Clarence felt the first feverish and overmastering thrill of the gold-seekers. Breathlessly he followed the breathless questions and careless replies. The gold had been dug out of a *placer* only thirty miles away. It might be worth, say, a hundred and fifty dollars; it was only *his* share of a week's work with two partners. It was not much; "the country was getting played out with fresh arrivals and greenhorns." All this falling carelessly from the unshaven lips of a dusty, roughly dressed man, with a long-handled shovel and pickaxe strapped on his back, and a frying-pan depending from his saddle. But no panoplied or armed knight ever seemed so heroic or independent a figure to Clarence. What could be finer than the noble scorn conveyed in his critical survey of the train, with its comfortable covered wagons and appliances of civilization? "Ye'll hev to get rid of them ther fixin's if yer goin' in for *placer* diggin'!" What a corroboration of Clarence's real thoughts! What a picture of independence was this! The picturesque scout, the all-powerful Judge Peyton, the daring young officer, all crumbled on their clayey pedestals before this hero in a red flannel shirt and high-topped boots. To stroll around in the open air all day, and pick up those shining bits of metal, without study, without method or routine—this was really life; to some day come upon that large nugget "you couldn't lift," that was worth as much as the train and horses—such a one as the stranger said was found the other day at Sawyer's Bar—this was worth giving up everything for. That rough man, with his smile of careless superiority, was the living link between Clarence and the Thousand and One Nights; in him were Aladdin and Sindbad incarnate.

Two days later they reached Stockton. Here Clarence, whose single suit of clothes had been reinforced by patching, odds and ends from Peyton's stores, and an extraordinary costume of army cloth, got up by the regimental tailor at Fort Ridge, was taken to be refitted at a general furnishing "emporium." But alas! in the selection of the clothing for that adult locality scant provision seemed to have been made for a boy of Clarence's years, and he was with difficulty fitted from an old condemned Government stores with "a boy's" seaman suit and a brass-buttoned pea-jacket. To this outfit Mr. Peyton added a small sum of money for his expenses, and a letter of explanation to his cousin. The stage-coach was to start at noon. It only remained for Clarence to take leave of the party. The final parting with Susy had been discounted on the two previous days with some tears, small frights and clingings, and the expressed determination on the child's part "to go with him;" but in the excitement of the arrival at Stockton it was still further mitigated, and under the influence of a little present from Clarence —his first disbursement of his small capital—had at last taken the form and promise of merely temporary separation. Nevertheless, when the boy's scanty pack was deposited under the stage-coach seat, and he had been left alone, he ran rapidly back to the train for one moment more with Susy. Panting and a little frightened, he reached Mrs. Peyton's car.

"Goodness! You're not gone yet," said Mrs. Peyton sharply. "Do you want to lose the stage?"

An instant before, in his loneliness, he might have answered, "Yes." But under the cruel sting of Mrs. Peyton's evident annoyance at his reappearance he felt his legs suddenly tremble, and his voice left him. He did not dare to look at Susy. But her voice rose comfortably from the depths of the wagon where she was sitting.

"The stage will be gone away, Kla'uns."

She too! Shame at his foolish weakness sent the yearning blood that had settled round his heart flying back into his face.

"I was looking for—for—for Jim, ma'am," he said at last, boldly.

He saw a look of disgust pass over Mrs. Peyton's face, and felt a malicious satisfaction as he turned and ran back to the stage. But here, to his surprise, he actually found Jim, whom he really hadn't thought of, darkly watching the last strapping of luggage. With a manner calculated to convey the impression to the other passengers that he was parting from a brother criminal, probably on his way to a state prison, Jim shook hands gloomily with Clarence, and eyed the other passengers furtively between his mated locks.

"Ef ye hear o' anythin' happenin', ye'll know what's up," he said, in a low, hoarse, but perfectly audible whisper. "Me and them's bound to part company afore long. Tell the fellows at Deadman's Gulch to look out for me at any time."

Although Clarence was not going to Deadman's Gulch, knew nothing of it, and had a faint suspicion that Jim was equally ignorant, yet as one or two of the passengers glanced anxiously at the demure, gray-eyed boy who seemed booked for such a baleful destination, he really felt the half-delighted, half-frightened consciousness that he was starting in life under fascinating immoral pretenses. But the forward spring of the fine-spirited horses, the quickened motion, the glittering sunlight, and the thought that he really was leaving behind him all the shackles of dependence and custom, and plunging into a life of freedom, drove all else from his mind. He turned at last from this hopeful, blissful future, and began to examine his fellow passengers with boyish curiosity. Wedged in between two silent men on the front seat, one of whom seemed a farmer, and the other, by his black attire, a professional man, Clarence was finally attracted by a black-mantled, dark-haired, bonnetless woman on the back seat, whose attention seemed to be monopolized by the jocular gallantries of her companions and the two men before her in the middle seat. From her position he could see little more than her dark eyes, which occasionally seemed to meet his frank curiosity in an amused sort of way, but he was chiefly struck by the pretty foreign sound of her musical voice, which was unlike anything he had ever heard before, and—alas for the inconstancy of youth—much finer than Mrs. Peyton's. Presently his farmer companion, casting a patronizing glance on Clarence's pea-jacket and brass buttons, said cheerily—

"Jest off a voyage, sonny?"

"No, sir," stammered Clarence; "I came across the plains."

"Then I reckon that's the rig-out for the crew of a prairie schooner, eh?" There was a laugh at this which perplexed Clarence. Observing it, the humorist kindly condescended to explain that "prairie schooner" was the current slang for an emigrant wagon.

"I couldn't," explained Clarence, naively looking at the dark eyes on the back seat, "get any clothes at Stockton but these; I suppose the folks didn't think there'd ever be boys in California."

The simplicity of this speech evidently impressed the others, for the two men in the middle seats turned at a whisper from the lady and regarded him curiously. Clarence blushed slightly and became silent. Presently the vehicle began to slacken its speed. They were ascending a hill; on either bank grew huge cottonwoods, from which occasionally depended a beautiful scarlet vine.

"Ah! eet ees pretty," said the lady, nodding her black-veiled head towards it. "Eet is good in ze hair."

One of the men made an awkward attempt to clutch a spray from the window. A brilliant inspiration flashed upon Clarence. When the stage began the ascent of the next hill, following the example of an outside passenger, he jumped down to walk. At the top of the hill he rejoined the stage, flushed and panting, but carrying a small branch of the vine in his scratched hands. Handing it to the man on the middle seat, he said, with grave, boyish politeness—"Please—for the lady."

A slight smile passed over the face of Clarence's neighbors. The bonnetless woman nodded a pleasant acknowledgment, and coquettishly wound the vine in her glossy hair. The dark man at his side, who hadn't spoken yet, turned to Clarence dryly.

"If you're goin' to keep up this gait, sonny, I reckon ye won't find much trouble gettin' a man's suit to fit you by the time you reach Sacramento."

Clarence didn't quite understand him, but noticed that a singular gravity seemed to overtake the two jocular men on the middle seat, and the lady looked out of the window. He came to the conclusion that he had made a mistake about alluding to his clothes and his size. He must try and behave more manly. That opportunity seemed to be offered two hours later, when the stage stopped at a wayside hotel or restaurant.

Two or three passengers had got down to refresh themselves at the bar. His right and left hand neighbors were, however, engaged in a drawling conversation on the comparative merits of San Francisco sandhill and water lots; the jocular occupants of the middle seat were still engrossed with the lady. Clarence slipped out of the stage and entered the bar-room with some ostentation. The complete ignoring of his person by the barkeeper and his customers, however, somewhat disconcerted him. He hesitated a moment, and then returned gravely to the stage door and opened it.

"Would you mind taking a drink with me, sir?" said Clarence politely, addressing the farmer-looking passenger who had been most civil to him. A dead silence followed. The two men on the middle seat faced entirely around to gaze at him.

"The Commodore asks if you'll take a drink with him," explained one of the men to Clarence's friend with the greatest seriousness.

"Eh? Oh, yes, certainly," returned that gentleman, changing his astonished expression to one of the deepest gravity, "seeing it's the Commodore."

"And perhaps you and your friend will join, too?" said Clarence timidly to the passenger who had explained; "and you too, sir?" he added to the dark man.

"Really, gentlemen, I don't see how we can refuse," said the latter, with the greatest formality, and appealing to the others. "A compliment of this kind from our distinguished friend is not to be taken lightly."

"I have observed, sir, that the Commodore's head is level," returned the other man with equal gravity.

Clarence could have wished they had not treated his first hospitable effort quite so formally, but as they stepped from the coach with unbending faces he led them, a little frightened, into the bar-room. Here, unfortunately, as he was barely able to reach over the counter, the barkeeper would have again overlooked him but for a quick glance from the dark man, which seemed to change even the barkeeper's perfunctory smiling face into supernatural gravity.

"The Commodore is standing treat," said the dark man, with unbroken seriousness, indicating Clarence, and leaning back with an air of respectful formality. "*I* will take straight whiskey. The Commodore, on account of just changing climate, will, I believe, for the present content himself with lemon soda."

Clarence had previously resolved to take whiskey, like the others, but a little doubtful of the politeness of countermanding his guest's order, and perhaps slightly embarrassed by the fact that all the other customers seemed to have gathered round him and his party with equally immovable faces, he said hurriedly:

"Lemon soda for me, please."

"The Commodore," said the barkeeper with impassive features, as he bent forward and wiped the counter with professional deliberation, "is right. No matter how much a man may be accustomed all his life to liquor, when he is changing climate, gentlemen, he says 'Lemon soda for me' all the time."

"Perhaps," said Clarence, brightening, "you will join too?"

"I shall be proud on this occasion, sir."

"I think," said the tall man, still as ceremoniously unbending as before, "that there can be but one toast here, gentlemen. I give you the health of the Commodore. May his shadow never be less."

The health was drunk solemnly. Clarence felt his cheeks tingle and in his excitement drank his own health with the others. Yet he was disappointed that there was not more joviality; he wondered if men always drank together so stiffly. And it occurred to him that it would be expensive. Nevertheless, he had his purse all ready ostentatiously in his hand; in fact, the paying for it out of his own money was not the least manly and independent pleasure he had promised himself. "How much?" he asked, with an affectation of carelessness.

The barkeeper cast his eye professionally over the barroom. "I think you said treats for the crowd; call it twenty dollars to make even change."

Clarence's heart sank. He had heard already of the exaggeration of California prices. Twenty dollars! It was half his fortune. Nevertheless, with an heroic effort, he controlled himself, and with slightly nervous fingers counted out the money. It struck him, however, as curious, not to say ungentlemanly, that the bystanders craned their necks over his shoulder to look at the contents of his purse, although some slight explanation was offered by the tall man.

"The Commodore's purse, gentlemen, is really a singular one. Permit me," he said, taking it from Clarence's hand with great politeness. "It is one of the new pattern, you observe, quite worthy of inspection." He

handed it to a man behind him, who in turn handed it to
another, while a chorus of "suthin quite new," "the
latest style," followed it in its passage round the room,
and indicated to Clarence its whereabouts. It was presently handed back to the barkeeper, who had begged
also to inspect it, and who, with an air of scrupulous
ceremony insisted upon placing it himself in Clarence's
side pocket, as if it were an important part of his func-
tion. The driver here called "all aboard." The
passengers hurriedly reseated themselves, and the episode
abruptly ended. For, to Clarence's surprise, these attentive friends of a moment ago at once became interested
in the views of a new passenger concerning the local
politics of San Francisco, and he found himself utterly
forgotten. The bonnetless woman had changed her position, and her head was no longer visible. The disillusion and depression that overcame him suddenly were as
complete as his previous expectations and hopefulness
had been extravagant. For the first time his utter unim-
portance in the world and his inadequacy to this new
life around him came upon him crushingly.

The heat and jolting of the stage caused him to fall
into a slight slumber and when he awoke he found his
two neighbors had just got out at a wayside station.
They had evidently not cared to waken him to say
"Good-by." From the conversation of the other passengers he learned that the tall man was a well-known
gambler, and the one who looked like a farmer was a
ship captain who had become a wealthy merchant. Clarence thought he understood now why the latter had
asked him if he came off a voyage, and that the nick-
name of "Commodore" given to him, Clarence, was some
joke intended for the captain's understanding. He
missed them, for he wanted to talk to them about his
relative at Sacramento, whom he was now so soon to
see. At last, between sleeping and waking, the end of
his journey was unexpectedly reached. It was dark,
but, being "steamer night," the shops and business places
were still open, and Mr. Peyton had arranged that the
stage-driver should deliver Clarence at the address of his

relative in "J Street,"—an address which Clarence had luckily remembered. But the boy was somewhat discomfited to find that it was a large office or banking-house. He, however, descended from the stage, and with his small pack in his hand entered the building as the stage drove off, and, addressing one of the busy clerks, asked for "Mr. Jackson Brant."

There was no such person in the office. There never had been any such person. The bank had always occupied that building. Was there not some mistake in the number? No; the name, number, and street had been deeply engrafted in the boy's recollection. Stop! it might be the name of a customer who had given his address at the bank. The clerk who made this suggestion disappeared promptly to make inquiries in the counting-room. Clarence, with a rapidly beating heart, awaited him. The clerk returned. There was no such name on the books. Jackson Brant was utterly unknown to every one in the establishment.

For an instant the counter against which the boy was leaning seemed to yield with his weight; he was obliged to steady himself with both hands to keep from falling. It was not his disappointment, which was terrible; it was not a thought of his future, which seemed hopeless; it was not his injured pride at appearing to have willfully deceived Mr. Peyton, which was more dreadful than all else; but it was the sudden, sickening sense that *he* himself had been deceived, tricked, and fooled! For it flashed upon him for the first time that the vague sense of wrong which had always haunted him was this—that this was the vile culmination of a plan to *get rid of him,* and that he had been deliberately lost and led astray by his relatives as helplessly and completely as a useless cat or dog!

Perhaps there was something of this in his face, for the clerk, staring at him, bade him sit down for a moment, and again vanished into the mysterious interior. Clarence had no conception how long he was absent, or indeed anything but his own breathless thoughts, for he was conscious of wondering afterwards why the clerk was leading him through a door in the counter into an inner room of many desks, and again through a glass door into a smaller office, where a preternaturally busy-looking man sat writing at a desk. Without looking up, but pausing only to apply a blotting-pad to the paper before him, the man said crisply—

"So you've been consigned to some one who don't seem to turn up, and can't be found, eh? Never mind that," as Clarence laid Peyton's letter before him. "Can't read it now. Well, I suppose you want to be shipped back to Stockton?"

"No!" said the boy, recovering his voice with an effort.

"Eh, that's business, though. Know anybody here?"

"Not a living soul; that's why they sent me," said the boy, in sudden reckless desperation. He was the more furious that he knew the tears were standing in his eyes.

The idea seemed to strike the man amusingly. "Looks a little like it, don't it?" he said, smiling grimly at the paper before him. "Got any money?"

"A little."

"How much?"

"About twenty dollars," said Clarence hesitatingly. The man opened a drawer at his side, mechanically, for he did not raise his eyes, and took out two ten-dollar gold pieces. "I'll go twenty better," he said, laying them down on the desk. "That'll give you a chance to look around. Come back here, if you don't see your way clear." He dipped his pen into the ink with a significant gesture as if closing the interview.

Clarence pushed back the coin. "I'm not a beggar," he said doggedly.

The man this time raised his head and surveyed the boy with two keen eyes. "You're not, hey? Well, do I look like one?"

"No," stammered Clarence, as he glanced into the man's haughty eyes.

"Yet, if I were in your fix, I'd take that money and be glad to get it."

"If you'll let me pay you back again," said Clarence,

a little ashamed, and considerably frightened at his implied accusation of the man before him.

"You can," said the man, bending over his desk again.

Clarence took up the money and awkwardly drew out his purse. But it was the first time he had touched it since it was returned to him in the bar-room, and it struck him that it was heavy and full—indeed, so full that on opening it a few coins rolled out on to the floor. The man looked up abruptly.

"I thought you said you had only twenty dollars?" he remarked grimly.

"Mr. Peyton gave me forty," returned Clarence, stupefied and blushing. "I spent twenty dollars for drinks at the bar—and," he stammered, "I—I—I don't know how the rest came here."

"You spent twenty dollars for *drinks?*" said the man, laying down his pen, and leaning back in his chair to gaze at the boy.

"Yes—that is—I treated some gentlemen of the stage, sir, at Davidson's Crossing."

"Did you treat the whole stage company?"

"No, sir, only about four or five—and the bar-keeper. But everything's so dear in California. *I* know that."

"Evidently. But it don't seem to make much difference with *you*," said the man, glancing at the purse.

"They wanted my purse to look at," said Clarence hurriedly, "and that's how the thing happened. Somebody put *his own money* back into *my* purse by accident."

"Of course," said the man grimly.

"Yes, that's the reason," said Clarence, a little relieved, but somewhat embarrassed by the man's persistent eyes.

"Then, of course," said the other quietly, "you don't require my twenty dollars now."

"But," returned Clarence hesitatingly, "this isn't *my* money. I must find out who it belongs to, and give it back again. Perhaps," he added timidly, "I might leave it here with you, and call for it when I find the man, or send him here."

With the greatest gravity he here separated the surplus from what was left of Peyton's gift and the twenty dollars he had just received. The balance unaccounted for was forty dollars. He laid it on the desk before the man, who, still looking at him, rose and opened the door.

"Mr. Reed."

The clerk who had shown Clarence in appeared.

"Open an account with—" He stopped and turned interrogatively to Clarence.

"Clarence Brant," said Clarence, coloring with excitement.

"With Clarence Brant. Take that deposit"—pointing to the money—"and give him a receipt." He paused as the clerk retired with a wondering gaze at the money, looked again at Clarence, said, "I think *you'll* do," and reëntered the private office, closing the door behind him.

I hope it will not be deemed inconceivable that Clarence, only a few moments before crushed with bitter disappointment and the hopeless revelation of his abandonment by his relatives, now felt himself lifted up suddenly into an imaginary height of independence and manhood. He was leaving the bank, in which he stood a minute before a friendless boy, not as a successful beggar, for this important man had disclaimed the idea, but absolutely as a customer! a depositor! a business man like the grown-up clients who were thronging the outer office, and before the eyes of the clerk who had pitied him! And he, Clarence, had been spoken to by this man, whose name he now recognized as the one that was on the door of the building—a man of whom his fellow-passengers had spoken with admiring envy— a banker famous in all California! Will it be deemed incredible that this imaginative and hopeful boy, forgetting all else, the object of his visit, and even the fact that he considered this money was not his own, actually put his hat a little on one side as he strolled out on his way to the streets and prospective fortune?

Two hours later the banker had another visitor. It chanced to be the farmer-looking man who had been Clarence's fellow-passenger. Evidently a privileged per-

son, he was at once ushered as "Captain Stevens" into
the presence of the banker. At the end of a familiar
business interview the captain asked carelessly—

"Any letters for me?"

The busy banker pointed with his pen to the letter
"S" in a row of alphabetically labeled pigeon-holes against
the wall. The captain, having selected his correspondence, paused with a letter in his hand.

"Look here, Carden, there are letters here for some
chap called 'John Silsbee.' They were here when I
called, ten weeks ago."

"Well?"

"That's the name of that Pike County man who was
killed by Injins in the plains. The 'Frisco papers had
all the particulars last night; may be it's for that fellow.
It hasn't got a postmark. Who left it here?"

Mr. Carden summoned a clerk. It appeared that the
letter had been left by a certain Brant Fauquier, to be
called for.

Captain Stevens smiled. "Brant's been too busy
dealin' faro to think of 'em agin, and since that shootin'
affair at Angels' I hear he's skipped to the southern
coast somewhere. Cal Johnson, his old chum, was in
the up stage from Stockton this afternoon."

"Did you come by the up stage from Stockton this
afternoon?" said Carden, looking up.

"Yes, as far as Ten-mile Station—rode the rest of the
way here."

"Did you notice a queer little old-fashioned kid—about
so high—like a runaway school-boy?"

"Did I? By G—d, sir, he treated me to drinks."

Carden jumped from his chair. "Then he wasn't
lying!"

"No! We let him do it; but we made it good for the
little chap afterwards. Hello! What's up?"

But Mr. Carden was already in the outer office beside
the clerk who had admitted Clarence.

"You remember that boy Brant who was here?"

"Yes, sir."

"Where did he go?"

"Don't know, sir."

"Go and find him somewhere and somehow. Go to all the hotels, restaurants, and gin-mills near here, and hunt him up. Take some one with you, if you can't do it alone. Bring him back here, quick !"

It was nearly midnight when the clerk fruitlessly returned. It was the fierce high noon of "steamer nights"; light flashed brilliantly from shops, counting-houses, drinking-saloons, and gambling-hells. The streets were yet full of eager, hurrying feet—swift of fortune, ambition, pleasure, or crime. But from among these deeper harsher footfalls the echo of the homeless boy's light, innocent tread seemed to have died out forever.

CHAPTER VIII

WHEN Clarence was once more in the busy street before the bank, it seemed clear to his boyish mind that, being now cast adrift upon the world and responsible to no one, there was no reason why he should not at once proceed to the nearest gold mines ! The idea of returning to Mr. Peyton and Susy, as a disowned and abandoned outcast, was not to be thought of. He would purchase some kind of an outfit, such as he had seen the miners carry, and start off as soon as he had got his supper. But although one of his most delightful anticipations had been the unfettered freedom of ordering a meal at a restaurant, on entering the first one he found himself the object of so much curiosity, partly from his size and partly from his dress, which the unfortunate boy was beginning to suspect was really preposterous, and he turned away with a stammered excuse, and did not try another. Further on he found a baker's shop, where he refreshed himself with some gingerbread and lemon soda. At an adjacent grocery he purchased some herrings, smoked beef, and biscuits, as future provisions for his "pack" or kit. Then began his real quest for an outfit. In an hour he had secured— ostensibly for some friend, to avoid curious inquiry—a pan, a blanket, a shovel and pick, all of which he deposited at the baker's, his unostentatious headquarters, with the exception of a pair of disguising high boots that half hid his sailor trousers, which he kept to put on at the last. Even to his inexperience the cost of these articles seemed enormous; when his purchases were complete, of his entire capital scarcely four dollars remained! Yet in the fond illusions of boyhood these rude appointments seemed possessed of far more value than the gold he had given in exchange for them, and he had enjoyed a child's delight in testing the transforming magic of money.

Meanwhile, the feverish contact of the crowded street had, strange to say, increased his loneliness, while the ruder joviality of its dissipations began to fill him with vague uneasiness. The passing glimpse of dancing halls and gaudily whirled figures that seemed only feminine in their apparel; the shouts and boisterous choruses from concert rooms; the groups of drunken roisterers that congregated around the doors of saloons or, hilariously charging down the streets, elbowed him against the wall, or humorously insisted on his company, discomposed and frightened him. He had known rude companionship before, but it was serious, practical, and under control. There was something in this vulgar degradation of intellect and power—qualities that Clarence had always boyishly worshiped—which sickened and disillusioned him. Later on a pistol shot in a crowd beyond, the rush of eager men past him, the disclosure of a limp and helpless figure against the wall, the closing of the crowd again around it, although it stirred him with a fearful curiosity, actually shocked him less hopelessly than their brutish enjoyments and abandonment.

It was in one of these rushes that he had been crushed against a swinging door, which, giving way to his pressure, disclosed to his wondering eyes a long, glitteringly adorned, and brightly lit room, densely filled with a silent, attentive throng in attitudes of decorous abstraction and preoccupation, that even the shouts and tumult at its very doors could not disturb. Men of all ranks and conditions, plainly or elaborately clad, were grouped together under this magic spell of silence and attention. The tables before them were covered with cards and loose heaps of gold and silver. A clicking, the rattling of an ivory ball, and the frequent, formal, lazy reiteration of some unintelligible sentence was all that he heard. But by a sudden instinct he *understood* it all. It was a gambling saloon!

Encouraged by the decorous stillness, and the fact that everybody appeared too much engaged to notice him, the boy drew timidly beside one of the tables. It was covered with a number of cards, on which were placed certain sums of money. Looking down, Clarence saw that he was standing before a card that as yet had nothing on it. A single player at his side looked up, glanced at Clarence curiously, and then placed half a dozen gold pieces on the vacant card. Absorbed in the general aspect of the room and the players, Clarence did not notice that his neighbor won twice, and even *thrice,* upon that card. Becoming aware, however, that the player while gathering in his gains, was smilingly regarding him he moved in some embarrassment to the other end of the table, where there seemed another gap in the crowd. It so chanced that there was also another vacant card. The previous neighbor of Clarence instantly shoved a sum of money across the table on the vacant card and won! At this the other players began to regard Clarence singularly, one or two of the spectators smiled, and the boy, coloring, moved awkwardly away. But his sleeve was caught by the successful player, who, detaining him gently, put three gold pieces into his hand.

"That's *your* share, sonny," he whispered.

"Share—for what?" stammered the astounded Clarence.

"For bringing me 'the luck,'" said the man.

Clarence stared. "Am I—to—to play with it?" he said, glancing at the coins and then at the table, in ignorance of the stranger's meaning.

"No, no!" said the man hurriedly, "don't do that,

You'll lose it, sonny, sure! Don't you see, *you bring the luck to others,* not to yourself. Keep it, old man, and run home!"

"I don't want it! I won't have it!" said Clarence with a swift recollection of the manipulation of his purse that morning, and a sudden distrust of all mankind.

"There!" He turned back to the table and laid the money on the first vacant card he saw. In another moment, as it seemed to him, it was raked away by the dealer. A sense of relief came over him.

"There!" said the man, with an awed voice and a strange, fatuous look in his eye. "What did I tell you? You see, it's allus so! Now," he added roughly, "get up and get out o' this, afore you lose the boots and shirt off ye."

Clarence did not wait for a second command. With another glance round the room, he began to make his way through the crowd towards the front. But in that parting glance he caught a glimpse of a woman presiding over a "wheel of fortune" in a corner, whose face seemed familiar. He looked again, timidly. In spite of an extraordinary head-dress or crown that she wore as the "Goddess of Fortune," he recognized, twisted in its tinsel, a certain scarlet vine which he had seen before; in spite of the hoarse formula which she was continually repeating, he recognized the foreign accent. It was the woman of the stage-coach! With a sudden dread that she might recognize him, and likewise demand his services "for luck," he turned and fled.

Once more in the open air, there came upon him a vague loathing and horror of the restless madness and feverish distraction of this half-civilized city. It was the more powerful that it was vague, and the outcome of some inward instinct. He found himself longing for the pure air and sympathetic loneliness of the plains and wilderness; he began to yearn for the companionship of his humble associates—the teamster, the scout Gildersleeve, and even Jim Hooker. But above all and before all was the wild desire to get away from these maddening streets and their bewildering occupants. He ran back to the baker's, gathered his purchases together, took advantage of a friendly doorway to strap them on his boyish shoulders, slipped into a side street, and struck out at once for the outskirts.

It had been his first intention to take stage to the nearest mining district, but the diminution of his small capital forbade that outlay, and he decided to walk there by the highroad, of whose general direction he had informed himself. In half an hour the lights of the flat, struggling city, and their reflection in the shallow, turbid river before it, had sunk well behind him. The air was cool and soft; a yellow moon swam in the slight haze that rose above the *tules;* in the distance a few scattered cottonwoods and sycamores marked like sentinels the road. When he had walked some distance he sat down beneath one of them to make a frugal supper from the dry rations in his pack, but in the absence of any spring he was forced to quench his thirst with a glass of water in a wayside tavern. Here he was good-humoredly offered something stronger, which he declined, and replied to certain curious interrogations by saying that he expected to overtake his friends in a wagon further on. A new distrust of mankind had begun to make the boy an adept in innocent falsehood, the more deceptive as his careless, cheerful manner, the result of his relief at leaving the city, and his perfect ease in the loving companionship of night and nature, certainly gave no indication of his homelessness and poverty.

It was long past midnight, when, weary in body, but still hopeful and happy in mind, he turned off the dusty road into a vast rolling expanse of wild oats, with the same sense of security of rest as a traveler to his inn. Here, completely screened from view by the tall stalks of grain that rose thickly around him to the height of a man's shoulder, he beat down a few of them for a bed, on which he deposited his blanket. Placing his pack for a pillow, he curled himself up in his blanket, and speedily fell asleep.

He awoke at sunrise, refreshed, invigorated, and hungry. But he was forced to defer his first self-prepared breakfast until he had reached water, and a less dangerous place than the wild-oat field to build his first camp fire. This he found a mile further on, near some dwarf willows on the bank of a half-dry stream. Of his various efforts to prepare his first meal, the fire was the most successful; the coffee was somewhat too substantially thick, and the bacon and herring lacked definiteness of quality from having been cooked in the same vessel. In this boyish picnic he missed Susy, and recalled, perhaps a little bitterly, her coldness at parting. But the novelty of his situation, the brilliant sunshine and sense of freedom, and the road already awakening to dusty life with passing teams, dismissed everything but the future from his mind. Readjusting his pack, he stepped on cheerily. At noon he was overtaken by a teamster, who in return for a match to light his pipe gave him a lift of a dozen miles. It is to be feared that Clarence's account of himself was equally fanciful with his previous story, and that the teamster parted from him with a genuine regret, and a hope that he would soon be overtaken by his friends along the road. "And mind that you ain't such a fool agin to let 'em make you tote their dod-blasted tools fur them!" he added unsuspectingly, pointing to Clarence's mining outfit. Thus saved the heaviest part of the day's journey, for the road was continually rising from the plains during the last six miles, Clarence was yet able to cover a considerable distance on foot before he halted for supper. Here he was again fortunate. An empty lumber team watering at the same spring, its driver offered to take Clarence's purchases— for the boy had profited by his late friend's suggestion to personally detach himself from his equipment—to Buckeye Mills for a dollar, which would also include a "shakedown passage" for himself on the floor of the wagon. "I reckon you've been foolin' away in Sacramento the money yer parents give yer for return stage fare, eh? Don't lie, sonny," he added grimly, as the now artful Clarence smiled diplomatically. "I've been thar myself!" Luckily, the excuse that he was "tired and sleepy" prevented further dangerous questioning, and the boy was soon really in deep slumber on the wagon floor.

He awoke betimes to find himself already in the mountains. Buckeye Mills was a straggling settlement, and Clarence prudently stopped any embarrassing inquiry from his friend by dropping off the wagon with his equipment as they entered it, and hurriedly saying "Good-by" from a crossroad through the woods. He had learned that the nearest mining camp was five miles away, and its direction was indicated by a long wooden "flume," or water-way, that alternately appeared and disappeared on the flank of the mountain opposite. The cooler and drier air, the grateful shadow of pine and bay, and the spicy balsamic odors that everywhere greeted him, thrilled and exhilarated him. The trail plunging sometimes into an undisturbed forest, he started the birds before him like a flight of arrows through its dim recesses; at times he hung breathlessly over the blue depths of cañons where the same forests were repeated a thousand feet below. Towards noon he struck into a rude road—evidently the thoroughfare of the locality—and was surprised to find that it, as well as the adjacent soil wherever disturbed, was a deep Indian red. Everywhere, along its sides, powdering the banks and boles of trees with its ruddy stain, in mounds and hillocks of piled dirt on the road, or in liquid paint-like pools, when a trickling stream had formed a gutter across it, there was always the same deep sanguinary color. Once or twice it became more vivid in contrast with the white teeth of quartz that peeped through it from the hillside or crossed the road in crumbled strata. One of those pieces Clarence picked up with a quickening pulse. It was veined and streaked with shining mica and tiny glittering cubes of mineral that *looked* like gold!

The road now began to descend towards a winding stream, shrunken by drought and ditching, that glared dazzlingly in the sunlight from its white bars of sand, or glistened in shining sheets and channels. Along its banks, and even encroaching upon its bed, were scattered a few mud cabins, strange-looking wooden troughs and gutters, and here and there, glancing through the leaves, the white canvas of tents. The stumps of felled trees and blackened spaces, as of recent fires, marked the stream on either side. A sudden sense of disappointment overcame Clarence. It looked vulgar, common, and worse than all—*familiar*. It was like the unlovely outskirts of a dozen other prosaic settlements he had seen in less romantic localities. In that muddy red stream, pouring out of a wooden gutter, in which three or four bearded, slouching, half-naked figures were raking like *chiffonniers,* there was nothing to suggest the royal metal. Yet he was so absorbed in gazing at the scene, and had walked so rapidly during the past few minutes, that he was startled, on turning a sharp corner of the road, to come abruptly upon an outlying dwelling.

It was a nondescript building, half canvas and half boards. The interior seen through the open door was fitted up with side shelves, a counter carelessly piled with provisions, groceries, clothing, and hardware—with no attempt at display or even ordinary selection—and a table, on which stood a demijohn and three or four dirty glasses. Two roughly dressed men, whose long, matted beards and hair left only their eyes and lips visible in the tangled hirsute wilderness below their slouched hats, were leaning against the opposite sides of the doorway, smoking. Almost thrown against them in the rapid momentum of his descent, Clarence halted violently.

"Well, sonny, you needn't capsize the shanty," said the first man, without taking his pipe from his lips.

"If yer looking fur yer ma, she and yer Aunt Jane hev jest gone over to Parson Doolittle's to take tea," observed the second man lazily. "She allowed that you'd wait."

"I'm—I'm—going to—to the mines," explained Clarence, with some hesitation. "I suppose this is the way."

The two men took their pipes from their lips, looked at each other, completely wiped every vestige of expression from their faces with the back of their hands, turned their eyes into the interior of the cabin, and said, "Will yer come yer, now *will* yer?" Thus adjured, half a dozen men, also bearded and carrying pipes in their mouths, straggled out of the shanty, and, filing in front of it, squatted down, with their backs against the boards, and gazed comfortably at the boy. Clarence began to feel uneasy.

"I'll give," said one, taking out his pipe and grimly eying Clarence, "a hundred dollars for him as he stands."

"And seein' as he's got that bran-new rig-out o' tools," said another, "I'll give a hundred and fifty—and the drinks. I've been," he added apologetically, "wantin' sunthin' like this a long time."

"Well, gen'lemen," said the man who had first spoken to him, "lookin' at him by and large; takin' in, so to speak, the gin'ral gait of him in single harness; bearin' in mind the perfect freshness of him, and the coolness and size of his cheek—the easy downyness, previousness, and utter don't-care-a-damnativeness of his coming yer, I think two hundred ain't too much for him, and we'll call it a bargain."

Clarence's previous experience of this grim, smileless Californian chaff was not calculated to restore his confidence. He drew away from the cabin, and repeated doggedly, "I asked you if this was the way to the mines."

"It *are* the mines, and these yere are the miners," said the first speaker gravely. "Permit me to interdoose 'em. This yere's Shasta Jim, this yere's Shotcard Billy, this is Nasty Bob, and this Slumgullion Dick. This yere's the Dook o' Chatham Street, the Livin' Skeleton, and me!"

"May we ask, fair young sir," said the Living Skeleton, who, however, seemed in fairly robust condition, "whence came ye on the wings of the morning, and whose Marble Halls ye hev left desolate?"

"I came across the plains, and got into Stockton two days ago on Mr. Peyton's train," said Clarence, indignantly, seeing no reason now to conceal anything. "I came to Sacramento to find my cousin, who isn't living there any more. I don't see anything funny in *that!*

I came here to the mines to dig gold—because—because Mr. Silsbee, the man who was to bring me here and might have found my cousin for me, was killed by Indians."

"Hold up, sonny. Let me help ye," said the first speaker, rising to his feet. "*You* didn't get killed by Injins because you got lost out of a train with Silsbee's infant darter. Peyton picked you up while you was takin' care of her, and two days arter you kem up to the broken-down Silsbee wagons, with all the folks lyin' there slartered."

"Yes, sir," said Clarence, breathlessly with astonishment.

"And," continued the man, putting his hand gravely to his head as if to assist his memory, "when you was all alone on the plains with that little child you saw one of those redskins, as near to you as I be, watchin' the train, and you didn't breathe or move while he was there?"

"Yes, sir," said Clarence eagerly.

"And you was shot at by Peyton, he thinkin' you was an Injun in the mesquite grass? And you once shot a buffalo that had been pitched with you down a gully— all by yourself?"

"Yes," said Clarence, crimson with wonder and pleasure. "You know me, then?"

"Well, ye-e-es," said the man gravely, parting his mustache with his fingers. "You see, *you've been here before.*"

"Before! Me?" repeated the astounded Clarence.

"Yes, before. Last night. You was taller then, and hadn't cut your hair. You cursed a good deal more than you do now. You drank a man's share of whiskey, and you borrowed fifty dollars to get to Sacramento with. I reckon you haven't got it about you now, eh?"

Clarence's brain reeled in utter confusion and hopeless terror.

Was he going crazy, or had these cruel men learned his story from his faithless friends, and this was a part of the plot? He staggered forward, but the men had risen

and quickly encircled him, as if to prevent his escape. In
vague and helpless desperation he gasped—

"What place is this?"

"Folks call it Deadman's Gulch."

Deadman's Gulch! A flash of intelligence lit up the
boy's blind confusion. Deadman's Gulch! Could it have
been Jim Hooker who had really run away, and had taken
his name? He turned half-imploringly to the first speaker.
"Wasn't he older than me, and bigger? Didn't he have
a smooth, round face and little eyes? Didn't he talk
hoarse? Didn't he—" He stopped hopelessly.

"Yes; oh, he wasn't a bit like you," said the man
musingly. "Ye see, that's the h—ll of it! You're altogether *too many* and *too various* fur this camp."

"I don't know who's been here before, or what they
have said," said Clarence desperately, yet even in that
desperation retaining the dogged loyalty to his old play-
mate, which was part of his nature. "I don't know, and
I don't care—there! I'm Clarence Brant of Kentucky;
I started in Silsbee's train from St. Jo, and I'm going
to the mines, and you can't stop me!"

The man who had first spoken started, looked keenly at
Clarence, and then turned to the others. The gentleman
known as the living skeleton had obtruded his huge
bulk in front of the boy, and, gazing at him, said reflectively, "Darned if it don't look like one of Brant's pups—
sure!"

"Air ye any relation to Kernel Hamilton Brant of
Looeyville?" asked the first speaker.

Again that old question! Poor Clarence hesitated,
despairingly. Was he to go through the same cross-
examination he had undergone with the Peytons? "Yes,"
he said doggedly, "I am—but he's dead, and you know it."

"Dead—of course." "Sartin." "He's dead." "The
Kernel's planted," said the men in chorus.

"Well, yes," reflected the Living Skeleton ostentatiously, as one who spoke from experience. "Ham Brant's
about as bony now as they make 'em."

"You bet! About the dustiest, deadest corpse you kin
turn out," corroborated Slumgullion Dick, nodding his

head gloomily to the others; "in point o' fack, es a corpse, about the last one I should keer to go huntin' fur."

"The Kernel's tech 'ud be cold and clammy," concluded the Duke of Chatham Street, who had not yet spoken, "sure. But what did yer mammy say about it? Is she gettin' married agin? Did *she* send ye here?"

It seemed to Clarence that the Duke of Chatham Street here received a kick from his companions; but the boy repeated doggedly—

"I came to Sacramento to find my cousin, Jackson Brant; but he wasn't there."

"Jackson Brant!" echoed the first speaker, glancing at the others. "Did your mother say he was your cousin?"

"Yes," said Clarence wearily. "Good-by."

"Hullo, sonny, where are you going?"

"To dig gold," said the boy. "And you know you can't prevent me, if it isn't on your claim. I know the law." He had heard Mr. Peyton discuss it at Stockton, and he fancied that the men, who were whispering among themselves, looked kinder than before, and as if they were no longer "acting" to him. The first speaker laid his hand on his shoulder, and said, "All right, come with me, and I'll show you where to dig."

"Who are you?" said Clarence. "You called yourself only 'me.'"

"Well, you can call me Flynn—Tom Flynn."

"And you'll show me where I can dig—myself?"

"I will."

"Do you know," said Clarence timidly, yet with a half-conscious smile, "that I—I kinder bring luck?"

The man looked down upon him, and said gravely, but, as it struck Clarence, with a new kind of gravity, "I believe you."

"Yes," said Clarence eagerly, as they walked along together, "I brought luck to a man in Sacramento the other day." And he related with great earnestness his experience in the gambling saloon. Not content with that—the sealed fountains of his childish deep being broken up by some mysterious sympathy—he spoke of his hospitable exploit with the passengers at the wayside bar, of the finding of his Fortunatus purse and his deposit at the bank. Whether that characteristic old-fashioned reticence which had been such an important factor for good or ill in his future had suddenly deserted him, or whether some extraordinary prepossession in his companion had affected him, he did not know; but by the time the pair had reached the hillside Flynn was in possession of all the boy's history. On one point only was his reserve unshaken. Conscious although he was of Jim Hooker's duplicity, he affected to treat it as a comrade's joke.

They halted at last in the middle of an apparently fertile hillside. Clarence shifted his shovel from his shoulders, unslung his pan, and looked at Flynn. "Dig anywhere here, where you like," said his companion carelessly, "and you'll be sure to find the color. Fill your pan with the dirt, go to that sluice, and let the water run in on the top of the pan—workin' it round so," he added, illustrating a rotary motion with the vessel. "Keep doing that until all the soil is washed out of it, and you have only the black sand at the bottom. Then work that the same way until you see the color. Don't be afraid of washing the gold out of the pan—you couldn't do it if you tried. There, I'll leave you here, and you wait till I come back." With another grave nod and something like a smile in the only visible part of his bearded face—his eyes—he strode rapidly away.

Clarence did not lose time. Selecting a spot where the grass was less thick, he broke through the soil and turned up two or three spadefuls of red soil. When he had filled the pan and raised it to his shoulder, he was astounded at its weight. He did not know that it was due to the red precipitate of iron that gave it its color. Staggering along with his burden to the running sluice, which looked like an open wooden gutter, at the foot of the hill, he began to carefully carry out Flynn's direction. The first dip of the pan in the running water carried off half the contents of the pan in liquid paint-like ooze. For a moment he gave way to boyish satisfaction in the sight and touch of this unctuous solution, and dabbled his fingers in it. A few moments more of rinsing and he came to the sediment of fine black sand that was beneath it. Another plunge and swilling of water in the pan, and—could he believe his eyes!—a few yellow tiny scales, scarcely larger than pins' heads, glittered among the sand. He poured it off. But his companion was right; the lighter sand shifted from side to side with the water, but the glittering points remained adhering by their own tiny specific gravity to the smooth surface of the bottom. It was "the color"—gold!

Clarence's heart seemed to give a great leap within him. A vision of wealth, of independence, of power, sprang before his dazzled eyes, and—a hand lightly touched him on the shoulder.

He started. In his complete preoccupation and excitement, he had not heard the clatter of horse-hoofs, and to his amazement Flynn was already beside him, mounted, and leading a second horse.

"You kin ride?" he said shortly.

"Yes," stammered Clarence; "but—"

"*But*—we've only got two hours to reach Buckeye Mills in time to catch the down stage. Drop all that, jump up, and come with me!"

"But I've just found gold," said the boy excitedly.

"And I've just found your—cousin. Come!"

He spurred his horse across Clarence's scattered implements, half helped, half lifted, the boy into the saddle of the second horse, and, with a cut of his riata over the animal's haunches, the next moment they were both galloping furiously away.

CHAPTER IX

TORN suddenly from his prospective future, but too much dominated by the man beside him to protest, Clarence was silent until a rise in the road, a few minutes later, partly abated their headlong speed, and gave him chance to recover his breath and courage.

"Where is my cousin?" he asked.

"In the Southern county, two hundred miles from here."

"Are we going to him?"

"Yes."

They rode furiously forward again. It was nearly half an hour before they came to a longer ascent. Clarence could see that Flynn was from time to time examining him curiously under his slouched hat. This somewhat embarrassed him, but in his singular confidence in the man no distrust mingled with it.

"Ye never saw your—cousin?" he asked.

"No," said Clarence; "nor he me. I don't think he knew me much, any way."

"How old mout ye be, Clarence?"

"Eleven."

"Well, as you're suthin of a pup"—Clarence started, and recalled Peyton's first criticism of him—"I reckon to tell ye suthin. Ye ain't goin' to be skeert, or afeard, or lose yer sand, I kalkilate, for skunkin' ain't in your breed. Well, wot ef I told ye that thish yer—thish yer—*cousin* o' yours was the biggest devil onhung; that he'd just killed a man, and had to lite out elsewhere, and *thet's* why he didn't show up in Sacramento—what if I told you that?"

Clarence felt that this was somehow a little too much. He was perfectly truthful, and lifting his frank eyes to Flynn, he said,

"I should think you were talking a good deal like Jim Hooker!"

His companion stared, and suddenly reined up his horse; then, bursting into a shout of laughter, he galloped ahead, from time to time shaking his head, slapping his legs, and making the dim woods ring with his boisterous mirth. Then as suddenly becoming thoughtful again, he rode on rapidly for half an hour, only speaking to Clarence to urge him forward, and assisting his progress by lashing the haunches of his horse. Luckily, the boy was a good rider—a fact which Flynn seemed to thoroughly appreciate—or he would have been unseated a dozen times.

At last the straggling sheds of Buckeye Mills came into

softer purple view on the opposite mountain. Then laying his hand on Clarence's shoulder as he reined in at
his side, Flynn broke the silence.

"There, boy," he said, wiping the mirthful tears from
his eyes. "I was only foolin'—only tryin' yer grit! This
yer cousin I'm taking you to be as quiet and soft-spoken
and as old-fashioned ez you be. Why, he's that wrapped
up in books and study that he lives alone in a big *adobe
rancherie* among a lot o' Spanish, and he don't keer to see
his own countrymen! Why, he's even changed his name,
and calles himself Don Juan Robinson! But he's very
rich; he owns three leagues of land and heaps of cattle
and horses, and," glancing approvingly at Clarence's seat
in the saddle, "I reckon you'll hev plenty of fun thar."

"But," hesitated Clarence, to whom this proposal
seemed only a repetition of Peyton's charitable offer, "I
think I'd better stay here and dig gold—*with you.*"

"And I think you'd better not," said the man, with a
gravity that was very like a settled determination.

"But my cousin never came for me to Sacramento—
nor sent, nor even wrote," persisted Clarence indignantly.

"Not to *you,* boy; but he wrote to the man whom he
reckoned would bring you there—Jack Silsbee—and left
it in the care of the bank. And Silsbee, being dead, didn't
come for the letter; and as you didn't ask for it when you
came, and didn't even mention Silsbee's name, that same
letter was sent back to your cousin through me, because
the bank thought we knew his whereabouts. It came to
the gulch by an express rider, whilst you were prospectin'
on the hillside. Rememberin' your story, I took the liberty of opening it, and found out that your cousin had
told Silsbee to bring you straight to him. So I'm only
doin' now what Silsbee would have done."

Any momentary doubt or suspicion that might have
risen in Clarence's mind vanished as he met his companion's steady and masterful eye. Even his disappointment was forgotten in the charm of this new-found
friendship and protection. And as its outset had been
marked by an unusual burst of confidence on Clarence's

part, the boy, in his gratitude, now felt something of the timid shyness of a deeper feeling, and once more became reticent.

They were in time to snatch a hasty meal at Buckeye Mills before the stage arrived, and Clarence noticed that his friend, despite his rough dress and lawless aspect, provoked a marked degree of respect from those he met—in which, perhaps, a wholesome fear was mingled. It is certain that the two best places in the stage were given up to them without protest, and that a careless, almost supercilious invitation to drink from Flynn was responded to with singular alacrity by all, including even two fastidiously dressed and previously reserved passengers. I am afraid that Clarence enjoyed this proof of his friend's singular dominance with a boyish pride, and, conscious of the curious eyes of the passengers, directed occasionally to himself, was somewhat ostentatious in his familiarity with this bearded autocrat.

At noon the next day they left the stage at a wayside road station, and Flynn briefly informed Clarence that they must again take horses. This at first seemed dificult in that out-of-the-way settlement, where they alone had stopped, but a whisper from the driver in the ear of the station-master produced a couple of fiery mustangs, with the same accompaniment of cautious awe and mystery. For the next two days they traveled on horseback, resting by night at the lodgings of one or other of Flynn's friends in the outskirts of a large town, where they arrived in the darkness, and left before day. To any one more experienced than the simple-minded boy it would have been evident that Flynn was purposely avoiding the more traveled roads and conveyances; and when they changed horses again the next day's ride was through an apparently unbroken wilderness of scattered wood and rolling plain. Yet to Clarence, with his pantheistic reliance and joyous sympathy with nature, the change was filled with exhilarating pleasure. The vast seas of tossing wild oats, the hillside still variegated with strange flowers, the virgin freshness of untrodden woods and leafy aisles, whose floors of moss or bark were undisturbed by human footprint, were a keen delight and novelty. More than this, his quick eye, trained perceptions, and frontier knowledge now stood him in good stead. His intuitive sense of distance, instincts of woodcraft, and his unerring detection of those signs, landmarks, and guideposts of nature, undistinguishable to aught but birds and beasts and some children, were now of the greatest service to his less favored companion. In this part of their strange pilgrimage it was the boy who took the lead. Flynn, who during the past two days seemed to have fallen into a mood of watchful reserve, nodded his approbation. "This sort of thing's yer best holt, boy," he said. "Men and cities ain't your little game."

At the next stopping-place Clarence had a surprise. They had again entered a town at nightfall, and lodged with another friend of Flynn's in rooms which from vague sounds appeared to be over a gambling saloon. Clarence woke late in the morning, and, descending into the street to mount for the day's journey, was startled to find that Flynn was not on the other horse, but that a well-dressed and handsome stranger had taken his place. But a laugh, and the familiar command, "Jump up, boy," made him look again. It *was* Flynn, but completely shaven of beard and mustache, closely clipped of hair, and in a fastidiously cut suit of black!

"Then you didn't know me?" said Flynn.

"Not till you spoke," replied Clarence.

"So much the better," said his friend sententiously, as he put spurs to his horse. But as they cantered through the street, Clarence, who had already become accustomed to the stranger's hirsute adornment, felt a little more awe of him. The profile of the mouth and chin now exposed to his sidelong glance was hard and stern, and slightly saturnine. Although unable at the time to identify it with anybody he had ever known, it seemed to the imaginative boy to be vaguely connected with some sad experience. But the eyes were thoughtful and kindly, and the boy later believed that if he had been more familiar with the face he would have loved it better. For it was the last and only day he was to see it, as, late that afternoon, after a dusty ride along more traveled highways, they reached their journey's end.

It was a low-walled house, with red-tiled roofs showing against the dark green of venerable pear and fig trees, and a square court-yard in the centre, where they had dismounted. A few words in Spanish from Flynn to one of the lounging peons admitted them to a wooden corridor, and thence to a long, low room, which to Clarence's eyes seemed literally piled with books and engravings. Here Flynn hurriedly bade him stay while he sought the host in another part of the building. But Clarence did not miss him; indeed, it may be feared, he forgot even the object of their journey in the new sensations that suddenly thronged upon him, and the boyish vista of the future that they seemed to open. He was dazed and intoxicated. He had never seen so many books before; he had never conceived of such lovely pictures. And yet in some vague way he thought he must have dreamt of them at some time. He had mounted a chair, and was gazing spellbound at an engraving of a sea-fight when he heard Flynn's voice.

His friend had quietly reëntered the room, in company with an oldish, half-foreign-looking man, evidently his relation. With no helping recollection, with no means of comparison beyond a vague idea that his cousin might look like himself, Clarence stood hopelessly before him. He had already made up his mind that he would have to go through the usual cross-questioning in regard to his father and family; he had even forlornly thought of inventing some innocent details to fill out his imperfect and unsatisfactory recollection. But, glancing up, he was surprised to find that his elderly cousin was as embarrassed as he was, Flynn, as usual, masterfully interposed.

"Of course ye don't remember each other, and thar ain't much that either of you knows about family matters, I reckon," he said grimly; "and as your cousin calls himself Don Juan Robinson," he added to Clarence, "it's just as well that you let 'Jackson Brant' slide. I know him better than you, but you'll get used to him, and he to you, soon enough. At least, you'd better," he concluded, with his singular gravity.

As he turned as if to leave the room with Clarence's embarrassed relative—much to that gentleman's apparent relief—the boy looked up at the latter and said timidly—

"May I look at those books?"

His cousin stopped, and glanced at him with the first expression of interest he had shown.

"Ah, you read; you like books?"

"Yes," said Clarence. As his cousin remained still looking at him thoughtfully, he added, "My hands are pretty clean, but I can wash them first, if you like."

"You may look at them," said Don Juan smilingly; "and as they are old books you can wash your hands afterwards." And, turning to Flynn suddenly, with an air of relief, "I tell you what I'll do—I'll teach him Spanish!"

They left the room together, and Clarence turned eagerly to the shelves. They were old books, some indeed very old, queerly bound, and worm-eaten. Some were in foreign languages, but others in clear, bold English type, with quaint wood-cuts and illustrations. One seemed to be a chronicle of battles and sieges, with pictured representations of combatants spitted with arrows, cleanly lopped off in limb, or toppled over distinctly by visible cannon-shot. He was deep in its perusal when he heard the clatter of a horse's hoofs in the court-yard and the voice of Flynn. He ran to the window, and was astonished to see his friend already on horseback, taking leave of his host.

For one instant Clarence felt one of those sudden revulsions of feeling common to his age, but which he had always timidly hidden under dogged demeanor. Flynn, his only friend! Flynn, his only boyish confidant! Flynn, his latest hero, was going away and forsaking him without a word of parting! It was true that he had only agreed to take him to his guardian, but still Flynn need not have left him without a word of hope or encouragement! With any one else Clarence would probably have taken refuge in his usual Indian stoicism, but the same feeling that had impelled him to offer Flynn his boyish confidences on their first meeting now overpowered him. He dropped his book, ran out into the corridor, and made his way to the court-yard, just as Flynn galloped out from the arch.

But the boy uttered a despairing shout that reached the rider. He drew rein, wheeled, halted, and sat facing Clarence impatiently. To add to Clarence's embarrassment his cousin had lingered in the corridor, attracted by the interruption, and a peon, lounging in the archway, obsequiously approached Flynn's bridle-rein. But the rider waved him off, and, turning sternly to Clarence, said:—

"What's the matter now?"

"Nothing," said Clarence, striving to keep back the hot tears that rose in his eyes. "But you were going away without saying 'good-by.' You've been very kind to me, and—and—I want to thank you!"

A deep flush crossed Flynn's face. Then glancing suspiciously towards the corridor, he said hurriedly,—

"Did *he* send you?"

"No, I came myself. I heard you going."

"All right. Good-by." He leaned forward as if about to take Clarence's outstretched hand, checked himself suddenly with a grim smile, and taking from his pocket a gold coin handed it to the boy.

Clarence took it, tossed it with a proud gesture to the waiting peon, who caught it thankfully, drew back a step from Flynn, and saying, with white cheeks, "I only wanted to say good-by," dropped his hot eyes to the ground. But it did not seem to be his own voice that had spoken, nor his own self that had prompted the act.

There was a quick interchange of glances between the departing guest and his late host, in which Flynn's eyes flashed with an odd, admiring fire, but when Clarence raised his head again he was gone. And as the boy turned back with a broken heart towards the corridor, his cousin laid his hand upon his shoulder.

"*Muy hidalgamente,* Clarence," he said pleasantly. "Yes, we shall make something of you!"

CHAPTER X

THEN followed to Clarence three uneventful years.
During that interval he learnt that Jackson Brant, or
Don Juan Robinson—for the tie of kinship was the least
factor in their relations to each other, and after the departure of Flynn was tacitly ignored by both—was more
Spanish than American. An early residence in Lower
California, marriage with a rich Mexican widow, whose
dying childless left him sole heir, and some strange re-
straining idiosyncrasy of temperament had quite dena-
tionalized him. A bookish recluse, somewhat superfas-
tidious towards his own countrymen, the more Clarence
knew him the more singular appeared his acquaintance
with Flynn; but as he did not exhibit more communi-
cativeness on this point than upon their own kinship,
Clarence finally concluded that it was due to the dominant
character of his former friend, and thought no more about
it. He entered upon the new life at El Refugio with no
disturbing past. Quickly adapting himself to the lazy
freedom of this *hacienda* existence, he spent the mornings
on horseback ranging the hills among his cousin's cattle,
and the afternoons and evenings busied among his cousin's
books with equally lawless and undisciplined independence.
The easy-going Don Juan, it is true, attempted to make
good his rash promise to teach the boy Spanish, and
actually set him a few tasks; but in a few weeks the
quick-witted Clarence acquired such a colloquial pro-
ficiency from his casual acquaintance with vaqueros and
small traders that he was glad to leave the matter in his
young kinsman's hands. Again, by one of those illogical
sequences which make a lifelong reputation depend upon
a single trivial act, Clarence's social status was settled
forever at El Refugio Rancho by his picturesque diversion
of Flynn's parting gift. The grateful peon to whom the
boy had scornfully tossed the coin repeated the act, gesture, and spirit of the scene to his companion, and Don
Juan's unknown and youthful relation was at once recognized as *hijo de la familia,* and undeniably a hidalgo

born and bred. But in the more vivid imagination of feminine El Refugio the incident reached its highest poetic form. "It is true, Mother of God," said Chucha of the Mill; "it was Domingo who himself relates it as it were the Creed. When the American escort had arrived with the young gentleman, this escort, look you, being not of the same quality, he is departing again without a word of permission. Comes to him at this moment my little hidalgo. 'You have yourself forgotten to take from me your demission,' he said. This escort, thinking to make his peace with a mere *muchacho,* gives to him a gold piece of twenty pesos. The little hidalgo has taken it *so,* and with the words, 'Ah! you would make of me your almoner to my cousin's people,' has given it at the moment to Domingo, and with a grace and fire admirable." But it is certain that Clarence's singular simplicity and truthfulness, a faculty of being picturesquely indolent in a way that suggested a dreamy abstraction of mind rather than any vulgar tendency to bodily ease and comfort, and possibly the fact that he was a good horseman, made him a popular hero at El Refugio. At the end of three years Don Juan found that this inexperienced and apparently idle boy of fourteen knew more of the practical ruling of the rancho than he did himself; also that this unlettered young rustic had devoured nearly all the books in his library with boyish recklessness of digestion. He found, too, that in spite of his singular independence of action, Clarence was possessed of an invincible loyalty of principle, and that, asking no sentimental affection, and indeed yielding none, he was, without presuming on his relationship, devoted to his cousin's interest. It seemed that from being a glancing ray of sunshine in the house, evasive but never obtrusive, he had become a daily necessity of comfort and security to his benefactor.

Clarence was, however, astonished, when, one morning, Don Juan, with the same embarrassed manner he had shown at their first meeting, suddenly asked him, "what business he expected to follow." It seemed the more singular, as the speaker, like most abstracted men, had hitherto always studiously ignored the future, in their daily intercourse. Yet this might have been either the habit of security or the caution of doubt. Whatever it was, it was some sudden disturbance of Don Juan's equanimity, as disconcerting to himself as it was to Clarence. So conscious was the boy of this that, without replying to his cousin's question, but striving in vain to recall some delinquency of his own, he asked, with his usual boyish directness —

"Has anything happened? Have I done anything wrong?"

"No, no," returned Don Juan hurriedly. "But, you see, it's time that you should think of your future—or at least prepare for it. I mean you ought to have some more regular education. You will have to go to school. It's too bad," he added fretfully, with a certain impatient forgetfulness of Clarence's presence, and as if following his own thought. "Just as you are becoming of service to me, and justifying your ridiculous position here—and all this d——d nonsense that's gone before—I mean, of course, Clarence," he interrupted himself, catching sight of the boy's whitening cheek and darkening eye, "I mean, you know—this ridiculousness of my keeping you from school at your age, and trying to teach you myself—don't you see."

"You think it is—ridiculous," repeated Clarence, with dogged persistency.

"I mean *I* am ridiculous," said Don Juan hastily. "There! there! let's say no more about it. To-morrow we'll ride over to San José and see the Father Secretary at the Jesuits' College about your entering at once. It's a good school, and you'll always be near the rancho!" And so the interview ended.

I am afraid that Clarence's first idea was to run away. There are few experiences more crushing to an ingenuous nature than the sudden revelation of the aspect in which it is regarded by others. The unfortunate Clarence, conscious only of his loyalty to his cousin's interest and what he believed were the duties of his position, awoke to find that position "ridiculous." In an afternoon's

gloomy ride through the lonely hills, and later in the
sleepless solitude of his room at night, he concluded that
his cousin was right. He would go to school; he would
study hard—so hard that in a little, a very little while,
he could make a living for himself. He awoke contented.
It was the blessing of youth that this resolve and execution seemed as one and the same thing.

The next day found him installed as a pupil and boarder
in the college. Don Juan's position and Spanish predilec-
tions naturally made his relation acceptable to the faculty;
but Clarence could not help perceiving that Father Sobriente, the Principal, regarded him at times with a
thoughtful curiosity that made him suspect that his cousin
had especially bespoken that attention, and that he occasionally questioned him on his antecedents in a way that
made him dread a renewal of the old questioning about
his progenitor. For the rest, he was a polished, cultivated
man; yet, in the characteristic, material criticism of
youth, I am afraid that Clarence chiefly identified him
as a priest with large hands, whose soft palms seemed to
be cushioned with kindness, and whose equally large feet,
encased in extraordinary shapeless shoes of undyed
leather, seemed to tread down noiselessly—rather than to
ostentatiously crush—the obstacles that beset the path of
the young student. In the cloistered galleries of the
court-yard Clarence sometimes felt himself borne down by
the protecting weight of this paternal hand; in the midnight silence of the dormitory he fancied he was often
conscious of the soft browsing tread and snuffly muffled
breathing of his elephantine-footed mentor.

His relations with his school-fellows were at first far
from pleasant. Whether they suspected favoritism;
whether they resented that old and unsympathetic manner
which sprang from his habits of association with his
elders; or whether they rested their objections on the
broader grounds of his being a stranger, I do not know,
but they presently passed from cruel sneers to physical
opposition. It was then found that this gentle and reserved youth had retained certain objectionable, rude,
direct, rustic qualities of fist and foot, and that, violating

all rules and disdaining the pomp and circumstance of school-boy warfare, of which he knew nothing, he simply thrashed a few of his equals out of hand, with or without ceremony, as the occasion or the insult happened. In this emergency one of the seniors was selected to teach this youthful savage his proper position. A challenge was given, and accepted by Clarence with a feverish alacrity that surprised himself as much as his adversary. This was a youth of eighteen, his superior in size and skill.

The first blow bathed Clarence's face in his own blood. But the sanguinary chrism, to the alarm of the spectators, effected an instantaneous and unhallowed change in the boy. Instantly closing with his adversary, he sprang at his throat like an animal, and locking his arm around his neck began to strangle him. Blind to the blows that rained upon him, he eventually bore his staggering enemy by sheer onset and surprise to the earth. Amidst the general alarm, the strength of half a dozen hastily summoned teachers was necessary to unlock his hold. Even then he struggled to renew the conflict. But his adversary had disappeared, and from that day forward Clarence was never again molested.

Seated before Father Sobriente in the infirmary, with swollen and bandaged face, and eyes that still seemed to see everything in the murky light of his own blood, Clarence felt the soft weight of the father's hand upon his knee.

"My son," said the priest gently, "you are not of our religion, or I should claim as a right to ask a question of your own heart at this moment. But as to a good friend, Claro, a good friend," he continued, patting the boy's knee, "you will tell me, old Father Sobriente, frankly and truthfully, as is your habit, one little thing. Were you not afraid?"

"No," said Clarence doggedly. "I'll lick him again to-morrow."

"Softly, my son! It was not of *him* I speak, but of something more terrible and awful. Were you not afraid of—of—" he paused, and suddenly darting his clear eyes into the very depths of Clarence's soul, added—"of *yourself?*"

The boy started, shuddered, and burst into tears.

"So, so," said the priest gently, "we have found our real enemy. Good! Now, by the grace of God, my little warrior, we shall fight *him* and conquer."

Whether Clarence profited by this lesson, or whether this brief exhibition of his quality prevented any repetition of the cause, the episode was soon forgotten. As his school-fellows had never been his associates or confidants, it mattered little to him whether they feared or respected him, or were hypocritically obsequious, after the fashion of the weaker.   His studies, at all events, profited by this lack of distraction.   Already his two years of desultory and omnivorous reading had given him a facile familiarity with many things, which left him utterly free of the timidity, awkwardness, or non-interest of a beginner. His usually reserved manner, which had been lack of expression rather than of conviction, had deceived his tutors.   The audacity of a mind that had never been dominated by others, and owed no allegiance to precedent, made his merely superficial progress something marvelous.

At the end of the first year he was a phenomenal scholar, who seemed capable of anything.   Nevertheless, Father Sobriente had an interview with Don Juan, and as a result Clarence was slightly kept back in his studies, a little more freedom from the rules was conceded to him, and he was even encouraged to take some diversion.   Of such was the privilege to visit the neighboring town of Santa Clara unrestricted and unattended.   He had always been liberally furnished with pocket-money, for which, in his companionless state and Spartan habits, he had a singular and unboyish contempt.   Nevertheless, he always appeared dressed with scrupulous neatness, and was rather distinguished-looking in his older reserve and melancholy self-reliance.

Lounging one afternoon along the Alameda, a leafy avenue set out by the early Mission Fathers between the village of San José and the convent of Santa Clara, he saw a double file of young girls from the convent approaching, on their usual promenade. A view of this procession being the fondest ambition of the San José collegian, and especially interdicted and circumvented by the good Fathers attending the college excursions, Clarence felt for it the profound indifference of a boy who, in the intermediate temperate zone of fifteen years, thinks that he is no longer young and romantic! He was passing them with a careless glance, when a pair of deep violet eyes caught his own under the broad shade of a coquettishly beribboned hat, even as it had once looked at him from the depths of a calico sunbonnet. Susy! He started, and would have spoken; but with a quick little gesture of caution and a meaning glance at the two nuns who walked at the head and foot of the file, she indicated him to follow. He did so at a respectful distance, albeit wondering. A little further on Susy dropped her handkerchief, and was obliged to dart out and run back to the end of the file to recover it. But she gave another swift glance of her blue eyes as she snatched it up and demurely ran back to her place. The procession passed on, but when Clarence reached the spot where she had paused he saw a three-cornered bit of paper lying in the grass. He was too discreet to pick it up while the girls were still in sight, but continued on, returning to it later. It contained a few words in a schoolgirl's hand, hastily scrawled in pencil: "Come to the south wall near the big pear-tree at six."

Delighted as Clarence felt, he was at the same time embarrassed. He could not understand the necessity of this mysterious rendezvous. He knew that if she was a scholar she was under certain conventual restraints; but with the privileges of his position and friendship with his teachers, he believed that Father Sobriente would easily procure him an interview with this old play-fellow, of whom he had often spoken, and who was, with himself, the sole survivor of his tragical past. And trusted as he was by Sobriente, there was something in this clandestine though innocent rendezvous that went against his loyalty. Nevertheless, he kept the appointment, and at the stated time was at the south wall of the convent, over which the gnarled boughs of the distinguishing pear-tree hung. Hard by in the wall was a grated wicket door that seemed unused.

Would she appear among the boughs or on the edge of the wall? Either would be like the old Susy. But to his surprise he heard the sound of the key turning in the lock. The grated door suddenly swung on its hinges, and Susy slipped out. Grasping his hand, she said, "Let's run, Clarence," and before he could reply she started off with him at a rapid pace. Down the lane they flew— very much, as it seemed to Clarence's fancy, as they had flown from the old emigrant wagon on the prairie, four years before. He glanced at the fluttering, fairy-like figure beside him. She had grown taller and more graceful; she was dressed in exquisite taste, with a minuteness of luxurious detail that bespoke the spoilt child; but there was the same prodigal outburst of rippling, golden hair down her back and shoulders, violet eyes, capricious little mouth, and the same delicate hands and feet he had remembered. He would have preferred a more deliberate survey, but with a shake of her head and an hysteric little laugh she only said, "Run, Clarence, run," and again darted forward. Arriving at the cross-street, they turned the corner, and halted breathlessly.

"But you're not running away from school, Susy, are you?" said Clarence anxiously.

"Only a little bit. Just enough to get ahead of the other girls," she said, rearranging her brown curls and tilted hat. "You see, Clarence," she condescended to explain, with a sudden assumption of older superiority, "mother's here at the hotel all this week, and I'm allowed to go home every night, like a day scholar. Only there's three or four other girls that go out at the same time with me, and one of the Sisters, and to-day I got ahead of 'em just to see *you*."

"But" began Clarence.

"Oh, it's all right; the other girls knew it, and helped me. They don't start out for half an hour yet, and they'll say I've just run ahead, and when they and the Sister get to the hotel I'll be there already—don't you see?"

"Yes," said Clarence dubiously.

"And we'll go to an ice-cream saloon now, shan't we? There's a nice one near the hotel. I've got some money," she added quickly, as Clarence looked embarrassed.

"So have I," said Clarence, with a faint accession of color. "Let's go!" She had relinquished his hand to smooth out her frock, and they were walking side by side at a more moderate pace. "But," he continued, clinging to his first idea with masculine persistence, and anxious to assure his companion of his power, of his position, "I'm in the college, and Father Sobriente, who knows your lady superior, is a good friend of mine and gives me privileges; and—and—when he knows that you and I used to play together—why, he'll fix it that we may see each other whenever we want."

"Oh, you silly!" said Susy. *"What!—*when you're—"

"When I'm *what?*"

The young girl shot a violet blue ray from under her broad hat. "Why—when we're grown up now?" Then with a certain precision, "Why, they're *very* particular about young gentlemen! Why, Clarence, if they suspected that you and I were—" Another violet ray from under the hat completed this unfinished sentence.

Pleased and yet confused, Clarence looked straight ahead with deepening color. "Why," continued Susy, "Mary Rogers, that was walking with me, thought you were ever so old—and a distinguished Spaniard! And I," she said abruptly—"haven't I grown? Tell me, Clarence," with her old appealing impatience, "haven't I grown? Do tell me!"

"Very much," said Clarence.

"And isn't this frock pretty—it's only my second best—but I've a prettier one with lace all down in front; but isn't this one pretty, Clarence, tell me?"

Clarence thought the frock and its fair owner perfection, and said so. Whereat Susy, as if suddenly aware of the presence of passers-by, assumed an air of severe propriety, dropped her hands by her side, and with an affected conscientiousness walked on, a little further from Clarence's side, until they reached the ice-cream saloon.

"Get a table near the back, Clarence," she said, in a confidential whisper, "where they can't see us—and strawberry, you know, for the lemon and vanilla here are just horrid!"

They took their seats in a kind of rustic arbor in the rear of the shop, which gave them the appearance of two youthful but somewhat over-dressed and over-conscious shepherds. There was an interval of slight awkwardness, which Susy endeavored to displace. "There has been," she remarked, with easy conversational lightness, "quite an excitement about our French teacher being changed. The girls in our class think it most disgraceful."

And this was all she could say after a separation of four years! Clarence was desperate, but as yet idealess and voiceless. At last, with an effort over his spoon, he gasped a floating recollection: "Do you still like flapjacks, Susy?"

"Oh, yes," with a laugh, "but we don't have them now."

"And Mose" (a black pointer, who used to yelp when Susy sang), "does he still sing with you?"

"Oh, *he's* been lost ever so long," said Susy composedly; "but I've got a Newfoundland and a spaniel and a black pony;" and here, with a rapid inventory of her other personal effects, she drifted into some desultory details of the devotion of her adopted parents, whom she now readily spoke of as "papa" and "mamma," with evidently no disturbing recollection of the dead. From which it appeared that the Peytons were very rich, and, in addition to their possessions in the lower country, owned a rancho in Santa Clara and a house in San Francisco. Like all children, her strongest impressions were the most recent. In the vain hope to lead her back to this material yesterday, he said—

"You remember Jim Hooker?"

"Oh, *he* ran away, when you left. But just think of it! The other day, when papa and I went into a big restaurant in San Francisco, who should be there *waiting* on the table—yes, Clarence, a real waiter—but Jim Hooker! Papa spoke to him; but of course," with a slight elevation of her pretty chin, "*I* couldn't, you know; fancy—a waiter!"

The story of how Jim Hooker had personated him stopped short upon Clarence's lips. He could not bring himself now to add that revelation to the contempt of his small companion, which, in spite of its *naïveté,* somewhat grated on his sensibilities.

"Clarence," she said, suddenly turning towards him mysteriously, and indicating the shopman and his assistants, "I really believe these people suspect us."

"Of what?" said the practical Clarence.

"Don't be silly! Don't you see how they are staring?"

Clarence was really unable to detect the least curiosity on the part of the shopman, or that any one exhibited the slightest concern in him or his companion. But he felt a return of the embarrassed pleasure he was conscious of a moment before.

"Then you're living with your father?" said Susy, changing the subject.

"You mean my *cousin,*" said Clarence, smiling. "You know my father died long before I ever knew you."

"Yes; that's what *you* used to say, Clarence, but papa says it isn't so." But seeing the boy's wondering eyes fixed on her with a troubled expression, she added quickly, "Oh, then, he *is* your cousin!"

"Well, I think I ought to know," said Clarence, with a smile, that was, however, far from comfortable, and a quick return of his old unpleasant recollections of the Peytons. "Why, I was brought to him by one of his friends." And Clarence gave a rapid boyish summary of his journey from Sacramento, and Flynn's discovery of the letter addressed to Silsbee. But before he had concluded he was conscious that Susy was by no means interested in these details, nor in the least affected by the passing allusion to her dead father and his relation to Clarence's misadventures. With her rounded chin in her hand, she was slowly examining his face, with a certain mischievous yet demure abstraction. "I tell you what, Clarence," she said, when he had finished, "you ought to make your cousin get you one of those *sombreros,* and a

nice gold-braided *serape*. They'd just suit you. And then
—then you could ride up and down the Alameda when we
are going by."

"But I'm coming to see you at—at your house, and at
the convent," he said eagerly. "Father Sobriente and my
cousin will fix it all right."

But Susy shook her head, with superior wisdom. "No;
they must never know our secret!—neither papa nor
mamma, especially mamma. And they mustn't know that
we've met again—*after these years!*" It is impossible to
describe the deep significance which Susy's blue eyes gave
to this expression. After a pause she went on—

"No! We must never meet again, Clarence, unless
Mary Rogers helps. She is my best, my *onliest* friend,
and older than I; having had trouble herself, and being
expressly forbidden to see him again. You can speak to
her about Suzette—that's my name now; I was re-
christened Suzette Alexandra Peyton by mamma. And
now, Clarence," dropping her voice and glancing shyly
around the saloon, "you may kiss me just once under my
hat, for good-by." She adroitly slanted her broad-
brimmed hat towards the front of the shop, and in its
shadow advanced her fresh young cheek to Clarence.

Coloring and laughing, the boy pressed his lips to it
twice. Then Susy arose, with the faintest affectation of
a sigh, shook out her skirt, drew on her gloves with the
greatest gravity, and saying, "Don't follow me further
than the door—they're coming now," walked with supercilious dignity past the preoccupied proprietor and waiters
to the entrance. Here she said, with marked civility,
"Good-afternoon, Mr. Brant," and tripped away towards
the hotel. Clarence lingered for a moment to look after
the lithe and elegant little figure, with its shining un-
dulations of hair that fell over the back and shoulders
of her white frock like a golden mantle, and then turned
away in the opposite direction.

He walked home in a state, as it seemed to him, of absurd perplexity. There were many reasons why his encounter with Susy should have been of unmixed pleasure.
She had remembered him of her own free will, and, in

spite of the change in her fortune, had made the first
advances. Her doubts about her future interviews had
affected him but little; still less, I fear, did he think of
the other changes in her character and disposition, for
he was of that age when they added only a piquancy and
fascination to her—as of one who, in spite of her weakness of nature, was still devoted to him! But he was
painfully conscious that this meeting had revived in him
all the fears, vague uneasiness, and sense of wrong that
had haunted his first boyhood, and which he thought he
had buried at El Refugio four years ago. Susy's allusion
to his father and the reiteration of Peyton's skepticism
awoke in his older intellect the first feeling of suspicion
that was compatible with his open nature. Was this recurring reticence and mystery due to any act of his
father's? But, looking back upon it in after-years, he concluded that the incident of that day was a premonition
rather than a recollection.

CHAPTER XI

WHEN he reached the college the Angelus had long
since rung. In the corridor he met one of the Fathers,
who, instead of questioning him, returned his salutation
with a grave gentleness that struck him. He had turned
into Father Sobriente's quiet study with the intention of
reporting himself, when he was disturbed to find him in
consultation with three or four of the faculty, who seemed
to be thrown into some slight confusion by his entrance.
Clarence was about to retire hurriedly when Father
Sobriente, breaking up the council with a significant
glance at the others, called him back. Confused and embarrassed, with a dread of something impending, the boy
tried to avert it by a hurried account of his meeting with
Susy, and his hopes of Father Sobriente's counsel and
assistance. Taking upon himself the idea of suggesting
Susy's escapade, he confessed the fault. The old man
gazed into his frank eyes with a thoughtful, half-com-
passionate smile. "I was just thinking of giving you a

holiday with—with Don Juan Robinson." The unusual substitution of this final title for the habitual "your cousin" struck Clarence uneasily. "But we will speak of that later. Sit down, my son; I am not busy. We shall talk a little. Father Pedro says you are getting on fluently with your translations. That is excellent, my son, excellent."

Clarence's face beamed with relief and pleasure. His vague fears began to dissipate.

"And you translate even from dictation! Good! We have an hour to spare, and you shall give to me a specimen of your skill. Eh? Good! I will walk here and dictate to you in my poor English, and you shall sit there and render it to me in your good Spanish. Eh? So we shall amuse and instruct ourselves."

Clarence smiled. These sporadic moments of instruction and admonition were not unusual to the good Father. He cheerfully seated himself at the Padre's table before a blank sheet of paper, with a pen in his hand. Father Sobriente paced the apartment, with his usual heavy but noiseless tread. To his surprise, the good priest, after an exhaustive pinch of snuff, blew his nose, and began, in his most lugubrious style of pulpit exhortation:—

"It has been written that the sins of the father shall be visited upon the children, and the unthinking and worldly have sought refuge from this law by declaring it harsh and cruel. Miserable and blind! For do we not see that the wicked man, who in the pride of his power and vainglory is willing to risk punishment to *himself*— and believes it to be courage—must pause before the awful mandate that condemns an equal suffering to those he loves, which he cannot withhold or suffer for? In the spectacle of these innocents struggling against disgrace, perhaps disease, poverty, or desertion, what avails his haughty, all-defying spirit? Let us imagine, Clarence."

"Sir?" said the literal Clarence, pausing in his exercise.

"I mean," continued the priest, with a slight cough, "let the thoughtful man picture a father: a desperate, self-willed man, who scorned the laws of God and society

—keeping only faith with a miserable subterfuge he called 'honor,' and relying only on his own courage and his knowledge of human weakness. Imagine him cruel and bloody—a gambler by profession, an outlaw among men, an outcast from the Church; voluntarily abandoning friends and family,—the wife he should have cherished, the son he should have reared and educated—for the gratification of his deadly passions. Yet imagine that man suddenly confronted with the thought of that heritage of shame and disgust which he had brought upon his innocent offspring—to whom he cannot give even his own desperate recklessness to sustain its vicarious suffering. What must be the feelings of a parent—"

"Father Sobriente," said Clarence softly.

To the boy's surprise, scarcely had he spoken when the soft protecting palm of the priest was already upon his shoulder, and the snuffy but kindly upper lip, trembling with some strange emotion, close beside his cheek.

"What is it, Clarence?" he said hurriedly. "Speak, my son, without fear! You would ask—"

"I only wanted to know if 'padre' takes a masculine verb here," replied Clarence naively.

Father Sobriente blew his nose violently. "Truly— though used for either gender, by the context masculine," he responded gravely. "Ah," he added, leaning over Clarence, and scanning his work hastily, "Good, very good! And now, possibly," he continued, passing his hand like a damp sponge over his heated brow, "we shall reverse our exercise. I shall deliver to you in Spanish what you shall render back in English, eh? And—let us consider— we shall make something more familiar and narrative, eh?"

To this Clarence, somewhat bored by these present solemn abstractions, assented gladly, and took up his pen. Father Sobriente, resuming his noiseless pacing, began:

"On the fertile plains of Guadalajara lived a certain caballero, possessed of flocks and lands, and a wife and son. But, being also possessed of a fiery and roving nature, he did not value them as he did perilous adventure, feats of arms, and sanguinary encounters. To

this may be added riotous excesses, gambling and drunk-
enness, which in time decreased his patrimony, even as his
rebellious and quarrelsome spirit had alienated his family
and neighbors. His wife, borne down by shame and sorrow, died while her son was still an infant. In a fit of
equal remorse and recklessness the caballero married
again within the year. But the new wife was of a temper
and bearing as bitter as her consort. Violent quarrels
ensued between them, ending in the husband abandoning
his wife and son, and leaving St. Louis—I should say
Guadalajara—for ever. Joining some adventurers in a
foreign land, under an assumed name, he pursued his
reckless course, until, by one or two acts of outlawry, he
made his return to civilization impossible. The deserted
wife and step-mother of his child coldly accepted the situation, forbidding his name to be spoken again in her
presence, announced that he was dead, and kept the
knowledge of his existence from his own son, whom she
placed under the charge of her sister. But the sister
managed to secretly communicate with the outlawed
father, and, under a pretext, arranged between them, of
sending the boy to another relation, actually dispatched
the innocent child to his unworthy parent. Perhaps
stirred by remorse, the infamous man—"

"Stop!" said Clarence suddenly.

He had thrown down his pen, and was standing erect
and rigid before the Father.

"You are trying to tell me something, Father Sobriente," he said, with an effort. "Speak out, I implore you.
I can stand anything but this mystery. I am no longer a
child. I have a right to know all. This that you are
telling me is no fable—I see it in your face, Father
Sobriente; it is the story of—of—"

"Your father, Clarence!" said the priest, in a trembling
voice.

The boy drew back, with a white face. "My father!"
he repeated. "Living, or dead?"

"Living, when you first left your home," said the old
man hurriedly, seizing Clarence's hand, "for it was he
who in the name of your cousin sent for you. Living—

yes, while you were here, for it was he who for the past three years stood in the shadow of this assumed cousin, Don Juan, and at last sent you to this school. Living, Clarence, yes; but living under a name and reputation that would have blasted you! And now *dead*—dead in Mexico, shot as an insurgent and in a still desperate career! May God have mercy on his soul!"

"Dead!" repeated Clarence, trembling, "only now?"

"The news of the insurrection and his fate came only an hour since," continued the Padre quickly; "his complicity with it and his identity were known only to Don Juan. He would have spared you any knowledge of the truth, even as this dead man would; but I and my brothers thought otherwise. I have broken it to you badly, my son, but forgive me?"

An hysterical laugh broke from Clarence and the priest recoiled before him. "Forgive *you!* What was this man to me?" he said, with boyish vehemence. "He never *loved* me! He deserted me; he made my life a lie. He never sought me, came near me, or stretched a hand to me that I could take?"

"Hush! hush!" said the priest, with a horrified look, laying his huge hand upon the boy's shoulder and bearing him down to his seat. "You know not what you say. Think—think, Clarence! Was there none of all those who have befriended you—who were kind to you in your wanderings—to whom your heart turned unconsciously? Think, Clarence! You yourself have spoken to me of such a one. Let your heart speak again, for his sake—for the sake of the dead."

A gentler light suffused the boy's eyes, and he started. Catching convulsively at his companion's sleeve, he said in an eager, boyish whisper, "There was one, a wicked, desperate man, whom they all feared—Flynn, who brought me from the mines. Yes, I thought that he was my cousin's loyal friend—more than all the rest; and I told him everything—all, that I never told the man I thought my cousin, or anyone, or even you; and I think, I think, Father, I liked him best of all. I thought since it was wrong," he continued, with a trembling smile, "for I was foolishly fond even of the way the others feared him, he that I feared not, and who was so kind to me. Yet he, too, left me without a word, and when I would have followed him—" But the boy broke down, and buried his face in his hands.

"No, no," said Father Sobriente, with eager persistence, "that was his foolish pride to spare you the knowledge of your kinship with one so feared, and part of the blind and mistaken penance he had laid upon himself. For even at that moment of your boyish indignation, he never was so fond of you as then. Yes, my poor boy, this man, to whom God led your wandering feet at Deadman's Gulch; the man who brought you here, and by some secret hold—I know not what—on Don Juan's past, persuaded him to assume to be your relation; this man Flynn, this Jackson Brant the gambler, this Hamilton Brant the outlaw—*was your father!* Ah, yes! Weep on, my son; each tear of love and forgiveness from thee hath vicarious power to wash away his sin."

With a single sweep of his protecting hand he drew Clarence towards his breast, until the boy slowly sank upon his knees at his feet. Then, lifting his eyes towards the ceiling, he said softly in an older tongue, "And *thou,* too, unhappy and perturbed spirit, rest!"

.   .   .   .

It was nearly dawn when the good Padre wiped the last tears from Clarence's clearer eyes. "And now, my son," he said, with a gentle smile, as he rose to his feet, "let us not forget the living. Although your step-mother has, through her own act, no legal claim upon you, far be it from me to indicate your attitude towards her. Enough that *you* are independent." He turned, and, opening a drawer in his secretaire, took out a bank-book, and placed it in the hands of the wondering boy.

"It was *his* wish, Clarence, that even after his death you should never have to prove your kinship to claim your rights. Taking adantage of the boyish deposit you had left with Mr. Carden at the bank, with his connivance and in your name he added to it, month by month and year by year; Mr. Carden cheerfully accepting the trust and management of the fund. The seed thus sown has produced a thousandfold, Clarence, beyond all expectations. You are not only free, my son, but of yourself and in whatever name you choose—your own master."

"I shall keep my father's name," said the boy simply.

"Amen!" said Father Sobriente.

Here closes the chronicle of Clarence Brant's boyhood. How he sustained his name and independence in after years, and who, of those already mentioned in these pages, helped him to make or mar it, may be a matter for future record.

IN THE CARQUINEZ WOODS

IN THE CARQUINEZ WOODS

CHAPTER I.

THE sun was going down on the Carquinez Woods. The few shafts of sunlight that had pierced their pillared gloom were lost in unfathomable depths, or splintered their ineffectual lances on the enormous trunks of the redwoods. For a time the dull red of their vast columns, and the dull red of their cast-off bark which matted the echoless aisles, still seemed to hold a faint glow of the dying day. But even this soon passed. Light and color fled upwards. The dark interlaced tree-tops, that had all day made an impenetrable shade, broke into fire here and there; their lost spires glittered, faded, and went utterly out. A weird twilight that did not come from the outer world, but seemed born of the wood itself, slowly filled and possessed the aisles. The straight, tall, colossal trunks rose dimly like columns of upward smoke. The few fallen trees stretched their huge length into obscurity, and seemed to lie on shadowy trestles. The strange breath that filled these mysterious vaults had neither coldness nor moisture; a dry, fragrant dust arose from the noiseless foot that trod their bark-strewn floor; the aisles might have been tombs, the fallen trees enormous mummies; the silence the solitude of a forgotten past.

And yet this silence was presently broken by a recurring sound like breathing, interrupted occasionally by inarticulate and stertorous gasps. It was not the quick, panting, listening breath of some stealthy feline or canine animal, but indicated a larger, slower, and more powerful organization, whose progress was less watchful and guarded, or as if a fragment of one of the fallen monsters had become animate. At times this life seemed to take visible form, but as vaguely, as misshapenly, as the phantom of a nightmare. Now it was a square object moving sideways, endways, with neither head nor tail and scarcely visible feet; then an arched bulk rolling against the trunks of the trees and recoiling again, or an upright cylindrical mass, but always oscillating and unsteady, and striking the trees on either hand. The frequent occurrence of the movement suggested the figures of some weird rhythmic dance to music heard by the shape alone. Suddenly it either became motionless or faded away.

There was the frightened neighing of a horse, the sudden jingling of spurs, a shout and outcry, and the swift apparition of three dancing torches in one of the dark aisles; but so intense was the obscurity that they shed no light on surrounding objects, and seemed to advance of their own volition without human guidance, until they disappeared suddenly behind the interposing bulk of one of the largest trees. Beyond its eighty feet of circumference the light could not reach, and the gloom remained inscrutable. But the voices and jingling spurs were heard distinctly.

"Blast the mare! She's shied off that cursed trail again."

"Ye ain't lost it again, hev ye?" growled a second voice.

"That's jist what I hev. And these blasted pine-knots don't give light an inch beyond 'em. D——d if I don't think they make this cursed hole blacker."

There was a laugh — a woman's laugh — hysterical, bitter, sarcastic, exasperating. The second speaker, without heeding it, went on:—

"What in thunder skeert the hosses? Did you see or hear anything?"

"Nothin'. The wood is like a graveyard."

The woman's voice again broke into a hoarse, contemptuous laugh. The man resumed angrily:—

"If you know anything, why in h—ll don't you say so,

instead of cackling like a d——d squaw there? P'raps you reckon you ken find the trail too."

"Take this rope off my wrist," said the woman's voice, "untie my hands, let me down, and I'll find it." She spoke quickly and with a Spanish accent.

It was the men's turn to laugh. "And give you a show to snatch that six-shooter and blow a hole through me, as you did to the Sheriff of Calaveras, eh? Not if this court understands itself," said the first speaker dryly.

"Go to the devil, then," she said curtly.

"Not before a lady," responded the other. There was another laugh from the men, the spurs jingled again, the three torches reappeared from behind the tree, and then passed away in the darkness.

For a time silence and immutability possessed the woods; the great trunks loomed upwards, their fallen brothers stretched their slow length into obscurity. The sound of breathing again became audible; the shape reappeared in the aisle, and recommenced its mystic dance. Presently it was lost in the shadow of the largest tree, and to the sound of breathing succeeded a grating and scratching of bark. Suddenly, as if riven by lightning, a flash broke from the center of the tree-trunk, lit up the woods, and a sharp report rang through it. After a pause the jingling of spurs and the dancing of torches were revived from the distance.

"Hallo?"

No answer.

"Who fired that shot?"

But there was no reply. A slight veil of smoke passed away to the right, there was the spice of gunpowder in the air, but nothing more.

The torches came forward again, but this time it could be seen they were held in the hands of two men and a woman. The woman's hands were tied at the wrist to the horse-hair reins of her mule, while a *riata*, passed around her waist and under the mule's girth, was held by one of the men, who were both armed with rifles and revolvers. Their frightened horses curveted, and it was with difficulty they could be made to advance.

"Ho! stranger, what are you shooting at?"

The woman laughed and shrugged her shoulders. "Look yonder at the roots of the tree. You're a d——d smart man for a sheriff, ain't you?"

The man uttered an exclamation and spurred his horse forward, but the animal reared in terror. He then sprang to the ground and approached the tree. The shape lay there, a scarcely distinguishable bulk.

"A grizzly, by the living Jingo! Shot through the heart."

It was true. The strange shape lit up by the flaring torches seemed more vague, unearthly, and awkward in its dying throes, yet the small shut eyes, the feeble nose, the ponderous shoulders, and half-human foot armed with powerful claws were unmistakable. The men turned by a common impulse and peered into the remote recesses of the wood again.

"Hi, Mister! come and pick up your game. Hallo there!"

The challenge fell unheeded on the empty woods.

"And yet," said he whom the woman had called the sheriff, "he can't be far off. It was a close shot, and the bear hez dropped in his tracks. Why, wot's this sticking in his claws?"

The two men bent over the animal. "Why, it's sugar, brown sugar—look!" There was no mistake. The huge beast's fore paws and muzzle were streaked with the unromantic household provision, and heightened the absurd contrast of its incongruous members. The woman, apparently indifferent, had taken that opportunity to partly free one of her wrists.

"If we hadn't been cavorting round this yer spot for the last half hour, I'd swear there was a shanty not a hundred yards away," said the sheriff.

The other man, without replying, remounted his horse instantly.

"If there is, and it's inhabited by a gentleman that kin make centre shots like that in the dark, and don't care to explain how, I reckon I won't disturb him."

The sheriff was apparently of the same opinion, for he

followed his companion's example, and once more led the way. The spurs tinkled, the torches danced, and the cavalcade slowly reëntered the gloom. In another moment it had disappeared.

The wood sank again into repose, this time disturbed by neither shape nor sound. What lower forms of life might have crept close to its roots were hidden in the ferns, or passed with deadened tread over the bark-strewn floor. Towards morning a coolness like dew fell from above, with here and there a dropping twig or nut, or the crepitant awakening and stretching-out of cramped and weary branches. Later a dull, lurid dawn, not unlike the last evening's sunset, filled the aisles. This faded again, and a clear gray light, in which every object stood out in sharp distinctness, took its place. Morning was waiting outside in all its brilliant, youthful coloring, but only entered as the matured and sobered day.

Seen in that stronger light, the monstrous tree near which the dead bear lay revealed its age in its denuded and scarred trunk, and showed in its base a deep cavity, a foot or two from the ground, partly hidden by hanging strips of bark which had fallen across it. Suddenly one of these strips was pushed aside, and a young man leaped lightly down.

But for the rifle he carried and some modern peculiarities of dress, he was of a grace so unusual and unconventional that he might have passed for a faun who was quitting his ancestral home. He stepped to the side of the bear with a light elastic movement that was as unlike customary progression as his face and figure were unlike the ordinary types of humanity. Even as he leaned upon his rifle, looking down at the prostrate animal, he unconsciously fell into an attitude that in any other mortal would have been a pose, but with him was the picturesque and unstudied relaxation of perfect symmetry.

"Hallo, Mister!"

He raised his head so carelessly and listlessly that he did not otherwise change his attitude. Stepping from behind the tree, the woman of the preceding night stood before him. Her hands were free except for a thong of

the *riata,* which was still knotted around one wrist, the
end of the thong having been torn or burnt away. Her
eyes were bloodshot, and her hair hung over her
shoulders in one long black braid.

"I reckoned all along it was *you* who shot the bear,"
she said; "at least some one hiding yer," and she indicated the hollow tree with her hand. "It wasn't no chance
shot." Observing that the young man, either from mis-
conception or indifference, did not seem to comprehend
her, she added, "We came by here, last night, a minute
after you fired."

"Oh, that was *you* kicked up such a row, was it?" said
the young man, with a shade of interest.

"I reckon," said the woman, nodding her head, "and
them that was with me."

"And who are they?"

"Sheriff Dunn, of Yolo, and his deputy."

"And where are they now?"

"The deputy—in h—ll, I reckon; I don't know about
the sheriff."

"I see," said the young man quietly; "and you?"

"I—got away," she said savagely. But she was taken
with a sudden nervous shiver, which she at once repressed
by tightly dragging her shawl over her shoulders and
elbows, and folding her arms defiantly.

"And you're going?"

"To follow the deputy, may be," she said gloomily.
"But come, I say, ain't you going to treat? It's cursed
cold here."

"Wait a moment." The young man was looking at her,
with his arched brows slightly knit and a half smile of
curiosity. "Ain't you Teresa?"

She was prepared for the question, but evidently was
not certain whether she would reply defiantly or confidently. After an exhaustive scrutiny of his face she
chose the latter, and said, "You can bet your life on it,
Johnny."

"I don't bet, and my name isn't Johnny. Then you're
the woman who stabbed Dick Curson over at Lagrange's?"

She became defiant again.

"That's me, all the time. What are you going to do about it?"

"Nothing. And you used to dance at the Alhambra?"

She whisked the shawl from her shoulders, held it up like a scarf, and made one or two steps of the *sembicuacua*. There was not the least gayety, recklessness, or spontaneity in the action; it was simply mechanical bravado. It was so ineffective, even upon her own feelings, that her arms presently dropped to her side, and she coughed embarrassedly. "Where's that whiskey, pardner?" she asked.

The young man turned toward the tree he had just quitted, and without further words assisted her to mount to the cavity. It was an irregular-shaped vaulted chamber, pierced fifty feet above by a shaft or cylindrical opening in the decayed trunk, which was blackened by smoke, as if it had served the purpose of a chimney. In one corner lay a bearskin and blanket; at the side were two alcoves or indentations, one of which was evidently used as a table, and the other as a cupboard. In another hollow, near the entrance, lay a few small sacks of flour, coffee, and sugar, the sticky contents of the latter still strewing the floor. From this storehouse the young man drew a wicker flask of whiskey, and handed it, with a tin cup of water, to the woman. She waved the cup aside, placed the flask to her lips, and drank the undiluted spirit. Yet even this was evidently bravado, for the water started to her eyes, and she could not restrain the paroxysm of coughing that followed.

"I reckon that's the kind that kills at forty rods," she said, with a hysterical laugh. "But I say, pardner, you look as if you were fixed here to stay," and she stared ostentatiously around the chamber. But she had already taken in its minutest details, even to observing that the hanging strips of bark could be disposed so as to completely hide the entrance.

"Well, yes," he replied; "it wouldn't be very easy to pull up the stakes and move the shanty further on."

Seeing that either from indifference or caution he had

not accepted her meaning, she looked at him fixedly, and said,—

"What is your little game?"

"Eh?"

"What are you hiding for—here, in this tree?"

"But I'm not hiding."

"Then why didn't you come out when they hailed you last night?"

"Because I didn't care to."

Teresa whistled incredulously. "All right—then if you're not hiding, I'm going to." As he did not reply, she went on: "If I can keep out of sight for a couple of weeks, this thing will blow over here, and I can get across into Yolo. I could get a fair show there, where the boys know me. Just now the trails are all watched, but no one would think of lookin' here."

"Then how did you come to think of it?" he asked carelessly.

"Because I knew that bear hadn't gone far for that sugar; because I know he hadn't stole it from a *cache*— it was too fresh, and we'd have seen the torn-up earth; because we had passed no camp; and because I knew there was no shanty here. And, besides," she added in a low voice, "maybe I was huntin' a hole myself to die in— and spotted it by instinct."

There was something in this suggestion of a hunted animal that, unlike anything she had previously said or suggested, was not exaggerated, and caused the young man to look at her again. She was standing under the chimney-like opening, and the light from above illuminated her head and shoulders. The pupils of her eyes had lost their feverish prominence, and were slightly suffused and softened as she gazed abstractedly before her. The only vestige of her previous excitement was in her left-hand fingers, which were incessantly twisting and turning a diamond ring upon her right hand, but without imparting the least animation to her rigid attitude. Suddenly, as if conscious of his scrutiny, she stepped aside out of the revealing light and by a swift feminine instinct raised her hand to her head as if to adjust her straggling hair. It was only for a moment, however, for, as if aware of the weakness, she struggled to resume her aggressive pose.

"Well," she said. "Speak up. Am I goin' to stop here, or have I got to get up and get?"

"You can stay," said the young man quietly; "but as I've got my provisions and ammunition here, and haven't any other place to go to just now, I suppose we'll have to share it together."

She glanced at him under her eyelids, and a half-bitter, half-contemptuous smile passed across her face. "All right, old man," she said, holding out her hand, "it's a go. We'll start in housekeeping at once, if you like."

"I'll have to come here once or twice a day," he said, quite composedly, "to look after my things, and get something to eat; but I'll be away most of the time, and what with camping out under the trees every night I reckon my share won't incommode you."

She opened her black eyes upon him, at this original proposition. Then she looked down at her torn dress. "I suppose this style of thing ain't very fancy, is it?" she said, with a forced laugh.

"I think I know where to beg or borrow a change for you, if you can't get any," he replied simply.

She stared at him again. "Are you a family man?"

"No."

She was silent for a moment. "Well," she said, "you can tell your girl I'm not particular about its being in the latest fashion."

There was a slight flush on his forehead as he turned toward the little cupboard, but no tremor in his voice as he went on: "You'll find tea and coffee here, and, if you're bored, there's a book or two. You read, don't you—I mean English?"

She nodded, but cast a look of undisguised contempt upon the two worn, coverless novels he held out to her. "You haven't got last week's 'Sacramento Union,' have you? I hear they have my case all in; only them lying reporters made it out against me all the time."

"I don't see the papers," he replied curtly.

"They say there's a picture of me in the 'Police Ga-zette,' taken in the act," and she laughed.

He looked a little abstracted, and turned as if to go. "I think you'll do well to rest a while just now, and keep as close hid as possible until afternoon. The trail is a mile away at the nearest point, but some one might miss it and stray over here. You're quite safe if you're care-ful, and stand by the tree. You can build a fire here," he stepped under the chimney-like opening, "without its being noticed. Even the smoke is lost and cannot be seen so high."

The light from above was falling on his head and shoulders, as it had on hers. She looked at him intently.

"You travel a good deal on your figure, pardner, don't you?" she said, with a certain admiration that was quite sexless in its quality; "but I don't see how you pick up a living by it in the Carquinez Woods. So you're going, are you? You might be more sociable. Good-by."

"Good-by!" He leaped from the opening.

"I say pardner!"

He turned a little impatiently. She had knelt down at the entrance, so as to be nearer his level, and was holding out her hand. But he did not notice it, and she quietly withdrew it.

"If anybody dropped in and asked for you, what name will they say?"

He smiled. "Don't wait to hear."

"But suppose *I* wanted to sing out for you, what will I call you?"

He hesitated. "Call me—Lo."

"Lo, the poor Indian?"[1]

"Exactly."

It suddenly occurred to the woman, Teresa, that in the young man's height, supple, yet erect carriage, color, and singular gravity of demeanor there was a refined, aborigi-nal suggestion. He did not look like any Indian she had ever seen, but rather as a youthful chief might have looked. There was a further suggestion in his fringed

[1] The first word of Pope's familiar apostrophe is humorously used in the Far West as a distinguishing title for the Indian.

buckskin shirt and moccasins; but before she could utter the half-sarcastic comment that rose to her lips he had glided noiselessly away, even as an Indian might have done.

She readjusted the slips of hanging bark with feminine ingenuity, dispersing them so as to completely hide the entrance. Yet this did not darken the chamber, which seemed to draw a purer and more vigorous light through the soaring shaft that pierced the roof than that which came from the dim woodland aisles below. Nevertheless, she shivered, and drawing her shawl closely around her began to collect some half-burnt fragments of wood in the chimney to make a fire. But the preoccupation of her thoughts rendered this a tedious process, as she would from time to time stop in the middle of an action and fall into an attitude of rapt abstraction, with far-off eyes and rigid mouth. When she had at last succeeded in kindling a fire and raising a film of pale blue smoke, that seemed to fade and dissipate entirely before it reached the top of the chimney shaft, she crouched beside it, fixed her eyes on the darkest corner of the cavern, and became motionless.

What did she see through that shadow?

Nothing at first but a confused medley of figures and incidents of the preceding night; things to be put away and forgotten; things that would not have happened but for another thing—the thing before which everything faded! A ball-room; the sounds of music; the one man she had cared for insulting her with the flaunting ostentation of his unfaithfulness; herself despised, put aside, laughed at, or worse, jilted. And then the moment of delirium, when the light danced; the one wild act that lifted her, the despised one, above them all—made her the supreme figure, to be glanced at by frightened women, stared at by half-startled, half-admiring men! "Yes," she laughed; but struck by the sound of her own voice, moved twice round the cavern nervously, and then dropped again into her old position.

As they carried him away he had laughed at her—like a hound that he was; he who had praised her for her

spirit, and incited her revenge against others; he who
had taught her to strike when she was insulted; and it
was only fit he should reap what he had sown. She was
what he, what other men, had made her. And what was
she now? What had she been once?

She tried to recall her childhood: the man and woman
who might have been her father and mother; who fought
and wrangled over her precocious little life; abused or
caressed her as she sided with either; and then left her
with a circus troupe, where she first tasted the power of
her courage, her beauty, and her recklessness. She remembered those flashes of triumph that left a fever in
her veins—a fever that when it failed must be stimulated
by dissipation, by anything, by everything that would
keep her name a wonder in men's mouths, an envious fear
to women. She recalled her transfer to the strolling
players; her cheap pleasures, and cheaper rivalries and
hatred—but always Teresa! the daring Teresa! the reckless Teresa! audacious as a woman, invincible as a boy;
dancing, flirting, fencing, shooting, swearing, drinking,
smoking, fighting Teresa! "Oh, yes; she had been loved,
perhaps—who knows?—but always feared. Why should
she change now? Ha, he should see."

She had lashed herself in a frenzy, as was her wont,
with gestures, ejaculations, oaths, adjurations, and passionate apostrophes, but with this strange and unexpected
result. Heretofore she had always been sustained and
kept up by an audience of some kind or quality, if only
perhaps a humble companion; there had always been
some one she could fascinate or horrify, and she could
read her power mirrored in their eyes. Even the half-
abstracted indifference of her strange host had been something. But she was alone now. Her words fell on apa-
thetic solitude; she was acting to viewless space. She
rushed to the opening, dashed the hanging bark aside,
and leaped to the ground.

She ran forward wildly a few steps, and stopped.

"Hallo!" she cried. "Look, 'tis I, Teresa!"

The profound silence remained unbroken. Her shrillest
tones were lost in an echoless space, even as the smoke

of her fire had faded into pure ether. She stretched out her clenched fists as if to defy the pillared austerities of the vaults around her.

"Come and take me if you dare!"

The challenge was unheeded. If she had thrown herself violently against the nearest tree-trunk, she could not have been stricken more breathless than she was by the compact, embattled solitude that encompassed her. The hopelessness of impressing these cold and passive vaults with her selfish passion filled her with a vague fear. In her rage of the previous night she had not seen the wood in its profound immobility. Left alone with the majesty of those enormous columns, she trembled and turned faint. The silence of the hollow tree she had just quitted seemed to her less awful than the crushing presence of these mute and monstrous witnesses of her weakness. Like a wounded quail with lowered crest and trailing wing, she crept back to her hiding place.

Even then the influence of the wood was still upon her. She picked up the novel she had contemptuously thrown aside, only to let it fall again in utter weariness. For a moment her feminine curiosity was excited by the discovery of an old book, in whose blank leaves were pressed a variety of flowers and woodland grasses. As she could not conceive that these had been kept for any but a sentimental purpose, she was disappointed to find that underneath each was a sentence in an unknown tongue, that even to her untutored eye did not appear to be the language of passion. Finally she rearranged the couch of skins and blankets, and, imparting to it in three clever shakes an entirely different character, lay down to pursue her reveries. But nature asserted herself, and ere she knew it she was asleep.

So intense and prolonged had been her previous excitement that, the tension once relieved, she passed into a slumber of exhaustion so deep that she seemed scarce to breathe. High noon succeeded morning, the central shaft received a single ray of upper sunlight, the afternoon came and went, the shadows gathered below, the sunset fires began to eat their way through the groined roof, and she still slept. She slept even when the bark hangings of the chamber were put aside, and the young man reëntered.

He laid down a bundle he was carrying and softly approached the sleeper. For a moment he was startled from his indifference; she lay so still and motionless. But this was not all that struck him; the face before him was no longer the passionate, haggard visage that confronted him that morning; the feverish air, the burning color, the strained muscles of mouth and brow, and the staring eyes were gone; wiped away, perhaps, by the tears that still left their traces on cheek and dark eyelash. It was the face of a handsome woman of thirty, with even a suggestion of softness in the contour of the cheek and arching of her upper lip, no longer rigidly drawn down in anger, but relaxed by sleep on her white teeth.

With the lithe, soft tread that was habitual to him, the young man moved about, examining the condition of the little chamber and its stock of provisions and necessaries, and withdrew presently, to reappear as noiselessly with a tin bucket of water. This done, he replenished the little pile of fuel with an armful of bark and pine cones, cast an approving glance about him, which included the sleeper, and silently departed.

It was night when she awoke. She was surrounded by a profound darkness, except where the shaft-like opening made a nebulous mist in the corner of her wooden cavern. Providentially she struggled back to consciousness slowly, so that the solitude and silence came upon her gradually, with a growing realization of the events of the past twenty-four hours, but without a shock. She was alone here, but safe still, and every hour added to her chances of ultimate escape. She remembered to have seen a candle among the articles on the shelf, and she began to grope her way towards the matches. Suddenly she stopped. What was that panting?

Was it her own breathing, quickened with a sudden nameless terror? or was there something outside? Her heart seemed to stop beating while she listened. Yes! it was a panting outside—a panting now increased, multi-

plied, redoubled, mixed with the sounds of rustling, tearing, craunching, and occasionally a quick, impatient snarl.
She crept on her hands and knees to the opening and
looked out. At first the ground seemed to be undulating
between her and the opposite tree. But a second glance
showed her the black and gray, bristling, tossing backs
of tumbling beasts of prey, charging the carcass of the
bear that lay at its roots, or contesting for the prize with
gluttonous, choked breath, sidelong snarls, arched spines,
and recurved tails. One of the boldest had leaped upon
a buttressing root of her tree within a foot of the opening. The excitement, awe, and terror she had undergone
culminated in one wild, maddened scream, that seemed to
pierce even the cold depths of the forest, as she dropped
on her face, with her hands clasped over her eyes in an
agony of fear.

Her scream was answered, after a pause, by a sudden
volley of firebrands and sparks into the midst of the
panting, crowding pack; a few smothered howls and
snaps, and a sudden dispersion of the concourse. In
another moment the young man, with a blazing brand
in either hand, leaped upon the body of the bear.

Teresa raised her head, uttered a hysterical cry, slid
down the tree, flew wildly to his side, caught convulsively
at his sleeve, and fell on her knees beside him.

"Save me! save me!" she gasped, in a voice broken by
terror. "Save me from those hideous creatures. No,
no!" she implored, as he endeavored to lift her to her
feet. "No—let me stay here close beside you. So,"
clutching the fringe of his leather hunting-shirt, and
dragging herself on her knees nearer him—"so—don't
leave me, for God's sake!"

"They are gone," he replied, gazing down curiously at
her, as she wound the fringe around her hand to
strengthen her hold; "they're only a lot of cowardly
coyotes and wolves, that dare not attack anything that
lives and can move."

The young woman responded with a nervous shudder.
"Yes, that's it," she whispered, in a broken voice; "it's
only the dead they want. Promise me—swear to me, if

I'm caught, or hung, or shot, you won't let me be left here to be torn and—ah! my God! what's that?"

She had thrown her arms around his knees, completely pinioning him to her frantic breast. Something like a smile of disdain passed across his face as he answered, "It's nothing. They will not return. Get up!"

Even in her terror she saw the change in his face. "I know, I know!" she cried. "I'm frightened—but I cannot bear it any longer. Hear me! Listen! Listen—but don't move! I didn't mean to kill Curson—no! I swear to God, no! I didn't mean to kill the sheriff—and I didn't. I was only bragging—do you hear? I lied! I lied—don't move, I swear to God I lied. I've made myself out worse than I was. I have. Only don't leave me now—and if I die—and it's not far off, may be—get me away from here—and from *them*. Swear it!"

"All right," said the young man, with a scarcely concealed movement of irritation. "But get up now, and go back to the cabin."

"No; not *there* alone." Nevertheless, he quietly but firmly released himself.

"I will stay here," he replied. "I would have been nearer to you, but I thought it better for your safety that my camp-fire should be further off. But I can build it here, and that will keep the coyotes off."

"Let me stay with you—beside you," she said imploringly.

She looked so broken, crushed, and spiritless, so unlike the woman of the morning that, albeit with an ill grace, he tacitly consented, and turned away to bring his blankets. But in the next moment she was at his side, following him like a dog, silent and wistful, and even offering to carry his burden. When he had built the fire, for which she had collected the pine-cones and broken branches near them, he sat down, folded his arms, and leaned back against the tree in reserved and deliberate silence.

Humble and submissive, she did not attempt to break in upon a reverie she could not help but feel had little kindliness to herself. As the fire snapped and sparkled, she pillowed her head upon a root, and lay still to watch it.

It rose and fell, and dying away at times to a mere lurid glow, and again, agitated by some breath scarcely perceptible to them, quickening into a roaring flame. When only the embers remained, a dead silence filled the wood. Then the first breath of morning moved the tangled canopy above, and a dozen tiny sprays and needles detached from the interlocked boughs winged their soft way noiselessly to the earth. A few fell upon the prostrate woman like a gentle benediction, and she slept. But even then, the young man, looking down, saw that the slender fingers were still aimlessly but rigidly twisted in the leather fringe of his hunting-shirt.

CHAPTER II.

IT was a peculiarity of the Carquinez Wood that it stood apart and distinct in its gigantic individuality. Even where the integrity of its own singular species was not entirely preserved, it admitted no inferior trees. Nor was there any diminishing fringe on its outskirts; the sentinels that guarded the few gateways of the dim trails were as monstrous as the serried ranks drawn up in the heart of the forest. Consequently, the red highway that skirted the eastern angle was bare and shadeless, until it slipped a league off into a watered valley and refreshed itself under lesser sycamores and willows. It was here the newly born city of Excelsior, still in its cradle, had, like an infant Hercules, strangled the serpentine North Fork of the American river, and turned its life current into the ditches and flumes of the Excelsior mines.

Newest of the new houses that seemed to have accidentally formed its single, straggling street was the residence of the Rev. Winslow Wynn, not unfrequently known as "Father Wynn," pastor of the First Baptist church. The "pastorage," as it was cheerfully called, had the glaring distinction of being built of brick, and was, as had been wickedly pointed out by idle scoffers, the only "fireproof" structure in town. This sarcasm was not, however, supposed to be particularly distasteful to "Father Wynn," who enjoyed the reputation of being "hail fellow, well met" with the rough mining element, who called them by their Christian names, had been known to drink at the bar of the Polka Saloon while engaged in the conversion of a prominent citizen, and was popularly said to have no "gospel starch" about him. Certain conscious outcasts and transgressors were touched at this apparent unbending of the spiritual authority. The rigid tenets of Father Wynn's faith were lost in the supposed catholicity of his humanity. "A preacher that can jine a man when he's histin' liquor into him, without jawin' about it, ought to be allowed to wrestle with sinners and splash about in as much cold water as he likes," was the criticism of one of his converts. Nevertheless, it was true that Father Wynn was somewhat loud and intolerant in his tolerance. It was true that he was a little more rough, a little more frank, a little more hearty, a little more impulsive than his disciples. It was true that often the proclamation of his extreme liberality and brotherly equality partook somewhat of an apology. It is true that a few who might have been most benefited by this kind of gospel regarded him with a singular disdain. It is true that his liberality was of an ornamental, insinuating quality, accompanied with but little sacrifice; his acceptance of a collection taken up in a gambling saloon for the rebuilding of his church, destroyed by fire, gave him a popularity large enough, it must be confessed, to cover the sins of the gamblers themselves, but it was not proven that *he* had ever organized any form of relief. But it was true that local history somehow accepted him as an exponent of mining Christianity, without the least reference to the opinions of the Christian miners themselves.

The Rev. Mr. Wynn's liberal habits and opinions were not, however, shared by his only daughter, a motherless young lady of eighteen. Nellie Wynn was in the eye of Excelsior an unapproachable divinity, as inaccessible and cold as her father was impulsive and familiar. An atmos-

phere of chaste and proud virginity made itself felt even
in the starched integrity of her spotless skirts, in her
neatly gloved finger-tips, in her clear amber eyes, in her
imperious red lips, in her sensitive nostrils. Need it be
said that the youth and middle age of Excelsior were
madly, because apparently hopelessly, in love with her?
For the rest, she had been expensively educated, was profoundly ignorant in two languages, with a trained misun-
derstanding of music and painting, and a natural and
faultless taste in dress.

The Rev. Mr. Wynn was engaged in a characteristic
hearty parting with one of his latest converts, upon his
own doorstep, with admirable *al fresco* effect. He had
just clapped him on the shoulder. "Good-by, good-by,
Charley, my boy, and keep in the right path; not up, or
down, or round the gulch, you know—ha, ha!—but
straight across lots to the shining gate." He had raised
his voice under the stimulus of a few admiring spectators,
and backed his convert playfully against the wall. "You
see! we're goin' in to win, you bet. Good-by! I'd ask
you to step in and have a chat, but I've got my work to
do, and so have you. The gospel mustn't keep us from
that, must it, Charley? Ha, ha!"

The convert (who elsewhere was a profane expressman, and had become quite imbecile under Mr. Wynn's
active heartiness and brotherly horse-play before spectators) managed, however, to feebly stammer with a blush
something about "Miss Nellie."

"Ah, Nellie. She, too, is at her tasks—trimming her
lamp—you know, the parable of the wise virgins," continued Father Wynn hastily, fearing that the convert
might take the illustration literally. "There, there —
good-by. Keep in the right path." And with a parting
shove he dismissed Charley and entered his own house.

That "wise virgin," Nellie, had evidently finished with
the lamp, and was now going out to meet the bridegroom,
as she was fully dressed and gloved, and had a pink
parasol in her hand, as her father entered the sitting-
room. His bluff heartiness seemed to fade away as he
removed his soft, broad-brimmed hat and glanced across

the too fresh-looking apartment. There was a smell of mortar still in the air, and a faint suggestion that at any moment green grass might appear between the interstices of the red-brick hearth. The room, yielding a little in the point of coldness, seemed to share Miss Nellie's fresh virginity, and, barring the pink parasol, set her off as in a vestal's cell.

"I supposed you wouldn't care to see Brace, the expressman, so I got rid of him at the door," said her father, drawing one of the new chairs towards him slowly, and sitting down carefully, as if it were a hitherto untried experiment.

Miss Nellie's face took a tint of interest. "Then he doesn't go with the coach to Indian Spring to-day?"

"No; why?"

"I thought of going over myself to get the Burnham girls to come to choir-meeting," replied Miss Nellie carelessly, "and he might have been company."

"He'd go now, if he knew you were going," said her father; "but it's just as well he shouldn't be needlessly encouraged. I rather think that Sheriff Dunn is a little jealous of him. By the way, the sheriff is much better. I called to cheer him up to-day" (Mr. Wynn had in fact tumultuously accelerated the sick man's pulse), "and he talked of you, as usual. In fact, he said he had only two things to get well for. One was to catch and hang that woman Teresa, who shot him; the other—can't you guess the other?" he added archly, with a faint suggestion of his other manner.

Miss Nellie coldly could not.

The Rev. Mr. Wynn's archness vanished. "Don't be a fool," he said dryly. "He wants to marry you, and you know it."

"Most of the men here do," responded Miss Nellie, without the least trace of coquetry. "Is the wedding or the hanging to take place first, or together, so he can officiate at both?"

"His share in the Union Ditch is worth a hundred thousand dollars," continued her father; "and if he isn't nominated for district judge this fall, he's bound to go to the legislature, anyway. I don't think a girl with your advantages and education can afford to throw away the chance of shining in Sacramento, San Francisco, or, in good time, perhaps even Washington."

Miss Nellie's eyes did not reflect entire disapproval of this suggestion, although she replied with something of her father's practical quality.

"Mr. Dunn is not out of his bed yet, and they say Teresa's got away to Arizona, so there isn't any particular hurry."

"Perhaps not; but see here, Nellie, I've some important news for you. You know your young friend of the Carquinez Woods — Dorman, the botanist, eh? Well, Brace knows all about him. And what do you think he is?"

Miss Nellie took upon herself a few extra degrees of cold, and didn't know.

"An Injin! Yes, an out-and-out Cherokee. You see he calls himself Dorman—Low Dorman. That's only French for 'Sleeping Water,' his Injin name!—'Low Dorman.'"

"You mean 'L'Eau Dormante,'" said Nellie.

"That's what I said. The chief called him 'Sleeping Water' when he was a boy, and one of them French Canadian trappers translated it into French when he brought him to California to school. But he's an Injin, sure. No wonder he prefers to live in the woods."

"Well?" said Nellie.

"Well," echoed her father impatiently, "he's an Injin, I tell you, and you can't of course have anything to do with him. He mustn't come here again."

"But you forget," said Nellie imperturbably, "that it was you who invited him here, and were so much exercised over him. You remember you introduced him to the Bishop and those Eastern clergymen as a magnificent specimen of a young Californian. You forget what an occasion you made of his coming to church on Sunday, and how you made him come in his buckskin shirt and walk down the street with you after service!"

"Yes, yes," said the Rev. Mr. Wynn, hurriedly.

"And," continued Nellie carelessly, "how you made us sing out of the same book 'Children of our Father's Fold,' and how you preached at him until he actually got a color!"

"Yes," said her father; "but it wasn't known then he was an Injin, and they are frightfully unpopular with those Southwestern men among whom we labor. Indeed, I am quite convinced that when Brace said 'the only good Indian was a dead one' his expression, though extravagant, perhaps, really voiced the sentiments of the majority. It would be only kindness to the unfortunate creature to warn him from exposing himself to their rude but conscientious antagonism."

"Perhaps you'd better tell him, then, in your own popular way, which they all seem to understand so well," responded the daughter. Mr. Wynn cast a quick glance at her, but there was no trace of irony in her face—nothing but a half-bored indifference as she walked toward the window.

"I will go with you to the coach-office," said her father, who generally gave these simple paternal duties the pronounced character of a public Christian example.

"It's hardly worth while," replied Miss Nellie. "I've to stop at the Watsons', at the foot of the hill, and ask after the baby; so I shall go on to the Crossing and pick up the coach when it passes. Good-by."

Nevertheless, as soon as Nellie had departed, the Rev. Mr. Wynn proceeded to the coach-office, and publicly grasping the hand of Yuba Bill, the driver, commended his daughter to his care in the name of the universal brotherhood of man and the Christian fraternity. Carried away by his heartiness, he forgot his previous caution, and confided to the expressman Miss Nellie's regrets that she was not to have that gentleman's company. The result was that Miss Nellie found the coach with its passengers awaiting her with uplifted hats and wreathed smiles at the Crossing, and the box seat (from which an unfortunate stranger, who had expensively paid for it, had been summarily ejected) at her service beside Yuba Bill, who had thrown away his cigar and donned a new pair

of buckskin gloves to do her honor.   But a more serious
result to the young beauty was the effect of the Rev.
Mr. Wynn's confidences upon the impulsive heart of Jack
Brace, the expressman.   It has been already intimated
that it was his "day off."   Unable to summarily reassume
his usual functions beside the driver without some practical reason, and ashamed to go so palpably as a mere
passenger, he was forced to let the coach proceed without
him.   Discomfited for the moment, he was not, however,
beaten.   He had lost the blissful journey by her side,
which would have been his professional right, but—she
was going to Indian Spring! could he not anticipate her
there?   Might they not meet in the most accidental manner?   And what might not come from that meeting away
from the prying eyes of their own town?   Mr. Brace did
not hesitate, but saddling his fleet Buckskin, by the time
the stage-coach had passed the Crossing in the high-road
he had mounted the hill and was dashing along the "cut-
off" in the same direction, a full mile in advance.   Arriving at Indian Spring, he left his horse at a Mexican
posada on the confines of the settlement, and from the
piled *débris* of a tunnel excavation awaited the slow
arrival of the coach.   On mature reflection he could give
no reason why he had not boldly awaited it at the express
office, except a certain bashful consciousness of his own
folly, and a belief that it might be glaringly apparent to
the bystanders.   When the coach arrived and he had overcome this consciousness, it was too late.   Yuba Bill had
discharged his passengers for Indian Spring and driven
away.   Miss Nellie was in the settlement, but where?   As
time passed he became more desperate and bolder.   He
walked recklessly up and down the main street, glancing
in at the open doors of shops, and even in the windows
of private dwellings.   It might have seemed a poor compliment to Miss Nellie, but it was an evidence of his
complete preoccupation, when the sight of a female face
at a window, even though it was plain or perhaps painted,
caused his heart to bound, or the glancing of a skirt in the
distance quickened his feet and his pulses.   Had Jack
contented himself with remaining at Excelsior he might

have vaguely regretted, but as soon become as vaguely accustomed to, Miss Nellie's absence. But it was not until his hitherto quiet and passive love took this first step of action that it fully declared itself. When he had made the tour of the town a dozen times unsuccessfully, he had perfectly made up his mind that marriage with Nellie or the speedy death of several people, including possibly himself, was the only alternative. He regretted he had not accompanied her; he regretted he had not demanded where she was going; he contemplated a course of future action that two hours ago would have filled him with bashful terror. There was clearly but one thing to do—to declare his passion the instant he met her, and return with her to Excelsior an accepted suitor, or not to return at all.

Suddenly he was vexatiously conscious of hearing his name lazily called, and looking up found that he was on the outskirts of the town, and interrogated by two horsemen.

"Got down to walk, and the coach got away from you, Jack, eh?"

A little ashamed of his preoccupation, Brace stammered something about "collections." He did not recognize the men, but his own face, name, and business were familiar to everybody for fifty miles along the stage-road.

"Well, you can settle a bet for us, I reckon. Bill Dacre thar bet me five dollars and the drinks that a young gal we met at the edge of the Carquinez Woods, dressed in a long brown duster and half muffled up in a hood, was the daughter of Father Wynn of Excelsior. I did not get a fair look at her, but it stands to reason that a high-toned young lady like Nellie Wynn don't go trap'sing along the wood like a Pike County tramp. I took the bet. May be you know if she's here or in Excelsior?"

Mr. Brace felt himself turning pale with eagerness and excitement. But the near prospect of seeing her presently gave him back his caution, and he answered truthfully that he had left her in Excelsior, and that in his two hours' sojourn in Indian Spring he had not met her once. "But," he added, with a Californian's reverence for the sanctity of a bet, "I reckon you'd better make it a stand-off for twenty-four hours, and I'll find out and let you know." Which, it is only fair to say, he honestly intended to do.

With a hurried nod of parting, he continued in the direction of the Woods. When he had satisfied himself that the strangers had entered the settlement, and would not follow him for further explanation, he quickened his pace. In half an hour he passed between two of the gigantic sentinels that guarded the entrance to a trail. Here he paused to collect his thoughts. The Woods were vast in extent, the trail dim and uncertain—at times apparently breaking off, or intersecting another trail as faint as itself. Believing that Miss Nellie had diverged from the highway only as a momentary excursion into the shade, and that she would not dare to penetrate its more sombre and unknown recesses, he kept within sight of the skirting plain. By degrees the sedate influence of the silent vaults seemed to depress him. The ardor of the chase began to flag. Under the calm of their dim roof the fever of his veins began to subside; his pace slackened; he reasoned more deliberately. It was by no means probable that the young woman in a brown duster was Nellie; it was not her habitual traveling dress; it was not like her to walk unattended in the road; there was nothing in her tastes and habits to take her into this gloomy forest, allowing that she had even entered it; and on this absolute question of her identity the two witnesses were divided. He stopped irresolutely, and cast a last, long, half-despairing look around him. Hitherto he had given that part of the wood nearest the plain his greatest attention. His glance now sought its darker recesses. Suddenly he became breathless. Was it a beam of sunlight that had pierced the groined roof above, and now rested against the trunk of one of the dimmer, more secluded giants? No, it was moving; even as he gazed it slipped away, glanced against another tree, passed across one of the vaulted aisles, and then was lost again. Brief as was the glimpse, he was not mistaken— it was the figure of a woman.

In another moment he was on her track, and soon had

10

the satisfaction of seeing her reappear at a lesser distance.
But the continual intervention of the massive trunks
made the chase by no means an easy one, and as he could
not keep her always in sight he was unable to follow or
understand the one intelligent direction which she seemed
to invariably keep. Nevertheless, he gained upon her
breathlessly, and, thanks to the bark-strewn floor, noiselessly. He was near enough to distinguish and recognize
the dress she wore, a pale yellow, that he had admired
when he first saw her. It was Nellie, unmistakably; if it
were she of the brown duster, she had discarded it, perhaps for greater freedom. He was near enough to call
out now, but a sudden nervous timidity overcame him;
his lips grew dry. What should he say to her? How
account for his presence? "Miss Nellie, one moment!"
he gasped. She darted forward and—vanished.

At this moment he was not more than a dozen yards
from her. He rushed to where she had been standing,
but her disappearance was perfect and complete. He
made a circuit of the group of trees within whose radius
she had last appeared, but there was neither trace of her,
nor a suggestion of her mode of escape. He called aloud
to her; the vacant Woods let his helpless voice die in
their unresponsive depths. He gazed into the air and
down at the bark-strewn carpet at his feet. Like most
of his vocation, he was sparing of speech, and epigram-
matic after his fashion. Comprehending in one swift but
despairing flash of intelligence the existence of some fateful power beyond his own weak endeavor, he accepted its
logical result with characteristic grimness, threw his hat
upon the ground, put his hands in his pockets, and said—

"Well, I'm d——d!"

CHAPTER III.

Out of compliment to Miss Nellie Wynn, Yuba Bill,
on reaching Indian Spring, had made a slight detour to
enable him to ostentatiously set down his fair passenger
before the door of the Burnhams. When it had closed
on the admiring eyes of the passengers and the coach had

rattled away, Miss Nellie, without any undue haste or apparent change in her usual quiet demeanor, managed, however, to dispatch her business promptly, and, leaving an impression that she would call again before her return to Excelsior, parted from her friends and slipped away through a side street to the General Furnishing Store of Indian Spring. In passing this emporium, Miss Nellie's quick eye had discovered a cheap brown linen duster hanging in its window. To purchase it, and put it over her delicate cambric dress, albeit with a shivering sense that she looked like a badly folded brown-paper parcel, did not take long. As she left the shop it was with mixed emotions of chagrin and security that she noticed that her passage through the settlement no longer turned the heads of its male inhabitants. She reached the outskirts of Indian Spring and the high-road at about the time Mr. Brace had begun his fruitless patrol of the main street. Far in the distance a faint olive-green table mountain seemed to rise abruptly from the plain. It was the Carquinez Woods. Gathering her spotless skirts beneath her extemporized brown domino, she set out briskly towards them.

But her progress was scarcely free or exhilarating. She was not accustomed to walking in a country where "buggy-riding" was considered the only genteel young-lady-like mode of progression, and its regular provision the expected courtesy of mankind. Always fastidiously booted, her low-quartered shoes were charming to the eye, but hardly adapted to the dust and inequalities of the high-road. It was true that she had thought of buying a coarser pair at Indian Spring, but once face to face with their uncompromising ugliness, she had faltered and fled. The sun was unmistakably hot, but her parasol was too well known and offered too violent a contrast to the duster for practical use. Once she stopped with an exclamation of annoyance, hesitated, and looked back. In half an hour she had twice lost her shoe and her temper; a pink flush took possession of her cheeks, and her eyes were bright with suppressed rage. Dust began to form grimy circles around their orbits; with cat-like shivers she even felt it pervade the roots of her blond hair. Gradually her breath grew more rapid and hysterical, her smarting eyes became humid, and at last, encountering two observant horsemen in the road, she turned and fled, until, reaching the wood, she began to cry.

Nevertheless she waited for the two horsemen to pass, to satisfy herself that she was not followed; then pushed on vaguely, until she reached a fallen tree, where, with a gesture of disgust, she tore off her hapless duster and flung it on the ground. She then sat down sobbing, but after a moment dried her eyes hurriedly and started to her feet. A few paces distant, erect, noiseless, with out-stretched hand, the young solitary of the Carquinez Woods advanced towards her. His hand had almost touched hers, when he stopped.

"What has happened?" he asked gravely.

"Nothing," she said, turning half away, and searching the ground with her eyes, as if she had lost something. "Only I must be going back now."

"You shall go back at once, if you wish it," he said, flushing slightly. "But you have been crying; why?"

Frank as Miss Nellie wished to be, she could not bring herself to say that her feet hurt her, and the dust and heat were ruining her complexion. It was therefore with a half-confident belief that her troubles were really of a moral quality that she answered, "Nothing—nothing, but —but—it's wrong to come here."

"But you did not think it was wrong when you agreed to come, at our last meeting," said the young man, with that persistent logic which exasperates the inconse-quent feminine mind. "It cannot be any more wrong to-day."

"But it was not so far off," murmured the young girl, without looking up.

"Oh, the distance makes it more improper, then," he said abstractedly; but after a moment's contemplation of her half-averted face, he asked gravely, "Has anyone talked to you about me?"

Ten minutes before, Nellie had been burning to un-burthen herself of her father's warning, but now she felt

she would not. "I wish you wouldn't call yourself Low,"
she said at last.

"But it's my name," he replied quietly.

"Nonsense! It's only a stupid translation of a stupid
nickname. They might as well call you 'Water' at once."

"But you said you liked it."

"Well, so I do. But don't you see—I—oh dear! you
don't understand."

Low did not reply, but turned his head with resigned
gravity towards the deeper woods. Grasping the barrel
of his rifle with his left hand, he threw his right arm
across his left wrist and leaned slightly upon it with the
habitual ease of a Western hunter—doubly picturesque in
his own lithe, youthful symmetry. Miss Nellie looked
at him from under her eyelids, and then half defiantly
raised her head and her dark lashes. Gradually an almost
magical change came over her features; her eyes grew
larger and more and more yearning, until they seemed to
draw and absorb in their liquid depths the figure of the
young man before her; her cold face broke into an ecstasy
of light and color; her humid lips parted in a bright, wel-
coming smile, until, with an irresistible impulse, she arose,
and throwing back her head stretched towards him two
hands full of vague and trembling passion.

In another moment he had seized them, kissed them,
and, as he drew her closer to his embrace, felt them
tighten around his neck. "But what name do you wish to
call me?" he asked, looking down into her eyes.

Miss Nellie murmured something confidentially to the
third button of his hunting shirt. "But that," he replied,
with a smile, "*that* wouldn't be any more practical, and
you wouldn't want others to call me dar—" Her fingers
loosened around his neck, she drew her head back, and
a singular expression passed over her face, which to any
calmer observer than a lover would have seemed, however, to indicate more curiosity than jealousy.

"Who else *does* call you so?" she added earnestly.
"How many, for instance?"

Low's reply was addressed not to her ear, but her lips.
She did not avoid it, but added, "And do you kiss them

all like that?" Taking him by the shoulders, she held
him a little way from her, and gazed at him from head
to foot. Then drawing him again to her embrace, she
said, "I don't care, at least no woman has kissed you like
that." Happy, dazzled, and embarrassed, he was beginning to stammer the truthful protestation that rose to
his lips, but she stopped him: "No, don't protest! say
nothing! Let *me* love *you*—that is all. It is enough."
He would have caught her in his arms again, but she
drew back. "We are near the road," she said quietly.
"Come! You promised to show me where you camped.
Let us make the most of our holiday. In an hour I must
leave the woods."

"But I shall accompany you, dearest."

"No, I must go as I came—alone."

"But Nellie—"

"I tell you no," she said, with an almost harsh practical
decision, incompatible with her previous abandonment.
"We might be seen together."

"Well, suppose we are; we must be seen together
eventually," he remonstrated.

The young girl made an involuntary gesture of impatient negation, but checked herself. "Don't let us talk
of that now. Come, while I am here under your own
roof—" she pointed to the high interlaced boughs above
them—"you must be hospitable. Show me your home;
tell me, isn't it a little gloomy sometimes?"

"It never has been; I never thought it *would* be until
the moment you leave it to-day."

She pressed his hand briefly and in a half-perfunctory
way, as if her vanity had accepted and dismissed the
compliment. "Take me somewhere," she said inquisi-
tively, "where you stay most; I do not seem to see you
here," she added, looking around her with a slight shiver.
"It is so big and so high. Have you no place where you
eat and rest and sleep?"

"Except in the rainy season, I camp all over the place—
at any spot where I may have been shooting or collecting."

"Collecting?" queried Nellie.

"Yes; with the herbarium, you know."

"Yes," said Nellie dubiously. "But you told me once—the first time we ever talked together," she added, looking in his eyes—"something about your keeping your things like a squirrel in a tree. Could we not go there? Is there not room for us to sit and talk without being brow-beaten and looked down upon by these supercilious trees?"

"It's too far away," said Low truthfully, but with a somewhat pronounced emphasis, "much too far for you just now; and it lies on another trail that enters the wood beyond. But come, I will show you a spring known only to myself, the wood ducks, and the squirrels. I dis-covered it the first day I saw you, and gave it your name. But you shall christen it yourself. It will be all yours, and yours alone, for it is so hidden and secluded that I defy any feet but my own or whoso shall keep step with mine to find it. Shall that foot be yours, Nellie?"

Her face beamed with a bright assent. "It may be difficult to track it from here," he said, "but stand where you are a moment, and don't move, rustle, nor agitate the air in any way. The woods are still now." He turned at right angles with the trail, moved a few paces into the ferns and underbrush, and then stopped with his finger on his lips. For an instant both remained motion-less; then with his intent face bent forward and both arms extended, he began to sink slowly upon one knee and one side, inclining his body with a gentle, perfectly-graduated movement until his ear almost touched the ground. Nellie watched his graceful figure breathlessly, until, like a bow unbent, he stood suddenly erect again, and beck-oned to her without changing the direction of his face.

"What is it?" she asked eagerly.

"All right; I have found it," he continued, moving for-ward without turning his head.

"But how? What did you kneel for?" He did not reply, but taking her hand in his continued to move slowly on through the underbrush, as if obeying some magnetic attraction. "How did you find it?" again asked the half-awed girl, her voice unconsciously falling to a whisper. Still silent, Low kept his rigid face and for-ward tread for twenty yards further; then he stopped and released the girl's half-impatient hand. "How did you find it?" she repeated sharply.

"With my ears and nose," replied Low gravely.

"With your nose?"

"Yes; I smelt it."

Still fresh with the memory of his picturesque attitude, the young man's reply seemed to involve something more irritating to her feelings than even that absurd anti-climax. She looked at him coldly and critically, and appeared to hesitate whether to proceed. "Is it far?" she asked.

"Not more than ten minutes now, as I shall go."

"And you won't have to smell your way again?"

"No; it is quite plain now," he answered seriously, the young girl's sarcasm slipping harmlessly from his Indian stolidity. "Don't you smell it yourself?"

But Miss Nellie's thin, cold nostrils refused to take that vulgar interest.

"Nor hear it? Listen!"

"You forget I suffer the misfortune of having been brought up under a roof," she replied coldly.

"That's true," repeated Low, in all seriousness; "it's not your fault. But do you know, I sometimes think I am peculiarly sensitive to water; I feel it miles away. At night, though I may not see it or even know where it is, I am conscious of it. It is company to me when I am alone, and I seem to hear it in my dreams. There is no music as sweet to me as its song. When you sang with me that day in church, I seemed to hear it ripple in your voice. It says to me more than the birds do, more than the rarest plants I find. It seems to live with me and for me. It is my earliest recollection; I know it will be my last, for I shall die in its embrace. Do you think, Nellie," he continued, stopping short and gazing earnestly in her face—"do you think that the chiefs knew this when they called me 'Sleeping Water'?"

To Miss Nellie's several gifts I fear the gods had not added poetry. A slight knowledge of English verse of a select character, unfortunately, did not assist her in the interpretation of the young man's speech, nor relieve her from the momentary feeling that he was at times deficient in intellect. She preferred, however, to take a personal view of the question, and expressed her sarcastic regret that she had not known before that she had been indebted to the great flume and ditch at Excelsior for the pleasure of his acquaintance. This pert remark occasioned some explanation, which ended in the girl's accepting a kiss in lieu of more logical argument. Nevertheless, she was still conscious of an inward irritation—always distinct from her singular and perfectly material passion—which found vent as the difficulties of their undeviating progress through the underbrush increased. At last she lost her shoe again, and stopped short. "It's a pity your Indian friends did not christen you 'Wild Mustard' or 'Clover,'" she said satirically, "that you might have had some sympathies and longings for the open fields instead of these horrid jungles! I know we will not get back in time."

Unfortunately, Low accepted this speech literally and with his remorseless gravity. "If my name annoys you, I can get it changed by the legislature, you know, and I can find out what my father's name was, and take that. My mother, who died in giving me birth, was the daughter of a chief."

"Then your mother was really an Indian?" said Nellie, "and you are—" She stopped short.

"But I told you all this the day we first met," said Low, with grave astonishment. "Don't you remember our long talk coming from church?"

"No," said Nellie coldly, "you didn't tell me." But she was obliged to drop her eyes before the unwavering, undeniable truthfulness of his.

"You have forgotten," he said calmly; "but it is only right you should have your own way in disposing of a name that I have cared little for; and as you're to have a share of it—"

"Yes, but it's getting late, and if we are not going forward—" interrupted the girl impatiently.

"We *are* going forward," said Low imperturbably; "but I wanted to tell you, as we were speaking on *that* subject"

(Nellie looked at her watch), "I've been offered the place of botanist and naturalist in Professor Grant's survey of Mount Shasta, and if I take it—why, when I come back, darling—well—"

"But you're not going just yet," broke in Nellie, with a new expression in her face.

"No."

"Then we need not talk of it now," she said, with animation.

Her sudden vivacity relieved him. "I see what's the matter," he said gently, looking down at her feet; "these little shoes were not made to keep step with a moccasin. We must try another way." He stooped as if to secure the erring buskin, but suddenly lifted her like a child to his shoulder. "There," he continued, placing her arm round his neck, "you are clear of the ferns and brambles now, and we can go on. Are you comfortable?" He looked up, read her answer in her burning eyes and the warm lips pressed to his forehead at the roots of his straight dark hair, and again moved onward as in a mesmeric dream. But he did not swerve from his direct course, and with a final dash through the undergrowth parted the leafy curtain before the spring.

At first the young girl was dazzled by the strong light that came from a rent in the interwoven arches of the wood. The breach had been caused by the huge bulk of one of the great giants that had half fallen, and was lying at a steep angle against one of its mightiest brethren, having borne down a lesser tree in the arc of its downward path. Two of the roots, as large as younger trees, tossed their blackened and bare limbs high in the air. The spring—the insignificant cause of this vast disruption—gurgled, flashed, and sparkled at the base; the limpid baby fingers that had laid bare the foundations of that fallen column played with the still clinging rootlets, laved the fractured and twisted limbs, and, widening, filled with sleeping water the graves from which they had been torn.

"It had been going on for years, down there," said Low, pointing to a cavity from which the fresh water now slowly welled, "but it had been quickened by the rising of the subterranean springs and rivers which always occurs at a certain stage of the dry season. I remember that on that very night—for it happened a little after midnight, when all sounds are more audible—I was troubled and oppressed in my sleep by what you would call a nightmare; a feeling as if I was kept down by bonds and pinions that I longed to break. And then I heard a crash in this direction, and the first streak of morning brought me the sound and scent of water. Six months afterwards I chanced to find my way here, as I told you, and gave it your name. I did not dream that I should ever stand beside it with you, and have you christen it yourself."

He unloosened the cup from his flask, and filling it at the spring handed it to her. But the young girl leant over the pool, and pouring the water idly back said, "I'd rather put my feet in it. Mayn't I?"

"I don't understand you," he said wonderingly.

"My feet are *so* hot and dusty. The water looks deliciously cool. May I?"

"Certainly."

He turned away as Nellie, with apparent unconsciousness, seated herself on the bank, and removed her shoes and stockings. When she had dabbled her feet a few moments in the pool, she said over her shoulder—

"We can talk just as well, can't we?"

"Certainly."

"Well, then, why didn't you come to church more often, and why didn't you think of telling father that you were convicted of sin and wanted to be baptized?"

"I don't know," hesitated the young man.

"Well, you lost the chance of having father convert you, baptize you, and take you into full church fellowship."

"I never thought—" he began.

"You never thought. Aren't you a Christian?"

"I suppose so."

"He supposes so! Have you no convictions—no profession?"

"But, Nellie, I never thought that you—"

"Never thought that I—what? Do you think that I could ever be anything to a man who did not believe in justification by faith, or in the covenant of church fellowship? Do you think father would let me?"

In his eagerness to defend himself he stepped to her side. But seeing her little feet shining through the dark water, like outcroppings of delicately veined quartz, he stopped embarrassed. Miss Nellie, however, leaped to one foot, and, shaking the other over the pool, put her hand on his shoulder to steady herself. "You haven't got a towel—or," she said dubiously, looking at her small handkerchief, "anything to dry them on?"

But Low did not, as she perhaps expected, offer his own handkerchief.

"If you take a bath after our fashion," he said gravely, "you must learn to dry yourself after our fashion."

Lifting her again lightly in his arms, he carried her a few steps to the sunny opening, and bade her bury her feet in the dried mosses and baked withered grasses that were bleaching in a hollow. The young girl uttered a cry of childish delight, as the soft ciliated fibres touched her sensitive skin.

"It is healing, too," continued Low; "a moccasin filled with it after a day on the trail makes you all right again,"

But Miss Nellie seemed to be thinking of something else.

"Is that the way the squaws bathe and dry themselves?"

"I don't know; you forget I was a boy when I left them."

"And you're sure you never knew any?"

"None."

The young girl seemed to derive some satisfaction in moving her feet up and down for several minutes among the grasses in the hollow; then, after a pause, said, "You are quite certain I am the first woman that ever touched this spring?"

"Not only the first woman, but the first human being, except myself."

"How nice!"

They had taken each other's hands; seated side by side, they leaned against a curving elastic root that half supported, half encompassed, them. The girl's capricious, fitful manner succumbed as before to the near contact of her companion. Looking into her eyes, Low fell into a sweet, selfish lover's monologue, descriptive of his past and present feelings towards her, which she accepted with a heightened color, a slight exchange of sentiment, and a strange curiosity. The sun had painted their half-embraced silhouettes against the slanting tree-trunk, and began to decline unnoticed; the ripple of the water mingling with their whispers came as one sound to the listening ear; even their eloquent silences were as deep, and, I wot, perhaps as dangerous, as the darkened pool that filled so noiselessly a dozen yards away. So quiet were they that the tremor of invading wings once or twice shook the silence, or the quick scamper of frightened feet rustled the dead grass. But in the midst of a prolonged stillness the young man sprang up so suddenly that Nellie was still half clinging to his neck as he stood erect. "Hush!" he whispered; "some one is near!"

He disengaged her anxious hands gently, leaped upon the slanting tree-trunk, and running half-way up its incline with the agility of a squirrel, stretched himself at full length upon it and listened.

To the impatient, inexplicably startled girl, it seemed an age before he rejoined her.

"You are safe," he said; "he is going by the western trail towards Indian Spring."

"Who is *he?*" she asked, biting her lips with a poorly restrained gesture of mortification and disappointment.

"Some stranger," replied Low.

"As long as he wasn't coming here, why did you give me such a fright?" she said pettishly. "Are you nervous because a single wayfarer happens to stray here?"

"It was no wayfarer, for he tried to keep near the trail," said Low. "He was a stranger to the wood, for he lost his way every now and then. He was seeking or expecting some one, for he stopped frequently and waited or listened. He had not walked far, for he wore spurs that tinkled and caught in the brush; and yet he had not ridden here, for no horse's hoofs passed the road since we have been here. He must have come from Indian Spring."

"And you heard all that when you listened just now?" asked Nellie, half disdainfully.

Impervious to her incredulity Low turned his calm eyes on her face. "Certainly, I'll bet my life on what I say. Tell me: do you know anybody in Indian Spring who would likely spy upon you?"

The young girl was conscious of a certain ill-defined uneasiness, but answered, "No."

"Then it was not *you* he was seeking," said Low thoughtfully. Miss Nellie had not time to notice the emphasis, for he added, "You must go at once, and lest you have been followed I will show you another way back to Indian Spring. It is longer, and you must hasten. Take your shoes and stockings with you until we are out of the bush."

He raised her again in his arms and strode once more out through the covert into the dim aisles of the wood. They spoke but little; she could not help feeling that some other discordant element, affecting him more strongly than it did her, had come between them, and was half perplexed and half frightened. At the end of ten minutes he seated her upon a fallen branch, and telling her he would return by the time she had resumed her shoes and stockings glided from her like a shadow. She would have uttered an indignant protest at being left alone, but he was gone ere she could detain him. For a moment she thought she hated him. But when she had mechanically shod herself once more, not without nervous shivers at every falling needle, he was at her side.

"Do you know anyone who wears a frieze coat like that?" he asked, handing her a few torn shreds of wool affixed to a splinter of bark.

Miss Nellie instantly recognized the material of a certain sporting coat worn by Mr. Jack Brace on festive occasions, but a strange yet infallible instinct that was part of her nature made her instantly disclaim all knowledge of it.

"No," she said.

"Not anyone who scents himself with some doctor's stuff like cologne?" continued Low, with the disgust of keen olfactory sensibilities.

Again Miss Nellie recognized the perfume with which the gallant expressman was wont to make redolent her little parlor, but again she avowed no knowledge of its possessor. "Well," returned Low with some disappointment, "such a man has been here. Be on your guard. Let us go at once."

She required no urging to hasten her steps, but hurried breathlessly at his side. He had taken a new trail by which they left the wood at right angles with the highway, two miles away. Following an almost effaced mule track along a slight depression of the plain, deep enough, however, to hide them from view, he accompanied her, until, rising to the level again, she saw they were beginning to approach the highway and the distant roofs of Indian Spring. "Nobody meeting you now," he whispered, "would suspect where you had been. Good night! until next week—remember."

They pressed each other's hands, and standing on the slight ridge outlined against the paling sky, in full view of the highway, parting carelessly, as if they had been chance met travelers. But Nellie could not restrain a parting backward glance as she left the ridge. Low had descended to the deserted trail, and was running swiftly in the direction of the Carquinez Woods.

CHAPTER IV

Teresa awoke with a start. It was day already, but how far advanced the even, unchanging, soft twilight of the woods gave no indication. Her companion had vanished, and to her bewildered senses so had the camp-fire, even to its embers and ashes. Was she awake, or had she wandered away unconsciously in the night? One glance at the tree above her dissipated the fancy. There was the opening of her quaint retreat and the hanging strips of bark, and at the foot of the opposite treee lay the carcass of the bear. It had been skinned, and, as Teresa thought with an inward shiver, already looked half its former size.

Not yet accustomed to the fact that a few steps in either direction around the circumference of those great trunks produced the sudden appearance or disappearance of any figure, Teresa uttered a slight scream as her young companion unexpectedly stepped to her side. "You see a change here," he said; "the stamped-out ashes of the camp-fire lie under the brush," and he pointed to some cleverly scattered boughs and strips of bark which completely effaced the traces of last night's bivouac. "We can't afford to call the attention of any packer or hunter who might straggle this way to this particular spot and this particular tree; the more naturally," he added, "as they always prefer to camp over an old fire." Accepting this explanation meekly, as partly a reproach for her caprice of the previous night, Teresa hung her head.

"I'm very sorry," she said, "but wouldn't that," pointing to the carcass of the bear, "have made them curious?"

But Low's logic was relentless.

"By this time there would have been little left to excite curiosity, if you had been willing to leave those beasts to their work."

"I'm very sorry," repeated the woman, her lips quivering.

"They are the scavengers of the wood," he continued in a lighter tone; "if you stay here you must try to use them to keep your house clean."

Teresa smiled nervously.

"I mean that they shall finish their work to-night," he added, "and I shall build another camp-fire for us a mile from here until they do."

But Teresa caught his sleeve.

"No," she said hurriedly, "don't, please, for me. You must not take the trouble, nor the risk. Hear me; do, please. I can bear it, I *will* bear it—to-night. I would have borne it last night, but it was so strange—and"— she passed her hands over her forehead—"I think I must have been half mad. But I am not so foolish now."

She seemed so broken and despondent that he replied reassuringly: "Perhaps it would be better that I should find another hiding-place for you, until I can dispose of that carcass so that it will not draw dogs after the wolves, and men after *them*. Besides, your friend the sheriff will probably remember the bear when he remembers anything, and try to get on its track again."

"He's a conceited fool," broke in Teresa in a high voice, with a slight return of her old fury, "or he'd have guessed where that shot came from; and," she added in a lower tone, looking down at her limp and nerveless fingers, "he wouldn't have let a poor, weak, nervous wretch like me get away."

"But his deputy may put two and two together, and connect your escape with it."

Teresa's eyes flashed. "It would be like the dog, just to save his pride, to swear it was an ambush of my friends, and that he was overpowered by numbers. Oh yes! I see it all!" she almost screamed, lashing herself into a rage at the bare contemplation of this diminution of her glory. "That's the dirty lie he tells everywhere, and is telling now."

She stamped her feet and glanced savagely around, as if at any risk to proclaim the falsehood. Low turned his impassive, truthful face towards her.

"Sheriff Dunn," he began gravely, "is a politician, and a fool when he takes to the trail as a hunter of man or beast. But he is not a coward nor a liar. Your chances would be better if he were—if he laid your escape to an ambush of your friends, than if his pride held you alone responsible."

"If he's such a good man, why do you hesitate?" she replied bitterly. "Why don't you give me up at once, and do a service to one of your friends?"

"I do not even know him," returned Low opening his clear eyes upon her. "I've promised to hide you here, and I shall hide you as well from him as from anybody."

Teresa did not reply, but suddenly dropping down upon the ground buried her face in her hands and began to sob convulsively. Low turned impassively away, and putting aside the bark curtain climbed into the hollow tree. In a few moments he reappeared, laden with provisions and a few simple cooking utensils, and touched her lightly on the shoulder. She looked up timidly; the paroxysm had passed, but her lashes yet glittered.

"Come," he said, "come and get some breakfast. I find you have eaten nothing since you have been here—twenty-four hours."

"I didn't know it," she said, with a faint smile. Then seeing his burden, and possessed by a new and strange desire for some menial employment, she said hurriedly, "Let me carry something—do, please," and even tried to disencumber him.

Half annoyed, Low at last yielded, and handing his rifle said, "There, then, take that; but be careful—it's loaded!"

A cruel blush burnt the woman's face to the roots of her hair as she took the weapon hesitatingly in her hand.

"No!" she stammered, hurriedly lifting her shame-suffused eyes to his; "no! no!"

He turned away with an impatience which showed her how completely gratuitous had been her agitation and its significance, and said, "Well, then, give it back if you are afraid of it." But she as suddenly declined to return it; and shouldering it deftly, took her place by his side. Silently they moved from the hollow tree together.

During their walk she did not attempt to invade his taciturnity. Nevertheless she was as keenly alive and watchful of his every movement and gesture as if she had hung enchanted on his lips. The unerring way with which he pursued a viewless, undeviating path through those trackless woods, his quick reconnaissance of certain trees or openings, his mute inspection of some almost imperceptible footprint of bird or beast, his critical examination of certain plants which he plucked and deposited in his deerskin haversack, were not lost on the quick-witted woman. As they gradually changed the clear, unencumbered aisles of the central woods for a more tangled undergrowth, Teresa felt that subtle admiration which culminates in imitation, and simulating perfectly the step, tread, and easy swing of her companion, followed so accurately his lead that she won a gratified exclamation from him when their goal was reached—a broken, blackened shaft, splintered by long-forgotten lightning, in the centre of a tangled carpet of wood-clover.

"I don't wonder you distanced the deputy," he said cheerfully, throwing down his burden, "if you can take the hunting-path like that. In a few days, if you stay here, I can venture to trust you alone for a little *pasear* when you are tired of the tree."

Teresa looked pleased, but busied herself with arrangements for the breakfast, while he gathered the fuel for the roaring fire which soon blazed beside the shattered tree.

Teresa's breakfast was a success. It was a revelation to the young nomad, whose ascetic habits and simple tastes were usually content with the most primitive forms of frontier cookery. It was at least a surprise to him to know that without extra trouble kneaded flour, water, and saleratus need not be essentially heavy; that coffee need not be boiled with sugar to the consistency of syrup; that even that rarest delicacy, small shreds of venison covered with ashes and broiled upon the end of a ramrod boldly thrust into the flames, would be better and even more expeditiously cooked upon burning coals. Moved in his practical nature, he was surprised to find this curious creature of disorganized nerves and useless impulses informed with an intelligence that did not preclude the welfare of humanity or the existence of a soul. He respected her for some minutes, until in the midst of a culinary triumph a big tear dropped and spluttered in the saucepan. But he forgave the irrelevancy by taking no notice of it, and by doing full justice to that particular dish.

Nevertheless, he asked several questions based upon these recently discovered qualities. It appeared that in the old days of her wanderings with the circus troupe she had often been forced to undertake this nomadic housekeeping. But she "despised it," had never done it since, and always had refused to do it for "him"—the personal pronoun referring, as Low understood, to her lover, Curson. Not caring to revive these memories further, Low briefly concluded: "I don't know what you were, or what you may be, but from what I see of you you've got all the *sabe* of a frontierman's wife."

She stopped and looked at him, and then with an impulse of imprudence that only half concealed a more serious vanity, asked, "Do you think I might have made a good squaw?"

"I don't know," he replied quietly. "I never saw enough of them to know."

Teresa, confident from his clear eyes that he spoke the truth, but having nothing ready to follow this calm disposal of her curiosity, relapsed into silence.

The meal finished, Teresa washed their scant table equipage in a little spring near the camp-fire; where, catching sight of her disordered dress and collar, she rapidly threw her shawl, after the national fashion, over her shoulder and pinned it quickly. Low *cached* the remaining provisions and the few cooking utensils under the dead embers and ashes, obliterating all superficial indication of their camp-fire as deftly and artistically as he had before.

"There isn't the ghost of a chance," he said in explanation, "that anybody but you or I will set foot here before we come back to supper, but it's well to be on guard. I'll take you back to the cabin now, though I bet you could find your way there as well as I can."

On their way back Teresa ran ahead of her companion, and plucking a few tiny leaves from a hidden oasis in the bark-strewn trail brought them to him.

"That's the kind you're looking for, isn't it?" she said, half timidly.

"It is," responded Low, in gratified surprise; "but how did you know it? You're not a botanist, are you?"

"I reckon not," said Teresa; "but you picked some when we came, and I noticed what they were."

Here was indeed another revelation. Low stopped and

gazed at her with such frank, open, utterly unabashed curiosity that her black eyes fell before him.

"And do you think," he asked with logical deliberation, "that you could find any plant from another I should give you?"

"Yes."

"Or from a drawing of it"

"Yes; perhaps even if you described it to me."

A half-confidential, half-fraternal silence followed.

"I tell you what. I've got a book—"

"I know it," interrupted Teresa; "full of these things."

"Yes. Do you think you could—"

"Of course I could," broke in Teresa, again.

"But you don't know what I mean," said the imperturbable Low.

"Certainly I do. Why, find 'em, and preserve all the different ones for you to write under—that's it, isn't it?"

Low nodded his head, gratified but not entirely convinced that she had fully estimated the magnitude of the endeavor.

"I suppose," said Teresa, in the feminine postscriptum voice which it would seem entered even the philosophical calm of the aisles they were treading—"I suppose that *she* places great value on them?"

Low had indeed heard Science personified before, nor was it at all impossible that the singular woman walking by his side had also. He said "Yes;" but added, in mental reference to the Linnean Society of San Francisco, that "*they* were rather particular about the rarer kinds."

Content as Teresa had been to believe in Low's tender relations with some favored *one* of her sex, this frank confession of a plural devotion staggered her.

"They?" she repeated.

"Yes," he continued calmly. "The Botanical Society I correspond with are more particular than the Government Survey."

"Then you are doing this for a society?" demanded Teresa, with a stare.

"Certainly. I'm making a collection and classification of specimens. I intend—but what are you looking at?"

Teresa had suddenly turned away. Putting his hand lightly on her shoulder, the young man brought her face to face him again.

She was laughing.

"I thought all the while it was for a girl," she said; "and—" But here the mere effort of speech sent her off into an audible and genuine outburst of laughter. It was the first time he had seen her even smile other than bitterly. Characteristically unconscious of any humor in her error, he remained unembarrassed. But he could not help noticing a change in the expression of her face, her voice, and even her intonation. It seemed as if that fit of laughter had loosed the last ties that bound her to a self-imposed character, had swept away the last barrier between her and her healthier nature, had dispossessed a painful unreality, and relieved the morbid tension of a purely nervous attitude. The change in her utterance and the resumption of her softer Spanish accent seemed to have come with her confidences, and Low took leave of her before their sylvan cabin with a comrade's heartiness, and a complete forgetfulness that her voice had ever irritated him.

When he returned that afternoon he was startled to find the cabin empty. But instead of bearing any appearance of disturbance or hurried flight, the rude interior seemed to have magically assumed a decorous order and cleanliness unknown before. Fresh bark hid the inequalities of the floor. The skins and blankets were folded in the corners, the rude shelves were carefully arranged, even a few tall ferns and bright but quickly fading flowers were disposed around the blackened chimney. She had evidently availed herself of the change of clothing he had brought her, for her late garments were hanging from the hastily-devised wooden pegs driven in the wall. The young man gazed around him with mixed feelings of gratification and uneasiness. His presence had been dispossessed in a single hour; his ten years of lonely habitation had left no trace that this woman had not effaced with a deft move of her hand. More than that, it looked as if she had always occupied it; and it was with a singular conviction that even when she should occupy it no longer it would only revert to him as her dwelling that he dropped the bark shutters athwart the opening, and left it to follow her.

To his quick ear, fine eye, and abnormal senses, this was easy enough. She had gone in the direction of this' morning's camp. Once or twice he paused with a half-gesture of recognition and a characteristic "Good!" at the place where she had stopped, but was surprised to find that her main course had been as direct as his own. Deviating from this direct line with Indian precaution, he first made a circuit of the camp, and approached the shattered trunk from the opposite direction. He consequently came upon Teresa unawares. But the momentary astonishment and embarrassment were his alone.

He scarcely recognized her. She was wearing the garments he had brought her the day before—a certain discarded gown of Miss Nellie Wynn, which he had hurriedly begged from her under the pretext of clothing the wife of a distressed overland emigrant then on the way to the mines. Although he had satisfied his conscience with the intention of confessing the pious fraud to her when Teresa was gone and safe from pursuit, it was not without a sense of remorse that he witnessed the sacrilegious transformation. The two women were nearly the same height and size; and although Teresa's maturer figure accented the outlines more strongly, it was still becoming enough to increase his irritation.

Of this becomingness she was doubtless unaware at the moment that he surprised her. She was conscious of having "a change," and this had emboldened her to "do her hair" and otherwise compose herself. After their greeting she was the first to allude to the dress, regretting that it was not more of a rough disguise, and that, as she must now discard the national habit of wearing her shawl "manta" fashion over her head, she wanted a hat. "But you must not," she said, "borrow any more dresses for me from your young woman. Buy them for me at some shop. They left me enough money for that." Low gently put aside the few pieces of gold she had drawn from her pocket, and briefly reminded her of the suspicion such a purchase by him would produce. "That's so," she said, with a laugh. *"Carámba!* what a mule I'm becoming! Ah! wait a moment. I have it! Buy me a common felt hat—a man's hat—as if for yourself, as a change to that animal," pointing to the fox-tailed cap he wore summer and winter, "and I'll show you a trick. I haven't run a theatrical wardrobe for nothing." Nor had she, for the hat thus procured, a few days later, became, by the aid of a silk handkerchief and a bluejay's feather, a fascinating "pork pie."

Whatever cause of annoyance to Low still lingered in Teresa's dress, it was soon forgotten in a palpable evidence of Teresa's value as a botanical assistant. It appeared that during the afternoon she had not only duplicated his specimens, but had discoverd one or two rare plants as yet unclassified in the flora of the Carquinez Woods. He was delighted, and in turn, over the campfire, yielded up some details of his present life and some of his earlier recollections.

"You don't remember anything of your father?" she asked. "Did he ever try to seek you out?"

"No! Why should he?" replied the imperturbable Low; "he was not a Cherokee."

"No, he was a beast," responded Teresa promptly. "And your mother—do you remember her?"

"No, I think she died."

"You *think* she died? Don't you know?"

"No!"

"Then you're another!" said Teresa. Notwithstanding this frankness, they shook hands for the night: Teresa nestling like a rabbit in a hollow by the side of the campfire; Low with his feet towards it, Indian-wise, and his head and shoulders pillowed on his haversack, only half distinguishable in the darkness beyond.

With such trivial details three uneventful days slipped by. Their retreat was undisturbed, nor could Low detect, by the least evidence to his acute perceptive faculties, that any intruding feet had since crossed the belt of shade. The echoes of passing events at Indian Spring had recorded the escape of Teresa as occurring at a remote and purely imaginative distance, and her probable direction the county of Yolo.

"Can you remember," he one day asked her, "what time it was when you cut the *riata* and got away?"

Teresa pressed her hands upon her eyes and temples.

"About three, I reckon."

"And you were here at seven; you could have covered some ground in four hours?"

"Perhaps—I don't know," she said, her voice taking up its old quality again. "Don't ask me—I ran all the way."

Her face was quite pale as she removed her hands from her eyes, and her breath came as quickly as if she had just finished that race for life.

"Then you think I am safe here?" she added, after a pause.

"Perfectly—until they find you are *not* in Yolo. Then they'll look here. And *that's* the time for you to go *there*." Teresa smiled timidly.

"It will take them some time to search Yolo—unless," she added, "you're tired of me here." The charming *non sequitur* did not, however, seem to strike the young man. "I've got time yet to find a few more plants for you," she suggested.

"Oh, certainly!"

"And give you a few more lessons in cooking."

"Perhaps."

The conscientious and literal Low was beginning to doubt if she were really practical. How otherwise could she trifle with such a situation?

It must be confessed that that day and the next she did trifle with it. She gave herself up to a grave and delicious languor that seemed to flow from shadow and silence and permeate her entire being. She passed hours in a thoughtful repose of mind and spirit that seemed to fall like balm from those steadfast guardians, and distill their gentle ether in her soul; or breathed into her listening ear immunity from the forgotten past, and security for the present. If there was no dream of the future in this calm, even recurrence of placid existence, so much the

better. The simple details of each succeeding day, the
quaint housekeeping, the brief companionship and coming
and going of her young host—himself at best a crystal-
lized personification of the sedate and hospitable woods—
satisfied her feeble cravings. She no longer regretted the
inferior position that her fears had obliged her to take the
first night she came; she began to look up to this young
man—so much younger than herself—without knowing
what it meant; it was not until she found that this attitude
did not detract from his picturesqueness that she discovered herself seeking for reasons to degrade him from
this seductive eminence.

A week had elapsed with little change. On two days he
had been absent all day, returning only in time to sup in
the hollow tree, which, thanks to the final removal of the
dead bear from its vicinity, was now considered a safer
retreat than the exposed camp-fire. On the first of these
occasions she received him with some preoccupation, paying but little heed to the scant gossip he brought from Indian Spring, and retiring early under the plea of fatigue,
that he might seek his own distant camp-fire, which,
thanks to her stronger nerves and regained courage, she
no longer required so near. On the second occasion, he
found her writing a letter more or less blotted with her
tears. When it was finished, she begged him to post it at
Indian Spring, where in two days an answer would be
returned, under cover, to him.

"I hope you will be satisfied then," she added.

"Satisfied with what?" queried the young man.

"You'll see," she replied, giving him her cold hand.
"Good-night."

"But can't you tell me now?" he remonstrated, retaining
her hand.

"Wait two days longer—it isn't much," was all she
vouchsafed to answer.

The two days passed. Their former confidence and
good fellowship were fully restored when the morning
came on which he was to bring the answer from the
post-office at Indian Spring. He had talked again of his
future, and had recorded his ambition to procure the ap-

pointment of naturalist to a Government Surveying Expedition. She had even jocularly proposed to dress herself in man's attire and "enlist" as his assistant.

"But you will be safe with your friends, I hope, by that time," responded Low.

"Safe with my friends," she repeated in a lower voice. "Safe with my friends—yes!" An awkward silence followed; Teresa broke it gayly: "But your girl, your sweetheart, my benefactor—will *she* let you go?"

"I haven't told her yet," said Low, gravely, "but I don't see why she should object."

"Object, indeed!" interrupted Teresa in a high voice and a sudden and utterly gratuitous indignation; "how should she? I'd like to see her do it!"

She accompanied him some distance to the intersection of the trail, where they parted in good spirits. On the dusty plain without a gale was blowing that rocked the high tree-tops above her, but, tempered and subdued, entered the low aisles with a fluttering breath of morning and a sound like the cooing of doves. Never had the wood before shown so sweet a sense of security from the turmoil and tempest of the world beyond; never before had an intrusion from the outer life—even in the shape of a letter—seemed so wicked a desecration. Tempted by the solicitation of air and shade, she lingered, with Low's herbarium slung on her shoulder.

A strange sensation, like a shiver, suddenly passed across her nerves, and left them in a state of rigid tension. With every sense morbidly acute, with every faculty strained to its utmost, the subtle instincts of Low's woodcraft transformed and possessed her. She knew it now! A new element was in the wood—a strange being—another life—another man approaching! She did not even raise her head to look about her, but darted with the precision and fleetness of an arrow in the direction of her tree. But her feet were arrested, her limbs paralzyed, her very existence suspended, by the sound of voice:—

"Teresa!"

It was a voice that had rung in her ears for the last

two years in all phases of intensity, passion, tenderness, and anger; a voice upon whose modulations, rude and unmusical though they were, her heart and soul had hung in transport or anguish. But it was a chime that had rung its last peal to her senses as she entered the Carquinez Woods, and for the last week had been as dead to her as a voice from the grave. It was the voice of her lover—Dick Curson!

CHAPTER V

THE wind was blowing towards the stranger, so that he was nearly upon her when Teresa first took the alarm. He was a man over six feet in height, strongly built, with a slight tendency to a roundness of bulk which suggested reserved rather than impeded energy. His thick beard and mustache were closely cropped around a small and handsome mouth that lisped except when he was excited, but always kept fellowship with his blue eyes in a perpetual smile of half-cynical good-humor. His dress was superior to that of the locality; his general expression that of a man of the world, albeit a world of San Francisco, Sacramento, and Murderer's Bar. He advanced towards her with a laugh and an outstretched hand.

"*You* here!" she gasped, drawing back.

Apparently neither surprised nor mortified at this reception, he answered frankly, "Yeth. You didn't expect me, I know. But Doloreth showed me the letter you wrote her, and—well—here I am, ready to help you, with two men and a thpare horthe waiting outside the woodth on the blind trail."

"You—*you*—here?" she only repeated.

Curson shrugged his shoulders. "Yeth." Of courth you never expected to thee me again, and leath of all *here*. I'll admit that; I'll thay I wouldn't if I'd been in your plathe. I'll go further, and thay you didn't want to thee me again—anywhere. But it all cometh to the thame thing; here I am. I read the letter you wrote Doloreth. I read how you were hiding here, under Dunn'th very nothe, with his whole pothe out, cavorting

round and barkin' up the wrong tree. I made up my
mind to come down here with a few nathty friends of
mine and cut you out under Dunn'th nothe, and run you
over into Yuba—that'th all."

"How dared she show you my letter—*you* of all men?
How dared she ask *your* help?" continued Teresa, fiercely.

"But she didn't athk my help," he responded coolly.
"D——d if I don't think she jutht calculated I'd be glad
to know you were being hunted down and thtarving, that
I might put Dunn on your track."

"You lie!" said Teresa, furiously; "she was my friend.
A better friend than those who professed—*more,*" she
added, with a contemptuous drawing away of her skirt
as if she feared Curson's contamination.

"All right. Thettle that with her when you go back,"
continued Curson philosophically. "We can talk of that
on the way. The thing now ith to get up and get out of
thethe woods. Come!"

Teresa's only reply was a gesture of scorn.

"I know all that," continued Curson half soothingly,
"but they're waiting."

"Let them wait. I shall not go."

"What will you do?"

"Stay here—till the wolves eat me."

"Teresa, listen. D—— it all—Teresa—Tita! see here,"
he said with sudden energy. "I swear to God it's all
right. I'm willing to let by-gones be by-gones and take a
new deal. You shall come back as if nothing had happened, and take your old place as before. I don't mind
doing the square thing, all round. If that's what you
mean, if that's all that stands in the way, why, look upon
the thing as settled. There, Tita, old girl, come."

Careless or oblivious of her stony silence and starting
eyes, he attempted to take her hand. But she disengaged
herself with a quick movement, drew back, and suddenly
crouched like a wild animal about to spring. Curson
folded his arms as she leaped to her feet; the little dagger
she had drawn from her garter flashed menacingly in the
air, but she stopped.

The man before her remained erect, impassive, and

silent; the great trees around and beyond her remained erect, impassive, and silent; there was no sound in the dim aisles but the quick panting of her mad passion, no movement in the calm, motionless shadow but the trembling of her uplifted steel. Her arm bent and slowly sank, her fingers relaxed, the knife fell from her hand.

"That'th quite enough for a thow," he said, with a return to his former cynical ease and a perceptible tone of relief in his voice. "It'th the thame old Theretha. Well, then, if you won't go with me, go without me; take the led horthe and cut away. Dick Athley and Petereth will follow you over the county line. If you want thome money, there it ith." He took a buckskin purse from his pocket. "If you won't take it from me—" he hesitated as she made no reply—"Athley'th flush and ready to lend you thome."

She had not seemed to hear him, but had stooped in some embarrassment, picked up the knife and hastily hid it, then with averted face and nervous fingers was beginning to tear strips of loose bark from the nearest trunk.

"Well, what do you thay?"

"I don't want any money, and I shall stay here." She hesitated, looked around her, and then added, with an effort, "I suppose you meant well. Be it so! Let by-gones be by-gones. You said just now, 'It's the same old Teresa.' So she is, and seeing she's the same she's better here than anywhere else."

There was enough bitterness in her tone to call for Curson's half-perfunctory sympathy.

"That be d——d," he responded quickly. "Jutht thay you'll come, Tita, and—"

She stopped his half-spoken sentence with a negative gesture. "You don't understand. I shall stay here."

"But even if they don't theek you here, you can't live here forever. The friend that you wrote about who wath tho good to you, you know, can't keep you here alwayth; and are you thure you can alwayth trutht her?"

"It isn't a woman; it's a man." She stopped short, and colored to the line of her forehead. "Who said it was a woman?" she continued fiercely, as if to cover her confusion with a burst of gratuitous anger. "Is that another of your lies?"

Curson's lips, which for a moment had completely lost their smile, were now drawn together in a prolonged whistle. He gazed curiously at her gown, at her hat, at the bow of bright ribbon that tied her black hair, and said, "Ah!"

"A poor man who has kept my secret," she went on hurriedly—"a man as friendless and lonely as myself. Yes," disregarding Curson's cynical smile, "a man who has shared everything—"

"Naturally," suggested Curson.

"And turned himself out of his only shelter to give me a roof and covering," she continued mechanically, struggling with the new and horrible fancy that his words awakened.

"And thlept every night at Indian Thpring to save your reputation," said Curson. "Of courthe."

Teresa turned very white. Curson was prepared for an outburst of fury—perhaps even another attack. But the crushed and beaten woman only gazed at him with frightened and imploring eyes. "For God's sake, Dick, don't say that!"

The amiable cynic was staggered. His good-humor and a certain chivalrous instinct he could not repress got the better of him. He shrugged his shoulders. "What I thay, and what you *do,* Teretha, needn't make us quarrel. I've no claim on you—I know it. Only—" a vivid sense of the ridiculous, powerful in men of his stamp, completed her victory—"only don't thay anything about my coming down here to cut you out from the—the—*the sheriff.*" He gave utterance to a short but unaffected laugh, made a slight grimace, and turned to go.

Teresa did not join in his mirth. Awkward as it would have been if he had taken a severer view of the subject, she was mortified even amidst her fears and embarrassment at his levity. Just as she had become convinced that his jealousy had made her over-conscious, his apparent good-humored indifference gave that over-consciousness a guilty significance. Yet this was lost in her sudden alarm as her companion, looking up, uttered an exclamation, and placed his hand upon his revolver. With a sinking conviction that the climax had come, Teresa turned her eyes. From the dim aisles beyond, Low was approaching. The catastrophe seemed complete.

She had barely time to utter an imploring whisper: "In the name of God, not a word to him." But a change had already come over her companion. It was no longer a parley with a foolish woman; he had to deal with a man like himself. As Low's dark face and picturesque figure came nearer, Mr. Curson's proposed method of dealing with him was made audible.

"Ith it a mulatto or a Thircuth, or both?" he asked, with affected anxiety.

Low's Indian phlegm was impervious to such assault. He turned to Teresa, without apparently noticing her companion. "I turned back," he said quietly, "as soon as I knew there were strangers here; I thought you might need me." She noticed for the first time that, in addition to his rifle, he carried a revolver and hunting knife in his belt.

"Yeth," returned Curson, with an ineffectual attempt to imitate Low's phlegm; "but ath I didn't happen to be a sthranger to this lady, perhaps it wathn't nethethary, particularly ath I had two friends—"

"Waiting at the edge of the wood with a led horse," interrupted Low, without addressing him, but apparently continuing his explanation to Teresa. But she turned to Low with feverish anxiety.

"That's so—he is an old friend—" she gave a quick, imploring glance at Curson—"an old friend who came to help me away—he is very kind," she stammered, turning alternately from the one to the other; "but I told him there was no hurry—at least to-day—that you—were— very good—too, and would hide me a little longer, until your plan—you know *your* plan," she added, with a look of beseeching significance to Low—"could be tried." And then, with a helpless conviction that her excuses, motives, and emotions were equally and perfectly transparent to both men, she stopped in a tremble.

"Perhapth it 'th jutht ath well, then, that the gentleman came thtraight here, and didn't tackle my two friendth when he pathed them," observed Curson, half sarcastically.

"I have not passed your friends, nor have I been near them," said Low, looking at him for the first time, with the same exasperating calm, "or perhaps I should not be *here* or they *there*. I knew that one man entered the wood a few moments ago, and that two men and four horses remained outside."

"That's true," said Teresa to Curson excitedly—"that's true. He knows all. He can see without looking, hear without listening. He—he—" she stammered, colored, and stopped.

The two men had faced each other. Curson, after his first good-natured impulse, had retained no wish to regain Teresa, whom he felt he no longer loved, and yet who, for that very reason perhaps, had awakened his chivalrous instincts. Low, equally on his side, was altogether unconscious of any feeling which might grow into a passion, and prevent him from letting her go with another if for her own safety. They were both men of a certain taste and refinement. Yet, in spite of all this, some vague instinct of the baser male animal remained with them, and they were moved to a mutually aggressive attitude in the presence of the female.

One word more, and the opening chapter of a sylvan Iliad might have begun. But this modern Helen saw it coming, and arrested it with an inspiration of feminine genius. Without being observed, she disengaged her knife from her bosom and let it fall as if by accident. It struck the ground with the point of its keen blade, bounded and rolled between them. The two men started and looked at each other with a foolish air. Curson laughed.

"I reckon she can take care of herthelf," he said, extending his hand to Low. "I'm off. But if I'm wanted *she'll* know where to find me." Low took the proffered hand, but neither of the two men looked at Teresa. The reserve of antagonism once broken, a few words of

11

caution, advice, and encouragement passed between them, in apparent obliviousness of her presence or her personal responsibility. As Curson at last nodded a farewell to her, Low insisted upon accompanying him as far as the horses, and in another moment she was again alone.

She had saved a quarrel between them at the sacrifice of herself, for her vanity was still keen enough to feel that this exhibition of her old weakness had degraded her in their eyes, and, worse, had lost the respect her late restraint had won from Low. They had treated her like a child or a crazy woman, perhaps even now were exchanging criticisms upon her—perhaps pitying her! Yet she had prevented a quarrel, a fight; possibly the death of either one or the other of these men who despised her, for none better knew than she the trivial beginning and desperate end of these encounters. Would they—would Low ever realize it, and forgive her? Her small, dark hands went up to her eyes and she sank upon the ground. She looked through tear-veiled lashes upon the mute and giant witnesses of her deceit and passion, and tried to draw, from their immovable calm, strength and consolation as before. But even they seemed to stand apart, reserved and forbidding.

When Low returned she hoped to gather from his eyes and manner what had passed between him and her former lover. But beyond a mere gentle abstraction at times he retained his usual calm. She was at last forced to allude to it herself with simulated recklessness.

"I suppose I didn't get a very good character from my last place?" she said, with a laugh.

"I don't understand you," he replied, in evident sincerity.

She bit her lip and was silent. But as they were returning home, she said gently, "I hope you were not angry with me for the lie I told when I spoke of 'your plan.' I could not give the real reason for not returning with—with—that man. But it's not all a lie. I have a plan—if you haven't. When you are ready to go to Sacramento to take your place, dress me as an Indian boy, paint my face, and let me go with you. You can leave me—there—you know."

"It's not a bad idea," he responded gravely. "We will see."

On the next day, and the next, the *rencontre* seemed to be forgotten. The herbarium was already filled with rare specimens. Teresa had even overcome her feminine repugnance to "bugs" and creeping things so far as to assist in his entomological collection. He had drawn from a sacred *cache* in the hollow of a tree the few worn text-books from which he had studied.

"They seem very precious," she said, with a smile.

"Very," he replied gravely. "There was one with plates that the ants ate up. and it will be six months before I can afford to buy another."

Teresa glanced hurriedly over his well-worn buckskin suit, at his calico shirt with its pattern almost obliterated by countless washings, and became thoughtful.

"I suppose you couldn't buy one at Indian Spring?" she said innocently.

For once Low was startled out of his phlegm. "Indian Spring!" he ejaculated; "perhaps not even in San Francisco. These came from the States."

"How did you get them?" persisted Teresa.

"I bought them for skins I got over the ridge."

"I didn't mean that—but no matter. Then you mean to sell that bearskin, don't you?" she added.

Low had, in fact, already sold it, the proceeds having been invested in a gold ring for Miss Nellie, which she scrupulously did not wear except in his presence. In his singular truthfulness he would have frankly confessed it to Teresa, but the secret was not his own. He contented himself with saying that he had disposed of it at Indian Spring.

Teresa started, and communicated unconsciously some of her nervousness to her companion. They gazed in each other's eyes with a troubled expression.

"Do you think it was wise to sell that particular skin, which might be identified?" she asked timidly.

Low knitted his arched brows, but felt a strange sense

of relief. "Perhaps not," he said carelessly; "but it's too late now to mend matters."

That afternoon she wrote several letters, and tore them up. One, however, she retained, and handed it to Low to post at Indian Spring, whither he was going. She called his attention to the superscription, being the same as the previous letter, and added, with affected gayety, "But if the answer isn't as prompt, perhaps it will be pleasanter than the last." Her quick feminine eye noticed a little excitement in his manner and a more studious attention to his dress. Only a few days before she would not have allowed this to pass without some mischievous allusion to his mysterious sweetheart; it troubled her greatly now to find that she could not bring herself to this household pleasantry, and that her lip trembled and her eye grew moist as he parted from her.

The afternoon passed slowly; he had said he might not return to supper until late, nevertheless a strange restlessness took possession of her as the day wore on. She put aside her work, the darning of his stockings, and rambled aimlessly through the woods. She had wandered she knew not how far, when she was suddenly seized with the same vague sense of a foreign presence which she had felt before. Could it be Curson again, with a word of warning? No! she knew it was not he; so subtle had her sense become that she even fancied that she detected in the invisible aura projected by the unknown no significance or relation to herself or Low, and felt no fear. Nevertheless she deemed it wisest to seek the protection of her sylvan bower, and hurried swiftly thither.

But not so quickly nor directly that she did not once or twice pause in her flight to examine the new-comer from behind a friendly trunk. He was a stranger—a young fellow with a brown mustache, wearing heavy Mexican spurs in his riding-boots, whose tinkling he apparently did not care to conceal. He had perceived her, and was evidently pursuing her, but so awkwardly and timidly that she eluded him with ease. When she had reached the security of the hollow tree and pulled the curtain of bark before the narrow opening, with her eye to the interstices, she waited his coming. He arrived breathlessly in the open space before the tree where the bear once lay; the dazed, bewildered, and half-awed expression of his face, as he glanced around him and through the openings of the forest aisles, brought a faint smile to her saddened face. At last he called in a half-embarrassed voice:—

"Miss Nellie!"

The smile faded from Teresa's cheek. Who was "Miss Nellie?" She pressed her ear to the opening. "Miss Wynn!" the voice again called, but was lost in the echoless woods. Devoured with a new gratuitous curiosity, in another moment Teresa felt she would have disclosed herself at any risk, but the stranger rose and began to retrace his steps. Long after his tinkling spurs were lost in the distance, Teresa remained like a statue, staring at the place where he had stood. Then she suddenly turned like a mad woman, glanced down at the gown she was wearing, tore it from her back as if it had been a polluted garment, and stamped upon it in a convulsion of rage. And then, with her beautiful bare arms clasped together over her head, she threw herself upon her couch in a tempest of tears.

CHAPTER VI

WHEN Miss Nellie reached the first mining extension of Indian Spring, which surrounded it like a fosse, she descended for one instant into one of its trenches, opened her parasol, removed her duster, hid it under a bowlder, and with a few shivers and cat-like strokes of her soft hands not only obliterated all material traces of the stolen cream of Carquinez Woods, but assumed a feline demureness quite inconsistent with any moral dereliction. Unfortunately, she forgot to remove at the same time a certain ring from her third finger, which she had put on with her duster and had worn at no other time. With this slight exception, the benignant fate which always protected that young person brought her in contact with

the Burnham girls at one end of the main street as the
returning coach to Excelsior entered the other, and
enabled her to take leave of them before the coach office
with a certain ostentation of parting which struck Mr.
Jack Brace, who was lingering at the doorway, into a
state of utter bewilderment.

Here was Miss Nellie Wynn, the belle of Excelsior,
calm, quiet, self-possessed, her chaste cambric skirts and
dainty shoes as fresh as when she had left her father's
house; but where was the woman of the brown duster,
and where the yellow-dressed apparition of the woods?
He was feebly repeating to himself his mental adjuration
of a few hours before when he caught her eye, and was
taken with a blush and a fit of coughing. Could he have
been such an egregious fool, and was it not plainly written on his embarrassed face for her to read?

"Are we going down together?" asked Miss Nellie
with an exceptionally gracious smile.

There was neither affectation nor coquetry in this advance. The girl had no idea of Brace's suspicion of her,
nor did any uneasy desire to placate or deceive a possible
rival of Low's prompt her graciousness. She simply
wished to shake off in this encounter the already stale
excitement of the past two hours, as she had shaken the
dust of the woods from her clothes. It was characteristic
of her irresponsible nature and transient susceptibilities
that she actually enjoyed the relief of change; more than
that, I fear, she looked upon this infidelity to a past
dubious pleasure as a moral principle. A mild, open
flirtation with a recognized man like Brace, after her
secret passionate tryst with a nameless nomad like Low,
was an ethical equipoise that seemed proper to one of her
religious education.

Brace was only too happy to profit by Miss Nellie's condescension; he at once secured the seat by her side, and
spent the four hours and a half of their return journey to
Excelsior in blissful but timid communion with her. If he
did not dare to confess his past suspicions, he was equally
afraid to venture upon the boldness he had premeditated
a few hours before. He was therefore obliged to take a

middle course of slightly egotistical narration of his own personal adventures, with which he beguiled the young girl's ear. This he only departed from once, to describe to her a valuable grizzly bearskin which he had seen that day for sale at Indian Spring, with a view to divining her possible acceptance of it for a "buggy robe;" and once to comment upon a ring which she had inadvertently disclosed in pulling off her glove.

"It's only an old family keepsake," she added, with easy mendacity; and affecting to recognize in Mr. Brace's curiosity a not unnatural excuse for toying with her charming fingers, she hid them in chaste and virginal seclusion in her lap, until she could recover the ring and resume her glove.

A week passed—a week of peculiar and desiccating heat for even those dry Sierra table-lands. The long days were filled with impalpable dust and acrid haze suspended in the motionless air; the nights were breathless and dewless; the cold wind which usually swept down from the snow line was laid to sleep over a dark monotonous level, whose horizon was pricked with the eating fires of burning forest crests. The lagging coach of Indian Spring drove up at Excelsior, and precipitated its passengers with an accompanying cloud of dust before the Excelsior Hotel. As they emerged from the coach, Mr. Brace, standing in the doorway, closely scanned their begrimed and almost unrecognizable faces. They were the usual type of travelers: a single professional man in dusty black, a few traders in tweeds and flannels, a sprinkling of miners in red and gray shirts, a Chinaman, a negro, and a Mexican packer or muleteer. This latter for a moment mingled with the crowd in the bar-room, and even penetrated the corridor and dining-room of the hotel, as if impelled by a certain semi-civilized curiosity, and then strolled with a lazy, dragging step—half impeded by the enormous leather leggings, chains, and spurs, peculiar to his class—down the main street. The darkness was gathering, but the muleteer indulged in the same childish scrutiny of the dimly lighted shops, magazines, and saloons, and even of the occasional groups of citizens at the street corners. Apparently young, as far as the outlines of his figure could be seen, he seemed to show even more than the usual concern of masculine Excelsior in the charms of womankind. The few female figures about at that hour, or visible at window or veranda, received his marked attention; he respectfully followed the two auburn-haired daughters of Deacon Johnson on their way to choir meeting to the door of the church. Not content with that act of discreet gallantry, after they had entered he managed to slip unperceived behind them.

The memorial of the Excelsior gamblers' generosity was a modern building, large and pretentious, for even Mr. Wynn's popularity, and had been good-humoredly known, in the characteristic language of the generous donors, as one of the "biggest religious bluffs" on record. Its groined rafters, which were so new and spicy that they still suggested their native forest aisles, seldom covered more than a hundred devotees, and in the rambling choir, with its bare space for the future organ, the few choristers, gathered round a small harmonium, were lost in the deepening shadow of that summer evening. The muleteer remained hidden in the obscurity of the vestibule. After a few moments' desultory conversation, in which it appeared that the unexpected absence of Miss Nellie Wynn, their leader, would prevent their practicing, the choristers withdrew. The stranger, who had listened eagerly, drew back in the darkness as they passed out, and remained for a few moments a vague and motionless figure in the silent church. Then coming cautiously to the window, the flapping broad-brimmed hat was put aside, and the faint light of the dying day shone in the black eyes of Teresa! Despite her face, darkened with dye and disfigured with dust, the matted hair piled and twisted around her head, the strange dress and boyish figure, one swift glance from under her raised lashes betrayed her identity.

She turned aside mechanically into the first pew, picked up and opened a hymn-book. Her eyes became riveted on a name written on the title-page, "Nellie Wynn."

Her name, and *her* book. The instinct that had guided her here was right; the slight gossip of her fellow-passengers was right; this was the clergyman's daughter, whose praise filled all mouths. This was the unknown girl the stranger was seeking, but who in turn perhaps had been seeking Low—the girl who absorbed his fancy— the secret of his absences, his preoccupation, his coldness! This was the girl whom to see, perhaps in his arms, she was now periling her liberty and her life unknown to him! A slight odor, some faint perfume of its owner, came from the book; it was the same she had noticed in the dress Low had given her. She flung the volume to the ground, and, throwing her arms over the back of the pew before her, buried her face in her hands.

In that light and attitude she might have seemed some rapt acolyte abandoned to self-communion. But whatever yearning her soul might have had for higher sympathy or deeper consolation, I fear that the spiritual Tabernacle of Excelsior and the Reverend Mr. Wynn did not meet that requirement. She only felt the dry, oven-like heat of that vast shell, empty of sentiment and beauty, hollow in its pretense and dreary in its desolation. She only saw in it a chief altar for the glorification of this girl who had absorbed even the pure worship of her companion, and converted and degraded his sublime paganism to her petty creed. With a woman's withering contempt for her own art displayed in another woman, she thought how she herself could have touched him with the peace that the majesty of their woodland aisles—so unlike this pillared sham—had taught her own passionate heart, had she but dared. Mingling with this imperfect theology, she felt she could have proved to him also that a brunette and a woman of her experience was better than an immature blonde. She began to loathe herself for coming hither, and dreaded to meet his face. Here a sudden thought struck her. What if he had not come here? What if she had been mistaken? What if her rash interpretation of his absence from the wood that night was simple madness? What if he should return—if he had already returned? She rose to her feet, whitening yet joyful with the thought. She could return at once; what was the girl to her now? Yet there was time to satisfy herself if he were at *her* house. She had been told where it was; she could find it in the dark; an open door or window would betray some sign or sound of the occupants. She rose, replaced her hat over her eyes, knotted her flaunting scarf around her throat, groped her way to the door, and glided into the outer darkness.

CHAPTER VII

It was quite dark when Mr. Jack Brace stopped before Father Wynn's open door. The windows were also invitingly open to the wayfarer, as were the pastoral counsels of Father Wynn, delivered to some favored guest within, in a tone of voice loud enough for a pulpit. Jack Brace paused. The visitor was the convalescent sheriff, Jim Dunn, who had publicly commemorated his recovery by making his first call upon the father of his inamorata. The Reverend Mr. Wynn had been expatiating upon the unremitting heat of a possible precursor of forest fires, and exhibiting some catholic knowledge of the designs of a Deity in that regard, and what should be the policy of the Legislature, when Mr. Brace concluded to enter. Mr. Wynn and the wounded man, who occupied an arm-chair by the window, were the only occupants of the room. But in spite of the former's ostentatious greeting, Brace could see that his visit was inopportune and unwelcome. The sheriff nodded a quick, impatient recognition, which, had it not been accompanied by an anathema on the heat, might have been taken as a personal insult. Neither spoke of Miss Nellie, although it was patent to Brace that they were momentarily expecting her. All of which went far to strengthen a certain wavering purpose in his mind.

"Ah, ha! strong language, Mr. Dunn," said Father Wynn, referring to the sheriff's adjuration, "but 'out of the fullness of the heart the mouth speaketh.' Job, sir, cursed, we are told, and even expressed himself in vigorous

Hebrew regarding his birthday. Ha, ha! I'm not opposed to that. When I have often wrestled with the spirit I confess I have sometimes said, 'D——n you.' Yes, sir, 'D——n you.'"

There was something so unutterably vile in the reverend gentleman's utterance and emphasis of this oath that the two men, albeit both easy and facile blasphemers, felt shocked; as the purest of actresses is apt to overdo the rakishness of a gay Lothario, Father Wynn's immaculate conception of an imprecation was something terrible. But he added, "The law ought to interfere with the reckless use of camp-fires in the woods in such weather by packers and prospectors."

"It isn't so much the work of white men," broke in Brace, "as it is of Greasers, Chinamen, and Diggers, especially Diggers. There's that blasted Low, ranges the whole Carquinez Woods as if they were his. I reckon he ain't particular just where he throws his matches."

"But he's not a Digger; he's a Cherokee, and only a half-breed at that," interpolated Wynn. "Unless," he added, with the artful suggestion of the betrayed trust of a too credulous Christian, "he deceived me in this as in other things."

In what other things Low had deceived him he did not say; but, to the astonishment of both men, Dunn growled a dissent to Brace's proposition. Either from some secret irritation with that possible rival, or impatience at the prolonged absence of Nellie, he had "had enough of that sort of hog-wash ladled out to him for genuine liquor." As to the Carquinez Woods, he [Dunn] "didn't know why Low hadn't as much right there as if he'd grabbed it under a preëmption law and didn't live there." With this hint at certain speculations of Father Wynn in public lands for a homestead, he added that "If they [Brace and Wynn] could bring him along any older American settler than an Indian, they might rake down his [Dunn's] pile." Unprepared for this turn in the conversation, Wynn hastened to explain that he did not refer to the pure aborigine, whose gradual extinction no one regretted more than himself, but to the mongrel, who inherited only the vices of civilization. "There should be a law, sir, against the mingling of races. There are men, sir, who violate the laws of the Most High by living with Indian women—squaw men, sir, as they are called."

Dunn rose with a face livid with weakness and passion. "Who dares say that? They are a d——d sight better than sneaking Northern Abolitionists, who married their daughters to buck niggers like—" But a spasm of pain withheld this Parthian shot at the politics of his two companions, and he sank back helplessly in his chair.

An awkward silence ensued. The three men looked at each other in embarrassment and confusion. Dunn felt that he had given way to a gratuitous passion; Wynn had a vague presentiment that he had said something that imperiled his daughter's prospects; and Brace was divided between an angry retort and the secret purpose already alluded to.

"It's all the blasted heat," said Dunn, with a forced smile, pushing away the whisky which Wynn had ostentatiously placed before him.

"Of course," said Wynn hastily; "only it's a pity Nellie ain't here to give you her smelling-salts. She ought to be back now," he added, no longer mindful of Brace's presence; "the coach is over-due now, though I reckon the heat made Yuba Bill take it easy at the up grade."

"If you mean the coach from Indian Spring," said Brace quietly, "it's in already; but Miss Nellie didn't come on it."

"May be she got out at the Crossing," said Wynn cheerfully; "she sometimes does."

"She didn't take the coach at Indian Spring," returned Brace, "because I saw it leave, and passed it on Buckskin ten minutes ago, coming up the hills."

"She's stopped over at Burnham's," said Wynn reflectively. Then, in response to the significant silence of his guests, he added, in a tone of chagrin which his forced heartiness could not disguise, "Well, boys, it's a disappointment all round; but we must take the lesson as it comes. I'll go over to the coach office and see if she's sent any word. Make yourselves at home until I return."

When the door had closed behind him, Brace arose and took his hat as if to go. With his hand on the lock, he turned to his rival, who, half hidden in the gathering darkness, still seemed unable to comprehend his ill-luck.

"If you're waiting for that bald-headed fraud to come back with the truth about his daughter," said Brace coolly, "you'd better send for your things and take up your lodgings here."

"What do you mean?" said Dunn sternly.

"I mean that she's not at the Burnhams'; I mean that he either does or does not know *where* she is, and that in either case he is not likely to give you information. But *I* can."

"You can?"

"Yes."

"Then, where is she?"

"In the Carquinez Woods, in the arms of the man you were just defending—Low, the half-breed."

The room had become so dark that from the road nothing could be distinguished. Only the momentary sound of struggling feet was heard.

"Sit down," said Brace's voice, "and don't be a fool. You're too weak, and it ain't a fair fight. Let go your hold. I'm not lying—I wish to God I was!"

There was silence, and Brace resumed, "We've been rivals, I know. May be I thought my chance as good as yours. If what I say ain't truth, we'll stand as we stood before; and if you're on the shoot, I'm your man when you like, where you like, or on sight if you choose. But I can't bear to see another man played upon as I've been played upon—given dead away as I've been. It ain't on the square.

"There," he continued, after a pause, "that's right, now steady. Listen. A week ago that girl went down just like this to Indian Spring. It was given out, like this, that she went to the Burnhams'. I don't mind saying, Dunn, that I went down myself, all on the square, thinking I might get a show to talk to her, just as *you* might have done, you know, if you had my chance. I didn't come across her anywhere. But two men that I met thought they recognized her in a disguise going into the woods. Not suspecting anything, I went after her; saw her at a distance in the middle of the woods in another dress that I can swear to, and was just coming up to her when she vanished—went like a squirrel up a tree, or down like a gopher in the ground, but vanished."

"Is that all?" said Dunn's voice. "And just because you were a d——d fool, or had taken a little too much whisky, you thought—"

"Steady. That's just what I said to myself," interrupted Brace coolly, "particularly when I saw her that same afternoon in another dress, saying 'Good-by' to the Burnhams, as fresh as a rose and as cold as those snow-peaks. Only one thing—she had a ring on her finger she never wore before, and didn't expect me to see."

"What if she did? She might have bought it. I reckon she hasn't to consult you," broke in Dunn's voice sternly.

"She didn't buy it," continued Brace quietly. "Low gave that Jew trader a bearskin in exchange for it, and presented it to her. I found that out two days afterwards. I found out that out of the whole afternoon she spent less than an hour with the Burnhams. I found out that she bought a duster like the disguise the two men saw her in. I found the yellow dress she wore that day hanging up in Low's cabin—the place where I saw her go—the *rendezvous where she meets him.* Oh, you're listenin', are you? Stop! Sit Down!

"I discovered it by accident," continued the voice of Brace when all was again quiet; "it was hidden as only a squirrel or an Injin can hide when they improve upon nature. When I was satisfied that the girl had been in the woods, I was determined to find out where she vanished, and went there again. Prospecting around, I picked up at the foot of one of the biggest trees this yer old memorandum-book, with grasses and herbs stuck in it. I remembered that I'd heard old Wynn say that Low, like the d——d Digger that he was, collected these herbs; only he pretended it was for science. I reckoned the book was his and that he mightn't be far away. I lay low and waited. Bimeby I saw a lizard running down the root. When he got sight of me he stopped."

"D——n the lizard! What's that got to do with where she is now?"

"Everything. That lizard had a piece of sugar in his mouth. Where did it come from? I made him drop it, and calculated he'd go back for more. He did. He scooted up that tree and slipped in under some hanging strips of bark. I shoved 'em aside, and found an opening to the hollow where they do their housekeeping."

"But you didn't see her there—and how do you know she is there now?"

"I determined to make it sure. When she left to-day, I started an hour ahead of her, and hid myself at the edge of the woods. An hour after the coach arrived at Indian Spring, she came there in a brown duster and was joined by him. I'd have followed them, but the d——d hound has the ears of a squirrel, and though I was five hundred yards from him he was on his guard."

"Guard be blessed! Wasn't you armed? Why didn't you go for him?" said Dunn, furiously.

"I reckoned I'd leave that for you," said Brace coolly. "If he'd killed me, and if he'd even covered me with his rifle, he'd been sure to let daylight through me at double the distance. I shouldn't have been any better off, nor you either. If I'd killed *him,* it would have been your duty as sheriff to put me in jail; and I reckon it wouldn't have broken your heart, Jim Dunn, to have got rid of *two* rivals instead of one. Hullo! Where are you going?"

"Going?" said Dunn hoarsely. "Going to the Carquinez Woods, by God! to kill him before her. *I'll* risk it, if you daren't. Let me succeed, and you can hang *me* and take the girl yourself."

"Sit down, sit down. Don't be a fool, Jim Dunn! You wouldn't keep the saddle a hundred yards. Did I say I wouldn't help you? No. If you're willing, we'll run the risk together, but it must be in my way. Hear me. I'll drive you down there in a buggy before daylight, and we'll surprise them in the cabin or as they leave the wood. But you must come as if to arrest him for some offense—say, as an escaped Digger from the Reservation, a dangerous tramp, a destroyer of public property in the forests, a suspected road agent, or anything to give you the right to hunt him. The exposure of him and Nellie, don't you see, must be accidental. If he resists, kill him on the spot, and nobody'll blame you; if he goes peaceably with you, and you once get him in Excelsior jail, when the story gets out that he's taken the belle of Excelsior for his squaw, if you'd the angels for your *posse* you couldn't keep the boys from hanging him to the first tree. What's that?"

He walked to the window, and looked out cautiously.

"If it was the old man coming back and listening," he said, after a pause, "it can't be helped. He'll hear it soon enough, if he don't suspect something already."

"Look yer, Brace," broke in Dunn hoarsely. "D——d if I understand you or you me. That dog Low has got to answer to *me*, not to the *law!* I'll take my risk of killing him, on sight and on the square. I don't reckon to handicap myself with a warrant, and I am not going to draw him out with a lie. You hear me? That's me all the time!"

"Then you calkilate to go down thar," said Brace contemptuously, "yell out for him and Nellie, and let him line you on a rest from the first tree as if you were a grizzly."

There was a pause. "What's that you were saying just now about a bearskin he sold?" asked Dunn slowly, as if reflecting.

"He exchanged a bearskin," replied Brace, "with a single hole right over the heart. He's a dead shot, I tell you."

"D——n his shooting," said Dunn. "I'm not thinking of that. How long ago did he bring in that bearskin?"

"About two weeks, I reckon. Why?"

"Nothing! Look yer, Brace, you mean well—thar's .ny hand. I'll go down with you there, but not as the sheriff. I'm going there as Jim Dunn, and you can come along as a white man, to see things fixed on the square. Come!"

Brace hesitated. "You'll think better of my plan before you get there; but I've said I'd stand by you, and I will. Come, then. There's no time to lose."

They passed out into the darkness together.

"What are you waiting for?" said Dunn impatiently, as Brace, who was supporting him by the arm, suddenly halted at the corner of the house.

"Some one was listening—did you not see him? Was it the old man?" asked Brace hurriedly.

"Blast the old man! It was only one of them Mexican packers chock-full of whisky, and trying to hold up the house. What are you thinking of? We shall be late."

In spite of his weakness, the wounded man hurriedly urged Brace forward, until they reached the latter's lodgings . To his surprise, the horse and buggy were already before the door.

"Then you reckoned to go, any way?" said Dunn, with a searching look at his companion.

"I calkilated *somebody* would go," returned Brace, evasively, patting the impatient Buckskin; "but come in and take a drink before we leave."

Dunn started out of a momentary abstraction, put his hand on his hip, and mechanically entered the house. They had scarcely raised the glasses to their lips when a sudden rattle of wheels was heard in the street. Brace set down his glass and ran to the window.

"It's the mare bolted," he said, with an oath. "We've kept her too long standing. Follow me," and he dashed down the staircase into the street. Dunn followed with difficulty; when he reached the door he was already confronted by his breathless companion. "She's gone off on a run, and I'll swear there was a man in the buggy!" He stopped and examined the halter-strap, still fastened to the fence. "Cut! by God!"

Dunn turned pale with passion. "Who's got another horse and buggy?" he demanded.

"The new blacksmith in Main Street; but we won't get it by borrowing," said Brace.

"How then?" asked Dunn savagely.

"Seize it, as the sheriff of Yuba and his deputy, pursuing a confederate of the Injin Low—THE HORSE THIEF!"

CHAPTER VIII

THE brief hour of darkness that preceded the dawn was that night intensified by a dense smoke, which, after blotting out horizon and sky, dropped a thick veil on the high road and the silent streets of Indian Spring. As the buggy containing Sheriff Dunn and Brace dashed through the obscurity, Brace suddenly turned to his companion.

"Some one ahead!"

The two men bent forward over the dashboard. Above the steady plunging of their own horse-hoofs they could hear the quicker irregular beat of other hoofs in the darkness before them.

"It's that horse thief!" said Dunn, in a savage whisper. "Bear to the right, and hand me the whip."

A dozen cuts of the cruel lash, and their maddened horse, bounding at each stroke, broke into a wild canter. The frail vehicle swayed from side to side at each spring of the elastic shafts. Steadying himself by one hand on the low rail, Dunn drew his revolver with the other. "Sing out to him to pull up, or we'll fire. My voice is clean gone," he added, in a husky whisper.

They were so near that they could distinguish the bulk of a vehicle careering from side to side in the blackness ahead. Dunn deliberately raised his weapon. "Sing out!" he repeated impatiently. But Brace, who was still keeping in the shadow, suddenly grasped his companion's arm.

"Hush! It's *not* Buckskin," he whispered hurriedly.

"Are you sure?"

"Don't you see we're gaining on him?" replied the other contemptuously. Dunn grasped his companion's hand and pressed it silently. Even in that supreme moment

this horseman's tribute to the fugitive Buckskin fore-
stalled all baser considerations of pursuit and capture!

In twenty seconds they were abreast of the stranger,
crowding his horse and buggy nearly into the ditch;
Brace keenly watchful, Dunn suppressed and pale. In
half a minute they were leading him a length; and when
their horse again settled down to his steady work, the
stranger was already lost in the circling dust that followed them. But the victors seemed disappointed. The
obscurity had completely hidden all but the vague outlines
of the mysterious driver.

"He's not our game, anyway," whispered Dunn.
"Drive on."

"But if it was some friend of his," suggested Brace
uneasily, "what would you do?"

"What I *said* I'd do," responded Dunn savagely. "I
don't want five minutes to do it in, either; we'll be half
an hour ahead of that d——d fool, whoever he is. Look
here; all you've got to do is to put me in the trail to
that cabin. Stand back of me, out of gun-shot, alone, if
you like, as my deputy, or with any number you can pick
up as my *posse*. If he gets by me as Nellie's lover, you
may shoot him or take him as a horse thief, if you like."

"Then you won't shoot him on sight?"

"Not till I've had a word with him."

"But—"

"I've chirped," said the sheriff gravely. "**Drive on.**"

For a few moments only the plunging hoofs and rattling wheels were heard. A dull, lurid glow began to
define the horizon. They were silent until an abatement
of the smoke, the vanishing of the gloomy horizon line,
and a certain impenetrability in the darkness ahead
showed them they were nearing the Carquinez Woods.
But they were surprised on entering them to find the
dim aisles alight with a faint mystic Aurora. The tops of
the towering spires above them had caught the gleam of
the distant forest fires, and reflected it as from a gilded
dome.

"It would be hot work if the Carquinez Woods should
conclude to take a hand in this yer little game that's

going on over on the Divide yonder," said Brace, securing his horse and glancing at the spires overhead. "I reckon I'd rather take a back seat at Injin Spring when the show commences."

Dunn did not reply, but, buttoning his coat, placed one hand on his companion's shoulder, and sullenly bade him "lead the way." Advancing slowly and with difficulty the desperate man might have been taken for a peaceful invalid returning from an early morning stroll. His right hand was buried thoughtfully in the side pocket of his coat. Only Brace knew that it rested on the handle of his pistol.

From time to time the latter stopped and consulted the faint trail with a minuteness that showed recent careful study. Suddenly he paused. "I made a blaze hereabouts to show where to leave the trail. There it is," he added, pointing to a slight notch cut in the trunk of an adjoining tree.

"But we've just passed one," said Dunn, "if that's what you are looking after, a hundred yards back."

Brace uttered an oath, and ran back in the direction signified by his companion. Presently he returned with a smile of triumph.

"They've suspected something. It's a clever trick, but it won't hold water. That blaze which was done to muddle you was cut with an axe; this which I made was done with a bowie-knife. It's the real one. We're not far off now. Come on."

They proceeded cautiously, at right angles with the "blazed" tree, for ten minutes more. The heat was oppressive; drops of perspiration rolled from the forehead of the sheriff, and at times, when he attempted to steady his uncertain limbs, his hands shrank from the heated, blistering bark he touched with ungloved palms.

"Here we are," said Brace, pausing at last. "Do you see that biggest tree, with the root stretching out halfway across to the opposite one?"

"No, it's further to the right and abreast of the dead brush," interrupted Dunn quickly, with a sudden revelation that this was the spot where he had found the dead bear in the night Teresa escaped.

"That's so," responded Brace, in astonishment.

"And the opening is on the other side, opposite the dead brush," said Dunn.

"Then you know it?" said Brace suspiciously.

"I reckon!" responded Dunn, grimly. "That's enough! Fall back!"

To the surprise of his companion, he lifted his head erect, and with a strong, firm step walked directly to the tree. Reaching it, he planted himself squarely before the opening.

"Halloo!" he said.

There was no reply. A squirrel scampered away close to his feet. Brace, far in the distance, after an ineffectual attempt to distinguish his companion through the intervening trunks, took off his coat, leaned against a tree, and lit a cigar.

"Come out of that cabin!" continued Dunn, in a clear, resonant voice. "Come out before I drag you out!"

"All right, 'Captain Scott.' Don't shoot, and I'll come down," said a voice as clear and as high as his own. The hanging strips of bark were dashed aside, and a woman leaped lightly to the ground.

Dunn staggered back. "Teresa! by the Eternal!"

It was Teresa! the old Teresa! Teresa, a hundred times more vicious, reckless, hysterical, extravagant, and outrageous than before. Teresa, staring with tooth and eye, sunburnt and embrowned, her hair hanging down her shoulders, and her shawl drawn tightly around her neck.

"Teresa it is! the same old gal! Here we are again! Return of the favorite in her original character! For two weeks only! Houp là! Tshk!" and, catching her yellow skirt with her fingers, she pirouetted before the astounded man, and ended in a pose. Recovering himself with an effort, Dunn dashed forward and seized her by the wrist.

"Answer me, woman! Is that Low's cabin?"

"It is."

"Who occupies it besides?"

"I do."

"And who else?"

"Well," drawled Teresa slowly, with an extravagant affectation of modesty, "nobody else but us, I reckon. Two's company, you know, and three's none."

"Stop! Will you swear that there isn't a young girl, his—his sweetheart—concealed there with you?"

The fire in Teresa's eye was genuine as she answered steadily, "Well, it ain't my style to put up with that sort of thing; at least, it wasn't over at Yolo, and you know it, Jim Dunn, or I wouldn't be here."

"Yes, yes," said Dunn hurriedly. "But I'm a d——d fool, or worse, the fool of a fool. Tell me, Teresa, is this man Low your lover?"

Teresa lowered her eyes as if in maidenly confusion. "Well, if I'd known that *you* had any feeling of your own about it—if you'd spoken sooner—"

"Answer me, you devil!"

"He is."

"And he has been with you here—yesterday—to-night?"

"He has."

"Enough."   He laughed a weak, foolish laugh, and, turning pale, suddenly lapsed against a tree. He would have fallen, but with a quick instinct Teresa sprang to his side, and supported him gently to a root. The action over they both looked astounded.

"I reckon that wasn't much like either you or me," said Dunn slowly, "was it? But if you'd let me drop then you'd have stretched out the biggest fool in the Sierras." He paused, and looked at her curiously. "What's come over you; blessed if I seem to know you now."

She was very pale again, and quiet; that was all.

"Teresa! d——n it, look here! When I was laid up yonder in Excelsior I said I wanted to get well for only two things. One was to hunt you down, the other to marry Nellie Wynn. When I came here I thought that last thing could never be. I came here expecting to find her here with Low, and kill him—perhaps kill her too.

I never once thought of you; not once. You might have risen up before me—between me and him—and I'd have passed you by. And now that I find it's all a mistake, and it was you, not her, I was looking for, why—"

"Why," she interrupted bitterly, "you'll just take me, of course, to save your time and earn your salary. I'm ready."

"But *I'm* not, just yet," he said faintly. "Help me up."

She mechanically assisted him to his feet.

"Now stand where you are," he added, "and don't move beyond this tree till I return."

He straightened himself with an effort, clenched his fists until the nails were nearly buried in his palms, and strode with a firm, steady step in the direction he had come. In a few moments he returned and stood before her.

"I've sent away my deputy—the man who brought me here, the fool who thought you were Nellie. He knows now he made a mistake. But who it was he mistook for Nellie he does not know, nor shall ever know, nor shall any living being know, other than myself. And when I leave the wood to-day I shall know it no longer. You are safe here as far as I am concerned, but I cannot screen you from others prying. Let Low take you away from here as soon as he can."

"Let him take me away? Ah, yes. For what?"

"To save you," said Dunn. "Look here, Teresa! Without knowing it, you lifted me out of hell just now, and because of the wrong I might have done her—for *her* sake, I spare you and shirk my duty."

"For her sake!" gasped the woman—"for her sake! Oh, yes! Go on."

"Well," said Dunn gloomily, "I reckon perhaps you'd as lieve left me in hell, for all the love you bear me. And may be you've grudge enough agin me still to wish I'd found her and him together."

"You think so?" she said, turning her head away.

"There, d——n it! I didn't mean to make you cry. May be you wouldn't, then. Only tell that fellow to take you out of this, and not run away the next time he sees a man coming."

"He didn't run," said Teresa, with flashing eyes. "I—I—I sent him away," she stammered. Then, suddenly turning with fury upon him, she broke out, "Run! Run from you! Ha, ha! You said just now I'd a grudge against you. Well, listen, Jim Dunn. I'd only to bring you in range of that young man's rifle, and you'd have dropped in your tracks like—"

"Like that bar, the other night," said Dunn, with a short laugh. "So *that* was your little game?" He checked his laugh suddenly—a cloud passed over his face. "Look here, Teresa," he said, with an assumption of carelessness that was as transparent as it was utterly incompatible with his frank, open selfishness. "What became of that bar? The skin—eh? That was worth something?"

"Yes," said Teresa quietly. "Low exchanged it and got a ring for me from that trader Isaacs. It was worth more, you bet. And the ring didn't fit either—"

"Yes," interrupted Dunn, with an almost childish eagerness.

"And I made him take it back, and get the value in money. I hear that Isaacs sold it again and made another profit; but that's like those traders." The disingenuous candor of Teresa's manner was in exquisite contrast to Dunn. He rose and grasped her hand so heartily she was forced to turn her eyes away.

"Good-by!" he said.

"You look tired," she murmured, with a sudden gentleness that surprised him; "let me go with you a part of the way."

"It isn't safe for you just now," he said, thinking of the possible consequences of the alarm Brace had raised.

"Not the way *you* came," she replied; "but one known only to myself."

He hesitated only a moment. "All right, then," he said finally, "let us go at once. It's suffocating here, and I seem to feel this dead bark crinkle under my feet."

She cast a rapid glance around her, and then seemed to sound with her eyes the far-off depths of the aisles, beginning to grow pale with the advancing day, but still holding a strange quiver of heat in the air. When she had finished her half-abstracted scrutiny of the distance, she cast one backward glance at her own cabin and stopped.

"Will you wait a moment for me?" she asked gently.

"Yes—but—no tricks, Teresa! It isn't worth the time."

She looked him squarely in the eyes without a word.

"Enough," he said; "go!"

She was absent for some moments. He was beginning to become uneasy, when she made her appearance again, clad in her old faded black dress. Her face was very pale, and her eyes were swollen, but she placed his hand on her shoulder, and bidding him not to fear to lean upon her, for she was quite strong, led the way.

"You look more like yourself now, and yet—blast it all!—you don't either," said Dunn, looking down upon her. "You've changed in some way. What is it? Is it on account of that Injin? Couldn't you have found a white man in his place?"

"I reckon he's neither worse nor better for that," she replied bitterly; "and perhaps he wasn't as particular in his taste as a white man might have been. But," she added, with a sudden spasm of her old rage, "it's a lie; he's *not* an Indian, no more than I am. Not unless being born of a mother who scarcely knew him, of a father who never even saw him, and being brought up among white men and wild beasts—less cruel than they were—could make him one!"

Dunn looked at her in surprise not unmixed with admiration. "If Nellie," he thought, "could but love *me* like that!" But he only said:

"For all that, he's an Injin. Why, look at his name. It ain't Low. It's *L'Eau Dormante,* Sleeping Water, an Injin name."

"And what does that prove?" returned Teresa. "Only that Indians clap a nick-name on any stranger, white or red, who may camp with them. Why, even his own father, a white man, the wretch who begot him and abandoned him,—*he* had an Indian name—*Loup Noir.*"

"What name did you say?"

"Le Loup Noir, the Black Wolf. I suppose you'd call him an Indian, too? Eh! What's the matter? We're walking too fast. Stop a moment and rest. There—there, lean on me!"

She was none too soon; for, after holding him upright a moment, his limbs failed, and stooping gently she was obliged to support him half reclining against a tree.

"It's the heat!" he said. "Give me some whisky from my flask. Never mind the water," he added faintly, with a forced laugh, after he had taken a draught at the strong spirit. "Tell me more about the other water—the Sleeping Water—you know. How do you know all this about him and his—father?"

"Partly from him and partly from Curson, who wrote to me about him," she answered with some hesitation.

But Dunn did not seem to notice this incongruity of correspondence with a former lover. "And *he* told you?"

"Yes; and I saw the name on an old memorandum book he has, which he says belonged to his father. It's full of old accounts of some trading post on the frontier. It's been missing for a day or two, but it will turn up. But I can swear I saw it."

Dunn attempted to rise to his feet. "Put your hand in my pocket," he said in a hurried whisper. "No, there!—bring out a book. There, I haven't looked at it yet. Is that it?" he added, handing her the book Brace had given him a few hours before.

"Yes," said Teresa, in surprise. "Where did you find it?"

"Never mind! Now let me see it, quick. Open it, for my sight is failing. There—thank you—that's all!"

"Take more whisky," said Teresa, with a strange anxiety creeping over her. "You are faint again."

"Wait! Listen, Teresa—lower—put your ear lower. Listen! I came near killing that chap Low to-day. Wouldn't it have been ridiculous?"

He tried to smile, but his head fell back. He had fainted.

CHAPTER IX

FOR the first time in her life Teresa lost her presence of mind in an emergency. She could only sit staring at the helpless man, scarcely conscious of his condition, her mind filled with a sudden prophetic intuition of the significance of his last words. In the light of that new revelation she looked into his pale, haggard face for some resemblance to Low, but in vain. Yet her swift feminine instinct met the objection. "It's the mother's blood that would show," she murmured, "not this man's."

Recovering herself, she began to chafe his hands and temples, and moistened his lips with the spirit. When his respiration returned with a faint color to his cheeks, she pressed his hands eagerly and leaned over him.

"Are you sure?" she asked.

"Of what?" he whispered faintly.

"That Low is really your son?"

"Who said so?" he asked, opening his round eyes upon her.

"You did yourself, a moment ago," she said quickly. "Don't you remember?"

"Did I?"

"You did. Is it not so?"

He smiled faintly. "I reckon."

She held her breath in expectation. But only the ludicrousness of the discovery seemed paramount to his weakened faculties. "Isn't it just about the ridiculousest thing all round?" he said, with a feeble chuckle. "First *you* nearly kill me before you know I am Low's father; then I'm just spoilin' to kill him before I know he's my son; then that god-forsaken fool Jack Brace mistakes you for Nellie and Nellie for you. Ain't it just the biggest thing for the boys to get hold of? But we must keep it dark until after I marry Nellie, don't you see? Then we'll have a good time all round, and I'll stand the drinks. Think of it, Teresha! You don' no me, I do' no you, nobody knowsh anybody elsh. I try kill Lo'. Lo' wants

kill Nellie. No thath no ri—' " but the potent liquor, overtaking his exhausted senses, thickened, impeded, and at
last stopped his speech. His head slipped to her shoulder,
and he became once more unconscious.

Teresa breathed again. In that brief moment she had
abandoned herself to a wild inspiration of hope which
she could scarcely define. Not that it was entirely a wild
inspiration; she tried to reason calmly. What if she
revealed the truth to him? What if she told the wretched
man before her that she had deceived him; that she had
overheard his conversation with Brace; that she had
stolen Brace's horse to Bring Low warning; that, failing
to find Low in his accustomed haunts, or at the camp-
fire, she had left a note for him pinned to the herbarium,
imploring him to fly with his companion from the danger
that was coming; and that, remaining on watch, she had
seen them both—Brace and Dunn—approaching, and had
prepared to meet them at the cabin? Would this miserable and maddened man understand her self-abnegation?
Would he forgive Low and Nellie?—she did not ask for
herself. Or would the revelation turn his brain, if it did
not kill him outright? She looked at the sunken orbits
of his eyes and hectic on his cheek, and shuddered.

Why was this added to the agony she already suffered?
She had been willing to stand between them with her
life, her liberty, and even—the hot blood dyed her cheek
at the thought—with the added shame of being thought
the cast-off mistress of that man's son. Yet all this she
had taken upon herself in expiation of something—she
knew not clearly what; no, for nothing—only for *him.*
And yet this very situation offered her that gleam of hope
which had thrilled her; a hope so wild in its improba-
bility, so degrading in its possibility, that at first she
knew not whether despair was not preferable to its
shame. And yet was it unreasonable? She was no
longer passionate; she would be calm and think it out
fairly.

She would go to Low at once. She would find him
somewhere—and even if with that girl, what mattered?—
and she would tell him all. When he knew that the life

and death of his father lay in the scale, would he let his brief, foolish passion for Nellie stand in the way? Even if he were not influenced by filial affection or mere compassion, would his pride let him stoop to a rivalry with the man who had deserted his youth? Could he take Dunn's promised bride, who must have coquetted with him to have brought him to this miserable plight? Was this like the calm, proud young god she knew? Yet she had an uneasy instinct that calm, proud young gods and goddesses did things like this, and felt the weakness of her reasoning flush her own conscious cheek.

"Teresa!"

She started. Dunn was awake, and was gazing at her curiously.

"I was reckoning it was the only square thing for Low to stop this promiscuous picnicking here and marry you out and out."

"Marry me!" said Teresa in a voice that, with all her efforts, she could not make cynical.

"Yes," he repeated, "after I've married Nellie; tote you down to San Angeles, and there take my name like a man, and give it to you. Nobody'll ask after *Teresa,* sure—you bet your life. And if they do, and he can't stop their jaw, just you call on the old man. It's mighty queer, ain't it, Teresa, to think of your being my daughter-in-law?"

It seemed here as if he was about to lapse again into unconsciousness over the purely ludicrous aspect of the subject, but he haply recovered his seriousness. "He'll have as much money from me as he wants to go into business with. What's his line of business, Teresa?" asked this prospective father-in-law, in a large, liberal way.

"He is a botanist!" said Teresa, with a sudden childish animation that seemed to keep up the grim humor of the paternal suggestion; "and oh, he is too poor to buy books! I sent for one or two for him myself, the other day—" she hesitated—"it was all the money I had, but it wasn't enough for him to go on with his studies."

Dunn looked at her sparkling eyes and glowing cheeks,

and became thoughtful. "Curson must have been a d——d fool," he said finally.

Teresa remained silent. She was beginning to be impatient and uneasy, fearing some mischance that might delay her dreaded, yet longed-for meeting with Low. Yet she could not leave this sick and exhausted man, *his father*, now bound to her by more than mere humanity.

"Couldn't you manage," she said gently, "to lean on me a few steps further, until I could bring you to a cooler spot and nearer assistance?

He nodded. She lifted him almost like a child to his feet. A spasm of pain passed over his face. "How far is it?" he asked.

"Not more than ten minutes," she replied.

"I can make a spurt for that time," he said coolly, and began to walk slowly but steadily on. Only his face, which was white and set, and the convulsive grip of his hand on her arm betrayed the effort. At the end of ten minutes she stopped. They stood before the splintered, lightning-scarred shaft in the opening of the woods, where Low had built her first camp-fire. She carefully picked up the herbarium, but her quick eye had already detected in the distance, before she had allowed Dunn to enter the opening with her, that her note was gone. Low had been there before them; he had been warned, as his absence from the cabin showed; he would not return there. They were free from interruption—but where had he gone?

The sick man drew a long breath of relief as she seated him in the clover-grown hollow where she had slept the second night of her stay. "It's cooler than those cursed woods," he said. "I suppose it's because it's a little like a grave. What are you going to do now?" he added, as she brought a cup of water and placed it at his side.

"I am going to leave you here for a little while," she said cheerfully, but with a pale face and nervous hands. "I'm going to leave you while I seek Low."

The sick man raised his head. "I'm good for a spurt, Teresa, like that I've just got through, but I don't think I'm up to a family party. Couldn't you issue cards later on?"

"You don't understand," she said. "I'm going to get Low to send some one of your friends to you here. I don't think he'll begrudge leaving *her* a moment for that," she added to herself bitterly.

"What's that you're saying?" he queried, with the nervous quickness of an invalid.

"Nothing—but that I'm going now." She turned her face aside to hide her moistened eyes. "Wish me good luck, won't you?" she asked, half sadly, half pettishly.

"Come here!"

She came and bent over him. He suddenly raised his hands, and, drawing her face down to his own, kissed her forehead.

"Give that to *him*," he whispered, "from *me*."

She turned and fled, happily for her sentiment, not hearing the feeble laugh that followed, as Dunn, in sheer imbecility, again referred to the extravagant ludicrousness of the situation. "It is about the biggest thing in the way of a sell all round," he repeated, lying on his back, confidentially to the speck of smoke-obscured sky above him. He pictured himself repeating it, not to Nellie—her severe propriety might at last overlook the fact, but would not tolerate the joke—but to her father! It would be one of those characteristic Californian jokes Father Wynn would admire.

To his exhaustion fever presently succeeded, and he began to grow restless. The heat too seemed to invade his retreat, and from time to time the little patch of blue sky was totally obscured by clouds of smoke. He amused himself with watching a lizard who was investigating a folded piece of paper, whose elasticity gave the little creature lively apprehensions of its vitality. At last he could stand the stillness of his reatreat and his supine position no longer, and rolled himself out of the bed of leaves that Teresa had so carefully prepared for him. He rose to his feet stiff and sore, and, supporting himself by the nearest tree, moved a few steps from the dead ashes of the camp-fire. The movement fright-

ened the lizard, who abandoned the paper and fled
With a satirical recollection of Brace and his "ridiculous" discovery through the medium of this animal, he
stooped and picked up the paper. "Like as not," he said
to himself, with grim irony, "these yer lizards are in
the discovery business. P'r'aps this may lead to another
mystery," and he began to unfold the paper with a smile.
But the smile ceased as his eye suddenly caught his own
name.

A dozen lines were written in pencil on what seemed
to be a blank leaf originally torn from some book. He
trembled so that he was obliged to sit down to read
these words:—

"When you get this keep away from the woods. Dunn
and another man are in deadly pursuit of you and your
companion. I overheard their plan to surprise you in
our cabin. *Don't go there,* and I will delay them and
put them off the scent. Don't mind me. God bless you,
and if you never see me again think sometimes of

"TERESA."

His trembling ceased; he did not start, but rose in an
abstracted way, and made a few deliberate steps in the
direction Teresa had gone. Even then he was so confused that he was obliged to refer to the paper again,
but with so little effect that he could only repeat the last
words, "think sometimes of Teresa." He was conscious
that this was not all; he had a full conviction of being
deceived, and knew that he held the proof in his hand,
but he could not formulate it beyond that sentence.
"Teresa"—yes, he would think of her. She would explain it. And here she was returning.

In that brief interval her face and manner had again
changed. Her face was pale and quite breathless. She
cast a swift glance at Dunn and the paper he mechanically held out, walked up to him, and tore it from his hand.

"Well," she said hoarsely, "what are you going to do
about it?"

He attempted to speak, but his voice failed him. Even
then he was conscious that if he had spoken he would

have only repeated, "think sometimes of Teresa." He looked longingly but helplessly at the spot where she had thrown the paper, as if it had contained his unuttered words.

"Yes," she went on to herself, as if he was a mute, indifferent spectator—"yes, they're gone. That ends it all. The game's played out. Well!" suddenly turning upon him, "now you know it all. Your Nellie *was* here with him, and is with him now. Do you hear? Make the most of it; you've lost them—but here I am."

"Yes," he said eagerly—"yes, Teresa."

She stopped, stared at him; then taking him by the hand led him like a child back to his couch. "Well," she said, in half-savage explanation, "I told you the truth when I said the girl wasn't at the cabin last night, and that I didn't know her. What are you glowerin' at? No! I haven't lied to you, I swear to God, except in one thing. Did you know what that was? To save him I took upon me a shame I don't deserve. I let you think I was his mistress. You think so now, don't you? Well, before God to-day—and He may take me when He likes —I'm no more to him than a sister! I reckon your Nellie can't say as much."

She turned away, and with the quick, impatient stride of some caged animal made the narrow circuit of the opening, stopping a moment mechanically before the sick man, and again, without looking at him, continuing her monotonous round. The heat had become excessive, but she held her shawl with both hands drawn tightly over her shoulders. Suddenly a wood-duck darted out of the covert blindly into the opening, struck against the blasted trunk, fell half stunned near her feet, and then, recovering, fluttered away. She had scarcely completed another circuit before the irruption was followed by a whirring bevy of quail, a flight of jays, and a sudden tumult of wings swept through the wood like a tornado. She turned inquiringly to Dunn, who had risen to his feet, but the next moment she caught convulsively at his wrist; a wolf had just dashed through the underbrush not a dozen yards away, and on either side of them they could hear the scamper and rustle of hurrying feet like the outburst of a summer shower. A cold wind arose from the opposite direction, as if to contest this wild exodus, but it was followed by a blast of sickening heat. Teresa sank at Dunn's feet in an agony of terror.

"Don't let them touch me!" she gasped; "keep them off! Tell me, for God's sake, what has happened!"

He laid his hand firmly on her arm, and lifted her in his turn to her feet like a child. In that supreme moment of physical danger, his strength, reason, and manhood returned in their plenitude of power. He pointed coolly to the trail she had quitted, and said,

"The Carquinez Woods are on fire!"

CHAPTER X

THE nest of the tuneful Burnhams, although in the suburbs of Indian Spring, was not in ordinary weather and seasons hidden from the longing eyes of the youth of that settlement. That night, however, it was veiled in the smoke that encompassed the great highway leading to Excelsior. It is presumed that the Burnham brood had long since folded their wings, for there was no sign of life nor movement in the house as a rapidly-driven horse and buggy pulled up before it. Fortunately, the paternal Burnham was an early bird, in the habit of picking up the first stirring mining worm, and a resounding knock brought him half dressed to the street door. He was startled at seeing Father Wynn before him, a trifle flushed and abstracted.

"Ah ha! up betimes, I see, and ready. No sluggards here—ha, ha!" he said heartily, slamming the door behind him, and by a series of pokes in the ribs genially backing his host into his own sitting-room. "I'm up, too, and am here to see Nellie. She's here, eh—of course?" he added, darting a quick look at Burnham.

But Mr. Burnham was one of those large, liberal Western husbands who classified his household under the general title of "woman folk," for the integers of which he was not responsible. He hesitated, and then propounded over the balusters to the upper story the direct query—

"You don't happen to have Nellie Wynn up there, do ye?"

There was an interval of inquiry proceeding from half a dozen reluctant throats, more or less cottony and muffled, in those various degrees of grievance and mental distress which indicate too early roused young womanhood. The eventual reply seemed to be affirmative, albeit accompanied with a suppressed giggle, as if the young lady had just been discovered as an answer to an amusing conundrum.

"All right," said Wynn, with an apparent accession of boisterous geniality. "Tell her I must see her, and I've only got a few minutes to spare. Tell her to slip on anything and come down; there's no one here but myself, and I've shut the front door on Brother Burnham. Ha, ha!" and suiting the action to the word, he actually bundled the admiring Brother Burnham out on his own doorstep. There was a light pattering on the staircase, and Nellie Wynn, pink with sleep, very tall, very slim, hastily draped in a white counterpane with a blue border and a general classic suggestion, slipped into the parlor. At the same moment her father shut the door behind her, placed one hand on the knob, and with the other seized her wrist.

"Where were you yesterday?" he asked.

Nellie looked at him, shrugged her shoulders, and said, "Here."

"You were in the Carquinez Woods with Low Dorman; you went there in disguise; you've met him there before. He is your clandestine lover; you have taken pledges of affection from him; you have—"

"Stop!" she said.

He stopped.

"Did he tell you this?" she asked, with an expression of disdain.

"No; I overheard it. Dunn and Brace were at the house waiting for you. When the coach did not bring you, I went to the office to inquire. As I left our door I thought I saw somebody listening at the parlor windows. It was only a drunken Mexican muleteer leaning against the house; but if *he* heard nothing, *I* did. Nellie, I heard Brace tell Dunn that he had tracked you in your disguise to the woods—do you hear? that when you pretended to be here with the girls you were with Low— alone; that you wear a ring that Low got of a trader here; that there was a cabin in the woods—"

"Stop!" she repeated.

Wynn again paused.

"And what did *you* do?" she asked.

"I heard they were starting down there to surprise you and him together, and I harnessed up and got ahead of them in my buggy."

"And found me here," she said, looking full into his eyes.

He understood her and returned the look. He recognized the full importance of the culminating fact conveyed in her words, and was obliged to content himself with its logical and worldly significance. It was too late now to take her to task for mere filial disobedience; they must become allies.

"Yes," he said hurriedly; "but if you value your reputation, if you wish to silence both these men, answer me fully."

"Go on," she said.

"Did you go to the cabin in the woods yesterday?"

"No."

"Did you ever go there with Low?"

"No; I do not know even where it is."

Wynn felt that she was telling the truth. Nellie knew it; but as she would have been equally satisfied with an equally efficacious falsehood, her face remained unchanged.

"And when did he leave you?"

"At nine o'clock, here. He went to the hotel."

"He saved his life, then, for Dunn is on his way to the woods to kill him."

The jeopardy of her lover did not seem to affect the

young girl with alarm, although her eyes betrayed some interest.

"Then Dunn has gone to the woods?" she said thoughtfully.

"He has," replied Wynn.

"Is that all?" she asked.

"I want to know what you are going to do?"

"I *was* going back to bed."

"This is no time for trifling, girl."

"I should think not," she said, with a yawn; "it's too early, or too late."

Wynn grasped her wrist more tightly. "Hear me! Put whatever face you like on this affair, you are compromised—and compromised with a man you can't marry."

"I don't know that I ever wanted to marry Low, if you mean him," she said quietly.

"And Dunn wouldn't marry you now."

"I'm not so sure of that, either."

"Nellie," said Wynn excitedly, "do you want to drive me mad? Have you nothing to say — nothing to suggest?"

"Oh, you want me to help you, do you! Why didn't you say that first? Well, go and bring Dunn here."

"Are you mad? The man has gone already in pursuit of your lover, believing you with him."

"Then he will the more readily come and talk with me without him. Will you take the invitation — yes or no?"

"Yes, but—"

"Enough. On your way there you will stop at the hotel and give Low a letter from me."

"Nellie!"

"You shall read it, of course," she said scornfully, "for it will be your text for the conversation you will have with him. Will you please take your hand from the lock and open the door?"

Wynn mechanically opened the door. The young girl flew up-stairs. In a very few moments she returned with two notes: one contained a few lines of formal invitation to Dunn; the other read as follows:

"DEAR MR. DORMAN,—My father will tell you how deeply I regret that our recent botanical excursions in the Carquinez Woods have been a source of serious misapprehensions to those who had a claim to my consideration, and that I shall be obliged to discontinue them for the future. At the same time he wishes me to express my gratitude for your valuable instruction and assistance in that pleasing study, even though approaching events may compel me to relinquish it for other duties. May I beg you to accept the inclosed ring as a slight recognition of my obligations to you?

"Your grateful pupil,
"NELLIE WYNN."

When he had finished reading the letter, she handed him a ring, which he took mechanically. He raised his eyes to hers with perfectly genuine admiration. "You're a good girl, Nellie," he said, and, in a moment of parental forgetfulness, unconsciously advanced his lips towards her cheek. But she drew back in time to recall him to a sense of that human weakness.

"I suppose I'll have time for a nap yet," she said, as a gentle hint to her embarrassed parent. He nodded and turned towards the door.

"If I were you," she continued, repressing a yawn, "I'd manage to be seen on good terms with Low at the hotel; so perhaps you need not give the letter to him until the last thing. Good-by."

The sitting-room door opened and closed behind her as she slipped up-stairs, and her father, without the formality of leave-taking, quietly let himself out by the front door.

When he drove into the high road again, however, an overlooked possibility threatened for a moment to indefinitely postpone his amiable intentions regarding Low. The hotel was at the further end of the settlement towards the Carquinez Woods, and as Wynn had nearly reached it he was recalled to himself by the sounds of hoofs and wheels rapidly approaching from the direction of the Excelsior turnpike. Wynn made no doubt it was the sheriff and Brace. To avoid recognition at that moment, he whipped up his horse, intending to keep the lead until he could turn into the first cross-road. But the coming travelers had the fleetest horse, and finding it impossible to distance them he drove close to the ditch, pulling up suddenly as the strange vehicle was abreast of him, and forcing them to pass him at full speed, with the result already chronicled. When they had vanished in the darkness, Mr. Wynn, with a heart overflowing with Christian thankfulness and universal benevolence, wheeled round, and drove back to the hotel he had already passed. To pull up at the veranda with a stentorian shout, to thump loudly at the deserted bar, to hilariously beat the panels of the landlord's door, and commit a jocose assault and battery upon that half-dresssed and half-awakened man. was eminently characteristic of Wynn, and part of his amiable plans that morning.

"Something to wash this wood smoke from my throat, Brother Carter, and about as much again to prop open your eyes," he said, dragging Carter before the bar, "and glasses round for as many of the boys as are up and stirring after a hard-working Christian's rest. How goes the honest publican's trade, and who have we here?"

"Thar's Judge Robinson and two lawyers from Sacramento, Dick Curson over from Yolo," said Carter, "and that ar young Injin yarb doctor from the Carquinez Woods. I reckon he's jist up—I noticed a light under his door as I passed."

"He's my man for a friendly chat before breakfast," said Wynn. "You needn't come up. I'll find the way. I don't want a light; I reckon my eyes ain't as bright nor as young as his, but they'll see almost as far in the dark— he! he!" And, nodding to Brother Carter, he strode along the passage. and with no other introduction than a playful and preliminary "Boo!" burst into one of the rooms. Low, who by the light of a single candle was bending over the plates of a large quarto, merely raised his eyes and looked at the intruder. The young man's natural imperturbability, always exasperating to Wynn, seemed accented that morning by contrast with his own over-acted animation.

"Ah ha!—wasting the midnight oil instead of imbibing the morning dews," said Father Wynn archly, illustrating his metaphor with a movement of his hand to his lips. "What have we here?"

"An anonymous gift," replied Low simply, recognizing the father of Nellie by rising from his chair. "It's a volume I've longed to possess, but never could afford to buy. I cannot imagine who sent it to me."

Wynn was for a moment startled by the thought that this recipient of valuable gifts might have influential friends. But a glance at the bare room, which looked like a camp, and the strange, unconventional garb of its occupant, restored his former convictions. There might be a promise of intelligence, but scarcely of prosperity, in the figure before him.

"Ah! We must not forget that we are watched over in the night season," he said, laying his hand on Low's shoulder, with an illustration of celestial guardianship that would have been impious but for its palpable grotesqueness. "No, sir, we know not what a day may bring forth."

Unfortunately, Low's practical mind did not go beyond a mere human interpretation. It was enough, however, to put a new light in his eye and a faint color in his cheek.

"Could it have been Miss Nellie?" he asked, with half-boyish hesitation.

Mr. Wynn was too much of a Christian not to bow before what appeared to him the purely providential interposition of this suggestion. Seizing it and Low at the same moment, he playfully forced him down again in his chair.

"Ah, you rascal!" he said, with infinite archness; "that's your game, is it? You want to trap poor Father Wynn. You want to make him say 'No.' You want to tempt him to commit himself. No, sir!—never, sir!—no, no!"

Firmly convinced that the present was Nellie's, and that her father only good-humoredly guessed it, the young man's simple, truthful nature was embarrassed. He longed to express his gratitude, but feared to betray the young girl's trust. The Reverend Mr. Wynn speedily relieved his mind.

"No," he continued, bestriding a chair, and familiarly confronting Low over its back. "No, sir—no! And you want me to say 'No,' don't you, regarding the little walks of Nellie and a certain young man in the Carquinez Woods?—ha, ha! You'd like me to say that I knew nothing of the botanizings, and the herb collectings, and the picknickings there—he, he!—you sly dog! Perhaps you'd like to tempt Father Wynn further, and make him swear he knows nothing of his daughter disguising herself in a duster and meeting another young man—isn't it another young man?—all alone, eh? Perhaps you want poor old Father Wynn to say No. No, sir, nothing of the kind ever occurred. Ah, you young rascal!"

Slightly troubled, in spite of Wynn's hearty manner, Low, with his usual directness, however, said, "I do not want anyone to deny that I have seen Miss Nellie."

"Certainly, certainly," said Wynn, abandoning his method, considerably disconcerted by Low's simplicity, and a certain natural reserve that shook off his familiarity. "Certainly it's a noble thing to be able to put your hand on your heart and say to the world, 'Come on, all of you! Observe me; I have nothing to conceal. I walk with Miss Wynn in the woods as her instructor—her teacher, in fact. We cull a flower here and there; we pluck an herb fresh from the hands of the Creator. We look, so to speak, from Nature to Nature's God.' Yes, my young friend, we should be the first to repel the foul calumny that could misinterpret our most innocent actions."

"Calumny?" repeated Low, starting to his feet. "What calumny?"

"My friend, my noble young friend, I recognize your indignation. I know your worth. When I said to Nellie, my only child, my perhaps too simple offspring—a mere wildflower like yourself—when I said to her, 'Go, my child, walk in the woods with this young man, hand in hand. Let him instruct you from the humblest roots, for he has trodden in the ways of the Almighty. Gather wisdom from his lips, and knowledge from his simple woodman's craft. Make, in fact, a collection not only of herbs, but of moral axioms and experience'—I knew I could trust you, and, trusting you, my young friend, I felt I could trust the world. Perhaps I was weak, foolish. But I thought only of her welfare. I even recall how that to preserve the purity of her garments, I bade her don a simple duster; that, to secure her from the trifling companionship of others, I bade her keep her own counsel, and seek you at seasons known but to yourselves."

"But . . . did Nellie . . . understand you?" interrupted Low hastily.

"I see you read her simple nature. Understand me? No, not at first! Her maidenly instinct—perhaps her duty to another—took the alarm. I remember her words. 'But what will Dunn say?' she asked. 'Will he not be jealous?'"

"Dunn! jealous! I don't understand," said Low, fixing his eyes on Wynn.

"That's just what I said to Nellie. 'Jealous!' I said. 'What, Dunn, your affianced husband, jealous of a mere friend—a teacher, a guide, a philosopher. It is impossible.' Well, sir, she was right. He is jealous. And, more than that, he has imparted his jealousy to others! In other words, he has made a scandal!"

Low's eyes flashed. "Where is your daughter now?" he said sternly.

"At present in bed, suffering from a nervous attack brought on by these unjust suspicions. She appreciates your anxiety, and, knowing that you could not see her, told me to give you this." He handed Low the ring and the letter.

The climax had been forced, and, it must be confessed, was by no means the one Mr. Wynn had fully arranged in his own inner consciousness. He had intended to take an ostentatious leave of Low in the bar-room, deliver the letter with archness, and escape before a possible explosion. He consequently backed towards the door for an emergency. But he was again at fault. That unaffected stoical fortitude in acute suffering, which was the one remaining pride and glory of Low's race, was yet to be revealed to Wynn's civilized eyes.

The young man took the letter, and read it without changing a muscle, folded the ring in it, and dropped it into his haversack. Then he picked up his blanket, threw it over his shoulder, took his trusty rifle in his hand, and turned towards Wynn as if coldly surprised that he was still standing there.

"Are you—are you—going?" stammered Wynn.

"Are you *not?*" replied Low dryly, leaning on his rifle for a moment as if waiting for Wynn to precede him. The preacher looked at him a moment, mumbled something, and then shambled feebly and ineffectively down the staircase before Low, with a painful suggestion to the ordinary observer of being occasionally urged thereto by the moccasin of the young man behind him.

On reaching the lower hall, however, he endeavored to create a diversion in his favor by dashing into the bar-room and clapping the occupants on the back with indiscriminate playfulness. But here again he seemed to be disappointed. To his great discomfiture, a large man not only returned his salutation with powerful levity, but with equal playfulness seized him in his arms, and after an ingenious simulation of depositing him in the horse-trough set him down in affected amazement. "Bleth't if I didn't think from the weight of your hand it wath my old friend, Thacramento Bill," said Curson apologetically, with a wink at the bystanders. "That'th the way Bill alwayth uthed to tackle hith friendth, till he wath one day bounthed by a prithe-fighter in Frithco, whom he had mithtaken for a mithionary." As Mr. Curson's reputation was of a quality that made any form of apology from him instantly acceptable, the amused spectators made way for him as, recognizing Low, who was just leaving the hotel, he turned coolly from them and walked towards him.

"Halloo!" he said, extending his hand. "You're the man I'm waiting for. Did you get a book from the exthpreth offithe latht night?"

"I did. Why?"

"It'th all right. Ath I'm rethponthible for it, I only wanted to know."

"Did *you* send it?" asked Low, quickly fixing his eyes on his face.

"Well, not exactly *me*. But it'th not worth making a mythtery of it. Teretha gave me a commithion to buy it and thend it to you anonymouthly. That'th a woman'th nonthenth, for how could thee get a retheipt for it?"

"Then it was *her* present," said Low gloomily.

"Of courthe. It wathn't mine, my boy. I'd have thent you a Tharp'th rifle in plathe of that muthle loader you carry, or thomething thenthible. But, I thay! what'th up? You look ath if you had been running all night."

Low grasped his hand. "Thank you," he said hurriedly; "but it's nothing. Only I must be back to the woods early. Good-by."

But Curson retained Low's hand in his own powerful grip.

"I'll go with you a bit further," he said. "In fact, I've got thomething to thay to you; only don't be in thuch a hurry; the woodth can wait till you get there." Quietly compelling Low to alter his own characteristic Indian stride to keep pace with his, he went on: "I don't mind thaying I rather cottoned to you from the time you acted like a white man—no offenthe—to Teretha. She thayth you were left when a child lying round, jutht ath promithcuouthly ath she wath; and if I can do anything towardth putting you on the trail of your people, I'll do it. I know thome of the *voyageurth* who traded with the Cherokeeth, and your father wath one—wathn't he?" He glanced at Low's utterly abstracted and immobile face. "I thay, you don't theem to take a hand in thith game, pardner. What'th the row? Ith anything wrong over there?" and he pointed to the Carquinez Woods, which were just looming out of the morning horizon in the distance.

Low stopped. The last words of his companion seemed to recall him to himself. He raised his eyes automatically to the woods and started.

"There *is* something wrong over there," he said breathlessly. "Look!"

"I thee nothing," said Curson, beginning to doubt Low's sanity; "nothing more than I thaw an hour ago."

"Look again. Don't you see that smoke rising straight up? It isn't blown over there from the Divide; it's new smoke! The fire is in the woods!"

"I reckon that'th so," muttered Curson, shading his eyes with his hand. "But, hullo! wait a minute! We'll get hortheth. I say!" he shouted, forgetting his lisp in his excitement—"stop!" But Low had already lowered his head and darted forward like an arrow.

In a few moments he had left not only his companion but the last straggling houses of the outskirts far behind him, and had struck out in a long, swinging trot for the disused "cut-off." Already he fancied he heard the note of clamor in Indian Spring, and thought he distinguished the sound of hurrying hoofs on the great highway. But the sunken trail hid it from his view. From the column of smoke now plainly visible in the growing morning light he tried to locate the scene of the conflagration. It was evidently not a fire advancing regularly from the outer skirt of the wood, communicated to it from the Divide; it was a local outburst near its centre. It was not in the direction of his cabin in the tree. There was no immediate danger to Teresa, unless fear drove her beyond the confines of the wood into the hands of those who might recognize her. The screaming of jays and ravens above his head quickened his speed, as it heralded the rapid advance of the flames; and the unexpected apparition of a bounding body, flattened and flying over the yellow plain, told him that even the secure retreat of the mountain wild-cat had been invaded. A sudden recollection of Teresa's uncontrollable terror that first night smote him with remorse and redoubled his efforts. Alone in the track of these frantic and bewildered beasts, to what madness might she not be driven!

The sharp crack of a rifle from the high road turned his course momentarily in that direction. The smoke was curling lazily over the heads of the party of men in the road, while the huge bulk of a grizzly was disappearing in the distance. A battue of the escaping animals had commenced! In the bitterness of his heart he caught at the horrible suggestion, and resolved to save her from them or die with her there.

How fast he ran, or the time it took him to reach the woods, has never been known. Their outlines were already hidden when he entered them. To a sense less keen, a courage less desperate, and a purpose less unaltered than Low's, the wood would have been impenetrable. The central fire was still confined to the lofty tree tops, but the downward rush of wind from time to time drove the smoke into the aisles in blinding and suffocating volumes. To simulate the creeping animals, and fall to the ground on hands and knees, feel his way through the underbrush when the smoke was densest, or take advantage of its momentary lifting, and without uncertainty, mistake, or hesitation glide from tree to tree in one undeviating course, was possible only to an experienced woodsman. To keep his reason and insight so clear as to be able in the midst of this bewildering confusion to shape that course so as to intersect the wild and unknown tract of an inexperienced, frightened wanderer belonged to Low, and Low alone. He was making his way against the wind towards the fire. He had reasoned that she was either in comparative safety to windward of it, or he should meet her being driven towards him by it, or find her succumbed and fainting at its feet. To do this he must penetrate the burning belt, and then pass under the blazing dome. He was already upon it; he could see the falling fire dropping like rain or blown like gorgeous blossoms of the conflagration across his path. The space was lit up brilliantly. The vast shafts of dull copper cast no shadow below, but there was no sign nor token of any human being. For a moment the young man was at fault. It was true this hidden heart of the forest bore no undergrowth; the cool matted carpet of the aisles seemed to quench the glowing fragments as they fell. Escape might be difficult, but not impossible, yet every moment was precious. He leaned against a tree, and sent his voice like a clarion before him: "Teresa!" There was no reply. He called again. A faint cry at his back from the trail he had just traversed made him turn. Only a few paces behind him, blinded and staggering, but following like a beaten and wounded animal, Teresa, halted, knelt, clasped her hands, and dumbly held them out before her. "Teresa!" he cried again, and sprang to her side.

She caught him by the knees, and lifted her face imploringly to his.

"Say that again!" she cried, passionately. "Tell me it was Teresa you called, and no other! You have come back for me! You would not let me die here alone!"

He lifted her tenderly in his arms, and cast a rapid glance around him. It might have been his fancy, but there seemed a dull glow in the direction he had come.

"You do not speak!" she said. "Tell me! You did not come here to seek her?"

"Whom?" he said quickly.

"Nellie!"

With a sharp cry he let her slip to the ground. All the pent-up agony, rage, and mortification of the last hour broke from him in that inarticulate outburst. Then, catching her hands again, he dragged her to his level.

"Hear me!" he cried, disregarding the whirling smoke and the fiery baptism that sprinkled them—"hear me! If you value your life, if you value your soul, and if you do not want me to cast you to the beasts like Jezebel of old, never—never take that accursed name again upon your lips. Seek her—*her?* Yes! Seek her to tie her like a witch's daughter of hell to that blazing tree!" He stopped. "Forgive me," he said in a changed voice. "I'm mad, and forgetting myself and you. Come."

Without noticing the expression of half-savage delight that had passed across her face, he lifted her in his arms.

"Which way are you going?" she asked, passing her hands vaguely across his breast, as if to reassure herself of his identity.

"To our camp by the scarred tree," he replied.

"Not there, not there," she said, hurriedly. "I was

driven from there just now. I thought the fire began there until I came here."

Then it was as he feared. Obeying the same mysterious law that had launched this fatal fire like a thunderbolt from the burning mountain crest five miles away into the heart of the Carquinez Woods, it had again leaped a mile beyond, and was hemming them between two narrowing lines of fire. But Low was not daunted. Retracing his steps through the blinding smoke, he strode off at right angles to the trail near the point where he had entered the wood. It was the spot where he had first lifted Nellie in his arms to carry her to the hidden spring. If any recollection of it crossed his mind at that moment, it was only shown in his redoubled energy. He did not glide through the thick underbrush, as on that day, but seemed to take a savage pleasure in breaking through it with sheer brute force. Once Teresa insisted upon relieving him of the burden of her weight, but after a few steps she staggered blindly against him, and would fain have recourse once more to his strong arms. And so, alternately staggering, bending, crouching, or bounding and crashing on, but always in one direction, they burst through the jealous rampart, and came upon the sylvan haunt of the hidden spring. The great angle of the half-fallen tree acted as a barrier to the wind and drifting smoke, and the cool spring sparkled and bubbled in the almost translucent air. He laid her down beside the water, and bathed her face and hands. As he did so his quick eye caught sight of a woman's handkerchief lying at the foot of the disrupted root. Dropping Teresa's hand, he walked towards it, and with the toe of his moccasin gave it one vigorous kick into the ooze at the overflow of the spring. He turned to Teresa, but she evidently had not noticed the act.

"Where are you?" she asked, with a smile.

Something in her movement struck him! He came towards her, and bending down looked into her face. "Teresa! Good God!—look at me! What has happened?"

She raised her eyes to his. There was a slight film

across them; the lids were blackened; the beautiful lashes gone forever!

"I see you a little now, I think," she said, with a smile, passing her hands vaguely over his face. "It must have happened when he fainted, and I had to drag him through the blazing brush; both my hands were full, and I could not cover my eyes."

"Drag whom?" said Low, quickly.

"Why, Dunn."

"Dunn! He here?" said Low, hoarsely.

"Yes; didn't you read the note I left on the herbarium? Didn't you come to the camp-fire?" she asked hurriedly, clasping his hands. "Tell me quickly!"

"No!"

"Then you were not there—then you didn't leave me to die?"

"No! I swear it, Teresa!" the stoicism that had upheld his own agony breaking down before her strong emotion.

"Thank God!" She threw her arms around him, and hid her aching eyes in his troubled breast.

"Tell me all, Teresa," he whispered in her listening ear. "Don't move; stay there, and tell me all."

With her face buried in his bosom, as if speaking to his heart alone, she told him part, but not all. With her eyes filled with tears, but a smile on her lips, radiant with new-found happiness, she told him how she had overheard the plans of Dunn and Brace, how she had stolen their conveyance to warn him in time. But here she stopped, dreading to say a word that would shatter the hope she was building upon his sudden revulsion of feeling for Nellie. She could not bring herself to repeat their interview—that would come later, when they were safe and out of danger; now not even the secret of his birth must come between them with its distraction, to mar their perfect communion. She faltered that Dunn had fainted from weakness, and that she had dragged him out of danger. "He will never interfere with us—I mean," she said softly, "with *me* again. I can promise you that as well as if he had sworn it."

"Let him pass, now," said Low; "that will come later on," he added, unconsciously repeating her thought in a tone that made her heart sick. "But tell me, Teresa, why did you go to Excelsior?"

She buried her head still deeper, as if to hide it. He felt her broken heart beat against his own; he was conscious of a depth of feeling her rival had never awakened in him. The possibility of Teresa loving him had never occurred to his simple nature. He bent his head and kissed her. She was frightened, and unloosed her clinging arms; but he retained her hand, and said, "We will leave this accursed place, and you shall go with me as you said you would; nor need you ever leave me, unless you wish it."

She could hear the beating of her own heart through his words; she longed to look at the eyes and lips that told her this, and read the meaning his voice alone could not entirely convey. For the first time she felt the loss of her sight. She did not know that it was, in this moment of happiness, the last blessing vouchsafed to her miserable life.

A few moments of silence followed, broken only by the distant rumor of the conflagration and the crash of falling boughs.

"It may be an hour yet," he whispered, "before the fire has swept a path for us to the road below. We are safe here, unless some sudden current should draw the fire down upon us. You are not frightened?" She pressed his hand; she was thinking of the pale face of Dunn, lying in the secure retreat she had purchased for him at such a sacrifice. Yet the possibility of danger to him now for a moment marred her present happiness and security. "You think the fire will not go north of where you found me?" she asked softly.

"I think not," he said, "but I will reconnoitre. Stay where you are."

They pressed hands, and parted. He leaped upon the slanting trunk and ascended it rapidly. She waited in mute expectation.

There was a sudden movement of the root on which

she sat, a deafening crash, and she was thrown forward on her face.

The vast bulk of the leaning tree, dislodged from its aerial support by the gradual sapping of the spring at its roots, or by the crumbling of the bark from the heat, had slipped, made a half revolution, and, falling, overbore the lesser trees in its path, and tore, in its resistless momentum, a broad opening to the underbrush.

With a cry to Low, Teresa staggered to her feet. There was an interval of hideous silence, but no reply. She called again. There was a sudden deepening roar, the blast of a fiery furnace swept through the opening, a thousand luminous points around her burst into fire, and in an instant she was lost in a whirlwind of smoke and flame! From the onset of its fury to its culmination twenty minutes did not elapse; but in that interval a radius of two hundred yards around the hidden spring was swept of life and light and motion.

For the rest of that day and part of the night a pall of smoke hung above the scene of desolation. It lifted only towards the morning, when the moon, rising high, picked out in black and silver the shrunken and silent columns of those roofless vaults, shorn of base and capital. It flickered on the still, overflowing pool of the hidden spring, and shone upon the white face of Low, who, with a rootlet of the fallen tree holding him down like an arm across his breast, seemed to be sleeping peacefully in the sleeping water.

* * * * * * *

Contemporaneous history touched him as briefly, but not as gently. "It is now definitely ascertained," said "The Slumgullion Mirror," "that Sheriff Dunn met his fate in the Carquinez Woods in the performance of his duty; that fearless man having received information of the concealment of a band of horse thieves in their recesses. The desperadoes are presumed to have escaped, as the only remains found are those of two wretched tramps, one of whom is said to have been a digger, who supported himself upon roots and herbs, and the other a degraded half-white woman. It is not unreasonable to suppose that the fire originated through their carelessness, although Father Wynn of the First Baptist Church, in his powerful discourse of last Sunday, pointed at the warning and lesson of such catastrophes. It may not be out of place here to say that the rumors regarding an engagement between the pastor's accomplished daughter and the late lamented sheriff are utterly without foundation, as it has been an *on dit* for some time in all well-informed circles that the indefatigable Mr. Brace, of Wells, Fargo and Co.'s Express, will shortly lead the lady to the hymeneal altar."

SNOW-BOUND AT EAGLE'S

SNOW-BOUND AT EAGLE'S

CHAPTER I

FOR some moments profound silence and darkness had accompanied a Sierran stage-coach towards the summit. The huge, dim bulk of the vehicle, swaying noiselessly on its straps, glided onward and upward as if obeying some mysterious impulse from behind, so faint and indefinite appeared its relation to the viewless and silent horses ahead. The shadowy trunks of tall trees that seemed to approach the coach windows, look in, and then move hurriedly away, were the only distinguishable objects. Yet even these were so vague and unreal that they might have been the mere phantoms of some dream of the half-sleeping passengers; for the thickly-strewn needles of the pine, that choked the way and deadened all sound, yielded under the silently-crushing wheels a faint soporific odor that seemed to benumb their senses, already slipping back into unconsciousness during the long ascent. Suddenly the stage stopped.

Three of the four passengers inside struggled at once into upright wakefulness. The fourth passenger, John Hale, had not been sleeping, and turned impatiently towards the window. It seemed to him that two of the moving trees had suddenly become motionless outside. One of them moved again, and the door opened quickly but quietly, as of itself.

"Git down," said a voice in the darkness.

All the passengers except Hale started. The man next to him moved his right hand suddenly behind him, but as quickly stopped. One of the motionless trees had apparently closed upon the vehicle, and what had seemed to be a bough projecting from it at right angles changed slowly into the faintly shining double-barrels of a gun at the window.

"Drop that!" said the voice.

The man who had moved uttered a short laugh, and returned his hand empty to his knees. The two others perceptibly shrugged their shoulders as over a game that was lost. The remaining passenger, John Hale, fearless by nature, inexperienced by habit, awaking suddenly to the truth, conceived :. desperate resistance. But without his making a gesture this was instinctively felt by the others; the muzzle of the gun turned spontaneously on him, and he was vaguely conscious of a certain contempt and impatience of him in his companions.

"Git down," repeated the voice imperatively.

The three passengers descended. Hale, furious, alert, but helpless of any opportunity, followed. He was surprised to find the stage-driver and express messenger standing beside him; he had not heard them dismount. He instinctively looked towards the horses. He could see nothing.

"Hold up your hands!"

One of the passengers had already lifted his, in a weary, perfunctory way. The others did the same reluctantly and awkwardly, but apparently more from the consciousness of the ludicrousness of their attitude than from any sense of danger. The rays of a bull's-eye lantern, deftly managed by invisible hands, while it left the intruders in shadow, completely illuminated the faces and figures of the passengers. In spite of the majestic obscurity and silence of surrounding nature, the group of humanity thus illuminated was more farcical than dramatic. A scrap of newspaper, part of a sandwich, and an orange peel that had fallen from the floor of the coach, brought into equal prominence by the searching light, completed the absurdity.

"There's a man here with a package of greenbacks," said the voice, with an official coolness that lent a certain suggestion of Custom House inspection to the transaction;

"who is it?" The passengers looked at each other, and their glance finally settled on Hale.

"It's not *him*," continued the voice, with a slight tinge of contempt on the emphasis. "You'll save time and searching, gentlemen, if you'll tote it out. If we've got to go through every one of you we'll try to make it pay."

The significant threat was not unheeded. The passenger who had first moved when the stage stopped put his hand to his breast.

"T'other pocket first, if you please," said the voice.

The man laughed, drew a pistol from his hip pocket, and, under the strong light of the lantern, laid it on a spot in the road indicated by the voice. A thick envelope, taken from his breast pocket, was laid beside it. "I told the d—d fools that gave it to me, instead of sending it by express, it would be at their own risk," he said apologetically.

"As it's going with the express now it's all the same," said the inevitable humorist of the occasion, pointing to the despoiled express treasure-box already in the road.

The intention and deliberation of the outrage was plain enough to Hale's inexperience now. Yet he could not understand the cool acquiescence of his fellow-passengers, and was furious. His reflections were interrupted by a voice which seemed to come from a greater distance. He fancied it was even softer in tone, as if a certain austerity was relaxed.

"Step in as quick as you like, gentlemen. You've five minutes to wait, Bill."

The passengers reëntered the coach; the driver and express messenger hurriedly climbed to their places. Hale would have spoken, but an impatient gesture from his companions stopped him. They were evidently listening for something; he listened too.

Yet the silence remained unbroken. It seemed incredible that there should be no indication near or far of that forceful presence which a moment ago had been so dominant. No rustle in the wayside "brush," nor echo from the rocky cañon below, betrayed a sound of their flight. A faint breeze stirred the tall tips of the pines, a cone dropped on the stage roof, one of the invisible horses that seemed to be listening too moved slightly in his harness. But this only appeared to accentuate the profound stillness. The moments were growing interminable, when the voice, so near as to startle Hale, broke once more from the surrounding obscurity.

"Good-night!"

It was the signal that they were free. The driver's whip cracked like a pistol shot, the horses sprang furiously forward, the huge vehicle lurched ahead, and then bounded violently after them. When Hale could make his voice heard in the confusion—a confusion which seemed greater from the colorless intensity of their last few moments' experience—he said hurriedly, "Then that fellow was there all the time?"

"I reckon," returned his companion, "he stopped five minutes to cover the driver with his double-barrel, until the two other men got off with the treasure."

"The *two* others!" gasped Hale. "Then there were only *three* men, and we *six*."

The man shrugged his shoulders. The passenger who had given up the greenbacks drawled, with a slow, irritating tolerance, "I reckon you're a stranger here?"

"I am—to this sort of thing, certainly, though I live a dozen miles from here, at Eagle's Court," returned Hale scornfully.

"Then you're the chap that's doin' that fancy ranchin' over at Eagle's," continued the man lazily.

"Whatever I'm doing at Eagle's Court, I'm not ashamed of it," said Hale tartly; "and that's more than I can say of what I've done—or *haven't* done—to-night. I've been one of six men overawed and robbed by *three*."

"As to the over-awin', ez you call it—mebbee you know more about it than us. As to the robbin'—ez far as I kin remember, *you* haven't onloaded much. Ef you're talkin' about what *oughter* have been done, I'll tell you what *could* have happened. P'r'aps ye noticed that when he pulled up I made a kind of grab for my wepping behind me?"

"I did; and you wern't quick enough," said Hale shortly.

"I wasn't quick enough, and that saved *you*. For ef I got that pistol out and in sight o' that man that held the gun—"

"Well," said Hale impatiently, "he'd have hesitated."

"He'd hev blown *you* with both barrels outer the window, and that before I'd got a half-cock on my revolver."

"But that would have been only one man gone, and there would have been five of you left," said Hale haughtily.

"That might have been, ef you'd contracted to take the hull charge of two handfuls of buck-shot and slugs; but ez one eighth o' that amount would have done your business, and yet left enough to have gone round, promiskiss, and satisfied the other passengers, it wouldn't do to kalkilate upon."

"But the express messenger and the driver were armed," continued Hale.

"They were armed, but not *fixed;* that makes all the difference."

"I don't understand."

"I reckon you know what a duel is?"

"Yes."

"Well, the chances agin *us* was about the same as you'd have ef you was put up agin another chap who was allowed to draw a bead on you, and the signal to fire was *your drawin' your weapon.* You may be a stranger to this sort o' thing, and p'r'aps you never fought a duel, but even then you wouldn't go foolin' your life away on any such chances."

Something in the man's manner, as in a certain sly amusement the other passengers appeared to extract from the conversation, impressed Hale, already beginning to be conscious of the ludicrous insufficiency of his own grievance beside that of his interlocutor.

"Then you mean to say this thing is inevitable," said he bitterly, but less aggressively.

"Ez long ez they hunt *you;* when you hunt *them* you've

got the advantage, allus provided you know how to get at them ez well as they know how to get at you. This yer coach is bound to go regular, and on certain days. *They* ain't. By the time the sheriff gets out his *posse* they've skedaddled, and the leader, like as not, is takin' his quiet cocktail at the Bank Exchange, or mebbe losin' his earnings to the sheriff over draw poker, in Sacramento. You see you can't prove anything agin them unless you take them 'on the fly.' It may be a part of Joaquim Murietta's band, though I wouldn't swear to it."

"The leader might have been Gentleman George, from up-country," interposed a passenger. "He seemed to throw in a few fancy touches, particlerly in that 'Good night.' Sorter chucked a little sentiment in it. Didn't seem to be the same thing ez, 'Git, yer d—d suckers,' on the other line."

"Whoever he was, he knew the road and the men who travelled on it. Like ez not, he went over the line beside the driver on the box on the down trip, and took stock of everything. He even knew I had those greenbacks; though they were handed to me in the bank at Sacramento. He must have been hanging' round there."

For some moments Hale remained silent. He was a civic-bred man, with an intense love of law and order; the kind of man who is the first to take that law and order into his own hands when he does not find it existing to please him. He had a Bostonian's respect for respectability, tradition, and propriety, but was willing to face irregularity and impropriety to create order elsewhere. He was fond of Nature with these limitations, never quite trusting her unguided instincts, and finding her as an instructress greatly inferior to Harvard University, though possibly not to Cornell. With dauntless enterprise and energy he had built and stocked a charming cottage farm in a nook in the Sierras, whence he opposed, like the lesser Englishman that he was, his own tastes to those of the alien West. In the present instance he felt it incumbent upon him not only to assert his principles, but to act upon them with his usual energy. How far he was impelled by the half-contemptuous passiveness of his companions it would be difficult to say.

"What is to prevent the pursuit of them at once?" he asked suddenly. "We are a few miles from the station, where horses can be procured."

"Who's to do it?" replied the other lazily. "The stage company will lodge the complaint with the authorities, but it will take two days to get the county officers out, and it's nobody else's funeral."

"I will go for one," said Hale quietly. "I have a horse waiting for me at the station, and can start at once."

There was an instant of silence. The stage-coach had left the obscurity of the forest, and by the stronger light Hale could perceive that his companion was examining him with two colorless, lazy eyes. Presently he said, meeting Hale's clear glance, but rather as if yielding to a careless reflection,—

"It *might* be done with four men. We oughter raise one man at the station." He paused. "I don't know ez I'd mind taking a hand myself," he added, stretching out his legs with a slight yawn.

"Ye can count *me* in, if you're goin', Kernel. I reckon I'm talkin' to Kernel Clinch," said the passenger beside Hale with sudden alacrity. "I'm Rawlins, of Frisco. Heerd of ye afore, Kernel, and kinder spotted you jist now from your talk."

To Hale's surprise the two men, after awkwardly and perfunctorily grasping each other's hand, entered at once into a languid conversation on the recent election at Fresno, without the slightest further reference to the pursuit of the robbers. It was not until the remaining and undenominated passenger turned to Hale, and, re-gretting that he had immediate business at the Summit, offered to accompany the party if they would wait a couple of hours, that Colonel Clinch briefly returned to the subject.

"*Four* men will do, and ez we'll hev to take horses from the station we'll hev to take the fourth man from there."

With these words he resumed his uninteresting con-versation with the equally uninterested Rawlins, and the undenominated passenger subsided into an admiring and dreamy contemplation of them both. With all his principle and really high-minded purpose, Hale could not help feeling constrained and annoyed at the sudden subordinate and auxiliary position to which he, the projector of the enterprise, had been reduced. It was true that he had never offered himself as their leader; it was true that the principle he wished to uphold and the effect he sought to obtain would be equally demonstrated under another; it was true that the execution of his own conception gravitated by some occult impulse to the man who had not sought it, and whom he had always regarded as an incapable. But all this was so unlike precedent or tradition that, after the fashion of conservative men, he was suspicious of it, and only that his honor was now involved he would have withdrawn from the enterprise. There was still a chance of reasserting himself at the station, where he was known, and where some authority might be deputed to him.

But even this prospect failed. The station, half hotel and half stable, contained only the landlord, who was also express agent, and the new volunteer who Clinch had suggested would be found among the stable-men. The nearest justice of the peace was ten miles away, and Hale had to abandon even his hope of being sworn in as a deputy constable. This introduction of a common and illiterate ostler into the party on equal terms with himself did not add to his satisfaction, and a remark from Rawlins seemed to complete his embarrassment.

"Ye had a mighty narrer escape down there just now," said that gentleman confidentially, as Hale buckled his saddle girths.

"I thought, as we were not supposed to defend ourselves, there was no danger," said Hale scornfully.

"Oh, I don't mean them road agents. But *him.*"

"Who?"

"Kernel Clinch. You jist ez good as allowed he hadn't any grit."

"Whatever I said, I suppose I am responsible for it," answered Hale haughtily.

"That's what gits me," was the imperturbable reply. "He's the best shot in Southern California, and hez let daylight through a dozen chaps afore now for half what you said."

"Indeed!"

"Howsummever," continued Rawlins philosophically, "ez he's concluded to go *with* ye instead of *for* ye, you're likely to hev your ideas on this matter carried out up to the handle. He'll make short work of it, you bet. Ef, ez I suspect, the leader is an airy young feller from Frisco, who hez took to the road lately, Clinch hez got a personal grudge agin him from a quarrel over draw poker."

This was the last blow to Hale's ideal crusade. Here he was—an honest, respectable citizen—engaged as simple accessory to a lawless vendetta originating at a gambling table! When the first shock was over that grim philosophy which is the reaction of all imaginative and sensitive natures came to his aid. He felt better; oddly enough he began to be conscious that he was thinking and acting like his companions. With this feeling a vague sympathy, before absent, faintly showed itself in their actions. The Sharpe's rifle put into his hands by the stable-man was accompanied by a familiar word of suggestion as to an equal, which he was ashamed to find flattered him. He was able to continue the conversation with Rawlins more coolly.

"Then you suspect who is the leader?"

"Only on giniral principles. There was a finer touch, so to speak, in this yer robbery that wasn't in the old-fashioned style. Down in my country they hed crude ideas about them things—used to strip the passengers of everything, includin' their clothes. They say that at the station hotels, when the coach came in, the folks used to stand round with blankets to wrap up the passengers so ez not to skeer the wimen. Thar's a story that the driver and express manager drove up one day with only a copy of the *Alty Californy* wrapped around 'em; but thin," added Rawlins grimly, "there *was* folks ez said the hull story was only an advertisement got up for the *Alty*."

"Time's up."

"Are you ready, gentlemen?" said Colonel Clinch.

Hale started. He had forgotten his wife and family at Eagle's Court, ten miles away. They would be alarmed at his absence, would perhaps hear some exaggerated version of the stage coach robbery, and fear the worst.

"Is there any way I could send a line to Eagle's Court before daybreak?" he asked eagerly.

The station was already drained of its spare men and horses. The undenominated passenger stepped forward and offered to take it himself when his business, which he would despatch as quickly as possible, was concluded.

"That ain't a bad idea," said Clinch reflectively, "for ef yer hurry you'll head 'em off in case they scent us, and try to double back on the North Ridge. They'll fight shy of the trail if they see anybody on it, and one man's as good as a dozen."

Hale could not help thinking that he might have been that one man, and had his opportunity for independent action but for his rash proposal, but it was too late to withdraw now. He hastily scribbled a few lines to his wife on a sheet of the station paper, handed it to the man, and took his place in the little cavalcade as it filed silently down the road.

They had ridden in silence for nearly an hour, and had passed the scene of the robbery by a higher track. Morning had long ago advanced its colors on the cold white peaks to their right, and was taking possession of the spur where they rode.

"It looks like snow," said Rawlins quietly.

Hale turned towards him in astonishment. Nothing on earth or sky looked less likely. It had been cold, but that might have been only a current from the frozen peaks beyond, reaching the lower valley. The ridge on which they had halted was still thick with yellowish-green summer foliage, mingled with the darker evergreen of pine and fir. Oven-like cañons in the long flanks of the mountain seemed still to glow with the heat of yesterday's noon; the breathless air yet trembled and quivered over stifling gorges and passes in the granite rocks, while far at their feet sixty miles of perpetual summer stretched away over the winding American River, now and then lost in a gossamer haze. It was scarcely ripe October where they stood; they could see the plenitude of August still lingering in the valleys.

"I've seen Thomson's Pass choked up with fifteen feet o' snow earlier than this," said Rawlins, answering Hale's gaze; "and last September the passengers sledded over the road we came last night, and all the time Thomson, a mile lower down over the ridge in the hollow, smoking his pipes under roses in his piazzy! Mountains is mighty uncertain; they make their own weather ez they want it. I reckon you ain't wintered here yet."

Hale was obliged to admit that he had only taken Eagle's Court in the early spring.

"Oh, you're all right at Eagle's—when you're there! But it's like Thomson's—it's the gettin' there that—— Hallo! What's that?"

A shot, distant but distinct, had rung through the keen air. It was followed by another so alike as to seem an echo.

"That's over yon, on the North Ridge," said the ostler, "about two miles as the crow flies and five by the trail. Somebody's shootin' b'ar."

"Not with a shot gun," said Clinch, quickly wheeling his horse with a gesture that electrified them. "It's *them,* and the've doubled on us! To the North Ridge, gentlemen, and ride all you know!"

It needed no second challenge to completely transform that quiet cavalcade. The wild man-hunting instinct, inseparable to most humanity, rose at their leader's look and word. With an incoherent and unintelligible cry, giving voice to the chase like the commonest hound of their fields, the order-loving Hale and the philosophical Rawlins wheeled with the others, and in another instant the little band swept out of sight in the forest.

An immense and immeasurable quiet succeeded. The sunlight glistened silently on cliff and scar, the vast distance below seemed to stretch out and broaden into repose. It might have been fancy, but over the sharp

13   v. 2

line of the North Ridge a light smoke lifted as of an escaping soul.

CHAPTER II

EAGLE'S COURT, one of the highest cañons of the Sierras, was in reality a plateau of table-land, embayed like a green lake in a semi-circular sweep of granite, that, lifting itself three thousand feet higher, became a foundation for the eternal snows. The mountain genii of space and atmosphere jealously guarded its seclusion and surrounded it with illusions; it never looked to be exactly what it was: the traveller who saw it from the North Ridge apparently at his feet in descending found himself separated from it by a mile-long abyss and a rushing river; those who sought it by a seeming direct trail at the end of an hour lost sight of it completely, or, abandoning the quest and retracing their steps, suddenly came upon the gap through which it was entered. That which from the Ridge appeared to be a copse of bushes beside the tiny dwelling were trees three hundred feet high; the cultivated lawn before it, which might have been covered by the traveller's handkerchief, was a field of a thousand acres.

The house itself was a long, low, irregular structure, chiefly of roof and veranda, picturesquely upheld by rustic pillars of pine, with the bark still adhering, and covered with vines and trailing roses. Yet it was evident that the coolness produced by this vast extent of cover was more than the architect, who had planned it under the influence of a staring and bewildering sky, had trustfully conceived, for it had to be mitigated by blazing fires in open hearths when the thermometer marked a hundred degrees in the field beyond. The dry, restless wind that continually rocked the tall masts of the pines with a sound like the distant sea, while it stimulated out-door physical exertion and defied fatigue, left the sedentary dwellers in these altitudes chilled in the shade they courted, or scorched them with heat when they ventured to bask supinely in the sun. White muslin curtains at the French windows, and rugs, skins, and heavy furs dispersed in the interior, with certain other charming but incongruous details of furniture, marked the inconsistencies of the climate.

There was a coquettish indication of this in the costume of Miss Kate Scott as she stepped out on the veranda that morning. A man's broad-brimmed Panama hat, partly unsexed by a twisted gayly-colored scarf, but retaining enough character to give piquancy to the pretty curves of the face beneath, protected her from the sun; a red flannel shirt—another spoil from the enemy—and a thick jacket shielded her from the austerities of the morning breeze. But the next inconsistency was peculiarly her own. Miss Kate always wore the freshest and lightest of white cambric skirts, without the least reference to the temperature. To the practical sanatory remonstrances of her brother-in-law, and to the conventional criticism of her sister, she opposed the same defence: "How else is one to tell when it is summer in this ridiculous climate? And then, woollen is stuffy, color draws the sun, and one at least knows when one is clean or dirty." Artistically the result was far from unsatisfactory. It was a pretty figure under the sombre pines, against the gray granite and the steely sky, and seemed to lend the yellowing fields from which the flowers had already fled a floral relief of color. I do not think the few masculine wayfarers of that locality objected to it; indeed, some had betrayed an indiscreet admiration, and had curiously followed the invitation of Miss Kate's warmly-colored figure until they had encountered the invincible indifference of Miss Kate's cold gray eyes. With these manifestations her brother-in-law did not concern himself; he had perfect confidence in her unqualified disinterest in the neighboring humanity, and permitted her to wander in her solitary picturesqueness, or accompanied her when she rode in her dark green habit, with equal freedom from anxiety.

For Miss Scott, although only twenty, had already subjected most of her maidenly illusions to mature critical analyses. She had voluntarily accompanied her sister and mother to California, in the earnest hope that nature contained something worth saying to her, and was disappointed to find she had already discounted its value in the pages of books. She hoped to find a vague freedom in this unconventional life thus opened to her, or rather to show others that she knew how intelligently to appreciate it, but as yet she was only able to express it in the one detail of dress already alluded to. Some of the men, and nearly all the women, she had met thus far, she was amazed to find, valued the conventionalities she believed she despised, and were voluntarily assuming the chains she thought she had thrown off. Instead of learning anything from them, these children of nature had bored her with eager questionings regarding the civilization she had abandoned, or irritated her with crude imitations of it for her benefit. "Fancy," she had written to a friend in Boston, "my calling on Sue Murphy, who remembered the Donner tragedy, and who once shot a grizzly that was prowling round her cabin, and think of her begging me to lend her my sack for a pattern, and wanting to know if 'polonays' were still worn." She remembered more bitterly the romance that had tickled her earlier fancy, told of two college friends of her brother-in-law's who were living the "perfect life" in the mines, laboring in the ditches with a copy of Homer in their pockets, and writing letters of the purest philosophy under the free air of the pines. How, coming unexpectedly on them in their Arcadia, the party found them unpresentable through dirt, and thenceforth unknowable through domestic complications that had filled their Arcadian cabin with half-breed children.

Much of this disillusion she had kept within her own heart, from a feeling of pride, or only lightly touched upon it in her relations with her mother and sister. For Mrs. Hale and Mrs. Scott had no idols to shatter, no enthusiasm to subdue. Firmly and unalterably conscious of their own superiority to the life they led and the community that surrounded them, they accepted their duties cheerfully, and performed them conscientiously. Those duties were loyalty to Hale's interests and a vague missionary work among the neighbors, which, like most missionary work, consisted rather in making their own ideas understood than in understanding the ideas of their audience. Old Mrs. Scott's zeal was partly religious, an inheritance from her Puritan ancestry; Mrs. Hale's was the affability of a gentlewoman and the obligation of her position. To this was added the slight languor of the cultivated American wife, whose health has been affected by the birth of her first child, and whose views of marriage and maternity were slightly tinged with gentle scepticism. She was sincerely attached to her husband, "who dominated the household" like the rest of his "women folk," with the faint consciousness of that division of service which renders the position of the sultan of a seraglio at once so prominent and so precarious. The attitude of John Hale in his family circle was dominant because it had never been subjected to criticism or comparison; and perilous for the same reason.

Mrs. Hale presently joined her sister in the veranda, and, shading her eyes with a narrow white hand, glanced on the prospect with a polite interest and ladylike urbanity. The searching sun, which, as Miss Kate once intimated, was "vulgarity itself," stared at her in return, but could not call a blush to her somewhat sallow cheek. Neither could it detract, however, from the delicate prettiness of her refined face with its soft gray shadows, or the dark gentle eyes, whose blue-veined lids were just ' then wrinkled into coquettishly mischievous lines by the strong light. She was taller and thinner than Kate, and had at times a certain shy, coy sinuosity of movement which gave her a more virginal suggestion than her unmarried sister. For Miss Kate, from her earliest youth, had been distinguished by that matronly sedateness of voice and step, and completeness of figure, which indicates some members of the gallinaceous tribe from their callow infancy.

"I suppose John must have stopped at the Summit on some business," said Mrs. Hale, "or he would have been here already. It's scarcely worth while waiting for him, unless you choose to ride over and meet him. You might

change your dress," she continued, looking doubtfully at
Kate's costume. "Put on your riding-habit, and take
Manuel with you."

"And take the only man we have, and leave you alone?"
returned Kate slowly. "No!"

"There are the Chinese field hands," said Mrs. Hale;
"you must correct your ideas, and really allow them some
humanity, Kate. John says they have a very good com-
pulsory school system in their own country, and can read
and write."

"That would be of little use to you here alone if—if—"
Kate hesitated.

"If what?" said Mrs. Hale smiling. "Are you thinking
of Manuel's dreadful story of the grizzly tracks across
the fields this morning? I promise you that neither I,
nor mother, nor Minnie shall stir out of the house until
you return, if you wish it."

"I wasn't thinking of that," said Kate; "though I don't
believe the beating of a gong and the using of strong
language is the best way to frighten a grizzly from the
house. Besides, the Chinese are going down the river
to-day to a funeral, or a wedding, or a feast of stolen
chickens—they're all the same—and won't be here."

"Then take Manuel," repeated Mrs. Hale. "We have
the Chinese servants and Indian Molly in the house to
protect us from Heaven knows what! I have the greatest confidence in Chy-Lee as a warrior, and in Chinese
warfare generally. One has only to hear him pipe in
time of peace to imagine what a terror he might become
in war time. Indeed, anything more deadly and soul-
harrowing than that love song he sang for us last night I
cannot conceive. But really, Kate, I am not afraid to
stay alone. You know what John says: we ought to be
always prepared for anything that might happen."

"My dear Josie," returned Kate, putting her arm around
her sister's waist, "I am perfectly convinced that if three-
fingered Jack, or two-toed Bill, or even Joaquim Murietta
himself, should step, red-handed, on that veranda, you
would gently invite him to take a cup of tea, inquire about
the state of the road, and refrain delicately from any

allusions to the sheriff. But I shan't take Manuel from you. I really cannot undertake to look after his morals at the station, and keep him from drinking *aguardiente* with suspicious characters at the bar. It is true he 'kisses my hand' in his speech, even when it is thickest, and offers his back to me for a horse-block, but I think I prefer the sober and honest familiarity of even that Pike County landlord who is satisfied to say, 'Jump, girl, and I'll ketch ye!'"

"I hope you didn't change your manner to either of them for that," said Mrs. Hale with a faint sigh. "John wants to be good friends with them, and they are behaving quite decently lately, considering that they can't speak a grammatical sentence nor know the use of a fork."

"And now the man puts on gloves and a tall hat to come here on Sundays, and the woman won't call until you've called first," retorted Kate; "perhaps you call that improvement. The fact is, Josephine," continued the young girl, folding her arms demurely, "we might as well admit it at once—these people don't like us."

"That's impossible!" said Mrs. Hale, with sublime simplicity. "You don't like them, you mean."

"I like them better than you do, Josie, and that's the reason why *I* feel it and *you* don't." She checked herself, and after a pause resumed in a lighter tone: "No; I sha'n't go to the station; I'll commune with nature to-day, and won't 'take any humanity in mine, thank you,' as Bill the driver says. *Adios.*"

"I wish Kate would not use that dreadful slang, even in jest," said Mrs. Scott, in her rocking-chair at the French window, when Josephine reëntered the parlor as her sister walked briskly away. "I am afraid she is being infected by the people at the station. She ought to have a change."

"I was just thinking," said Josephine, looking abstractedly at her mother, "that I would try to get John to take her to San Francisco this winter. The Careys are expected, you know; she might visit them."

"I'm afraid, if she stays here much longer, she won't care to see them at all. She seems to care for nothing

now that she ever liked before," returned the old lady
ominously.

Meantime the subject of these criticisms was carrying
away her own reflections tightly buttoned up in her short
jacket. She had driven back her dog Spot—another one
of her disillusions, who, giving way to his lower nature,
had once killed a sheep—as she did not wish her Jacques-
like contemplation of any wounded deer to be incon-
sistently interrupted by a fresh outrage from her companion. The air was really very chilly, and for the first
time in her mountain experience the direct rays of the
sun seemed to be shorn of their power. This compelled
her to walk more briskly than she was conscious of, for
in less than an hour she came suddenly and breathlessly
upon the mouth of the cañon, or natural gateway to
Eagle's Court.

To her always a profound spectacle of mountain mag-
nificence, it seemed to-day almost terrible in its cold,
strong grandeur. The narrowing pass was choked for
a moment between two gigantic buttresses of granite, approaching each other so closely at their towering summits
that trees growing in opposite clefts of the rock inter-
mingled their branches and pointed the soaring Gothic
arch of a stupendous gateway. She raised her eyes with
a quickly beating heart. She knew that the interlacing
trees above her were as large as those she had just
quitted; she knew also that the point where they met was
only half-way up the cliff, for she had once gazed down
upon them, dwindled to shrubs from the airy summit;
she knew that their shaken cones fell a thousand feet
perpendicularly, or bounded like shot from the scarred
walls they bombarded. She remembered that one of these
pines, dislodged from its high foundations, had once
dropped like a portcullis in the archway, blocking the pass,
and was only carried afterwards by assault of steel and
fire. Bending her head mechanically, she ran swiftly
through the shadowy passage, and halted only at the beginning of the ascent on the other side.

It was here that the actual position of the plateau, so
indefinite of approach, began to be realized. It now ap-

peared an independent elevation, surrounded on three sides by gorges and watercourses, so narrow as to be overlooked from the principal mountain range, with which it was connected by a long cañon that led to the ridge. At the outlet of this cañon—in bygone ages a mighty river—it had the appearance of having been slowly raised by the diluvium of that river, and the *débris* washed down from above—a suggestion repeated in miniature by the artificial plateaus of excavated soil raised before the mouths of mining tunnels in the lower flanks of the mountain. It was the realization of a fact—often forgotten by the dwellers in Eagle's Court—that the valley below them, which was their connecting link with the surrounding world, was only reached by ascending the mountain, and the nearest road was over the higher mountain ridge. Never before had this impressed itself so strongly upon the young girl as when she turned that morning to look upon the plateau below her. It seemed to illustrate the conviction that had been slowly shaping itself out of her reflections on the conversation of that morning. It was possible that the perfect understanding of a higher life was only reached from a height still greater, and that to those half-way up the mountain the summit was never as truthfully revealed as to the humbler dwellers in the valley.

I do not know that these profound truths prevented her from gathering some quaint ferns and berries, or from keeping her calm gray eyes open to certain practical changes that were taking place around her. She had noticed a singular thickening in the atmosphere that seemed to prevent the passage of the sun's rays, yet without diminishing the transparent quality of the air. The distant snow-peaks were as plainly seen, though they appeared as if in moonlight. This seemed due to no cloud or mist, but rather to a fading of the sun itself. The occasional flurry of wings overhead, the whirring of larger birds in the cover, and a frequent rustling in the undergrowth, as of the passage of some stealthy animal, began equally to attract her attention. It was so different from the habitual silence of these sedate solitudes. Kate had no vague fear of wild beasts; she had been long enough a mountaineer to understand the general immunity enjoyed by the unmolesting wayfarer, and kept her way undismayed. She was descending an abrupt trail when she was stopped by a sudden crash in the bushes. It seemed to come from the opposite incline, directly in a line with her, and apparently on the very trail that she was pursuing. The crash was then repeated again and again lower down, as of a descending body. Expecting the apparition of some fallen tree, or detached boulder bursting through the thicket, in its way to the bottom of the gulch, she waited. The foliage was suddenly brushed aside, and a large grizzly bear half rolled, half waddled, into the trail on the opposite side of the hill. A few moments more would have brought them face to face at the foot of the gulch; when she stopped there were not fifty yards between them.

She did not scream; she did not faint; she was not even frightened. There did not seem to be anything terrifying in this huge, stupid beast, who, arrested by the rustle of a stone displaced by her descending feet, rose slowly on his haunches and gazed at her with small, wondering eyes. Nor did it seem strange to her, seeing that he was in her way, to pick up a stone, throw it in his direction, and say simply, "Sho! get away!" as she would have done to an intruding cow. Nor did it seem odd that he should actually "go away" as he did, scrambling back into the bushes again, and disappearing like some grotesque figure in a transformation scene. It was not until after he had gone that she was taken with a slight nervousness and giddiness, and retraced her steps somewhat hurriedly, shying a little at every rustle in the thicket. By the time she had reached the great gateway she was doubtful whether to be pleased or frightened at the incident, but she concluded to keep it to herself.

It was still intensely cold. The light of the midday sun had decreased still more, and on reaching the plateau again she saw that a dark cloud, not unlike the precursor of a thunder-storm, was brooding over the snowy peaks beyond. In spite of the cold this singular suggestion of

summer phenomena was still borne out by the distant
smiling valley, and even in the soft grasses at her feet.
It seemed to her the crowning inconsistency of the climate,
and with a half-serious, half-playful protest on her lips
she hurried forward to seek the shelter of the house.

CHAPTER III

To Kate's surprise, the lower part of the house was
deserted, but there was an unusual activity on the floor
above, and the sound of heavy steps. There were alien
marks of dusty feet on the scrupulously clean passage, and
on the first step of the stairs a spot of blood. With a
sudden genuine alarm that drove her previous adventure
from her mind, she impatiently called her sister's name.
There was a hasty yet subdued rustle of skirts on the
staircase, and Mrs. Hale, with her finger on her lip,
swept Kate unceremoniously into the sitting-room, closed
the door, and leaned back against it, with a faint smile.
She had a crumpled paper in her hand.

"Don't be alarmed, but read that first," she said, handing her sister the paper. "It was brought just now."

Kate instantly recognized her brother's distinct hand.
She read hurriedly, "The coach was robbed last night;
nobody hurt. I've lost nothing but a day's time, as this
business will keep me here until to-morrow, when Manuel
can join me with a fresh horse. No cause for alarm.
As the bearer goes out of his way to bring you this,
see that he wants for nothing."

"Well," said Kate expectantly.

"Well, the 'bearer' was fired upon by the robbers, who
were lurking on the Ridge. He was wounded in the leg.
Luckily he was picked up by his friend, who was coming
to meet him, and brought here as the nearest place.
He's up-stairs in the spare bed in the spare room, with
his friend, who won't leave his side. He won't even
have mother in the room. They've stopped the bleeding
with John's ambulance things, and now, Kate, here's
a chance for you to show the value of your education

in the ambulance class. The ball has got to be extracted. Here's your opportunity."

Kate looked at her sister curiously. There was a faint pink flush on her pale cheeks, and her eyes were gently sparkling. She had never seen her look so pretty before.

"Why not have sent Manuel for a doctor at once?" asked Kate.

"The nearest doctor is fifteen miles away, and Manuel is nowhere to be found. Perhaps he's gone to look after the stock. There's some talk of snow; imagine the absurdity of it!"

"But who are they?"

"They speak of themselves as 'friends,' as if it were a profession. The wounded one was a passenger, I suppose."

"But what are they like?" continued Kate. "I suppose they're like them all."

Mrs. Hale shrugged her shoulders.

"The wounded one, when he's not fainting away, is laughing. The other is a creature with a moustache, and gloomy beyond expression."

"What are you going to do with them?" said Kate.

"What should I do? Even without John's letter I could not refuse the shelter of my house to a wounded and helpless man. I shall keep him, of course, until John comes. Why, Kate, I really believe you are so prejudiced against these people you'd like to turn them out. But I forget! It's because you *like* them so well. Well, you need not fear to expose yourself to the fascinations of the wounded Christy Minstrel—I'm sure he's that—or to the unspeakable one, who is shyness itself, and would not dare to raise his eyes to you."

There was a timid, hesitating step in the passage. It paused before the door, moved away, returned, and finally asserted its intentions in the gentlest of taps.

"It's him; I'm sure of it," said Mrs. Hale, with a suppressed smile.

Kate threw open the door smartly, to the extreme discomfiture of a tall, dark figure that already had slunk away from it. For all that, he was a good-looking enough fellow, with a moustache as long and almost as flexible as a ringlet. Kate could not help noticing also that his hand, which was nervously pulling the moustache, was white and thin.

"Excuse me," he stammered, without raising his eyes, "I was looking for—for—the old lady. I—I beg your pardon. I didn't know that you—the young ladies—company—were here. I intended—I only wanted to say that my friend—" He stopped at the slight smile that passed quickly over Mrs. Hale's mouth, and his pale face reddened with an angry flush.

"I hope he is not worse," said Mrs. Hale, with more than her usual languid gentleness. "My mother is not here at present. Can I—can *we*—this is my sister—do as well?"

Without looking up he made a constrained recognition of Kate's presence, that embarrassed and curt as it was, had none of the awkwardness of rusticity.

"Thank you; you're very kind. But my friend is a little stronger, and if you can lend me an extra horse I'll try to get him on the Summit to-night."

"But you surely will not take him away from us so soon?" said Mrs. Hale, with a languid look of alarm, in which Kate, however, detected a certain real feeling. "Wait at least until my husband returns to-morrow."

"He won't be here to-morrow," said the stranger hastily. He stopped, and as quickly corrected himself. "That is, his business is so very uncertain, my friend says."

Only Kate noticed the slip; but she noticed also that her sister was apparently unconscious of it. "You think," she said, "that Mr. Hale may be delayed?"

He turned upon her almost brusquely. "I mean that it is already snowing up there;" he pointed through the window to the cloud Kate had noticed; "if it comes down lower in the pass the roads will be blocked up. That is why it would be better for us to try and get on at once."

"But if Mr. Hale is likely to be stopped by snow, so are you," said Mrs. Hale playfully; "and you had better let us try to make your friend comfortable here rather than expose him to that uncertainty in his weak condition. We will do our best for him. My sister is dying for an opportunity to show her skill in surgery," she continued, with an unexpected mischievousness that only added to Kate's surprised embarrassment. "Aren't you, Kate?"

Equivocal as the young girl knew her silence appeared, she was unable to utter the simplest polite evasion. Some unaccountable impulse kept her constrained and speechless. The stranger did not, however, wait for her reply, but, casting a swift, hurried glance around the room, said, "It's impossible; we must go. In fact, I've already taken the liberty to order the horses round. They are at the door now. You may be certain," he added, with quick earnestness, suddenly lifting his dark eyes to Mrs. Hale, and as rapidly withdrawing them, "that your horse will be returned at once, and—and—we won't forget your kindness." He stopped and turned towards the hall. "I—I have brought my friend down-stairs. He wants to thank you before he goes."

As he remained standing in the hall the two women stepped to the door. To their surprise, half reclining on a cane sofa was the wounded man, and what could be seen of his slight figure was wrapped in a dark *serape*. His beardless face gave him a quaint boyishness quite inconsistent with the mature lines of his temples and forehead. Pale, and in pain, as he evidently was, his blue eyes twinkled with intense amusement. Not only did his manner offer a marked contrast to the sombre uneasiness of his companion, but he seemed to be the only one perfectly at his ease in the group around him.

"It's rather rough making you come out here to see me off," he said, with a not unmusical laugh that was very infectious, "but Ned there, who carried me down-stairs, wanted to tote me round the house in his arms like a baby to say ta-ta to you all. Excuse my not rising, but I feel as uncertain below as a mermaid, and as out of my element," he added, with a mischievous glance at his friend. "Ned concluded I must go on. But I must say good-by to the old lady first. Ah! here she is."

To Kate's complete bewilderment, not only did the utter familiarity of this speech, pass unnoticed and unrebuked by her sister, but actually her own mother advanced quickly with every expression of lively sympathy, and with the authority of her years and an almost maternal anxiety endeavored to dissuade the invalid from going. "This is not my house," she said, looking at her daughter, "but if it were I should not hear of your leaving, not only to-night, but until you were out of danger. Josephine! Kate! What are you thinking of to permit it? Well, then *I* forbid it—there!"

Had they become suddenly insane, or were they bewitched by this morose intruder and his insufferably familiar confidant? The man was wounded, it was true; they might have to put him up in common humanity; but here was her austere mother, who wouldn't come in the room when Whisky Dick called on business, actually pressing both of the invalid's hands, while her sister, who never extended a finger to the ordinary visiting humanity of the neighborhood, looked on with evident complacency.

The wounded man suddenly raised Mrs. Scott's hand to his lips, kissed it gently, and, with his smile quite vanished, endeavored to rise to his feet. "It's of no use—we must go. Give me your arm, Ned. Quick! Are the horses there?"

"Dear me," said Mrs. Scott quickly. "I forgot to say the horse cannot be found anywhere. Manuel must have taken him this morning to look up the stock. But he will be back to-night certainly, and if to-morrow—"

The wounded man sank back to a sitting position. "Is Manuel your man?" he asked grimly.

"Yes."

The two men exchanged glances.

"Marked on his left cheek and drinks a good deal?"

"Yes," said Kate, finding her voice. "Why?"

The amused look came back to the man's eyes. "That kind of man isn't safe to wait for. We must take our own horse, Ned. Are you ready?"

"Yes."

The wounded man again attempted to rise. He fell back, but this time quite heavily. He had fainted.

Involuntarily and simultaneously the three women rushed to his side. "He cannot go," said Kate suddenly.

"He will be better in a moment."

"But only for a moment. Will nothing induce you to change your mind?"

As if in reply a sudden gust of wind brought a volley of rain against the window.

"*That* will," said the stranger bitterly.

"The rain?"

"A mile from here it is *snow;* and before we could reach the Summit with these horses the road would be impassable."

He made a slight gesture to himself, as if accepting an inevitable defeat, and turned to his companion, who was slowly reviving under the active ministration of the two women. The wounded man looked around with a weak smile. "This is one way of going off," he said faintly, "but I could do this sort of thing as well on the road."

"You can do nothing now," said his friend, decidedly. "Before we get to the Gate the road will be impassable for our horses."

"For *any* horses?" asked Kate.

"For any horses. For any man or beast I might say. Where we cannot get out, no one can get in," he added, as if answering her thoughts. "I am afraid that you won't see your brother to-morrow morning. But I'll reconnoitre as soon as I can do so without torturing *him,*" he said, looking anxiously at the helpless man; "he's got about his share of pain, I reckon, and the first thing is to get him easier." It was the longest speech he had made to her; it was the first time he had fairly looked her in the face. His shy restlessness had suddenly given way to dogged resignation, less abstracted, but scarcely more flattering to his entertainers. Lifting his companion gently in his arms, as if he had been a child, he reascended the staircase, Mrs. Scott and the hastily-summoned Molly following with overflowing solicitude.

As soon as they were alone in the parlor Mrs. Hale turned to her sister: "Only that our guests seemed to be as anxious to go just now as you were to pack them off, I should have been shocked at your inhospitality. What has come over you, Kate? These are the very people you have reproached me so often with not being civil enough to."

"But *who* are they?"

"How do I know? There is *your brother's* letter."

She usually spoke of her husband as "John." This slight shifting of relationship and responsibility to the feminine mind was significant. Kate was a little frightened and remorseful.

"I only meant you don't even know their names."

"That wasn't necessary for giving them a bed and bandages. Do you suppose the good Samaritan ever asked the wounded Jew's name, and that the Levite did not excuse himself because the thieves had taken the poor man's card-case? Do the directions, 'In case of accident,' in your ambulance rules, read, 'First lay the sufferer on his back and inquire his name and family connections'? Besides, you can call one 'Ned' and the other 'George,' if you like."

"Oh, you know what I mean," said Kate, irrelevantly. "Which is George?"

"George is the wounded man," said Mrs. Hale; "*not* the one who talked to you more than he did to any one else. I suppose the poor man was frightened and read dismissal in your eyes."

"I wish John were here."

"I don't think we have anything to fear in his absence from men whose only wish is to get away from us. If it is a question of propriety, my dear Kate, surely there is the presence of mother to prevent any scandal—although really her own conduct with the wounded one is not above suspicion," she added, with that novel mischievousness that seemed a return of her lost girlhood. "We must try to do the best we can with them and for them," she said decidedly, "and meantime I'll see if I can't arrange John's room for them."

"John's room?"

"Oh, mother is perfectly satisfied; indeed, suggested it. It's larger and will hold two beds, for 'Ned,' the friend, must attend to him at night. And, Kate, don't you think, if you're not going out again, you might change your costume? It does very well while we are alone—"

"Well," said Kate indignantly, "as I am not going into his room—"

"I'm not so sure about that, if we can't get a regular doctor. But he is very restless, and wanders all over the house like a timid and apologetic spaniel."

"Who?"

"Why 'Ned.' But I must go and look after the patient. I suppose they've got him safe in his bed again," and with a nod to her sister she tripped up-stairs.

Uncomfortable and embarrassed, she knew not why, Kate sought her mother. But that good lady was already in attendance on the patient, and Kate hurried past that baleful centre of attraction with a feeling of loneliness and strangeness she had never experienced before. Entering her own room she went to the window—that first and last refuge of the troubled mind—and gazed out. Turning her eyes in the direction of her morning's walk, she started back with a sense of being dazzled. She rubbed first her eyes and then the rain-dimmed pane. It was no illusion! The whole landscape, so familiar to her, was one vast field of dead, colorless white! Trees, rocks, even distance itself, had vanished in those few hours. An even shadowless, motionless white sea filled the horizon. On either side a vast wall of snow seemed to shut out the world like a shroud. Only the green plateau before her, with its sloping meadows and fringe of pines and cottonwood, lay alone like a summer island in this frozen sea.

A sudden desire to view this phenomenon more closely, and to learn for herself the limits of this new tethered life, completely possessed her, and, accustomed to act upon her independent impulses, she seized a hooded waterproof cloak, and slipped out of the house unperceived. The rain was falling steadily along the descending trail where she walked, but beyond, scarcely a mile across the chasm, the wintry distance began to confuse her brain with the inextricable swarming of snow. Hurrying down with feverish excitement, she at last came in sight of the arching granite portals of their domain. But her first glance through the gateway showed it closed as if with a white portcullis. Kate remembered that the trail began to ascend beyond the arch, and knew that what she saw was only the mountain side she had partly climbed this morning. But the snow had already crept down its flank, and the exit by trail was practically closed. Breathlessly making her way back to the highest part of the plateau—the cliff behind the house that here descended abruptly to the rain-dimmed valley—she gazed at the dizzy depths in vain for some undiscovered or forgotten trail along its face. But a single glance convinced her of its inaccessibility. The gateway was indeed their only outlet to the plain below. She looked back at the falling snow beyond until she fancied she could see in the crossing and recrossing lines the moving meshes of a fateful web woven around them by viewless but inexorable fingers.

Half frightened, she was turning away, when she perceived, a few paces distant, the figure of the stranger, "Ned," also apparently absorbed in the gloomy prospect. He was wrapped in the clinging folds of a black *serape* braided with silver; the broad flap of a slouch hat beaten back by the wind exposed the dark, glistening curls on his white forehead. He was certainly very handsome and picturesque, and that apparently without effort or consciousness. Neither was there anything in his costume or appearance inconsistent with his surroundings, or, even with what Kate could judge were his habits or position. Nevertheless, she instantly decided that he was *too* handsome and too picturesque, without suspecting that her ideas of the limits of masculine beauty were merely personal experience.

As he turned away from the cliff they were brought face to face. "It doesn't look very encouraging over there," he said quietly, as if the inevitableness of the situation had relieved him of his previous shyness and effort; "it's even worse than I expected. The snow must have begun there last night, and it looks as if it meant to stay." He stopped for a moment, and then, lifting his eyes to her, said:— "I suppose you know what this means?"

"I don't understand you."

"I thought not. Well! it means that you are absolutely cut off here from any communication or intercourse with any one outside of that cañon. By this time the snow is five feet deep over the only trail by which one can pass in and out of that gateway. I am not alarming you, I hope, for there is no real physical danger; a place like this ought to be well garrisoned, and certainly is self-supporting so far as the mere necessities and even comforts are concerned. You have wood, water, cattle, and game at your command, but for two weeks at least you are completely isolated."

"For two weeks," said Kate, growing pale—"and my brother!"

"He knows all by this time, and is probably as assured as I am of the safety of his family."

"For two weeks," continued Kate; "impossible! You don't know my brother! He will find some way to get to us."

"I hope so," returned the stranger gravely, "for what is possible for him is possible for us."

"Then you are anxious to get away," Kate could not help saying.

"Very."

The reply was not discourteous in manner, but was so far from gallant that Kate felt a new and inconsistent resentment. Before she could say anything he added, "And I hope you will remember, whatever may happen, that I did my best to avoid staying here longer than was necessary to keep my friend from bleeding to death in the road."

"Certainly," said Kate; then added awkwardly, "I hope he'll be better soon." She was silent, and then, quickening her pace, said hurriedly, "I must tell my sister this dreadful news."

"I think she is prepared for it. If there is anything I can do to help you I hope you will let me know. Perhaps I may be of some service. I shall begin by exploring the trails to-morrow, for the best service we can do you possibly is to take ourselves off; but I can carry a gun, and the woods are full of game driven down from the mountains. Let me show you something you may not have noticed." He stopped, and pointed to a small knoll of sheltered shrubbery and granite on the opposite mountain, which still remained black against the surrounding snow. It seemed to be thickly covered with moving objects. "They are wild animals driven out of the snow," said the stranger. "That larger one is a grizzly; there is a panther, wolves, wild cats, a fox, and some mountain goats."

"An ill-assorted party," said the young girl.

"Ill luck makes them companions. They are too frightened to hurt one another now."

"But they will eat each other later on," said Kate, stealing a glance at her companion.

He lifted his long lashes and met her eyes. "Not on a haven of refuge."

CHAPTER IV

KATE found her sister, as the stranger had intimated, fully prepared. A hasty inventory of provisions and means of subsistence showed that they had ample resources for a much longer isolation.

"They tell me it is by no means an uncommon case, Kate; somebody over at somebody's place was snowed in for four weeks, and now it appears that even the Summit House is not always accessible. John ought to have known it when he bought the place; in fact, I was ashamed to admit that he did not. But that is like John, to prefer his own theories to the experience of others. However, I don't suppose we should even notice the privation except for the mails. It will be a lesson to

John, though. As Mr. Lee says, he is on the outside, and can probably go wherever he likes from the Summit except to come here."

"Mr. Lee?" echoed Kate.

"Yes, the wounded one; and the other's name is Falkner. I asked them in order that you might be properly introduced. There were very respectable Falkners in Charlestown, you remember; I thought you might warm to the name, and perhaps trace the connection, now that you are such good friends. It's providential they are here, as we haven't got a horse or a man in the place since Manuel disappeared, though Mr. Falkner says he can't be far away, or they would have met him on the trail if he had gone towards the Summit."

"Did they say anything more of Manuel?"

"Nothing; though I am inclined to agree with you that he isn't trustworthy. But that again is the result of John's idea of employing native skill at the expense of retaining native habits."

The evening closed early, and with no diminution in the falling rain and rising wind. Falkner kept his word, and unostentatiously performed the out-door work in the barn and stables, assisted by the only Chinese servant remaining, and under the advice and supervision of Kate. Although he seemed to understand horses, she was surprised to find that he betrayed a civic ignorance of the ordinary details of the farm and rustic household. It was quite impossible that she should retain her distrustful attitude, or he his reserve in their enforced companionship. They talked freely of subjects suggested by the situation, Falkner exhibiting a general knowledge and intuition of things without parade or dogmatism. Doubtful of all versatility as Kate was, she could not help admitting to herself that his truths were none the less true for their quantity or that he got at them without ostentatious processes. His talk certainly was more picturesque than her brother's, and less subduing to her faculties. John had always crushed her.

When they returned to the house he did not linger in the parlor or sitting-room, but at once rejoined his friend.

When dinner was ready in the dining-room, a little more deliberately arranged and ornamented than usual, the two women were somewhat surprised to receive an excuse from Falkner, begging them to allow him for the present to take his meals with the patient, and thus save the necessity of another attendant.

"It is all shyness, Kate," said Mrs. Hale, confidently, "and must not be permitted for a moment."

"I'm sure I should be quite willing to stay with the poor boy myself," said Mrs. Scott, simply, "and take Mr. Falkner's place while he dines."

"You are too willing, mother," said Mrs. Hale, pertly, "and your 'poor boy,' as you call him, will never see thirty-five again."

"He will never see any other birthday!" retorted her mother, "unless you keep him more quiet. He only talks when you're in the room."

"He wants some relief to his friend's long face and moustachios that make him look prematurely in mourning," said Mrs. Hale, with a slight increase of animation. "I don't propose to leave them too much together. After dinner we'll adjourn to their room and lighten it up a little. You must come, Kate, to look at the patient, and counteract the baleful effects of my frivolity."

Mrs. Hale's instincts were truer than her mother's experience; not only that the wounded man's eyes became brighter under the provocation of her presence, but it was evident that his naturally exuberant spirits were a part of his vital strength, and were absolutely essential to his quick recovery. Encouraged by Falkner's grave and practical assistance, which she could not ignore, Kate ventured to make an examination of Lee's wound. Even to her unpractised eye it was less serious than at first appeared. The great loss of blood had been due to the laceration of certain small vessels below the knee, but neither artery nor bone was injured. A recurrence of the hæmorrhage or fever was the only thing to be feared, and these could be averted by bandaging, repose, and simple nursing.

The unfailing good humor of the patient under this

manipulation, the quaint originality of his speech, the freedom of his fancy, which was, however, always controlled by a certain instinctive tact, began to affect Kate nearly as it had the others. She found herself laughing over the work she had undertaken in a pure sense of duty; she joined in the hilarity produced by Lee's affected terror of her surgical mania, and offered to undo the bandages in search of the thimble he declared she had left in the wound with a view to further experiments.

"You ought to broaden your practice," he suggested. "A good deal might be made out of Ned and a piece of soap left carelessly on the first step of the staircase, while mountains of surgical opportunities lie in a humble orange peel judiciously exposed. Only I warn you that you wouldn't find him as docile as I am. Decoyed into a snow-drift and frozen, you might get some valuable experiences in resuscitation by thawing him."

"I fancied you had done that already, Kate," whispered Mrs. Hale.

"Freezing is the new suggestion for painless surgery," said Lee, coming to Kate's relief with ready tact, "only the knowledge should be more generally spread. There was a man up at Strawberry fell under a sledge-load of wood in the snow. Stunned by the shock, he was slowly freezing to death, when, with a tremendous effort, he succeeded in freeing himself all but his right leg, pinned down by a small log. His axe happened to have fallen within reach, and a few blows on the log freed him."

"And saved the poor fellow's life," said Mrs. Scott, who was listening with sympathizing intensity.

"At the expense of his *left leg,* which he had unknowingly cut off under the pleasing supposition that it was a log," returned Lee demurely.

Nevertheless, in a few moments he managed to divert the slightly shocked susceptibilities of the old lady with some raillery of himself, and did not again interrupt the even good-humored communion of the party. The rain beating against the windows and the fire sparkling on the hearth seemed to lend a charm to their peculiar isolation, and it was not until Mrs. Scott rose with a warning that they were trespassing upon the rest of their patient that they discovered that the evening had slipped by unnoticed. When the door at last closed on the bright, sympathetic eyes of the two young women and the motherly benediction of the elder, Falkner walked to the window, and remained silent, looking into the darkness. Suddenly he turned bitterly to his companion.

"This is just h—ll, George."

George Lee, with a smile on his boyish face, lazily moved his head.

"I don't know! If it wasn't for the old woman, who is the one solid chunk of absolute goodness here, expecting nothing, wanting nothing, it would be good fun enough! These two women, cooped up in this house, wanted excitement. They've got it! That man Hale wanted to show off by going for us; he's had his chance, and will have it again before I've done with him. That d—d fool of a messenger wanted to go out of his way to exchange shots with me; I reckon he's the most satisfied of the lot! I don't know why *you* should growl. You did your level best to get away from here, and the result is, that little Puritan is ready to worship you."

"Yes—but this playing it on them—George—this—"

"Who's playing it? Not you; I see you've given away our names already."

"I couldn't lie, and they know nothing by that."

"Do you think they would be happier by knowing it? Do you think that soft little creature would be as happy as she was to-night if she knew that her husband had been indirectly the means of laying me by the heels here? Where is the swindle? This hole in my leg? If you had been five minutes under that girl's d—d sympathetic fingers you'd have thought it was genuine. Is it in our trying to get away? Do you call that ten-feet drift in the pass a swindle? Is it in the chance of Hale getting back while we're here? That's real enough, isn't it? I say, Ned, did you ever give your unfettered intellect to the contemplation of *that?*"

Falkner did not reply. There was an interval of silence, but he could see from the movement of George's shoulders that he was shaking with suppressed laughter.

"Fancy Mrs. Hale archly introducing her husband! My offering him a chair, but being all the time obliged to cover him with a derringer under the bedclothes. Your rushing in from your peaceful pastoral pursuits in the barn, with a pitchfork in one hand and the girl in the other, and dear old mammy sympathizing all round and trying to make everything comfortable."

"I should not be alive to see it, George," said Falkner gloomily.

"You'd manage to pitchfork me and those two women on Hale's horse and ride away; that's what you'd do, or I don't know you! Look here, Ned," he added more seriously, "the only swindling was our bringing that note here. That was *your* idea. You thought it would remove suspicion, and as you believed I was bleeding to death you played that game for all it was worth to save me. You might have done what I asked you to do—propped me up in the bushes, and got away yourself. I was good for a couple of shots yet, and after that—what mattered? That night, the next day, the next time I take the road, or a year hence? It will come when it will come, all the same!"

He did not speak bitterly, nor relax his smile. Falkner, without speaking, slid his hand along the coverlet. Lee grasped it, and their hands remained clasped together for a few minutes in silence.

"How is this to end? We cannot go on here in this way," said Falkner suddenly.

"If we cannot get away it must go on. Look here, Ned. I don't reckon to take anything out of this house that I didn't bring in it, or isn't freely offered to me; yet I don't otherwise, you understand, intend making myself out a d—d bit better than I am. That's the only excuse I have for not making myself out *just what* I am. I don't know the fellow who's obliged to tell every one the last company he was in, or the last thing he did! Do you suppose even these pretty little women tell *us* their whole story? Do you fancy that this St. John in the wilderness is canonized in his family? Perhaps, when I take the liberty to intrude in his affairs, as he has in mine, he'd see he isn't. I don't blame you for being sensitive, Ned. It's natural. When a man lives outside the revised statutes of his own State he is apt to be awfully fine on points of etiquette in his own household. As for me, I find it rather comfortable here. The beds of other people's making strike me as being more satisfactory than my own. Good-night."

In a few moments he was sleeping the peaceful sleep of that youth which seemed to be his own dominant quality. Falkner stood for a little space and watched him, following the boyish lines of his cheek on the pillow, from the shadow of the light brown lashes under his closed lids to the lifting of his short upper lip over his white teeth, with his regular respiration. Only a sharp accenting of the line of nostril and jaw and a faint depression of the temple betrayed his already tried manhood.

The house had long sunk to repose when Falkner returned to the window, and remained looking out upon the storm. Sudenly he extinguished the light, and passing quickly to the bed laid his hand upon the sleeper. Lee opened his eyes instantly.

"Are you awake?"

"Perfectly."

"Somebody is trying to get into the house!"

"Not *him*, eh?" said Lee gayly.

"No; two men. Mexicans, I think. One looks like Manuel."

"Ah," said Lee, drawing himself up to a sitting posture. "Well?"

"Don't you see? He believes the women are alone."

"The dog—d—d hound!"

"Speak respectfully of one of my people, if you please, and hand me my derringer. Light the candle again, and open the door. Let them get in quietly. They'll come here first. It's *his* room, you understand, and if there's any money it's here. Anyway, they must pass here to get to the women's rooms. Leave Manuel to me, and you take care of the other."

"I see."

"Manuel knows the house, and will come first. When he's fairly in the room shut the door and go for the other. But no noise. This is just one of the *sw-eetest* things out—if it's done properly."

"But *you,* George?"

"If I couldn't manage that fellow without turning down the bedclothes I'd kick myself. Hush. Steady now."

He lay down and shut his eyes as if in natural repose. Only his right hand, carelessly placed under his pillow, closed on the handle of his pistol. Falkner quietly slipped into the passage. The light of the candle faintly illuminated the floor and opposite wall, but left it on either side in pitchy obscurity.

For some moments the silence was broken only by the sound of the rain without. The recumbent figure in bed seemed to have actually succumbed to sleep. The multitudinous small noises of a house in repose might have been misinterpreted by ears less keen than the sleeper's; but when the apparent creaking of a far-off shutter was followed by the sliding apparition of a dark head of tangled hair at the door, Lee had not been deceived, and was as prepared as if he had seen it. Another step, and the figure entered the room. The door closed instantly behind it. The sound of a heavy body struggling against the partition outside followed, and then suddenly ceased.

The intruder turned, and violently grasped the handle of the door, but recoiled at a quiet voice from the bed.

"Drop that, and come here."

He started back with an exclamation. The sleeper's eyes were wide open; the sleeper's extended arm and pistol covered him.

"Silence! or I'll let that candle shine through you!"

"Yes, captain!" growled the astounded and frightened half-breed. "I didn't know you were here."

Lee raised himself, and grasped the long whip in his left hand and whirled it round his head.

"*Will you* dry up?"

The man sank back against the wall in silent terror.

"Open that door now—softly."

Manuel obeyed with trembling fingers.

"Ned," said Lee in a low voice, "bring him in here—quick."

There was a slight rustle, and Falkner appeared, backing in another gasping figure, whose eyes were starting under the strong grasp of the captor at his throat.

"Silence," said Lee, "all of you."

There was a breathless pause. The sound of a door hesitatingly opened in the passage broke the stillness, followed by the gentle voice of Mrs. Scott.

"Is anything the matter?"

Lee made a slight gesture of warning to Falkner, of menace to the others. "Everything's the matter," he called out cheerily. "Ned's managed to half pull down the house trying to get at something from my saddle-bags."

"I hope he has not hurt himself," broke in another voice mischievously.

"Answer, you clumsy villain," whispered Lee, with twinkling eyes.

"I'm all right, thank you," responded Falkner, with unaffected awkwardness.

There was a slight murmuring of voices, and then the door was heard to close. Lee turned to Falkner.

"Disarm that hound and turn him loose outside, and make no noise. And you, Manuel! tell him what his and your chances are if he shows his black face here again."

Manuel cast a single, terrified, supplicating glance, more suggestive than words, at his confederate, as Falkner shoved him before him from the room. The next moment they were silently descending the stairs.

"May I go too, captain?" entreated Manuel. "I swear to God—"

"Shut the door!" The man obeyed.

"Now, then," said Lee, with a broad, gratified smile, laying down his whip and pistol within reach, and comfortably settling the pillows behind his back, "we'll have a quiet confab. A sort of old-fashioned talk, eh? You're not looking well, Manuel. You're drinking too much again. It spoils your complexion."

"Let me go, captain," pleaded the man, emboldened

by the good-humored voice, but not near enough to notice a peculiar light in the speaker's eye.

"You've only just come, Manuel; and at considerable trouble, too. Well, what have you got to say? What's all this about? What are you doing here?"

The captured man shuffled his feet nervously, and only uttered an uneasy laugh of coarse discomfiture.

"I see. You're bashful. Well, I'll help you along. Come! You knew that Hale was away and these women were here without a man to help them. You thought you'd find some money here, and have your own way generally, eh?"

The tone of Lee's voice inspired him to confidence; unfortunately, it inspired him with familiarity also.

"I reckoned I had the right to a little fun on my own account, cap. I reckoned ez one gentleman in the profession wouldn't interfere with another gentleman's little game," he continued coarsely.

"Stand up."

"Wot for?"

"Up, I say!"

Manuel stood up and glanced at him.

"Utter a cry that might frighten these women, and by the living God they'll rush in here only to find you lying dead on the floor of the house you'd have polluted."

He grasped the whip and laid the lash of it heavily twice over the ruffian's shoulders. Writhing in suppressed agony, the man fell imploringly on his knees.

"Now, listen!" said Lee, softly twirling the whip in the air. "I want to refresh your memory. Did you ever learn, when you were with me—before I was obliged to kick you out of gentlemen's company—to break into a private house? Answer!"

"No," stammered the wretch.

"Did you ever learn to rob a woman, a child, or any but a man, and that face to face?"

"No," repeated Manuel.

"Did you ever learn from me to lay a finger upon a woman, old or young, in anger or kindness?"

"No."

"Then, my poor Manuel, it's as I feared; civilization has ruined you. Farming and a simple, bucolic life have perverted your morals. So you were running off with the stock and that mustang, when you got stuck in the snow; and the luminous idea of this little game struck you? Eh? That was another mistake, Manuel; I never allowed you to think when you were with me."

"No, captain."

"Who's your friend?"

"A d—d cowardly nigger from the Summit."

"I agree with you for once; but he hasn't had a very brilliant example. Where's he gone now?"

"To h—ll, for all I care!"

"Then I want you to go with him. Listen. If there's a way out of the place, you know it or can find it. I give you two days to do it—you and he. At the end of that time the order will be to shoot you on sight. Now take off your boots."

The man's dark face visibly whitened, his teeth chattered in superstitious terror.

"I'm not going to shoot you now," said Lee, smiling, "so you will have a chance to die with your boots on,[1] if you are superstitious. I only want you to exchange them for that pair of Hale's in the corner. The fact is I have taken a fancy to yours. That fashion of wearing the stockings outside strikes me as one of the neatest things out."

Manuel suddenly drew off his boots with their muffled covering, and put on the ones designated.

"Now open the door."

He did so. Falkner was already waiting at the threshold. "Turn Manuel loose with the other, Ned, but disarm him first. They might quarrel. The habit of carrying arms, Manuel," added Lee, as Falkner took a pistol and bowie-knife from the half-breed, "is of itself provocative of violence, and inconsistent with a bucolic and pastoral life."

---

[1] "To die with one's boots on." A synonym for death by violence, popular among Southwestern desperadoes, and the subject of superstitious dread.

When Falkner returned he said hurriedly to his companion, "Do you think it wise, George, to let those hell-hounds loose? Good God! I could scarcely let my grip of his throat go, when I thought of what they were hunting."

"My dear Ned," said Lee, luxuriously ensconcing himself under the bedclothes again with a slight shiver of delicious warmth, "I must warn you against allowing the natural pride of a higher walk to prejudice you against the general level of our profession. Indeed, I was quite struck with the justice of Manuel's protest that I was interfering with certain rude processes of his own towards results aimed at by others."

"George!" interrupted Falkner, almost savagely.

"Well. I admit it's getting rather late in the evening for pure philosophical inquiry, and you are tired. Practically, then, it *was* wise to let them get away before they discovered two things. One, our exact relations here with these women; and the other, *how many* of us were here. At present they think we are three or four in possession and with the consent of the women."

"The dogs!"

"They are paying us the highest compliment they can conceive of by supposing us cleverer scoundrels than themselves. You are very unjust, Ned."

"If they escape and tell their story?"

"We shall have the rare pleasure of knowing we are better than people believe us. And now put those boots away somewhere where we can produce them if necessary, as evidence of Manuel's evening call. At present we'll keep the thing quiet, and in the early morning you can find out where they got in and remove any traces they have left. It is no use to frighten the women. There's no fear of their returning."

"And if they get away?"

"We can follow in their tracks."

"If Manuel gives the alarm?"

"With his burglarious boots left behind in the house? Not much! Good-night, Ned. Go to bed."

With these words Lee turned on his side and quietly

resumed his interrupted slumber. Falkner did not, however, follow this sensible advice. When he was satisfied that his friend was sleeping he opened the door softly and looked out. He did not appear to be listening, for his eyes were fixed upon a small pencil of light that stole across the passage from the foot of Kate's door. He watched it until it suddenly disappeared, when, leaving the door partly open, he threw himself on his couch without removing his clothes. The slight movement awakened the sleeper, who was beginning to feel the accession of fever. He moved restlessly.

"George," said Falkner, softly.

"Yes."

"Where was it we passed that old Mission Church on the road one dark night, and saw the light burning before the figure of the Virgin through the window?"

There was a moment of crushing silence. "Does that mean you're wanting to light the candle again?"

"No."

"Then don't lie there inventing sacrilegious conundrums, but go to sleep."

Nevertheless, in the morning his fever was slightly worse. Mrs. Hale, offering her condolence, said, "I know that you have not been resting well, for even after your friend met with that mishap in the hall, I heard your voices, and Kate says your door was open all night. You have a little fever too, Mr. Falkner."

George looked curiously at Falkner's pale face—it was burning.

CHAPTER V

THE speed and fury with which Clinch's cavalcade swept on in the direction of the mysterious shot left Hale no chance for reflection. He was conscious of shouting incoherently with the others, of urging his horse irresistibly forward, of momentarily expecting to meet or overtake something, but without any further thought. The figures of Clinch and Rawlins immediately before him shut out the prospect of the narrowing trail. Once only, taking advantage of a sudden halt that threw them confusedly together, he managed to ask a question.

"Lost their track—found it again!" shouted the ostler, as Clinch, with a cry like the baying of a hound, again darted forward. Their horses were panting and trembling under them, the ascent seemed to be growing steeper, a singular darkness, which even the density of the wood did not sufficiently account for, surrounded them, but still their leader madly urged them on. To Hale's returning senses they did not seem in a condition to engage a single resolute man, who might have ambushed in the woods or beaten them in detail in the narrow gorge, but in another instant the reason of their furious haste was manifest. Spurring his horse ahead, Clinch dashed out into the open with a cheering shout—a shout that as quickly changed to a yell of imprecation. They were on the Ridge in a blinding snow-storm! The road had already vanished under their feet, and with it the fresh trail they had so closely followed! They stood helplessly on the shore of a trackless white sea, blank and spotless of any trace or sign of the fugitives.

" 'Pears to me, boys," said the ostler, suddenly ranging before them, "ef you're not kalkilatin' on gittin' another party to dig ye out, ye'd better be huntin' fodder and cover instead of road agents. 'Skuse me, gentlemen, but I'm responsible for the hosses, and this ain't no time for circus-ridin'. We're a matter o' six miles from the station in a bee line."

"Back to the trail, then," said Clinch, wheeling his horse towards the road they had just quitted.

" 'Skuse me, Kernel," said the ostler, laying his hand on Clinch's rein, "but that way only brings us back the road we kem—the stage road—three miles further from home. That three miles is on the divide, and by the time we get there it will be snowed up worse nor this. The shortest cut is along the Ridge. If we hump ourselves we ken cross the divide afore the road is blocked. And that, 'skuse me, gentlemen, is *my* road."

There was no time for discussion. The road was already palpably thickening under their feet. Hale's arm was stiffened to his side by a wet, clinging snow-wreath. The figures of the others were almost obliterated and shapeless. It was not snowing—it was snowballing! The huge flakes, shaken like enormous feathers out of a vast blue-black could, commingled and fell in sprays and patches. All idea of their former pursuit was forgotten; the blind rage and enthusiasm that had possessed them was gone. They dashed after their new leader with only an instinct for shelter and succor.

They had not ridden long when fortunately, as it seemed to Hale, the character of the storm changed. The snow no longer fell in such large flakes, nor as heavily. A bitter wind succeeded; the soft snow began to stiffen and crackle under the horses' hoofs; they were no longer weighted and encumbered by the drifts upon their bodies; the smaller flakes now rustled and rasped against them like sand, or bounded from them like hail. They seemed to be moving more easily and rapidly, their spirits were rising with the stimulus of cold and motion, when suddenly their leader halted.

"It's no use, boys. It can't be done! This is no blizzard, but a regular two days' snifter! It's no longer meltin', but packin' and driftin' now. Even if we get over the divide, we're sure to be blocked up in the pass."

It was true! To their bitter disappointment they could now see that the snow had not really diminished in quantity, but that the now finely-powdered particles were rapidly filling all inequalities of the surface, packing closely against projections, and swirling in long furrows across the levels. They looked with anxiety at their self-constituted leader.

"We must make a break to get down in the woods again before it's too late," he said briefly.

But they had already drifted away from the fringe of larches and dwarf pines that marked the sides of the Ridge, and lower down merged into the dense forest that clothed the flank of the mountain they had lately climbed, and it was with the greatest difficulty that they again reached it, only to find that at that point it was too precipitous for the descent of their horses. Benumbed and speechless, they continued to toil on, opposed to the full fury of the stinging snow, and at times obliged to turn their horses to the blast to keep from being blown over the Ridge. At the end of half an hour the ostler dismounted, and, beckoning to the others, took his horse by the bridle, and began the descent. When it came to Hale's turn to dismount he could not help at first recoiling from the prospect before him. The trail—if it could be so called—was merely the track or furrow of some fallen tree dragged, by accident or design, diagonally across the sides of the mountain. At times it appeared scarcely a foot in width; at other times a mere crumbling gully, or a narrow shelf made by the projections of dead boughs and collected *débris*. It seemed perilous for a foot passenger, it appeared impossible for a horse. Nevertheless, he had taken a step forward when Clinch laid his hand on his arm.

"You'll bring up the rear," he said not unkindly, "ez you're a stranger here. Wait until we sing out to you."

"But if I prefer to take the same risks as you all?" said Hale stiffly.

"You kin," said Clinch grimly. "But I reckoned, as you wern't familiar with this sort o' thing, you wouldn't keer, by any foolishness o' yours, to stampede the rocks ahead of us, and break down the trail, or send down an avalanche on top of us. But just ez you like."

"I will wait, then," said Hale hastily.

The rebuke, however, did him good service. It preoccupied his mind, so that it remained unaffected by the dizzy depths, and enabled him to abandon himself mechanically to the sagacity of his horse, who was contented simply to follow the hoofprints of the preceding animal, and in a few moments they reached the broader trail without a mishap. A discussion regarding their future movements was already taking place. The impossibility of regaining the station at the Summit was admitted; the way down the mountain to the next settlement was still left to them, or the adjacent woods, if they wished for an encampment. The ostler once more assumed authority.

"'Skuse me, gentlemen, but them horses don't take no *pasear* down the mountain to-night. The stage-road ain't a mile off, and I kalkilate to wait here till the up stage comes. She's bound to stop on account of the snow; and I've done my dooty when I hand the horses over to the driver."

"But if she hears of the block up yer, and waits at the lower station?" said Rawlins.

"Then I've done my dooty all the same. 'Skuse me, gentlemen, but them ez hez their own horses kin do ez they like."

As this clearly pointed to Hale, he briefly assured his companions that he had no intention of deserting them. "If I cannot reach Eagle's Court, I shall at least keep as near it as possible. I suppose any messenger from my house to the Summit will learn where I am and why I am delayed?"

"Messenger from your house!" gasped Rawlins. "Are you crazy, stranger? Only a bird would get outer Eagle's now; and it would hev to be an eagle at that! Between your house and the Summit the snow must be ten feet by this time, to say nothing of the drift in the pass."

Hale felt it was the truth. At any other time he would have worried over this unexpected situation, and utter violation of all his traditions. He was past that now, and even felt a certain relief. He knew his family were safe; it was enough. That they were locked up securely, and incapable of interfering with *him,* seemed to enhance his new, half-conscious, half-shy enjoyment of an adventurous existence.

The ostler, who had been apparently lost in contemplation of the steep trail he had just descended, suddenly clapped his hand to his leg with an ejaculation of gratified astonishment.

"Waal, darn my skin ef that ain't Hennicker's 'slide' all the time! I heard it was somewhat about here."

Rawlins briefly explained to Hale that a slide was a rude incline for the transit of heavy goods that could not be carried down a trail.

"And Hennicker's," continued the man, "ain't more nor a mile away. Ye might try Hennicker's at a push, eh?"

By a common instinct the whole party looked dubiously at Hale. "Who's Hennicker?" he felt compelled to ask.

The ostler hesitated, and glanced at the others to reply. "There *are* folks," he said lazily, at last, "ez beleeves that Hennicker ain't much better nor the crowd we're hunting; but they don't say it *to* Hennicker. We needn't let on what we're after."

"I for one," said Hale stoutly, "decidedly object to any concealment of our purpose."

"It don't follow," said Rawlins carelessly, "that Hennicker even knows of this yer robbery. It's his gineral gait we refer to. Ef yer think it more polite, and it makes it more sociable to discuss this matter afore him, I'm agreed."

"Hale means," said Clinch, "that it wouldn't be on the square to take and make use of any points we might pick up there agin the road agents."

"Certainly," said Hale. It was not at all what he had meant, but he felt singularly relieved at the compromise.

"And ez I reckon Hennicker ain't such a fool ez not to know who we are and what we're out for," continued Clinch, "I reckon there ain't any concealment."

"Then it's Hennicker's?" said the ostler, with swift deduction.

"Hennicker's it is! Lead on."

The ostler remounted his horse, and the others followed. The trail presently turned into a broader track, that bore some signs of approaching habitations, and at the end of five minutes they came upon a clearing. It was part of one of the fragmentary mountain terraces, and formed by itself a vast niche, or bracketed shelf, in the hollow flank of the mountain that, to Hale's first glance, bore a rude resemblance to Eagle's Court. But there was neither meadow nor open field; the few acres of ground had been wrested from the forest by axe and fire, and unsightly stumps everywhere marked the rude and difficult attempts at cultivation. Two or three rough buildings of unplaned and unpainted boards, connected by rambling sheds, stood in the centre of the amphi-theatre. Far from being protected by the encircling ram-part, it seemed to be the selected arena for the combating elements. A whirlwind from the outer abyss continually filled this cave of Æolus with driving snow, which, how-ever, melted as it fell, or was quickly whirled away again.

A few dogs barked and ran out to meet the cavalcade, but there was no other sign of any life disturbed or concerned at their approach.

"I reckon Hennicker ain't home, or he'd hev been on the lookout afore this," said the ostler, dismounting and rapping on the door.

After a silence, a female voice, unintelligibly to the others, apparently had some colloquy with the ostler, who returned to the party.

"Must go in through the kitchin—can't open the door for the wind."

Leaving their horses in the shed, they entered the kitchen, which communicated, and presently came upon a square room filled with smoke from a fire of green pine logs. The doors and windows were tightly fastened; the only air came in through the large-throated chimney in voluminous gusts, which seemed to make the hollow shell of the apartment swell and expand to the point of bursting. Despite the stinging of the resinous smoke, the temperature was grateful to the benumbed travellers. Several cushionless arm-chairs, such as were used in bar-rooms, two tables, a sideboard, half bar and half cupboard, and a rocking-chair comprised the furniture, and a few bear and buffalo skins covered the floor. Hale sank into one of the arm-chairs, and, with a lazy satis-faction, partly born of his fatigue and partly from some newly-discovered appreciative faculty, gazed around the room, and then at the mistress of the house, with whom the others were talking.

She was tall, gaunt, and withered; in spite of her

evident years, her twisted hair was still dark and full,
and her eyes bright and piercing; her complexion and
teeth had long since succumbed to the vitiating effects
of frontier cookery, and her lips were stained with the
yellow juice of a brier-wood pipe she held in her mouth.
The ostler had explained their intrusion, and veiled their
character under the vague epithet of a "hunting party,"
and was now evidently describing them personally. In
his new-found philosophy the fact that the interest of
his hostess seemed to be excited only by the names of his
companions, that he himself was carelessly, and even
deprecatingly, alluded to as the "stranger from Eagle's"
by the ostler, and completely overlooked by the old
woman, gave him no concern.

"You'll have to talk to Zenobia yourself. Dod rot ef
I'm gine to interfere. She knows Hennicker's ways, and
if she chooses to take in transients it ain't no funeral o'
mine. Zeenie! You, Zeenie! Look yer!"

A tall, lazy-looking, handsome girl appeared on the
threshold of the next room, and with a hand on each
door-post slowly swung herself backwards and forwards,
without entering. "Well, Maw?"

The old woman briefly and unalluringly pictured the
condition of the travellers.

"Paw ain't here," began the girl doubtfully, "and—
How dy, Dick! is that you?" The interruption was
caused by her recognition of the ostler, and she lounged
into the room. In spite of a skimp, slatternly gown,
whose straight skirt clung to her lower limbs, there was
a quaint, nymph-like contour to her figure. Whether
from languor, ill-health, or more probably from a morbid
consciousness of her own height, she moved with a
slightly affected stoop that had become a habit. It
did not seem ungraceful to Hale, already attracted by
her delicate profile, her large dark eyes, and a certain
weird resemblance she had to some half-domesticated
dryad.

"That'll do, Maw," she said, dismissing her parent
with a nod. "I'll talk to Dick."

As the door closed on the old woman, Zenobia leaned

her hands on the back of a chair, and confronted the admiring eyes of Dick with a goddess-like indifference.

"Now wot's the use of your playin' this yer game on me, Dick? Wot's the good of your ladlin' out that hog-wash about huntin'? *Huntin'!* I'll tell yer the huntin' you-uns hev been at! You've been huntin' George Lee and his boys since an hour before sun up. You've been followin' a blind trail up to the Ridge, until the snow got up and hunted *you* right here! You've been whoopin' and yellin' and circus-ridin' on the roads like ez yer wos Comanches, and frightening all the women folk within miles—that's your huntin'! You've been climbin' down Paw's old slide at last, and makin' tracks for here to save the skins of them condemned government horses of the Kempany! And *that's* your huntin'!"

To Hale's surprise, a burst of laughter from the party followed this speech. He tried to join in, but this ridiculous summary of the result of his enthusiastic sense of duty left him—the only earnest believer mortified and embarrassed. Nor was he the less concerned as he found the girl's dark eyes had rested once or twice upon him curiously. Zenobia laughed too, and, lazily turning the chair around, dropped into it. "And by this time George Lee's loungin' back in his chyar and smokin' his cigyar somewhar in Sacramento," she added, stretching her feet out to the fire, and suiting the action to the word with an imaginary cigar between the long fingers of a thin and not over-clean hand.

"We cave, Zeenie!" said Rawlins, when their hilarity had subsided to a more subdued and scarcely less flattering admiration of the unconcerned goddess before them. "That's about the size of it. You kin rake down the pile. I forgot you're an old friend of George's."

"He's a white man!" said the girl decidedly.

"Ye used to know him?" continued Rawlins.

"Once. Paw ain't in that line now," she said simply.

There was such a sublime unconsciousness of any moral degradation involved in this allusion that even Hale accepted it without a shock. She rose presently, and, going to the little sideboard, brought out a number of glasses;

these she handed to each of the party, and then, producing
a demijohn of whiskey, slung it dexterously and gracefully over her arm, so that it rested on her elbow like a
cradle, and, going to each one in succession, filled their
glasses. It obliged each one to rise to accept the libation,
and as Hale did so in his turn he met the dark eyes of
the girl full on his own. There was a pleased curiosity
in her glance that made this married man of thirty-five
color as awkwardly as a boy.

The tender of refreshment being understood as a tacit
recognition of their claims to a larger hospitality, all
further restraint was removed. Zenobia resumed her seat,
and placing her elbow on the arm of her chair. and her
small round chin in her hand, looked thoughtfully in the
fire. "When I say George Lee's a white man, it ain't
because I know him. It's his general gait. Wot's he
ever done that's underhanded or mean? Nothin'! You
kant show the poor man he's ever took a picayune from.
When he's helped himself to a pile it's been outer them
banks or them express companies, that think it mighty
fine to bust up themselves, and swindle the poor folks o'
their last cent, and nobody talks o' huntin' *them!* And
does he keep their money? No; he passes it round among
the boys that help him, and they put it in circulation. *He*
don't keep it for himself; he ain't got fine houses in
Frisco; he don't keep fast horses for show. Like ez
not the critter he did that job with—ef it was him—none
of you boys would have rid! And he takes all the risks
himself; you ken. bet your life that every man with him
was safe and away afore he turned his back on you-uns."

"He certainly drops a little of his money at draw poker,
Zeenie," said Clinch, laughing. "He lost five thousand
dollars to Sheriff Kelly last week."

"Well, I don't hear of the sheriff huntin' him to give it
back, nor do I reckon Kelly handed it over to the Express
it was taken from. I heard *you* won suthin' from him a
spell ago. I reckon you've been huntin' him to find out
whar you should return it." The laugh was clearly against
Clinch. He was about to make some rallying rejoinder
when the young girl suddenly interrupted him. "Ef

you're wantin' to hunt somebody, why don't you take higher game? Thar's that Jim Harkins: go for him, and I'll join you."

"Harkins!" exclaimed Clinch and Hale simultaneously.

"Yes, Jim Harkins; do you know him?" she said, glancing from one to the other.

"One of my friends do," said Clinch laughing; "but don't let that stop you."

"And *you*—over there," continued Zenobia, bending her head and eyes towards Hale.

"The fact is—I believe he was my banker," said Hale, with a smile. "I don't know him personally."

"Then you'd better hunt him before he does you."

"What's *he* done, Zeenie?" asked Rawlins, keenly enjoying the discomfiture of the others.

"What?" She stopped, threw her long black braids over her shoulder, clasped her knee wtih her hands, and rocking backwards and forwards, sublimely unconscious of the apparition of a slim ankle and half-dropped-off slipper from under her shortened gown, continued, "It mightn't please *him*," she said slyly, nodding towards Hale.

"Pray don't mind me," said Hale, with unnecessary eagerness.

"Well," said Zenobia, "I reckon you all know Ned Falkner and the Excelsior Ditch?"

"Yes, Falkner's the superintendent of it," said Rawlins. "And a square man too. Thar ain't anything mean about him."

"Shake," said Zenobia, extending her hand. Rawlins shook the proffered hand with eager spontaneousness, and the girl resumed: "He's about ez good ez they make 'em —you bet. Well, you know Ned has put all his money, and all his strength, and all his *sabe,* and—"

"His good looks," added Clinch mischievously.

"Into that Ditch," continued Zenobia, ignoring the interruption. "It's his mother, it's his sweetheart, it's his everything! When other chaps of his age was cavortin' round Frisco, and havin' high jinks, Ned was in his Ditch. 'Wait till the Ditch is done,' he used to say.

'Wait till she begins to boom, and then you just stand round.' Mor'n that, he got all the boys to put in their last cent—for they loved Ned, and love him now, like ez ef he wos a woman."

"That's so," said Clinch and Rawlins simultaneously, "and he's worth it."

"Well," continued Zenobia, "the Ditch didn't boom ez soon ez they kalkilated. And then the boys kept gettin' poorer and poorer, and Ned he kept gettin' poorer and poorer in everything but his hopefulness and grit. Then he looks around for more capital. And about this time, that coyote Harkins smelt suthin' nice up there, and he gits Ned to give him control of it, and he'll lend him his name and fix up a company. Soon ez he gets control, the first thing he does is to say that it wants half a million o' money to make it pay, and levies an assessment of two hundred dollars a share. That's nothin' for them rich fellows to pay, or pretend to pay, but for boys on grub wages it meant only ruin. They couldn't pay, and had to forfeit their shares for next to nothing. And Ned made one more desperate attempt to save them and himself by borrowing money on his shares; when that hound Harkins got wind of it, and let it be buzzed around that the Ditch is a failure, and that he was goin' out of it; that brought the shares down to nothing. As Ned couldn't raise a dollar, the new company swooped down on his shares for the debts *they* had put up. and left him and the boys to help themselves. Ned couldn't bear to face the boys that he'd helped to ruin, and put out, and ain't been heard from since. After Harkins had got rid of Ned and the boys he manages to pay off that wonderful debt, and sells out for a hundred thousand dollars. That money—Ned's money—he sends to Sacramento, for he don't dare to travel with it himself, and is kalkilatin' to leave the kentry, for some of the boys allow to kill him on sight. So ef you're wantin' to hunt suthin', thar's yer chance, and you needn't go inter the snow to do it."

"But surely the law can recover this money?" said Hale indignantly. "It is as infamous a robbery as—" He stopped as he caught Zenobia's eye.

"Ez last night's, you were goin' to say. I'll call it *more*. Them road agents don't pretend to be your friend —but take yer money and run their risks. For ez to the law—that can't help yer."

"It's a skin game, and you might ez well expect to recover a gambling debt from a short-card sharp," explained Clinch; "Falkner oughter shot him on sight."

"Or the boys lynched him," suggested Rawlins.

"I think," said Hale, more reflectively, "that in the absence of legal remedy a man of that kind should have been forced under strong physical menace to give up his ill-gotten gains. The money was the primary object, and if that could be got without bloodshed—which seems to me a useless crime—it would be quite as effective. Of course, if there was resistance or retaliation, it might be necessary to kill him."

He had unconsciously fallen into his old didactic and dogmatic habit of speech, and perhaps, under the spur of Zenobia's eyes, he had given it some natural emphasis. A dead silence followed, in which the others regarded him with amused and gratified surprise, and it was broken only by Zenobia rising and holding out her hand. "Shake!"

Hale raised it gallantly, and pressed his lips on the one spotless finger.

"That's gospel truth. And you ain't the first white man to say it."

"Indeed," laughed Hale. "Who was the other?"

"George Lee!"

CHAPTER VI

THE laughter that followed was interrupted by a sudden barking of the dogs in the outer clearing. Zenobia rose lazily and strode to the window. It relieved Hale of certain embarrassing reflections suggested by her comment.

"Ef it ain't that God-forsaken fool Dick bringing up passengers from the snow-bound up stage in the road! I reckon *I've* got suthin' to say to that!" But the later appearance of the apologetic Dick, with the assurance that the party carried a permission from her father, granted at the lower station in view of such an emergency, checked her active opposition. "That's like Paw," she soliloquized aggrievedly; "shuttin' us up and settin' dogs on everybody for a week, and then lettin' the whole stage service pass through one door and out at another. Well, it's *his* house and *his* whiskey, and they kin take it, but they don't get me to help 'em."

They certainly were not a prepossessing or good-natured acquisition to the party. Apart from the natural antagonism which, on such occasions, those in possession always feel towards the new-comer, they were strongly inclined to resist the dissatisfied querulousness and aggressive attitude of these fresh applicants for hospitality. The most offensive one was a person who appeared to exercise some authority over the others. He was loud, assuming, and dressed with vulgar pretension. He quickly disposed himself in the chair vacated by Zenobia, and called for some liquor.

"I reckon you'll hev to help yourself," said Rawlins dryly, as the summons met with no response. "There are only two women in the house, and I reckon their hands are full already."

"I call it d—d uncivil treatment," said the man, raising his voice; "and Hennicker had better sing smaller if he don't want his old den pulled down some day. He ain't any better than men that hev been picked up afore now."

"You oughter told him that, and mebbe he'd hev come over with yer," returned Rawlins. "He's a mild, soft, easy-going man, is Hennicker! Ain't he, Colonel Clinch?"

The casual mention of Clinch's name produced the effect which the speaker probably intended. The stranger stared at Clinch, who, apparently oblivious of the conversation, was blinking his cold gray eyes at the fire. Dropping his aggressive tone to mere querulousness, the man sought the whiskey demijohn, and helped himself and his companions. Fortified by liquor he returned to the fire.

"I reckon you've heard about this yer robbery, Colonel,"

he said, addressing Clinch, with an attempt at easy familiarity.

Without raising his eyes from the fire, Clinch briefly assented, "I reckon."

"I'm up yer, examining into it, for the Express."

"Lost much?" asked Rawlins.

"Not so much ez they might hev. That fool Harkins had a hundred thousand dollars in greenbacks sealed up like an ordinary package of a thousand dollars, and gave it to a friend, Bill Guthrie, in the bank to pick out some unlikely chap among the passengers to take charge of it to Reno. He wouldn't trust the Express. Ha! ha!"

The dead, oppressive silence that followed his empty laughter made it seem almost artificial. Rawlins held his breath and looked at Clinch. Hale, with the instincts of a refined, sensitive man, turned hot with the embarrassment Clinch should have shown. For that gentleman, without lifting his eyes from the fire, and with no apparent change in his demeanor, lazily asked—

"Ye didn't ketch the name o' that passenger?"

"Naturally, no! For when Guthrie heard what was said agin him he wouldn't give his name until he heard from him."

"And *what* was said agin him?" asked Clinch musingly.

"What would be said agin a man that give up that sum o' money, like a chaw of tobacco, for the asking? Why, there were but three men, as far ez we kin hear, that did the job. And there were four passengers inside, armed, and the driver and express messenger on the box. Six were robbed by *three!*—they were a sweet-scented lot! Reckon they must hev felt mighty small, for I hear they got up and skedaddled from the station under the pretext of lookin' for the robbers." He laughed again, and the laugh was noisily repeated by his five companions at the other end of the room.

Hale, who had forgotten that the stranger was only echoing a part of his own criticism of eight hours before, was on the point of rising with burning cheeks and angry indignation, when the lazily uplifted eye of Clinch caught his, and absolutely held him down with its paralyzing and deadly significance. Murder itself seemed to look from those cruelly quiet and remorseless gray pupils. For a moment he forgot his own rage in this glimpse of Clinch's implacable resentment; for a moment he felt a thrill of pity for the wretch who had provoked it. He remained motionless and fascinated in his chair as the lazy lids closed like a sheath over Clinch's eyes again. Rawlins, who had probably received the same glance of warning, remained equally still.

"They haven't heard the last of it yet, you bet," continued the infatuated stranger. "I've got a little statement here for the newspaper," he added, drawing some papers from his pocket; "suthin' I just run off in the coach as I came along. I reckon it'll show things up in a new light. It's time there should be some change. All the cussin' that's been usually done hez been by the passengers agin the express and stage companies. I propose that the Company should do a little cussin' themselves. See? P'r'aps you don't mind my readin' it to ye? It's just spicy enough to suit them newspaper chaps."

"Go on," said Colonel Clinch quietly.

The man cleared his throat, with the preliminary pose of authorship, and his five friends, to whom the composition was evidently not unfamiliar, assumed anticipatory smiles.

"I call it 'Prize Pusillanimous Passengers.' Sort of runs easy off the tongue, you know.

"'It now appears that the success of the late stagecoach robbery near the Summit was largely due to the pusillanimity—not to use a more serious word'"— He stopped, and looked explanatorily towards Clinch: "Ye'll see in a minit what I'm gettin' at by that pusillanimity of the passengers themselves. 'It now transpires that there were only three robbers who attacked the coach, and that although passengers, driver, and express messenger were fully armed, and were double the number of their assailants, not a shot was fired. We mean no reflections upon the well-known courage of Yuba Bill, nor the experience and coolness of Bracy Tibbetts, the courteous express messenger, both of whom have since confessed to have been more than astonished at the Christian and lamb-like submission of the insiders. Amusing stories of some laughable yet sickening incidents of the occasion—such as grown men kneeling in the road, and offering to strip themselves completely, if their lives were only spared; of one of the passengers hiding under the seat, and only being dislodged by pulling his coat-tails; of incredible sums promised, and even offers of menial service, for the preservation of their wretched carcases—are received with the greatest gusto; but we are in possession of facts which may lead to more serious accusations. Although one of the passengers is said to have lost a large sum of money intrusted to him, while attempting with barefaced effrontery to establish a rival "carrying" business in one of the Express Company's own coaches—' I call that a good point." He interrupted himself to allow the unrestrained applause of his own party. "Don't you?"

"It's just h—ll," said Clinch musingly.

" 'Yet the affair," resumed the stranger from his manuscript, " 'is locked up in great and suspicious mystery. The presence of Jackson N. Stanner, Esq.' (that's me), 'special detective agent to the Company, and his staff in town, is a guaranty that the mystery will be thoroughly probed.' Hed to put that in to please the Company," he again deprecatingly explained. " 'We are indebted to this gentleman for the facts.' "

"The pint you want to make in that article," said Clinch, rising, but still directing his face and his conversation to the fire, "ez far ez I ken see ez that no three men kin back down six unless they be cowards, or are willing to be backed down."

"That's the point what I start from," rejoined Stanner, "and work up. I leave it to you ef it ain't so."

"I can't say ez I agree with you," said the Colonel dryly. He turned, and still without lifting his eyes walked towards the door of the room which Zenobia had entered. The key was on the inside, but Clinch gently opened the door, removed the key, and closing the door again locked it from his side. Hale and Rawlins felt their hearts beat quickly; the others followed Clinch's slow movements and downcast mien with amused curiosity. After locking the other outlet from the room, and putting the keys in his pocket, Clinch returned to the fire. For the first time he lifted his eyes; the man nearest him shrank back in terror.

"I am the man," he said slowly, taking deliberate breath between his sentences, "who gave up those greenbacks to the robbers. I am one of the three passengers you have lampooned in that paper, and these gentlemen beside me are the other two." He stopped and looked around him. "You don't believe that three men can back down six! Well, I'll show you how it can be done. More than that, I'll show you how ONE man can do it; for, by the living G—d, if you don't hand over that paper I'll kill you where you sit! I'll give you until I count ten; if one of you moves he and you are dead men—but *you* first!"

Before he had finished speaking Hale and Rawlins had both risen, as if in concert, with their weapons drawn. Hale could not tell how or why he had done so, but he was equally conscious, without knowing why, of fixing his eye on one of the other party, and that he should, in the event of an affray, try to kill him. He did not attempt to reason; he only knew that he should do his best to kill that man and perhaps others.

"One," said Clinch, lifting his derringer, "two— three—"

"Look here, Colonel—I swear I didn't know it was you. Come—d—m it! I say—see here," stammered Stanner, with white cheeks, not daring to glance for aid to his stupefied party.

"Four—five—six—"

"Wait! Here!" He produced the paper and threw it on the floor.

"Pick it up and hand it to me. Seven—eight—"

Stanner hastily scrambled to his feet, picked up the paper, and handed it to the Colonel. "I was only joking, Colonel," he said, with a forced laugh.

"I'm glad to hear it. But as this joke is in black and white, you wouldn't mind saying so in the same fashion. Take that pen and ink and write as I dictate. 'I certify that I am satisfied that the above statement is a base calumny against the characters of Ringwood Clinch, Robert Rawlins, and John Hale, passengers, and that I do hereby apologize to the same.' Sign it. That'll do. Now let the rest of your party sign as witnesses."

They complied without hesitation; some, seizing the opportunity of treating the affair as a joke, suggested a drink.

"Excuse me," said Clinch quietly, "but ez this house ain't big enough for me and that man, and ez I've got business at Wild Cat Station with this paper, I think I'll go without drinkin'." He took the keys from his pocket, unlocked the doors, and taking up his overcoat and rifle turned as if to go.

Rawlins rose to follow him; Hale alone hesitated. The rapid occurrences of the last half hour gave him no time for reflection. But he was by no means satisfied of the legality of the last act he had aided and abetted, although he admitted its rude justice, and felt he would have done so again. A fear of this, and an instinct that he might be led into further complications if he continued to identify himself with Clinch and Rawlins; the fact that .they had professedly abandoned their quest, and that it was really supplanted by the presence of an authorized party whom they had already come in conflict with—all this urged him to remain behind. On the other hand, the apparent desertion of his comrades at the last moment was opposed both to his sense of honor and the liking he had taken to them. But he reflected that he had already shown his active partisanship, that he could be of little service to them at Wild Cat Station, and would be only increasing the distance from his home; and above all, an impatient longing for independent action finally decided him. "I think I'll stay here," he said to Clinch, "unless you want me."

Clinch cast a swift and meaning glance at the enemy, but looked approval. "Keep your eyes skinned, and you're good for a dozen of 'em," he said *sotto voce,* and then turned to Stanner. "I'm going to take this paper to Wild Cat. If you want to communicate with me hereafter you know where I am to be found, unless—" he smiled grimly

—"you'd like to see me outside for a few minutes before I go?"

"It is a matter that concerns the Stage Company, not me," said Stanner, with an attempt to appear at his ease.

Hale accompanied Clinch and Rawlins through the kitchen to the stables. The ostler, Dick, had already returned to the rescue of the snow-bound coach.

"I shouldn't like to leave many men alone with that crowd," said Clinch, pressing Hale's hand; "and I wouldn't have allowed your staying behind ef I didn't know I could bet my pile on you. Your offerin' to stay just puts a clean finish on it. Look yer, Hale, I didn't cotton much to you at first; but ef you ever want a friend, call on Ringwood Clinch."

"The same here, old man," said Rawlins, extending his hand as he appeared from a hurried conference with the old woman at the woodshed, "and trust to Zeenie to give you a hint ef there's anythin' underhanded goin' on. So long."

Half inclined to resent this implied suggestion of protection, yet half pleased at the idea of a confidence with the handsome girl he had seen, Hale returned to the room. A whispered discussion among the party ceased on his entering, and an awkward silence followed, which Hale did not attempt to break as he quietly took his seat again by the fire. He was presently confronted by Stanner, who with an affectation of easy familiarity crossed over to the hearth.

"The old Kernel's d—d peppery and high toned when he's got a little more than his reg'lar three fingers o' corn juice, eh?"

"I must beg you to understand distinctly, Mr. Stanner," said Hale, with a return of his habitual precision of statement, "that I regard any slighting allusion to the gentleman who has just left not only as in exceedingly bad taste coming from *you*, but very offensive to myself. If you mean to imply that he was under the influence of liquor, it is my duty to undeceive you; he was so perfectly in possession of his faculties as to express not only his own but *my* opinion of your conduct. You must also admit that he was discriminating enough to show his objection to your company by leaving it. I regret that circumstances do not make it convenient for me to exercise that privilege; but if I am obliged to put up with your presence in this room, I strongly insist that it is not made unendurable with the addition of your conversation."

The effect of this deliberate and passionless declaration was more discomposing to the party than Clinch's fury. Utterly unaccustomed to the ideas and language suddenly confronting them, they were unable to determine whether it was the real expression of the speaker, or whether it was a vague badinage or affectation to which any reply would involve them in ridicule. In a country terrorized by practical joking, they did not doubt but that this was a new form of hoaxing calculated to provoke some response that would constitute them as victims. The immediate effect upon them was that complete silence in regard to himself that Hale desired. They drew together again and conversed in whispers, while Hale, with his eyes fixed on the fire, gave himself up to somewhat late and useless reflection.

He could scarcely realize his position. For however he might look at it, within a space of twelve hours he had not only changed some of his most cherished opinions, but he had acted in accordance with that change in a way that made it seem almost impossible for him ever to recant. In the interests of law and order he had engaged in an unlawful and disorderly pursuit of criminals, and had actually come in conflict not with the criminals, but with the only party apparently authorized to pursue them. More than that, he was finding himself committed to a certain sympathy with the criminals. Twenty-four hours ago, if anyone had told him that he would have condoned an illegal act for its abstract justice, or assisted to commit an illegal act for the same purpose, he would have felt himself insulted. That he knew he would not now feel it as an insult perplexed him still more. In these circumstances the fact that he was separated from his family, and as it were from all his past life and traditions, by a chance accident, did not disturb him greatly; indeed, he was for the first time a little doubtful of their probable criticism on his inconsistency, and was by no means in a hurry to subject himself to it.

Lifting his eyes, he was suddenly aware that the door leading to the kitchen was slowly opening. He had thought he heard it creak once or twice during his deliberate reply to Stanner. It was evidently moving now so as to attract his attention, without disturbing the others. It presently opened sufficiently wide to show the face of Zeenie, who, with a gesture of caution towards his companions, beckoned him to join her. He rose carelessly as if going out, and, putting on his hat, entered the kitchen as the retreating figure of the young girl glided lightly towards the stables. She ascended a few open steps as if to a hay-loft, but stopped before a low door. Pushing it open, she preceded him into a small room, apparently under the roof, which scarcely allowed her to stand upright. By the light of a stable lantern hanging from a beam he saw that, though poorly furnished, it bore some evidence of feminine taste and habitation. Motioning to the only chair, she seated herself on the edge of the bed, with her hands clasping her knees in her familiar attitude. Her face bore traces of recent agitation, and her eyes were shining with tears. By the closer light of the lantern he was surprised to find it was from laughter.

"I reckoned you'd be right lonely down there with that Stanner crowd, particklerly after that little speech o' your'n, so I sez to Maw I'd get you up yer for a spell. Maw and I heerd you exhort 'em! Maw allowed you woz talkin' a furrin' tongue all along, but I—sakes alive!—I hed to hump myself to keep from bustin' into a yell when yer jist drawed them Webster-unabridged sentences on 'em." She stopped and rocked backwards and forwards with a laugh that, subdued by the proximity of the roof and the fear of being overheard, was by no means unmusical. "I'll tell ye whot got me, though! That part commencing, 'Suckamstances over which I've no controul.'"

"Oh, come! I didn't say that," interrupted Hale, laughing.

"'Don't make it convenient for me to exercise the privilege of kickin' yer out to that extent,'" she continued; "'but if I cannot dispense with your room, the least I can say is that it's a d—d sight better than your company—' or suthin' like that! And then the way you minded your stops, and let your voice rise and fall just ez easy ez if you wos a First Reader in large type. Why, the Kernel wasn't nowhere. *His* cussin' didn't come within a mile o' yourn. That Stanner jist turned yaller."

"I'm afraid you are laughing at me," said Hale, not knowing whether to be pleased or vexed at the girl's amusement.

"I reckon I'm the only one that dare do it, then," said the girl simply. "The Kernel sez the way you turned round after he'd done his cussin', and said yer believed you'd stay and take the responsibility of the whole thing— and did, in that kam, soft, did-anybody-speak-to-me style— was the neatest thing he'd seen yet. No! Maw says I ain't much on manners, but I know a man when I see him."

For an instant Hale gave himself up to the delicious flattery of unexpected, unintended, and apparently uninterested compliment. Becoming at last a little embarrassed under the frank curiosity of the girl's dark eyes, he changed the subject.

"Do you always come up here through the stables?" he asked, glancing round the room, which was evidently her own.

"I reckon," she answered half abstractedly. "There's a ladder down thar to Maw's room—" pointing to a trapdoor beside the broad chimney that served as a wall— "but it's handier the other way, and nearer the hosses if you want to get away quick."

This palpable suggestion—borne out by what he remembered of the other domestic details—that the house had been planned with reference to sudden foray or escape reawakened his former uneasy reflections. Zeenie, who had been watching his face, added, "It's no slouch, when

b'ar or painters hang round nights and stampede the
stock, to be able to swing yourself on to a hoss whenever
you hear a row going on outside."

"Do you mean that *you*—"

"Paw *used,* and I do *now,* sense I've come into the
room." She pointed to a nondescript garment, half cloak,
half habit, hanging on the wall. "I've been outer bed and
on Pitchpine's back as far ez the trail five minutes arter
I heard the first bellow."

Hale regarded her with undisguised astonishment.
There was nothing at all Amazonian or horsey in her
manners, nor was there even the robust physical contour
that might have been developed through such experiences.
On the contrary, she seemed to be lazily effeminate in
body and mind. Heedless of his critical survey of her,
she beckoned him to draw his chair nearer, and, looking
into his eyes, said—

"Whatever possessed *you* to take to huntin' men?"

Hale was staggered by the question, but nevertheless
endeavored to explain. But he was surprised to find that
his explanation appeared stilted even to himself, and, he
could not doubt, was utterly incomprehensible to the girl.
She nodded her head, however, and continued—

"Then you haven't anythin' agin' George?"

"I don't know George," said Hale, smiling. "My proceeding was against the highwayman."

"Well, *he* was the highwayman."

"I mean, it was the principle I objected to—a principle
that I consider highly dangerous."

"Well *he* is the principal, for the others only *helped,*
I reckon," said Zeenie with a sigh, "and I reckon he *is*
dangerous."

Hale saw it was useless to explain. The girl continued—

"What made you stay here instead of going on with
the Kernel? There was suthin' else besides your wanting
to make that Stanner take water. What is it?"

A light sense of the propinquity of beauty, of her confidence, of their isolation, of the eloquence of her dark
eyes, at first tempted Hale to a reply of simple gallantry;

a graver consideration of the same circumstances froze it upon his lips.

"I don't know," he returned awkwardly.

"Well, I'll tell you," she said. "You didn't cotton to the Kernel and Rawlins much more than you did to Stanner. They ain't your kind."

In his embarrassment Hale blundered upon the thought he had honorably avoided.

"Suppose," he said, with a constrained laugh, "I had stayed to see you."

"I reckon *I* ain't your kind, neither," she replied promptly. There was a momentary pause when she rose and walked to the chimney. "It's very quiet down there," she said, stooping and listening over the roughly-boarded floor that formed the ceiling of the room below. "I wonder what's going on."

In the belief that this was a delicate hint for his return to the party he had left, Hale rose, but the girl passed him hurriedly, and, opening the door, cast a quick glance into the stable beyond.

"Just as I reckoned—the horses are gone too. They've skedaddled," she said blankly.

Hale did not reply. In his embarrassment a moment ago the idea of taking an equally sudden departure had flashed upon him. Should he take this as a justification of that impulse, or how? He stood irresolutely gazing at the girl, who turned and began to descend the stairs silently. He followed. When they reached the lower room they found it as they had expected—deserted.

"I hope I didn't drive them away," said Hale, with an uneasy look at the troubled face of the girl. "For I really had an idea of going myself a moment ago."

She remained silent, gazing out of the window. Then, turning with a slight shrug of her shoulders, said half defiantly: "What's the use now? Oh, Maw! the Stanner crowd has vamosed the ranch, and this yer stranger kalkilates to stay!"

CHAPTER VII

A WEEK had passed at Eagle's Court—a week of mingled clouds and sunshine by day, of rain over the green plateau and snow on the mountain by night. Each morning had brought its fresh greenness to the winter-girt domain, and a fresh coat of dazzling white to the barrier that separated its dwellers from the world beyond. There was little change in the encompassing wall of their prison; if anything, the snowy circle round them seemed to have drawn its lines nearer day by day. The immediate result of this restricted limit had been to confine the range of cattle to the meadows nearer the house, and at a safe distance from the fringe of wilderness now invaded by the prowling tread of predatory animals.

Nevertheless, the two figures lounging on the slope at sunset gave very little indication of any serious quality in the situation. Indeed, so far as appearances were concerned, Kate, who was returning from an afternoon stroll with Falkner, exhibited, with feminine inconsistency, a decided return to the world of fashion and conventionality apparently just as she was effectually excluded from it. She had not only discarded her white dress as a concession to the practical evidence of the surrounding winter, but she had also brought out a feather hat and sable muff which had once graced a fashionable suburb of Boston. Even Falkner had exchanged his slouch hat and picturesque *serape* for a beaver overcoat and fur cap of Hale's which had been pressed upon him by Kate, under the excuse of the exigencies of the season. Within a stone's throw of the thicket, turbulent with the savage forces of nature, they walked with the abstraction of people hearing only their own voices; in the face of the solemn peaks clothed with white austerity they talked gravely of dress.

"I don't mean to say," said Kate demurely, "that you're to give up the *serape* entirely; you can wear it on rainy nights and when you ride over here from your friend's

house to spend the evening—for the sake of old times,"
she added, with an unconscious air of referring to an already antiquated friendship; "but you must admit it's a
little too gorgeous and theatrical for the sunlight of day
and the public highway."

"But why should that make it wrong, if the experience
of a people has shown it to be a garment best fitted for
their wants and requirements?" said Falkner argumenta-
tively.

"But you are not one of those people," said Kate, "and
that makes all the difference. You look differently and
act differently, so that there is something irreconcilable
between your clothes and you that makes you look odd."

"And to look odd, according to your civilized prejudices,
is to be wrong," said Falkner bitterly.

"It is to seem different from what one really is—which
is wrong. Now, you are a mining superintendent, you
tell me. Then you don't want to look like a Spanish
brigand, as you do in that *serape*. I am sure if you had
ridden up to a stage-coach while I was in it, I'd have
handed you my watch and purse without a word. There!
you are not offended?" she added, with a laugh, which did
not, however, conceal a certain earnestness. "I suppose
I ought to have said I would have given it gladly to such
a romantic figure, and perhaps have got out and danced a
saraband or bolero with you—if that is the thing to do
nowadays. Well!" she said, after a dangerous pause,
"consider that I've said it."

He had been walking a little before her, with his
face turned towards the distant mountain. Suddenly he
stopped and faced her. "You would have given enough of
your time to the highwayman, Miss Scott, as would have
enabled you to identify him for the police—and no more.
Like your brother, you would have been willing to sacrifice yourself for the benefit of the laws of civilization
and good order."

If a denial to this assertion could have been expressed
without the use of speech, it was certainly transparent in
the face and eyes of the young girl at that moment. If
Falkner had been less self-conscious he would have seen

it plainly. But Kate only buried her face in her lifted muff, slightly raised her pretty shoulders, and, dropping her tremulous eyelids, walked on. "It seems a pity," she said, after a pause, "that we cannot preserve our own miserable existence without taking something from others —sometimes even a life!" He started. "And it's horrid to have to remind you that you have yet to kill something for the invalid's supper," she continued. "I saw a hare in the field yonder."

"You mean that jackass rabbit?" he said, abstractedly.

"What you please. It's a pity you didn't take your gun instead of your rifle."

"I brought the rifle for protection."

"And a shot gun is only aggressive, I suppose?"

Falkner looked at her for a moment, and then, as the hare suddenly started across the open a hundred yards away, brought the rifle to his shoulder. A long interval— as it seemed to Kate—elapsed; the animal appeared to be already safely out of range, when the rifle suddenly cracked; the hare bounded in the air like a ball, and dropped motionless. The girl looked at the marksman in undisguised admiration. "Is it quite dead?" she said timidly.

"It never knew what struck it."

"It certainly looks less brutal than shooting it with a shot gun, as John does, and then not killing it outright," said Kate. "I hate what is called sport and sportsmen, but a rifle seems—"

"What?" said Falkner.

"More—gentlemanly."

She had raised her pretty head in the air, and, with her hand shading her eyes, was looking around the clear ether, and said meditatively, "I wonder—no matter."

"What is it?"

"Oh, nothing."

"It is something," said Falkner, with an amused smile, reloading his rifle.

"Well, you once promised me an eagle's feather for my hat. Isn't that thing an eagle?"

"I am afraid it's only a hawk."

"Well, that will do. Shoot that!"

Her eyes were sparkling. Falkner withdrew his own with a slight smile, and raised his rifle with provoking deliberation.

"Are you quite sure it's what you want?" he asked demurely.

"Yes—quick!"

Nevertheless, it was some minutes before the rifle cracked again. The wheeling bird suddenly struck the wind with its wings aslant, and then fell like a plummet at a distance which showed the difficulty of the feat. Falkner started from her side before the bird reached the ground. He returned to her after a lapse of a few moments, bearing a trailing wing in his hand. "You shall make your choice," he said gayly.

"Are you sure it was killed outright?"

"Head shot off," said Falkner briefly.

"And besides, the fall would have killed it," said Kate conclusively. "It's lovely. I suppose they call you a very good shot?"

"They—who?"

"Oh! the people you know — your friends, and their sisters."

"George shoots better than I do, and has had more experience. I've seen him do that with a pistol. Of course not such a long shot, but a more difficult one."

Kate did not reply, but her face showed a conviction that as an artistic and gentlemanly performance it was probably inferior to the one she had witnessed. Falkner, who had picked up the hare also, again took his place by her side, as they turned towards the house.

"Do you remember the day you came, when we were walking here, you pointed out that rock on the mountain where the poor animals had taken refuge from the snow?" said Kate suddenly.

"Yes," answered Falkner; "they seem to have diminished. I am afraid you were right; they have either eaten each other or escaped. Let us hope the latter."

"I looked at them with a glass every day," said Kate, "and they've got down to only four. There's a bear and that shabby, over-grown cat you call a California lion, and a wolf, and a creature like a fox or a squirrel."

"It's a pity they're not all of a kind," said Falkner.

"Why?"

"There'd be nothing to keep them from being comfortable together."

"On the contrary, *I* should think it would be simply awful to be shut up entirely with one's own kind."

"Then you believe it is possible for them, with their different natures and habits, to be happy together?" said Falkner, with sudden earnestness.

"I believe," said Kate hurriedly, "that the bear and the lion find the fox and the wolf very amusing, and that the fox and the wolf—"

"Well?" said Falkner, stopping short.

"Well, the fox and the wolf will carry away a much better opinion of the lion and bear than they had before."

They had reached the house by this time, and for some occult reason Kate did not immediately enter the parlor, where she had left her sister and the invalid, who had already been promoted to a sofa and a cushion by the window, but proceeded directly to her own room. As a manœuvre to avoid meeting Mrs. Hale, it was scarcely necessary, for that lady was already in advance of her on the staircase, as if she had left the parlor for a moment before they entered the house. Falkner, too, would have preferred the company of his own thoughts, but Lee, apparently the only unpreoccupied, all-pervading, and boyishly alert spirit in the party, hailed him from within, and obliged him to present himself on the threshold of the parlor with the hare and hawk's wing he was still carrying. Eying the latter with affected concern, Lee said gravely: "Of course, I *can* eat it, Ned, and I dare say it's the best part of the fowl, and the hare isn't more than enough for the women, but I had no idea we were so reduced. Three hours and a half gunning, and only one hare and a hawk's wing. It's terrible."

Perceiving that his friend was alone, Falkner dropped his burden in the hall and strode rapidly to his side. "Look here, George, we must, *I* must, leave this place at once. It's no use talking; I can stand this sort of thing no longer."

"Nor can I, with the door open. Shut it, and say what you want quick, before Mrs. Hale comes back. Have you found a trail?"

"No, no; that's not what I mean."

"Well, it strikes me it ought to be, if you expect to get away. Have you proposed to Beacon Street, and she thinks it rather premature on a week's acquaintance?"

"No; but—"

"But you *will,* you mean? *Don't,* just yet."

"But I cannot live this perpetual lie."

"That depends. I don't know *how* you're lying when I'm not with you. If you're walking round with that girl, singing hymns and talking of your class in Sunday-school, or if you're insinuating that you're a millionaire, and think of buying the place for a summer hotel, I should say you'd better quit that kind of lying. But, on the other hand, I don't see the necessity of your dancing round here with a shot gun, and yelling for Harkins's blood, or counting that package of greenbacks in the lap of Miss Scott, to be truthful. It seems to me there ought to be something between the two."

"But, George, don't you think—you are on such good terms with Mrs. Hale and her mother—that you might tell them the whole story? That is, tell it in your own way; they will hear anything from you, and believe it."

"Thank you; but suppose I don't believe in lying, either?"

"You know what I mean! You have a way, d—n it, of making everything seem like a matter of course, and the most natural thing going."

"Well, suppose I did. Are you prepared for the worst?"

Falkner was silent for a moment, and then replied, "Yes, anything would be better than this suspense."

"I don't agree with you. Then you would be willing to have them forgive us?"

"I don't understand you."

"I mean that their forgiveness would be the worst thing that could happen. Look here, Ned. Stop a moment;

listen at that door. Mrs. Hale has the tread of an angel, with the pervading capacity of a cat. Now listen! *I* don't pretend to be in love with anybody here, but if I were I should hardly take advantage of a woman's helplessness and solitude with a sensational story about myself. It's not giving her a fair show. You know she won't turn you out of the house."

"No," said Falkner, reddening; "but I should expect to go at once, and that would be my only excuse for telling her."

"Go! where? In your preoccupation with that girl you haven't even found the trail by which Manuel escaped. Do you intend to camp outside the house, and make eyes at her when she comes to the window?"

"Because you think nothing of flirting with Mrs. Hale," said Falkner bitterly, "you care little—"

"My dear Ned," said Lee, "the fact that Mrs. Hale has a husband, and knows that she can't marry me, puts us on equal terms. Nothing that she could learn about me hereafter would make a flirtation with me any less wrong than it would be now, or make her seem more a victim. Can you say the same of yourself and that Puritan girl?"

"But you did not advise me to keep aloof from her; on the contrary, you—"

"I thought you might make the best of the situation, and pay her some attention, *because* you could not go any further."

"You thought I was utterly heartless and selfish, like—"

"Ned!"

Falkner walked rapidly to the fireplace, and returned. "Forgive me, George—I'm a fool—and an ungrateful one."

Lee did not reply at once, although he took and retained the hand Falkner had impulsively extended. "Promise me," he said slowly, after a pause, "that you will say nothing yet to either of these women. I ask it for your own sake, and this girl's, not for mine. If, on the contrary, you are tempted to do so from any Quixotic idea of honor, remember that you will only precipitate something that will oblige you, from that same sense of honor, to separate from the girl forever."

"I don't understand."

"Enough!" said he, with a quick return of his old reckless gayety. "Shoot-Off-His-Mouth—the Beardless Boy Chief of the Sierras—has spoken! Let the Pale Face with the black moustache ponder and beware how he talks hereafter to the Rippling Cochituate Water! Go!"

Nevertheless, as soon as the door had closed upon Falkner, Lee's smile vanished. With his colorless face turned to the fading light at the window, the hollows in his temples and the lines in the corners of his eyes seemed to have grown more profound. He remained motionless and absorbed in thought so deep that the light rustle of a skirt, that would at other times have thrilled his sensitive ear, passed unheeded. At last, throwing off his reverie with the full and unrestrained sigh of a man who believes himself alone, he was startled by the soft laugh of Mrs. Hale, who had entered the room unperceived.

"Dear me! How portentous! Really, I almost feel as if I were interrupting a *tête-à-tête* between yourself and some old flame. I haven't heard anything so old-fashioned and conservative as that sigh since I have been in California. I thought you never had any Past out here?"

Fortunately his face was between her and the light, and the unmistakable expression of annoyance and impatience which was passed over it was spared her. There was, however, still enough dissonance in his manner to affect her quick feminine sense, and when she drew nearer to him it was with a certain maiden-like timidity.

"You are not worse, Mr. Lee, I hope? You have not over-exerted yourself?"

"There's little chance of that with one leg—if not in the grave at least mummified with bandages," he replied, with a bitterness new to him.

"Shall I loosen them? Perhaps they are too tight. There is nothing so irritating to one as the sensation of being tightly bound."

The light touch of her hand upon the rug that covered his knees, the thoughtful tenderness of the blue-veined

15   v. 2

lids, and the delicate atmosphere that seemed to surround her like a perfume cleared his face of its shadow and brought back the reckless fire into his blue eyes.

"I suppose I'm intolerant of all bonds," he said, looking at her intently, "in others as well as myself!"

Whether or not she detected any double meaning in his words, she was obliged to accept the challenge of his direct gaze, and, raising her eyes to his, drew back a little from him with a slight increase of color. "I was afraid you had heard bad news just now."

"What would you call bad news?" asked Lee, clasping his hands behind his head, and leaning back on the sofa, but without withdrawing his eyes from her face.

"Oh, any news that would interrupt your convalesence, or break up our little family party," said Mrs. Hale. "You have been getting on so well that really it would seem cruel to have anything interfere with our life of forgetting and being forgotten. But," she added with apprehensive quickness, "has anything happened? Is there really any news from—from the trails? Yesterday Mr. Falkner said the snow had recommenced in the pass. Has he seen anything, noticed anything different?"

She looked so very pretty, with the rare, genuine, and youthful excitement that transfigured her wearied and wearying regularity of feature, that Lee contented himself with drinking in her prettiness as he would have inhaled the perfume of some flower.

"Why do you look at me so, Mr. Lee?" she asked, with a slight smile. "I believe something *has* happened. Mr. Falkner *has* brought you some intelligence."

"He has certainly found out something I did not foresee."

"And that troubles you?"

"It does."

"Is it a secret?"

"No."

"Then I suppose you will tell it to me at dinner," she said, with a little tone of relief.

"I am afraid, if I tell it at all, I must tell it now," he said, glancing at the door.

"You must do as you think best," she said coldly, "as it seems to be a secret, after all." She hesitated. "Kate is dressing, and will not be down for some time."

"So much the better. For I'm afraid that Ned has made a poor return to your hospitality by falling in love with her."

"Impossible! He has known her for scarcely a week."

"I am afraid we won't agree as to the length of time necessary to appreciate and love a woman. I think it can be done in seven days and four hours, the exact time we have been here."

"Yes; but as Kate was not in when you arrived, and did not come until later, you must take off at least one hour," said Mrs. Hale gayly.

"Ned can. *I* shall not abate a second."

"But are you not mistaken in his feelings?" she continued hurriedly. "He certainly has not said anything to her."

"That is his last hold on honor and reason. And to preserve that little intact he wants to run away at once."

"But that would be very silly."

"Do you think so?" he said, looking at her fixedly.

"Why not?" she asked in her turn, but rather faintly.

"I'll tell you why," he said, lowering his voice with a certain intensity of passion unlike his usual boyish light-heartedness. "Think of a man whose life has been one of alternate hardness and aggression, of savage disappointment and equally savage successes, who has known no other relaxation than dissipation and extravagance; a man to whom the idea of the domestic hearth and family ties only meant weakness, effeminacy, or—worse; who had looked for loyalty and devotion only in the man who battled for him at his right hand in danger, or shared his privations and sufferings. Think of such a man, and imagine that an accident has suddenly placed him in an atmosphere of purity, gentleness, and peace, surrounded him by the refinements of a higher life than he had ever known, and that he found himself as in a dream, on terms of equality with a pure woman who had never known any other life, and yet would understand and pity his. Im-

agine his loving her! Imagine that the first effect of that
love was to show him his own inferiority and the immeasurable gulf that lay between his life and hers!
Would he not fly rather than brave the disgrace of her
awakening to the truth? Would he not fly rather than
accept even the pity that might tempt her to a sacrifice?"

"But—is Mr. Falkner all that?"

"Nothing of the kind, I assure you!" said he demurely.
"But that's the way a man in love feels."

"Really! Mr. Falkner should get you to plead his
cause with Kate," said Mrs. Hale with a faint laugh.

"I need all my persuasive powers in that way for myself," said Lee boldly.

Mrs. Hale rose. "I think I hear Kate coming," she
said. Nevertheless, she did not move away. "It *is* Kate
coming," she added hurriedly, stooping to pick up her
work-basket, which had slipped with Lee's hand from her
own.

It was Kate, who at once flew to her sister's assistance,
Lee deploring from the sofa his own utter inability to aid
her. "It's all my fault, too," he said to Kate, but looking
at Mrs. Hale. "It seems I have a faculty of upsetting
existing arrangements without the power of improving
them, or even putting them back in their places. What
shall I do? I am willing to hold any number of skeins
or rewind any quantity of spools. I am even willing to
forgive Ned for spending the whole day with you, and
only bringing me the wing of a hawk for supper."

"That was all my folly, Mr. Lee," said Kate, with
swift mendacity; "he was all the time looking after something for you, when I begged him to shoot a bird to get
a feather for my hat. And that wing is *so* pretty."

"It is a pity that mere beauty is not edible," said Lee,
gravely, "and that if the worst comes to the worst here
you would probably prefer me to Ned and his moustachios,
merely because I've been tied by the leg to this sofa and
slowly fattened like a Strasbourg goose."

Nevertheless, his badinage failed somehow to amuse
Kate, and she presently excused herself to rejoin her sister, who had already slipped from the room. For the first

time during their enforced seclusion a sense of restraint and uneasiness affected Mrs. Hale, her sister, and Falkner at dinner. The latter addressed himself to Mrs. Scott, almost entirely. Mrs. Hale was fain to bestow an exceptional and marked tenderness on her little daughter Minnie, who, however, by some occult childish instinct, insisted upon sharing it with Lee—her great friend—to Mrs. Hale's uneasy consciousness. Nor was Lee slow to profit by the child's suggestion, but responded with certain vicarious caresses that increased the mother's embarrassment. That evening they retired early, but in the intervals of a restless night Kate was aware, from the sound of voices in the opposite room, that the friends were equally wakeful.

A morning of bright sunshine and soft warm air did not, however, bring any change to their new and constrained relations. It only seemed to offer a reason for Falkner to leave the house very early for his daily rounds, and gave Lee that occasion for unaided exercise with an extempore crutch on the veranda which allowed Mrs. Hale to pursue her manifold duties without the necessity of keeping him company. Kate also, as if to avoid an accidental meeting with Falkner, had remained at home with her sister. With one exception, they did not make their guests the subject of their usual playful comments, nor, after the fashion of their sex, quote their ideas and opinions. That exception was made by Mrs. Hale.

"You have had no difference with Mr. Falkner?" she said carelessly.

"No," said Kate quickly. "Why?"

"I only thought he seemed rather put out at dinner last night, and you didn't propose to go and meet him to-day."

"He must be bored with my company at times, I dare say," said Kate, with an indifference quite inconsistent with her rising color. "I shouldn't wonder if he was a little vexed with Mr. Lee's chaffing him about his sport yesterday, and probably intends to go further to-day, and bring home larger game. I think Mr. Lee very amusing always, but I sometimes fancy he lacks feeling."

"Feeling! You don't know him, Kate," said Mrs. Hale

quickly. She stopped herself, but with a half-smiling recollection in her dropped eyelids.

"Well, he doesn't look very amiable now, stamping up and down the veranda. Perhaps you'd better go and soothe him."

"I'm really *so* busy just now," said Mrs. Hale, with sudden and inconsequent energy; "things have got dreadfully behind in the last week. You had better go, Kate, and make him sit down, or he'll be overdoing it. These men never know any medium—in anything."

Contrary to Kate's expectation, Falkner returned earlier than usual, and, taking the invalid's arm, supported him in a more ambitious walk along the terrace before the house. They were apparently absorbed in conversation, but the two women who observed them from the window could not help noticing the almost feminine tenderness of Falkner's manner towards his wounded friend, and the thoughtful tenderness of his ministering care.

"I wonder," said Mrs. Hale, following them with softly appreciative eyes, "if women are capable of as disinterested friendship as men? I never saw anything like the devotion of these two creatures. Look! if Mr. Falkner hasn't got his arm round Mr. Lee's waist, and Lee, with his own arm over Falkner's neck, is looking up in his eyes. I declare, Kate, it almost seems an indiscretion to look at them."

Kate, however, to Mrs. Hale's indignation, threw her pretty head back and sniffed the air contemptuously. "I really don't see anything but some absurd sentimentalism of their own, or some mannish wickedness they're concocting by themselves. I am by no means certain, Josephine, that Lee's influence over that young man is the best thing for him."

"On the contrary! Lee's influence seems the only thing that checks his waywardness," said Mrs. Hale quickly. "I'm sure, if anyone makes sacrifices, it is Lee; I shouldn't wonder that even now he is making some concession to Falkner, and all those caressing ways of your friend are for a purpose. They're not much different from us, dear."

"Well, *I* wouldn't stand there and let them see me looking at them as if I couldn't bear them out of my sight for a moment," said Kate, whisking herself out of the room. "They're conceited enough, Heaven knows, already."

That evening, at dinner, however, the two men exhibited no trace of the restraint or uneasiness of the previous day. If they were less impulsive and exuberant, they were still frank and interested, and if the term could be used in connection with men apparently trained to neither self-control nor repose, there was a certain gentle dignity in their manner which for the time had the effect of lifting them a little above the social level of their entertainers. For even with all their predisposition to the strangers, Kate and Mrs. Hale had always retained a conscious attitude of gentle condescension and superiority towards them —an attitude not inconsistent with a stronger feeling, nor altogether unprovocative of it; yet this evening they found themselves impressed with something more than an equality in the men who had amused and interested them, and they were perhaps a little more critical and doubtful of their own power. Mrs. Hale's little girl, who had appreciated only the seriousness of the situation, had made her own application of it. "Are you dow'in' away from aunt Kate and mamma?" she asked, in an interval of silence.

"How else can I get you the red snow we saw at sunset, the other day, on the peak yonder?" said Lee gayly. "I'll have to get up some morning very early, and catch it when it comes at sunrise."

"What is this wonderful snow, Minnie, that you are tormenting Mr. Lee for?" asked Mrs. Hale.

"Oh! it's a fairy snow that he told me all about; it only comes when the sun comes up and goes down, and if you catch ever so little of it in your hand it makes all you fink you want come true! Wouldn't that be nice?" But to the child's astonishment her little circle of auditors, even while assenting, sighed.

The red snow was there plain enough the next morning before the valley was warm with light, and while Minnie, her mother, and aunt Kate were still peacefully sleeping.

And Mr. Lee had kept his word, and was evidently seeking it, for he and Falkner were already urging their horses through the pass, with their faces towards and lit up by its glow.

CHAPTER VIII

KATE was stirring early, but not as early as her sister, who met her on the threshold of her room. Her face was quite pale, and she held a letter in her hand. "What does this mean, Kate?"

"What is the matter?" asked Kate, her own color fading from her cheek.

"They are gone—with their horses. Left before day, and left this."

She handed Kate an open letter. The girl took it hurriedly, and read—

"When you get this we shall be no more; perhaps not even as much. Ned found the trail yesterday, and we are taking the first advantage of it before day. We dared not trust ourselves to say 'Good-by!' last evening; we were too cowardly to face you this morning; we must go as we came, without warning, but not without regret. We leave a package and a letter for your husband. It is not only our poor return for your gentleness and hospitality, but, since it was accidentally the means of giving us the pleasure of your society, we beg you to keep it in safety until his return. We kiss your mother's hands. Ned wants to say something more, but time presses, and I only allow him to send his love to Minnie, and to tell her that he is trying to find the red snow.

"GEORGE LEE."

"But he is not fit to travel," said Mrs. Hale. "And the trail—it may not be passable."

"It was passable the day before yesterday," said Kate drearily, "for I discovered it, and went as far as the buck-eyes."

"Then it was you who told them about it," said Mrs. Hale reproachfully.

"No," said Kate indignantly. "Of course I didn't."
She stopped, and, reading the significance of her speech
in the glistening eyes of her sister, she blushed. Josephine kissed her, and said—

"It *was* treating us like children, Kate, but we must
make them pay for it hereafter. For that package and
letter to John means something, and we shall probably see
them before long. I wonder what the letter is about, and
what is in the package?"

"Probably one of Mr. Lee's jokes. He is quite capable
of turning the whole thing into ridicule. I dare say he
considers his visit here a prolonged jest."

"With his poor leg, Kate? You are as unfair to him
as you were to Falkner when they first came."

Kate, however, kept her dark eyebrows knitted in a
piquant frown.

"To think of his intimating *what* he would allow Falkner to say! And yet you believe he has no evil influence
over the young man."

Mrs. Hale laughed. "Where are you going so fast,
Kate?" she called mischievously, as the young lady
flounced out of the room.

"Where? Why, to tidy John's room. He may be coming at any moment now. Or do you want to do it yourself?"

"No, no," returned Mrs. Hale hurriedly; "you do it.
I'll look in a little later on."

She turned away with a sigh. The sun was shining
brilliantly outside. Through the half-open blinds its long
shafts seemed to be searching the house for the lost guests,
and making the hollow shell appear doubly empty. What
a contrast to the dear dark days of mysterious seclusion
and delicious security, lit by Lee's laughter and the sparkling hearth, which had passed so quickly! The forgotten outer world seemed to have returned to the house
through those open windows and awakened its dwellers
from a dream.

The morning seemed interminable, and it was past noon,
while they were deep in a sympathetic conference with
Mrs. Scott, who had drawn a pathetic word-picture of

the two friends perishing in the snow-drift, without flannels, brandy, smelling-salts, or jelly, which they had forgotten, when they were startled by the loud barking of "Spot" on the lawn before the house. The women looked hurriedly at each other.

"They have returned," said Mrs. Hale.

Kate ran to the window. A horseman was approaching the house. A single glance showed her that it was neither Falkner, Lee, nor Hale, but a stranger.

"Perhaps he brings some news of them," said Mrs. Scott quickly. So complete had been their preoccupation with the loss of their guests that they could not yet conceive of anything that did not pertain to it.

The stranger, who was at once ushered into the parlor, was evidently disconcerted by the presence of the three women.

"I reckoned to see John Hale yer," he began, awkwardly.

A slight look of disappointment passed over their faces. "He has not yet returned," said Mrs. Hale briefly.

"Sho! I wanter know. He's hed time to do it, I reckon," said the stranger.

"I suppose he hasn't been able to get over from the Summit," returned Mrs. Hale. "The trail is closed."

"It ain't now, for I kem over it this mornin' myself."

"You didn't—meet—anyone?" asked Mrs. Hale timidly, with a glance at the others.

"No."

A long silence ensued. The unfortunate visitor plainly perceived an evident abatement of interest in himself, yet he still struggled politely to say something. "Then I reckon you know what kept Hale away?" he said dubiously.

"Oh, certainly—the stage robbery."

"I wish I'd known that," said the stranger reflectively, "for I ez good ez rode over jist to tell it to ye. Ye see John Hale, he sent a note to ye 'splainin' matters by a gentleman; but the road agents tackled that man, and left him for dead in the road."

"Yes," said Mrs. Hale impatiently.

"Luckily he didn't die, but kem to, and managed to crawl inter the brush, whar I found him when I was lookin' for stock, and brought him to my house—"

"*You* found him? *Your* house?" interrupted Mrs. Hale.

"Inter *my* house," continued the man doggedly. "I'm Thompson of Thompson's Pass over yon; mebbe it ain't much of a house; but I brought him thar. Well, ez he couldn't find the note that Hale had guv him, and like ez not the road agents had gone through him and got it, ez soon ez the weather let up I made a break over yer to tell ye."

"You say Mr. Lee came to your house," repeated Mrs. Hale, "and is there now?"

"Not much," said the man grimly; "and I never said *Lee* was thar. I mean that Bilson waz shot by Lee and kem—"

"Certainly, Josephine!" said Kate, suddenly stepping between her sister and Thompson, and turning upon her a white face and eyes of silencing significance; "certainly —don't you remember?—that's the story we got from the Chinaman, you know, only muddled. Go on sir," she continued, turning to Thompson calmly; "you say that the man who brought the note from my brother was shot by Lee?"

"And another fellow they call Falkner. Yes, that's about the size of it."

"Thank you; it's nearly the same story that we heard. But you have had a long ride, Mr. Thompson; let me offer you a glass of whiskey in the dining-room. This way, please."

The door closed upon them none too soon. For Mrs. Hale already felt the room whirling around her, and sank back into her chair with a hysterical laugh. Old Mrs. Scott did not move from her seat, but, with her eyes fixed on the door, impatiently waited Kate's return. Neither spoke, but each felt that the young, untried girl was equal to the emergency, and would get at the truth.

The sound of Thompson's feet in the hall and the closing of the front door was followed by Kate's reappearance. Her face was still pale, but calm.

"Well?" said the two women in a breath.

"Well," returned Kate slowly; "Mr. Lee and Mr. Falkner were undoubtedly the two men who took the paper from John's messenger and brought it here."

"You are sure?" said Mrs. Scott.

"There can be no mistake, mother."

"*Then,*" said Mrs. Scott, with triumphant feminine logic, "I don't want anything more to satisfy me that they are *perfectly innocent!*"

More convincing than the most perfect masculine deduction, this single expression of their common nature sent a thrill of sympathy and understanding through each. They cried for a few moments on each other's shoulders. "To think," said Mrs. Scott, "what that poor boy must have suffered to have been obliged to do—that to—to—Bilson—isn't that the creature's name? I suppose we ought to send over there and inquire after him, with some chicken and jelly, Kate. It's only common humanity, and we must be just, my dear; for even if he shot Mr. Lee and provoked the poor boy to shoot him, he may have thought it his duty. And then, it will avert suspicions."

"To think," murmured Mrs. Hale, "what they must have gone through while they were here—momentarily expecting John to come, and yet keeping up such a light heart."

"I believe, if they had stayed any longer, they would have told us everything," said Mrs. Scott.

Both the younger women were silent. Kate was thinking of Falkner's significant speech as they neared the house on their last walk; Josephine was recalling the remorseful picture drawn by Lee, which she knew was his own portrait. Suddenly she started.

"But John will be here soon; what are we to tell him? And then that package and that letter."

"Don't be in a hurry to tell him anything at present, my child," said Mrs. Scott gently. "It is unfortunate this Mr. Thompson called here, but we are not obliged to understand what he says now about John's message, or to connect our visitors with his story. I'm sure, Kate, I should have treated them exactly as we did if they had come without any message from John; so I do not know why we should lay any stress on that, or even speak of it. The simple fact is that we have opened our house to two strangers in distress. Your husband," continued Mr. Hale's mother-in-law, "does not require to know more. As to the letter and package, we will keep that for further consideration. It cannot be of much importance, or they would have spoken of it before; it is probably some trifling present as a return for your hospitality. I should use no *indecorous* haste in having it opened."

The two women kissed Mrs. Scott with a feeling of relief, and fell back into the monotony of their household duties. It is to be feared, however, that the absence of their outlawed guests was nearly as dangerous as their presence in the opportunity it afforded for uninterrupted and imaginative reflection. Both Kate and Josephine were at first shocked and wounded by the discovery of the real character of the two men with whom they had associated so familiarly, but it was no disparagement to their sense of propriety to say that the shock did not last long, and was accompanied with the fascination of danger. This was succeeded by a consciousness of the delicate flattery implied in their indirect influence over the men who had undoubtedly risked their lives for the sake of remaining with them. The best woman is not above being touched by the effect of her power over the worst man, and Kate at first allowed herself to think of Falkner in that light. But if in her later reflections he suffered as a heroic experience to be forgotten, he gained something as an actual man to be remembered. Now that the proposed rides from "his friend's house" were a part of the illusion, would he ever dare to visit them again? Would she dare to see him? She held her breath with a sudden pain of parting that was new to her; she tried to think of something else, to pick up the scattered threads of her life before that eventful day. But in vain; that one week had filled the place with implacable memories, or more terrible, as it seemed to her and her sister, they had both lost their feeble, alien hold upon Eagle's Court in the sudden presence of the real genii of these solitudes, and henceforth they alone would be the strangers there. They

scarcely dared to confess it to each other, but this return
to the dazzling sunlight and cloudless skies of the past
appeared to them to be the one unreal experience; they
had never known the true wild flavor of their home, except in that week of delicious isolation. Without breathing it aloud, they longed for some vague *dénoûment* to
this experience that should take them from Eagle's Court
forever.

It was noon the next day when the little household be-
held the last shred of their illusion vanish like the melting
snow in the strong sunlight of John Hale's return. He
was accompanied by Colonel Clinch and Rawlins, two
strangers to the women. Was it fancy, or the avenging
spirit of their absent companions? but *he* too looked a
stranger, and as the little cavalcade wound its way up
the slope he appeared to sit his horse and wear his hat
with a certain slouch and absence of his usual restraint
that strangely shocked them. Even the old half-conde-
scending, half-punctilious gallantry of his greeting of his
wife and family was changed, as he introduced his companions with a mingling of familiarity and shyness that
was new to him. Did Mrs. Hale regret it, or feel a sense
of relief in the absence of his usual seignorial formality?
She only knew that she was grateful for the presence of
the strangers, which for the moment postponed a matrimonial confidence from which she shrank.

"Proud to know you," said Colonel Clinch, with a sudden outbreak of the antique gallantry of some remote
Huguenot ancestor. "My friend, Judge Hale, must be a
regular Roman citizen to leave such a family and such
a house at the call of public duty. Eh, Rawlins?"

"You bet," said Rawlins, looking from Kate to her
sister in undisguised admiration.

"And I suppose the duty could not have been a very
pleasant one," said Mrs. Hale, timidly, without looking
at her husband.

"Gad, madam, that's just it," said the gallant Colonel,
seating himself with a comfortable air, and an easy,
though by no means disrespectful, familiarity. "We went
into this fight a little more than a week ago. The only

scrimmage we've had has been with the detectives that
were on the robbers' track. Ha! ha! The best people
we've met have been the friends of the men we were
huntin', and we've generally come to the conclusion to
vote the other ticket! Ez Judge Hale and me agreed ez
we came along, the two men ez we'd most like to see
just now and shake hands with are George Lee and
Ned Falkner."

"The two leaders of the party who robbed the coach,"
explained Mr. Hale, with a slight return of his usual precision of statement.

The three women looked at each other with a blaze of
thanksgiving in their grateful eyes. Without comprehending all that Colonel Clinch had said, they understood
enough to know that their late guests were safe from the
pursuit of that party, and that their own conduct was
spared criticism. I hardly dare write it, but they instantly
assumed the appearance of aggrieved martyrs, and felt as
if they were!

"Yes, ladies!" continued the Colonel, inspired by the
bright eyes fixed upon him. "We haven't taken the road
ourselves yet, but—pohn honor—we wouldn't mind doing
it in a case like this." Then with the fluent, but somewhat exaggerated, phraseology of a man trained to
"stump" speaking, he gave an account of the robbery and
his own connection with it. He spoke of the swindling
and treachery which had undoubtedly provoked Falkner
to obtain restitution of his property by an overt act of
violence under the leadership of Lee. He added that he
had learned since at Wild Cat Station that Harkins had
fled the country, that a suit had been commenced by the
Excelsior Ditch Company, and that all available property
of Harkins had been seized by the sheriff.

"Of course it can't be proved yet, but there's no doubt
in my mind that Lee, who is an old friend of Ned Falkner's, got up that job to help him, and that Ned's off
with the money by this time—and I'm right glad of it.
I can't say ez we've done much towards it, except to keep
tumbling in the way of that detective party of Stanner's,
and so throw them off the trail—ha, ha! The Judge here,

I reckon, has had his share of fun, for while he was at
Hennicker's trying to get some facts from Hennicker's
pretty daughter, Stanner tried to get up some sort of vigilance committee of the stage passengers to burn down
Hennicker's ranch out of spite, but the Judge here stepped
in and stopped that."

"It was really a high-handed proceeding, Josephine, but
I managed to check it," said Hale, meeting somewhat con-
sciously the first direct look his wife had cast upon him,
and falling back for support on his old manner. "In its
way, I think it was worse than the robbery by Lee and
Falkner, for it was done in the name of law and order;
while, as far as I can judge from the facts, the affair that
we were following up was simply a rude and irregular
restitution of property that had been morally stolen."

"I have no doubt you did quite right, though I don't understand it," said Mrs. Hale languidly; "but I trust these
gentlemen will stay to luncheon, and in the meantime
excuse us for running away, as we are short of servants,
and Manuel seems to have followed the example of the
head of the house and left us, in pursuit of somebody or
something."

When the three women had gained the vantage-ground
of the drawing-room, Kate said, earnestly, "As it's all
right, hadn't we better tell him now?"

"Decidedly not, child," said Mrs. Scott, imperatively.
"Do you suppose they are in a hurry to tell us *their* whole
story? Who are those Hennicker people? and they were
there a week ago!"

"And did you notice John's hat when he came in, and
the vulgar familiarity of calling him 'Judge'?" said Mrs.
Hale.

"Well, certainly anything like the familiarity of this
man Clinch *I* never saw," said Kate. "Contrast his manner with Mr. Falkner's."

At luncheon the three suffering martyrs finally succeeded in reducing Hale and his two friends to an attitude
of vague apology. But their triumph was short-lived.
At the end of the meal they were startled by the trampling
of hoofs without, followed by loud knocking. In another

moment the door was opened, and Mr. Stanner strode into the room. Hale rose with a look of indignation.

"I thought, as Mr. Stanner understood that I had no desire for his company elsewhere, he would hardly venture to intrude upon me in my house, and certainly not after—"

"Ef you're alluding to the Vigilantes shakin' you and Zeenie up at Hennicker's, you can't make *me* responsible for that. I'm here now on business—you understand— reg'lar business. Ef you want to see the papers yer ken. I suppose you know what a warrant is?"

"I know what *you* are," said Hale hotly; "and if you don't leave my house—"

"Steady, boys," interrupted Stanner, as his five hench-men filed into the hall. "There's no backin' down here, Colonel Clinch, unless you and Hale kalkilate to back down the State of Californy! The matter stands like this. There's a half-breed Mexican, called Manuel, arrested over at the Summit, who swears he saw George Lee and Edward Falkner in this house the night after the robbery. He says that they were makin' themselves at home here, as if they were among friends, and con-siderin' the kind of help we've had from Mr. John Hale, it looks ez if it might be true."

"It's an infamous lie!" said Hale.

"It may be true, John," said Mrs. Scott, suddenly step-ping in front of her pale-cheeked daughters. "A wounded man was brought here out of the storm by his friend, who claimed the shelter of your roof. As your mother I should have been unworthy to stay beneath it and have denied that shelter or withheld it until I knew his name and what he was. He stayed here until he could be removed. He left a letter for you. It will probably tell you if he was the man this person is seeking."

"Thank you, mother," said Hale, lifting her hand to his lips quietly; "and perhaps you will kindly tell these gentlemen that, as your son does not care to know who or what the stranger was, there is no necessity for opening the letter, or keeping Mr. Stanner a moment longer."

"But you will oblige *me,* John, by opening it before

these gentlemen," said Mrs. Hale recovering her voice and color. "Please to follow me," she said preceding them to the staircase.

They entered Mr. Hale's room, now restored to its original condition. On the table lay a letter and a small package. The eyes of Mr. Stanner, a little abashed by the attitude of the two women, fastened upon it and glistened.

Josephine handed her husband the letter. He opened it in breathless silence and read—

"JOHN HALE,

"We owe you no return for voluntarily making yourself a champion of justice and pursuing us, except it was to offer you a fair field and no favor. We didn't get that much from you, but accident brought us into your house and into your family, where we *did* get it, and were fairly vanquished. To the victors belong the spoils. We leave the package of greenbacks which we took from Colonel Clinch in the Sierra coach, but which was first stolen by Harkins from forty-four shareholders of the Excelsior Ditch. We have no right to say what *you* should do with it, but if you aren't tired of following the same line of justice that induced you to run after *us,* you will try to restore it to its rightful owners.

"We leave you another trifle as an evidence that our intrusion into your affairs was not without some service to you, even if the service was as accidental as the intrusion. You will find a pair of boots in the corner of your closet. They were taken from the burglarious feet of Manuel, your *peon,* who, believing the three ladies were alone and at his mercy, entered your house with an accomplice at two o'clock on the morning of the 21st, and was kicked out by

"Your obedient servants,
"GEORGE LEE & EDWARD FALKNER."

Hale's voice and color changed on reading this last paragraph. He turned quickly towards his wife; Kate flew to the closet, where the muffled boots of Manuel confronted them. "We never knew it. I always suspected something that night," said Mrs. Hale and Mrs. Scott in the same breath.

"That's all very well, and like George Lee's high falutin'," said Stanner, approaching the table, "but as long ez the greenbacks are here he can make what capital he likes outer Manuel. I'll trouble you to pass over that package."

"Excuse me," said Hale, "but I believe this is the package taken from Colonel Clinch. Is it not?" he added, appealing to the Colonel.

"It is," said Clinch.

"Then take it," said Hale, handing him the package. "The first restitution is to you, but I believe you will fulfil Lee's instructions as well as myself."

"But," said Stanner, furiously interposing, "I've a warrant to seize that wherever found, and I dare you to disobey the law."

"Mr. Stanner," said Clinch, slowly, "there are ladies present. If you insist upon having that package I must ask them to withdraw, and I'm afraid you'll find me better prepared to resist a *second* robbery than I was the first. Your warrant, which was taken out by the Express Company, is supplanted by civil proceedings taken the day before yesterday against the property of the fugitive swindler Harkins! You should have consulted the sheriff before you came here."

Stanner saw his mistake. But in the faces of his grinning followers he was obliged to keep up his bluster. "You shall hear from me again, sir," he said, turning on his heel.

"I beg your pardon," said Clinch grimly, "but do I understand that at last I am to have the honor—"

"You shall hear from the Company's lawyers, sir," said Stanner, turning red, and noisily leaving the room.

"And so, my dear ladies," said Colonel Clinch, "you have spent a week with a highwayman. I say *a* highwayman, for it would be hard to call my young friend Falkner by that name for his first offence, committed under great provocation, and undoubtedly instigated by Lee, who was an old friend of his, and to whom he came, no doubt, in desperation."

Kate stole a triumphant glance at her sister, who dropped her lids over her glistening eyes. "And this Mr. Lee," she continued more gently, "is he really a highwayman?"

"George Lee," said Clinch, settling himself back oratorically in his chair, "my dear young lady, *is* a highwayman, but not of the common sort. He is a gentleman born, madam, comes from one of the oldest families of the Eastern Shore of Maryland. He never mixes himself up with anything but some of the biggest strikes, and he's an educated man. He is very popular with ladies and children; he was never known to do or say anything that could bring a blush to the cheek of beauty or a tear to the eye of innocence. I think I may say I'm sure you found him so."

"I shall never believe him anything but a gentleman," said Mrs. Scott, firmly.

"If he has a defect, it is perhaps a too reckless indulgence in draw poker," said the Colonel, musingly; "not unbecoming a gentleman, understand me, Mrs. Scott, but perhaps too reckless for his own good. George played a grand game, a glittering game, but pardon me if I say an *uncertain* game. I've told him so; it's the only point on which we ever differed."

"Then you know him?" said Mrs. Hale, lifting her soft eyes to the Colonel.

"I have that honor."

"Did his appearance, Josephine," broke in Hale, somewhat ostentatiously, "appear to—er—er—correspond with these qualities? You know what I mean."

"He certainly seemed very simple and natural," said Mrs. Hale, slightly drawing her pretty lips together. "He did not wear his trousers rolled up over his boots in the company of ladies, as you're doing now, nor did he make his first appearance in this house with such a hat as you wore this morning, or I should not have admitted him."

There were a few moments of embarrassing silence.

"Do you intend to give that package to Mr. Falkner yourself, Colonel?" asked Mrs. Scott.

"I shall hand it over to the Excelsior Company," said the Colonel, "but I shall inform Ned of what I have done."

"Then," said Mrs. Scott, "will you kindly take a message from us to him?"

"If you wish it."

"You will be doing *me* a great favor, Colonel," said Hale, politely.

Whatever the message was, six months later it brought Edward Falkner, the reëstablished superintendent of the Excelsior Ditch, to Eagle's Court. As he and Kate stood again on the plateau, looking towards the distant slopes once more green with verdure, Falkner said—

"Everything here looks as it did the first day I saw it, except your sister."

"The place does not agree with her," said Kate hurriedly. "That is why my brother thinks of leaving it before the winter sets in."

"It seems so sad," said Falkner, "for the last words poor George said to me, as he left to join his cousin's corps at Richmond, were: 'If I'm not killed, Ned, I hope some day to stand again beside Mrs. Hale, at the window in Eagle's Court, and watch you and Kate coming home!'"